CITY OF INNOCENT MONSTERS

Also by STACEY HORAN

OLD CITY MYSTERIES

A Place for Good and Evil

STANDALONES (Young Adult)

Inland

Sycamore Lane

THE ELIXIR VITAE ADVENTURES SERIES (Young Adult)

Book One: *Ortus*

Book Two: *Juvenis*

Book Three: *Adultus*

Book Four: *Senectus*

Book Five: *Mortem*

CITY OF INNOCENT MONSTERS

An Old City Mystery

STACEY HORAN

This book is a work of fiction. Names, characters, places and incidents either are the work of the author's imagination or are used fictitiously. Any resemblance to actual persons, living or dead, is entirely coincidental.

Copyright © 2024 by Stacey Horan

All rights reserved.

No part of this book may be reproduced in any form or by any electronic or mechanical means, including information storage and retrieval systems, without written permission from the author, except for the use of brief quotations in a book review.

Ghost Bridge Press LLC

Cover design by James T. Egan of Bookfly Design

ISBN: 978-1-964473-00-0

For Dad

CITY OF INNOCENT MONSTERS

What strange phenomena we find in a great city, all we need do is stroll about with our eyes open. Life swarms with innocent monsters.

—Charles Baudelaire, *Le Spleen de Paris*

Chapter One

The deep, rumbling growl could only have been made by a monster. Leo Roberts was used to all manner of scary things. Well, "used to" was probably too strong a description. But sitting here in the pitch-black night, this sound was altogether one of the scariest things he'd ever heard. The growl came again, a rumble in a bass octave that Leo could feel in his bones.

"What the hell is that?!" he hissed, trying his best to keep his voice to a whisper, though he really wanted to scream at the top of his lungs and run back to the car like a frightened little boy. Leo, however, was not a little boy. He was fifteen years old and an apprentice private investigator, and he dealt with eerie things all the time. He would not run. He might pee his pants, but he would not run.

Leo tugged the brim of his baseball cap down just a little farther and shifted his chair a few inches to the right so that he was closer to his boss, Sidney Stone. The deep growl was answered by another, this one slightly higher in pitch but still a low baritone. It sounded like it was right in front of him. Behind him. All around him, for that matter.

"Seriously, Sid. What is that?!" Leo wrapped his arms tightly around himself to keep from shaking too badly. He shook his head at the absurdity of the action, given Florida's warm temperatures and uncomfortably high humidity.

"Gators," Sid whispered.

Even though Leo was only a couple of feet away from Sid, he could barely make out her silhouette in the dark. "Gators?!" He snorted. "No way. There is no way that sound is coming from a little alligator."

Sid chuckled softly. "Well, for starters, it's probably not *little*. And it's not a single alligator but several. Maybe even dozens. They are all over this place. That's why we're here, remember?"

Leo growled in frustration, noting how the noise he made sounded like a kitten purring compared to the rumbling snarls coming from the monsters in the dark. "I remember," he whispered. "I just didn't think they were really that big . . . or that there'd be that many of them."

Leo's father had taken him to the alligator farm just up the road when Leo was little, on their one and only vacation together. He remembered seeing the alligators; some of them had been huge, but at the time he was skeptical that they were 100 percent real. After all, Florida was the land of theme parks and make-believe, so the giant alligators seemed about as realistic to him as fairy princesses and superheroes.

"Did you read the file?" asked Sid. "Or did you just pretend to read it when I asked you to?"

"No, I read it," Leo grumbled. "I just thought . . . I thought you were exaggerating. Besides, the file didn't say anything about them making noises."

Another growl came from Leo's left. Or was it right in front of him? It was followed by another and then another. The nearby swamp acted as an amplifier, and the effect was a symphony of demonic bellows, like rolling thunder. Leo gritted his teeth and wished that he hadn't agreed to join Sid on tonight's stakeout.

Sid's newest client was the exclusive Oakmire Golf and Country Club, specifically its board of directors. The club was located on Anastasia Island, a fourteen-mile-long, one-mile-wide island located just east of downtown St. Augustine, Florida.

After news broke a couple of weeks ago that Travis Colquitt, the St. Johns County sheriff, had been arrested on fraud and false impersonation charges as a direct result of Sidney Stone's private investigative work, her phone had started ringing and business had picked up. Sid had three new clients within a week of the sheriff's arrest, and all of them had been easy-to-close cases of spousal infidelity. She was still getting requests for help finding lost pets, and those she tossed to Leo. So far, he'd closed five of them all on his own—two cats, two dogs, and a chicken.

The Oakmire board of directors had called Sid this past Monday morning and set up an initial meeting with her. She returned from that meeting positively beaming and marched straight into the house to convince Leo's grandfather, Burt, to permit Leo to accompany her on stakeouts, which would begin on Friday night.

After the Sheriff Colquitt case, in which Leo had helped Sid solve the mystery behind the cold case of her own husband and daughter, Burt had forbidden him from helping Sid with any more PI work. During the Colquitt case, Leo—who had the unusual ability to see and speak to the spirits of people who had passed on—had communed with Sid's dead husband, Wes. Doing so had required him to relive Wes's fatal car crash, complete with the horrors of screams, searing pain, and mangled bodies. The encounter left Leo battered and bruised; Burt had been so furious that he almost kicked Sid out of the multi-purpose apartment/office he'd built for her in his garage.

Over the next two weeks, though, Sid had managed to negotiate a temporary truce with Burt. Leo was allowed to continue working on the lost pet cases as long as none of them involved a dangerous species like boa constrictors, Gila monsters, or chihuahuas. Much to Leo's disappointment, Sid had agreed to keep to Burt's condition that Leo be kept far away from cases involving cheating spouses. He'd enjoyed working on the case involving County Commissioner J. T. Clement and his now ex-wife, Josie. In fact, Leo had been the one to discover that the commissioner was the one doing the cheating, not his wife.

This week, when the Oakmire Golf and Country Club came calling, Sid asked Burt if they could renegotiate the terms of their peace accord, and Leo had jumped into the negotiations. Since the case appeared to involve no marital infidelity, Burt agreed that Leo could help, provided that he adhere to a strict no-spirits-allowed clause. Leo had said yes, but deep down he knew that clause would be broken at some point, especially in a town like the Old City, as St. Augustine was colloquially known.

Tonight was their first night on the Oakmire case, and Leo and Sid were sitting in a pair of black canvas camping chairs hidden among a spread of neatly trimmed azaleas under a stand of three giant live oaks. At sunset, this spot had been beautiful, but now in the pitch black of night, surrounded by alligators, it was the last place on earth Leo wanted to be. They were staking out the Oakmire golf course. More specifically, they were staking out the swampland that butted up against some of the holes on the course. Hence, the serenade from this evening's alligator chorus.

Earlier in the evening, from their vantage point under the oaks, Sid and Leo had been able to see the wide stretch of marshland that ran along the western edge of the first and second holes. The marsh extended west, as much as half a mile in some places, before flowing into the Matanzas River, which formed part of the Intracoastal Waterway along the east coast of Florida. The proximity of their stakeout site to the marsh had the added bonus of a faint onshore breeze that brought with it a veritable assault on one's sense of smell—a cocktail of chemicals used to treat the golf-course grass, the smell of reclaimed irrigation water, the muddy odor of the shallows, and all manner of decaying things hidden from view by the mangroves and swamp grass.

Leo slapped the back of his neck, hoping to have killed the mosquito he could hear buzzing around, and pulled the collar of his shirt up a little higher. Despite wearing one of his grandfather's dark, long-sleeved, button-down shirts, and a pair of faded black jeans that he'd bought at the thrift store for five dollars, he was still getting eaten alive. He'd been excited when he found the jeans, even though they were too big in the waist. His only other jeans were two pairs that he'd brought with him when he moved to the Old City about six weeks ago, and they were nearly two inches too short for him. His growth spurts this past year, combined with his dad's death and his mom's meager earnings, had meant there was never any money for new clothes. But now, since coming to live with Burt and starting work with Sid's PI business, he had his own money to pay for things like new (or at least new-to-him) clothes.

He waved a hand to shoo away another mosquito that was buzzing around his ear. "I don't think this bug spray is working."

Sid slapped the side of her face, clearly feeling the tell-tale sting from what should probably be Florida's official state bird. By tomorrow morning, there would be a big, red, angry mosquito bite on her cheek. "Guppy swore it was the best stuff out there. He said it's what he and his landscaping crew use."

Leo swatted at the buzzing sound by his ear. "Well, it's crap." His neck began to itch where he'd slapped it earlier, and he scratched even though he knew he shouldn't. "And it smells like cat piss."

Sid sighed. "I know. You'd think the smell alone would keep the mosquitos away."

It was almost midnight, and none of the houses along the eastern side of the first and second holes of the golf course had their lights on. One reason for this was an Oakmire homeowners' association rule that no outside lights were permitted after eleven o'clock along the back side of any house with a view of the marsh. No one wanted to encourage the monsters of the swamp to climb out of their bog and head for the nearest swimming pool.

The second reason was that the residents of the Oakmire Golf and Country Club—all of whom Leo assumed were filthy rich, given the size and splendor of the homes he'd seen—apparently liked to go to bed early. Frankly, it wasn't much different from the neighborhood where he and Sid lived, just a few blocks off of the Old City's historic downtown district. Those streets rolled up by eleven o'clock as well.

Leo slapped at another buzzing mosquito, and Sid sighed from boredom while the alligator choir continued its late-night concert. A deep growl that couldn't have been more than ten yards away almost made Leo jump out of his skin. "Are we safe here?"

"Yes," Sid whispered. She paused before adding, "I think so."

"You think so!"

"Shhhh!"

"What do you mean you think so?!"

"Shhhh! We're fine. They said this was a good location," Sid hissed. "Now be quiet, or I'll send you back to the car."

Leo was tempted to say something else, just for the opportunity to get out of the dark and sit in the safety of Sid's old sedan, but he was interrupted by a barrage of curse words. Looking to his left, Leo realized the profanity was coming from two golfers. But unlike golfers' usual reasons for swearing on the course—a bad tee shot, a missed putt—these two were swinging their clubs as if they were engaged in a sword fight. And they were dead.

Chapter Two

Leo tugged at the brim of his baseball cap, wishing the profanity would stop blaring in his head. He didn't always hear the voices of the spirits he encountered, but when he did, the sound was usually soft. These two, however, were so loud and angry that it seemed like they were shouting right in Leo's ear, and their language was so foul that it might have made his father, who had served in the navy for fourteen years, blush with embarrassment.

Leo was hearing two voices, if you could even call them that. One was a deep baritone or bass, the other a tenor, but Leo would have been hard-pressed to say which voice belonged to which golfer. It was actually more sensation than sound, if he had to try to describe it. More a feeling or a thought downloaded into his mind than someone actually speaking to him. But the dead golfers' swearing was angry and violent, and Leo could have done without their free tutorial on verbal obscenities.

Even in the dark, Sid could tell Leo was pulling at his hat

and rocking back and forth. "What's going on, Leo? Do you see something?"

"Yep." Leo hugged himself as he glanced sideways toward the first green as the two spirits continued fencing with their putters. "There are two over on the first hole." He kept his voice low, hoping the spirits wouldn't hear him. "They're fighting. Not sure why, but they're yelling and trying to hit each other with golf clubs."

Sid snorted with laughter. "Wish I could see that. So much for the game of golf being a gentlemen's sport. Do they know you can see them?" She covered her mouth to try to muffle her giggles.

"Not yet," Leo muttered, "but they might if you keep laughing."

"Sorry, sorry." Sid cleared her throat. "What do they look like?"

Leo hadn't told her that he'd seen the spirits when they'd first arrived at Oakmire. While Sid was inside the clubhouse, checking in with the club's management, Leo had waited on the back veranda and noticed two men standing by the starter's shack. One of them was wearing sharply creased khaki pants, two layered, short-sleeved polos—one navy-blue and one white —a white sun visor, and bright white golf shoes. Leo thought the man was maybe Sid's age, although he wasn't sure exactly what age that was. The man had curly, brown hair and a paunch that hung over his trousers. There was nothing unusual about his appearance, except for the fact that he was selecting a club from his bag and preparing to play golf while dead.

The other man was a much stranger sight, standing as he was with his head bowed and writing on a scorecard with a tiny pencil. He seemed younger than the first man and wore a white, short-sleeved golf shirt with a wide, light-blue collar, a pair of light-blue, bell-bottom slacks, and black-and-white oxford golf shoes. He was tall and slim with wavy, blond hair and long sideburns. Unlike his golf partner, this second man looked like he'd been burnt to a crisp along one side of his body.

Leo had studied the two golfers from his hiding place behind one of the numerous tall, white columns on the clubhouse's wraparound veranda. They ignored him as they studied their scorecards, selected clubs from their bags, and took practice swings. The spirits were still waiting by the guard shack when Sid emerged from the clubhouse and led the way to their stakeout spot. In fact, they must have waited for hours before finally teeing off. Now, here they were, shortly before midnight, taking swings at each other with their clubs and cursing up a storm.

Leo kept his voice low as he described the spirits for Sid. "At this rate, I doubt they'll ever finish all eighteen holes."

"Maybe they never do," Sid whispered. "Maybe this is what happens every night. They tee off and end up in a knockdown, drag-out fight before they even finish the first hole."

"Maybe." Leo turned his head and studied the spirits more closely. The fighting began to wane, so either they were wearing themselves out or had simply grown bored with the argument. When they finally stopped fighting and swearing, they collected their bags and headed in his direction. "They're coming this way."

"Really?" Sid shifted in her chair. "What are they doing?"

Leo waited until the spirits passed them and took up their positions on the tee box of the second hole. "They're getting ready to tee off over there." He pointed before realizing that Sid probably couldn't see him in the dark. "They're on hole number two now."

"Stopped their fighting, I guess." Sid turned her head toward the tee box but saw nothing and heard only the alligator chorus still singing in the swamp.

"I'm not sure. I don't think . . ." Leo stared at the two dead golfers. Something had seemed off about them all evening, and it was only in that moment that Leo finally realized it. "I don't think they know they're dead."

"What?!" Sid asked.

"Ghosts," whispered Leo. "I don't think they're regular spirits. I think they're ghosts." Leo wasn't very familiar with the rules surrounding ghosts, but he knew they were spirits who were trapped, usually for one of two reasons: either they didn't know they were dead or they did know but had unfinished scores to settle. Leo couldn't tell which applied to this pair, but based on their behavior, he assumed it was the former. In fact, they had looked like they were ready to enjoy a nice round of golf, at least until they had started fighting with one another.

Leo guessed that the man who was burnt had probably been killed by a bolt of lightning. The other man appeared unharmed. Heart attack, perhaps. Maybe a stroke. Whatever had killed him hadn't left a mark. In both cases, their deaths were probably very sudden and happened in the middle of play on this course. That's why they were here, perpetually playing their late-night round of golf.

"Why do you think they're ghosts?" whispered Sid, and Leo noted a slight tremor in her voice.

Leo shrugged into the darkness. "I don't really know. It's just a feeling I have. They don't seem like the usual spirits who have crossed over. These two guys haven't done that. They seem stuck, so I'm pretty sure they're ghosts."

As soon as those words left his lips, he regretted uttering them. In that moment, the two ghosts who were taking practice swings on the second tee turned to look at him.

"Uh-oh," Leo muttered.

"What? What's happening?" Sid asked.

Before he could respond, the two dead golfers raised their

clubs and came charging toward him. Leo leaped up from his chair, planted his feet in a wide stance, clamped his hands onto his baseball cap, and muttered the words that Mad Hattie, his unofficial tutor in all things mediumistic, had taught him: "You will not speak to me or approach me. Stay away!" The ghosts were undeterred. They came barreling toward him, and Leo heard what sounded like soldiers' battle cries in his head. Leo tried again but louder this time, "When I am wearing this hat, you will stay away from me. Now go!"

And that's when the ghosts began to beat him with their golf clubs. The sensation was like being whipped with an icicle. "Stop!" Leo cried as he tried to cover his head and neck with his arms. "Stop it!"

"Leo!" Sid bolted from her chair and reached for him in the dark. When she found him, she felt him cowering and shaking like a leaf. Sid wrapped her arms around him, and when she did, she felt like she was in an ice-cold windstorm, except that there was no actual breeze stirring. "What is that?!"

Leo was trying not to cry. "They're hitting me with their clubs." A sob broke loose, and he dropped to his knees, clinging to Sid. She was probably feeling the cold, but Leo doubted it was hurting her as much as it was hurting him. And she certainly couldn't hear the shouting.

"Right." Sid tightened her arms around the boy. "Where are they? Point to them so I know where they are." Leo lifted a shaking hand and pointed to a spot just off his left shoulder. Sid patted his back. "Got it. Stay down, Leo. I'm going to try something."

Sid stood up and stepped in front of Leo, facing the spot he had pointed to. Leo clutched her pant leg with one hand, holding on to her like a scared little boy. Sid's anger flared red-hot.

"Gentlemen!" she shouted. She summoned her best

teacher voice, the one she'd used in her classroom all those years ago when she needed to get the kids under control, the voice all her kids knew meant Sid was angry and they were in big trouble. She clapped her hands twice, the sound like gunshots in the night. "Stop that at once!"

Leo felt the ice-cold bludgeoning stop. He released his grip on her pant leg. "They're gone, Sid."

"Really?" Sid looked around and then instantly felt silly since she couldn't see ghosts, even when they were standing in front of her.

Leo stood and asked, "How did you do that?"

Sid couldn't see his face, but she could hear the awe in his voice. "Apparently, ghosts are a lot like unruly first graders."

Leo laughed and reached for her, wrapping his skinny arms around her in a tight hug. "Thank you," he whispered.

She patted his back. "Any time, Leo. Any time." He released her, and she heard him take a shuddering breath. "Why do you think they attacked you? Did something happen?"

"I don't know." Leo plopped down in his camp chair. "I think they might have heard us talking about them. They must have realized that I could see and hear them. If they're haunting this place, maybe they think it's their job to try to scare people away. Especially people who can see them." He fumbled with the lid of the cooler, pulling out a soda and holding it in Sid's direction. "Want one?"

Sid took her seat beside him. "No, thanks."

Leo popped the top of the can and took several gulps, trying to calm his nerves. "I just hope they don't come back."

"Well, I'm happy to yell at them again if necessary," Sid offered. "So, what were they saying? You mentioned they were shouting at each other before they started attacking you. What did they say?"

Leo shook his head. "I can't tell you."

"Hmm," said Sid. "Foreign language?"

Leo chuckled. "Cussing, actually."

"Pffft," huffed Sid. "I was married to a cop. I doubt that those two ghosts said anything I haven't heard before."

"I don't know about that. The stuff they were saying was pretty bad." He could feel his cheeks heating with embarrassment.

But before Leo could recite for Sid some of the dead golfers' more colorful phrases, somewhere in the distance, someone screamed.

Chapter Three

"That wasn't an alligator!" hissed Leo.

"Nope," Sid said, jumping to her feet. "It wasn't a ghost either." She scrambled in the dark for her backpack and yanked her flashlight from the side pocket. She flicked it on and turned the beam on Leo. "You should stay here. It's probably safer."

"Uh-uh. No way."

"Yes way."

"No! What if the ghosts come back?"

Sid muttered a few choice words under her breath.

"I heard that." Leo grinned. Sid's curse words were G-rated compared to what he'd heard from the two dead golfers.

"Fine." She flung her backpack full of cameras and equipment over her shoulder and turned to head toward the second green. "But you've got to keep up. I'm not waiting."

Leo grabbed his flashlight out of his own backpack and followed after Sid. They left their camp chairs and small cooler behind. Sid ran down the fairway of the short, par 3 second hole and crossed the green. Her backpack banged against her back, and she knew there would be bruises in the morning to accompany the mosquito bites. As best as Sid could determine, the scream had come from their right. That direction was north, and Sid knew from studying the map of the golf course that holes one, two, and three lined up from south to north along the edge of the marsh.

Leo swung his flashlight beam in all directions, searching for alligators as much as for the source of the scream. He followed Sid off the second green and into another small stand of oak trees and azalea bushes, emerging onto the tee box for the third hole. The low purr of an engine could be heard now, although its sound was fading.

"Come on!" yelled Sid. She took off in a full-out sprint, ignoring the painful banging of her bag against her spine.

Leo did his best to keep up with Sid. Running was her thing. It was what she did when she was stressed or upset or bored or trying to work out a problem in her head. It seemed to Leo like she was running most of the time. For him, running was something he liked to avoid. The last time he'd run full out was in middle school gym class. He was built like his father—tall and skinny with long legs—but he'd also inherited his father's lack of physical prowess. When Leo ran, he looked like a marionette whose arms and legs rarely moved with any sort of synchronicity. At this moment, he was very glad that no one could see him flailing his way down the middle of the fairway behind the marathon-runner form of his middle-aged boss.

Sid stopped when she reached the green, and Leo came to a halt next to her, huffing loudly. The third hole on this golf course was a long par 5 that extended farther into the marsh than any of the others. Its green and the northern half of the fairway formed a peninsula surrounded by water, swamp grass, and whatever creatures lived in the bog. A wooden bridge that was wide enough for a golf cart ran from the end of the cart path on the east side of the green to the tee box of the fourth hole, which was located back on dry land between two small mansions.

"Do you see anything?" Sid asked. She waved her flashlight to and fro, but its beam failed to illuminate much more than the bugs flying around them.

"No," Leo answered. He was looking for alligators, and he realized that Sid was probably expecting him to be scouting for something else. "What exactly are we looking for?"

"The source of the scream," she panted. "Or the boat that was here. You heard that engine, right?"

"Yeah, I did. It sounded like it was leaving, like it was moving away from us." Leo heard a splash and swung his flashlight beam toward the noise but saw nothing but ripples on the water. "Can we get out of here? This place is giving me the creeps."

Sid chuckled. "Really? You see and talk to dead people, and yet some alligator calls in the dark have you freaked out?"

Leo shown his flashlight into her face. "I shouldn't have to remind you that between a spirit and an alligator, only one of those two things can chomp onto your leg, drag you under the water, and eat you alive."

Sid shut her eyes against the bright light. "All right, all right." From behind her, just a few yards away, there was a loud growl followed by a series of splashes that sounded like something violently thrashing in the water. "Yeah, okay, let's get out of here."

They jogged back the way they had come and found their camping chairs and cooler right where they'd left them. Sid sighed. "I think whoever was out there is gone now. Let's head home. We can figure out our next moves in the morning."

Leo hesitated. "Look, I don't want to stick around, but do you think someone is hurt? Should we call someone for help?"

Sid pinched the bridge of her nose. She'd been thinking the same thing on the jog back to their stakeout spot. "Maybe. Probably. I don't know." She paced back and forth and then kicked herself for continuing to stall. "Do me a favor, Leo. Pack up our stuff, haul it back to the car, and wait for me there. I'll call the sheriff's office and let them know what we heard, and I'll look around a bit more."

Leo didn't have to be told twice. Sid could deal with the authorities while he waited in the mosquito-free—and hopefully ghost-free—comfort of the car. Leo folded the chairs, picked up the cooler, and walked briskly back toward the clubhouse. He made it all the way to the car without seeing any ghosts. Once everything was loaded in the trunk, Leo slipped into the passenger seat, pulled his headphones from his backpack, and began listening to his favorite playlist. It was the one with all the songs Burt and his bandmates had recommended, songs by The Allman Brothers Band and Lynyrd Skynyrd, songs that were familiar to him because he'd heard Burt and his band playing them in his living room.

As he listened to the music, he tried to ignore the fact that the baseball cap trick that Mad Hattie had taught him hadn't worked tonight. In fact, it had failed so spectacularly that he was afraid he might find bruises on his skin in the morning. What had gone wrong?

Leo shook his head. He was too tired to try to figure it out now. Whatever the problem was, it could wait until morning. Besides, he didn't want to do anything that would cause the ghosts to come find him again. Leo cranked up his music, reclined his seat, and closed his eyes. He was asleep within minutes. In fact, he was still asleep when the flashing lights of the patrol car pulled up behind him.

Chapter Four

By the time Sid finished her call with the sheriff's office and made her way back to the parking lot, Leo was sound asleep in the passenger seat of her car. She was tempted to sit in the car as well to avoid the mosquitos, but she didn't want to wake him. He'd had a rough night, what with all the alligators, the running, and the ass-kicking by a couple of ghosts. Instead, Sid leaned against the trunk and waited for the patrol car to arrive.

She'd been tempted to call Detective Tony Davis, who had been her late husband's partner in the marine unit and who had helped her solve the mystery surrounding Wes's death and the death of their daughter, Iris. It was late, though, and Sid knew Tony's wife, Naomi, would not appreciate her calling the house while their young son Dante, slept. Besides, what could Tony do? If Sid had found a dead body, that would be different—he would have been the first person she called—but tonight there had only been a scream. Granted, it was a loud, bloodcurdling scream, but there had been no dead body. At least none that she could find with a couple of flashlights.

There had also been the sound of an engine. Sid's best guess was that it had been a jon boat. One of the perks of being married to an officer in the marine unit was that you had a lot of exposure to boats and engines and all kinds of watercraft, whether you wanted it or not. Sid knew enough to know that no one would venture into a marshland like the one that bordered the west side of Anastasia Island unless they were in one of only a handful of boats: a canoe, a kayak, an airboat, or a jon boat. The first two wouldn't have had an engine, and no one would mistake the deafening sound of an airboat for the more muted outboard-engine noise she'd heard tonight. Thus, a jon boat seemed to be the answer.

Wes had been on Sid's mind a lot lately. This weekend was the third anniversary of his and their daughter's death. Iris had only been five years old when it happened. She'd been killed instantly. Wes was not so lucky. Thanks to Leo, Sid now knew the truth about what happened that night. The boy's gift for seeing and communicating with dead people had come in handy. Wes's spirit had shown Leo what transpired, and Leo had experienced it—actually felt it—in harrowing detail. For the pain Leo went through, Sid was truly sorry, but in doing so, Leo had given her a gift. Sid could finally move on, knowing the truth about that night and no longer having to guess, having to wonder, about what really happened to the people she loved most in the world. While Sid knew justice might never be fully served, she also knew that Wes and Iris were at peace. They were no longer in pain, no longer suffering, and that helped take the edge off her own heartbreak. The anniversary of their death was always difficult to bear, but this year it was just a tiny bit easier. Thanks to Leo.

Half an hour passed between Sid placing the call to the sheriff's office and a patrol car arriving. When it did, it pulled up behind Sid's car, ignoring the parking lines, and two deputies got out. Both of them, one male and one female, were so young that Sid wondered if she'd taught them in one of her first-grade classes. Surely she wasn't old enough, and they weren't young enough, for that to be true. At least, she hoped that was the case.

"Deputies," said Sid, by way of greeting. "Sorry to drag you out here in the middle of the night."

"It's a slow night." The male deputy shrugged. "I'm Deputy Weber. This is Deputy Adcock." He pointed to his partner.

Sid nodded as she studied the two deputies. They were the same height, a little shorter than Sid herself, and stocky. In the poorly lit parking lot, they appeared to have the same dirty-blond hair color and brown eyes. Even their facial features were similar. Sid tried to remember whether Wes had ever talked about there being twins in the sheriff's office, but she couldn't recall. And he'd died three years ago, so it was entirely possible that these two young deputies were twins who were recently hired.

"I'm Sidney Stone." Sid offered her hand, and both officers shook it. She suppressed a smile; even their handshakes felt the same.

"You reported hearing a scream, is that right?" asked Deputy Adcock.

Sid nodded. "Yes, we heard it coming from the direction of the third hole."

"Can you give us the house address?" asked Deputy Adcock, reaching for her notebook.

"Not a house. The third hole." Sid frowned. "Actually, it was probably from somewhere in the marsh along the third hole." The two deputies glanced at each other and sighed in unison. Again, Sid tried not to smirk. "I can show you if you'd like."

"Fine," muttered Deputy Adcock.

Deputy Weber made a sweeping gesture with his hands. "Please lead the way, ma'am."

Sid inwardly cringed. She hated being called "ma'am," but it was inevitable given the youth of these two deputies. Sid led them past the starter's shack and down the first fairway toward their stakeout position. She explained what she and Leo had been doing there. "We've been hired by the board of directors of the club to look into . . . a situation."

"What kind of situation?" asked Adcock as she scanned the stakeout area with her flashlight.

"I can't tell you that." Sid was not about to reveal client confidences to these two children, even if they were sheriff's deputies. When Adcock opened her mouth to object, Sid cut her off. "It involves some complaints by Oakmire residents who think people might be trespassing on the golf course at night." Sid held up her hands. "But that is all I'm at liberty to say."

"If there is criminal trespass involved," began Adcock.

But Sid interrupted her again. "The sheriff's office has been notified of this situation on four separate occasions. In each instance, a deputy such as yourselves was sent over, found nothing, and left. The board of directors hired me to stake out the place for a few nights to see if I could catch whoever was trespassing." Sid held up her hands again. "Just photos. Maybe video. Nothing more than that. I'm sure any evidence that is obtained proving criminal trespass would be turned over to the sheriff's office as promptly as possible."

Adcock raised an eyebrow, and Weber licked his lips in an attempt to hide a smile.

"Shall we continue with the tour?" asked Sid, and then she walked off in the direction of the second and third holes without waiting for an answer.

As they strolled down the fairway of the second hole,

Weber called out to her. "You know, I recognize you. You're that private eye who took down Sheriff Colquitt, aren't you?"

Without breaking her stride, Sid answered, "Sheriff Colquitt took himself down."

"Yeah, but you're the one that put the case together, right? You're the one who found out that he was posing as his dead twin brother, right?" asked Weber.

"Mmm," Sid grunted. She really didn't want to discuss the case with these two.

Weber jogged to catch up with her. "Your husband used to be a deputy, right?"

"Marine unit, yes."

"Cool."

"Yes, very cool." Sid picked up her pace, hoping to get this whole night over with as soon as possible.

"And didn't he—"

"Die?" asked Sid, adding an intentional sharpness to her voice. "Yes, he did. He was a marine deputy for many years, and Sheriff Colquitt lured him to a remote location under false pretenses where he and my five-year-old daughter were killed in a horrific car crash that should never ever have happened." She halted and spun to face Weber, shining her flashlight beam into his eyes. "Now, if you don't mind, I really don't want to talk about my dead husband and daughter or the bastard who was directly responsible for their deaths. If it's okay with you, I'd prefer to just tell you what happened tonight, show you what you need to see, and then go home. It's late. I'm tired. And I'm sure you both have much better things to do than traipse around a golf course in the middle of the night and get eaten alive by mosquitos."

As if on cue, Adcock slapped her cheek in an attempt to kill a mosquito. "Just show us where you think the scream came from."

Weber stepped aside, and Adcock took his place beside Sid as their little parade continued across the second green toward the third hole.

"Sorry about that," Adcock muttered. "It's just that it's all anyone is talking about in the office. I mean, the sheriff getting arrested and all. It's big news."

"Mmm," Sid grunted again.

"That was good work," Adcock whispered. "Takes balls to bring down someone like that."

Sid didn't bother to reply.

Once she led the deputies through the trees and onto the third hole's tee box, she stopped. "Okay, this is where I think the scream came from. Somewhere out there." She pointed her flashlight down the fairway, but it didn't illuminate much. "This is the last hole on the north side of the clubhouse that runs along the marsh. Holes four through nine weave through the neighborhood and head back toward the clubhouse. The other half of the course, holes ten through eighteen, are on the southside of the clubhouse, and the scream definitely didn't come from south of where I was sitting. It had to come from somewhere around here." She dropped her flashlight, letting it illuminate her feet. "When I heard it, I ran in the direction I thought it was coming from, but I never heard another scream. By the time I got here, I heard an engine, likely from a jon boat. The sound faded, so I assume whoever was in the boat was leaving the area."

"Why do you think it was a jon boat?" asked Adcock.

Sid told the deputies her theory about what kinds of boats would be used to venture into the marsh. "I'd been here since sunset. I didn't hear boat motors prior to the one I heard leaving. Whoever was driving that boat tonight probably used oars on their approach from the river, and whatever emergency caused someone to scream probably required them to leave in a hurry. Hence the use of an outboard motor. That boat, whatever it was and whoever was on it, has to be long gone by now."

Adcock nodded. "Okay, we'll take a look." She and Weber left Sid standing on the tee box as they made a sweep of the third hole, up the west side of the fairway, around the green, and back down the east side. Sid watched their flashlight beams sweeping side to side. By the time they returned to her, she had at least four more mosquito bites.

"Nothing," said Weber, scratching his elbow. "We're not going to be able to see anything tonight anyway." He looked up, shining his flashlight upward in a comical attempt to light up the sky. "Too cloudy. No moon."

Adcock sighed. "You're right that whoever was here is probably long gone. They either left on that boat you heard, or they ran into the neighborhood. We'll let dispatch know to send someone out right away if they get any more calls from this area tonight."

"Fine," said Sid. "You guys done then? Can we get out of here?"

Weber smacked the same arm he had been scratching. "Yeah, let's go before these things drain me completely."

They walked back to the parking lot, and Adcock pointed to a sleeping Leo in the passenger seat of Sid's car. "Was he with you tonight? Does he have anything to add?"

Sid shook her head. "Nope. Good night, Deputies."

As Sid reached for the door handle, Weber pointed to the only other car in the parking lot. "Any idea who that belongs to?"

All three of them glanced over at the sleek, black sports car that was parked in the last reserved spot right in front of the clubhouse.

"Nope," Sid answered. "It was here when I got here tonight." She didn't explain that the reason she knew the car was already parked at the club was because Leo had whistled when he saw it. She also didn't mention that she'd already jotted down the license plate number.

Chapter Five

The next morning, Leo waited until he heard his grandfather fire up his truck and pull out of the driveway before he crawled out of bed. It was early, a little before eight o'clock, and while Leo wanted nothing more than to sleep in until noon, he had something important to take care of this morning. He needed to understand why the situation with the ghosts had spiraled out of control the previous night, and he knew of only one person who could possibly shed some light on it. He dressed quickly and went downstairs. His grandfather had posted a note to the refrigerator letting Leo know that he would be working at La Señora, a bed-and-breakfast down at the end of Saragossa Street. Between La Señora and its rival, the Crane's Roost, directly across the street, Burt had a nice stream of part-time construction renovation work to keep him busy in retirement. If Leo had been awake before Burt had left for this latest job, he would have been roped into helping, but renovation work was not part of Leo's plans for the day. He also wanted to avoid his grandfather for another reason, namely last night's big, fat violation of Burt's no-spirits-allowed clause in his détente with Sid.

Leo grabbed his house key from the table by the front door and headed out into the late-summer morning. It was already hot and sticky, without a cloud in the sky. There'd been no rain for more than a week, and everything that was once vibrant green was now faded and brittle from the unforgiving Florida sunshine. The lawns smelled slightly burnt, and the ever-present birdsong on their street sounded subdued and sluggish.

As Leo walked, he scrolled through his mother's social media pages and read her latest blog post. PB&J Buffet was going strong, if his mom's photos and videos were to be believed. Leo's father had passed away a little over a year ago, and Trisha Paisley Roberts had changed her name to Paizley—with a Z, because it was apparently better for branding—and packed up their life in Norfolk, Virginia, to head south to St. Augustine. Her plans did not include staying put. No sooner had Paizley parked Leo with his grandfather than she had taken off with her childhood friend, the recently divorced Brooklyn Montecito, and Brooklyn's fluffy teacup dog named Jezebel, all in an effort to outrun the grief of losing her young husband.

Paizley Roberts was only thirty-three. She'd gotten pregnant at eighteen and been cut off by her parents shortly thereafter. She'd worked two jobs for as long as Leo could remember, trying to make ends meet with the meager salary his father brought home as an enlisted navy sailor. Leo didn't begrudge his mother's adventures—he knew she'd never had any before now—but he sometimes wished she would have taken him with her. He missed her, especially at times like this. Life was hard and very confusing, and he really needed one of her hugs and to hear her tell him that everything would be okay. Leo fired off a text, a quick one to say that he was all right and to ask how she was doing.

He put his phone back in his pocket and wondered how long it would be before he heard back from her. She never replied right away, and sometimes two or three days would pass before he'd get a response. He talked to her on the phone about once a week, and lately that was only because Leo had called her first. Paizley Roberts had largely abandoned her parenting duties. Leo knew it was because she was still grieving and because his grandfather Burt was taking good care of him. Still, it hurt to be left behind and all but forgotten.

By the time Leo arrived at his first destination, he was dripping with sweat. The line at Fire in the Hole was out the door, but it moved quickly. Leo bought three datil-pepper-glazed donuts and then went next door to Pirate Joe's, where he ordered a large coffee and ate one of the donuts while he waited. When his order was up, he added cream and copious amounts of sugar before heading out of the café and up Aviles Street to the Plaza de la Constitución.

He found Mad Hattie sitting under her usual tree in the only part of downtown St. Augustine with any reliable shade. Hattie's tree was a large live oak, its branches spreading wide and providing shelter from the sun if not the humidity. Hattie was sitting cross-legged on a blanket, wearing a bright yellow sun dress and her wide-brimmed straw hat. This morning, her feet were dirty, her long dreadlocks were tied back at the nape of her neck, and she was wearing oversize, dark sunglasses. Leo could smell the coconut scent of her sunscreen as he approached. Hattie didn't move a muscle.

Leo cleared his throat. "Miss Hattie," he whispered. "Miss Hattie, I brought you coffee and a donut."

A smile tugged at the corners of Hattie's mouth. "Boy, I told you that you don't need to bring me that no more."

"I know." Leo kneeled in front of her and held out the coffee cup. "I wanted to."

Hattie's face brightened into a smile that was more gums than teeth. "All right then." She took the cup and removed the lid, inhaling deeply. "What can I do for you, Leo?"

Leo plucked one of the donuts from the bag and handed the bag with the last donut over to Hattie. She set the bag and her cup down on her blanket and, without removing her sunglasses, studied him in silence for several moments. Leo grew uncomfortable under her gaze and absently scratched at the mosquito bite on his neck. Hattie pointed a crooked finger at him. "You look terrible, boy. Now, tell Ol' Hattie what's been goin' on."

Leo picked at the glaze on his donut. "I saw a ghost last night." He paused, but Hattie said nothing and merely sipped her coffee. "Two, actually." He turned around and lifted his shirt so that Hattie could see the faint bruises on his back. "They attacked me with golf clubs." He quickly lowered his shirt and sat facing her again. "It felt like . . . I don't know. It was cold, and it stung, but it wasn't like getting hit with an actual golf club, thankfully."

Hattie had gone still, the cup lifted halfway to her lips. "Where was this?"

"Oakmire golf course. It's over on Anastasia Island. You know it?" When Hattie nodded, Leo added, "We were sitting between the first and second holes."

Hattie cocked an eyebrow. "We?"

"My boss and me. She's a private investigator. Her name's Sidney Stone. Maybe you heard of her? She's been in the news lately because of that Sheriff Colquitt stuff. You know, him getting arrested and all." Leo shrugged. "I helped her out with that case. And I'm helping her with a new one out at Oakmire."

He took a bite of his donut, managing to fit about half of it in his mouth.

Hattie took another sip of coffee. "Are the ghosts connected with your case?"

Leo shook his head. "Don't think so." He told her about the two dead golfers and everything that had transpired prior to them beating him with their putters. "I did what you told me to do, but it didn't work, and I don't understand why."

Hattie sighed. "Ghosts don't play by the same rules as spirits. They are darker, especially the ones who like to haunt places. Those that don't know they're dead, they just keep doin' their thing, moving around like they used to when they were alive. But the ones that like haunting? Well. It takes a lot more to deal with them. And it sounds like your two ghosts like haunting that golf course." She clucked her tongue. "Best thing to do is not go back there."

"I can't do that." Leo shook his head again. "We have another stakeout tonight. I have to go back." He leaned forward. "What can I do, Miss Hattie? I really don't want them to attack me again."

Hattie nodded. "Come with me, boy. We got to go see someone."

Leo stood and helped Hattie to her feet, and then he carried her bag and rolled-up blanket as they left the shady park and began walking up St. George Street. At this early hour, very few shops were open, and only a few tourists were roaming the pedestrian-only section of the Old City's historic downtown. They turned down Cuna Street, a narrow, one-laned, cobblestone street that headed east toward the bay. When they reached a two-story, white-clapboard house with flamingo-pink trim, Hattie stepped up onto the front porch and knocked on the door. The house had been converted into a shop, like many of the buildings in the downtown district. According to both the wooden sign out front and the fancy script painted across the front windows, the shop was called Muy Local.

"It's closed, Miss Hattie." Leo pointed to a sign in the glass window of the front door. "They don't open until eleven o'clock."

Hattie winked. "She'll open for me." She knocked again and again, then paused and knocked a fourth time. Each series of knocks was a singsong pattern, but Leo couldn't quite place the tune. Hattie leaned against the porch railing and waited while Leo fidgeted from foot to foot, trying to peer into the windows.

A few minutes later, the door opened, and a woman poked her head out. "Well, happy birthday to you, too." Leo grinned as he realized that was the rhythm Hattie had beaten on the shop's door.

The woman standing in the doorway was short, barely five feet tall, with a mass of gray curls piled high on top of her head. Leo guessed she was probably his grandfather's age, so in her mid-sixties. She wore a long, red, silk scarf around her head that was tied at the nape of her neck so that its ends streamed down her back. She was dressed in a pale denim sundress and red espadrilles. Her skin was a light brown, and a dark mole sat atop her right cheekbone. She glanced over at Leo and smiled. "Come on in, Hattie, and bring this handsome young man with you." She winked at Leo and ducked back inside.

Hattie chuckled and followed her in. Leo rolled his eyes and entered the shop, closing the door behind him. The shop was an explosion of color in all manner of forms—jewelry, pottery, scarves, hats, T-shirts, paintings, and photographs. Wind chimes hung from the ceiling, clothing hung on a rolling rack in one corner, and a small bookshelf near the register contained a couple dozen books. One of the titles caught Leo's eye, *The Old City's Most Haunted*. He picked it up and began flipping through it, wondering if the Oakmire golf course made the list.

"That one's crap," said the woman. She pointed to the book Leo was holding. "That author doesn't know shit. She wouldn't recognize a spirit if it walked up and kissed her on the lips." The woman smiled at him and then at Hattie. "Come upstairs. I just made coffee." She beckoned them to follow, and the trio paraded single file up a narrow staircase at the back of the shop. The apartment on the second floor was homier than the shop below but no less colorful and cluttered. Boxes were stacked high on one side of the living room, the occupant of the apartment having given it over to storage for the shop.

Hattie and Leo sat at a dining table near the window overlooking Cuna Street. Leo watched as a young jogger ran down the street, his head bobbing along to whatever tune he was listening to in his earphones, and a bearded homeless man shuffled past the shop, his bedroll perched high on top of a military-issue backpack. Other than that, the street below was quiet.

The apartment, however, was anything but. The woman disappeared into the tiny galley kitchen and banged and clanged around in there for several minutes. The scent of toast and strong coffee wafted out, and Leo's stomach rumbled in response. He was hungry, and two donuts weren't enough for a growing fifteen-year-old boy. Eventually, the woman emerged and placed on the table an intricately carved serving tray loaded with a coffee carafe, three stacked cups, a sugar bowl, and thick slices of toasted, buttered Cuban bread. Before taking her own seat, she passed out plates and napkins to her guests.

Once seated, the woman turned to Leo and held out her hand. "I'm Valentina Ortiz, but everyone calls me Val."

Leo shook the woman's hand. "Nice to meet you. I'm Leo."

"Leo," Val repeated, cocking her head to the side. "You're not local, are you?"

"No, ma'am," Leo answered. "At least, I wasn't before last month. I live with my grandfather over on Saragossa. His name's Burt Roberts."

Val shook her head. "I don't think I've had the pleasure. What about your parents, Leo?"

Leo's gaze dropped to his lap. "My dad died a year ago, and my mom is in . . ." He paused to try to remember where her latest posts had pinned her. "Memphis, I think? No, wait. I think she's somewhere in Alabama. At some old recording studio."

"Muscle Shoals," Hattie muttered.

"Yeah, that one." Leo nodded. "My mom's a travel blogger, so I'm living with my grandfather for a while." He didn't want to go into any further details about how Paizley Roberts had abandoned her only son on her father-in-law's doorstep and run off with her old high school friend to travel around the United States in a tiny camper and post about it on social media.

"Well, that sounds exciting. I'm not local either, despite the name of my shop," said Val, and Leo was grateful to her for pivoting the conversation away from his absentee mother. Val picked up the coffee carafe and poured the dark, thick liquid into a cup, which she handed to Hattie. "I was born in Cuba, but I moved to Miami with my family when I was a little girl. I owned a small art gallery there for many years, but I sold it and moved up here after my husband died." She sighed. "And I opened my little shop downstairs. St. Augustine has a small but enthusiastic local art scene. I only sell work by local artists and artisans. Some of it is very good. The rest . . ." She shrugged and smiled. Picking up another cup from the tray, she asked, "Coffee, Leo?"

"Um," Leo hesitated. He didn't like coffee, but he didn't want to be rude. "Okay, sure."

She poured him a cup and handed it to him. Leo watched as Hattie heaped sugar into her cup and stirred vigorously.

Val did the same. "Cuban coffee is served very strong and very sweet, Leo."

Leo nodded and mimicked the two women, adding lots of sugar to his cup and stirring until a caramel-colored foam rested on top of the dark liquid. He took a tiny sip, and, though not completely repulsed, he decided he wasn't really a fan. He set his cup down, and Val passed him the plate of toast with a knowing smile.

"So, what brings you two to my door this early in the morning?" Val sat back in her chair, crossed her legs, and sipped her coffee. Leo took a bite of his toast, almost groaning with pleasure at its buttery flavor, and waited for Hattie to answer the woman's questions.

Hattie took a sip, placed her cup on the table, and pointed at Leo. "This boy picked a fight with some ghosts over at Oakmire last night."

"Really?" Val swung her gaze to Leo, her eyes lighting up as they went. "Do tell."

Leo shook his head at Hattie, who merely chuckled in response. "Don't worry, Leo. This woman here is just like us." She pointed to Val. "She has the gift, too."

Val nodded. "For as long as I can remember, I've been able to see spirits. Not like Hattie, mind you. I only see points of light, not full-bodied spirits, but I sometimes receive messages from them to pass along to their loved ones." She frowned. "And occasionally I get premonitions." Leo's eyebrows shot up, and Val nodded again. "I don't like those so much. They mostly come to me in daydreams, but occasionally I get them at night, too." She held up a finger. "I've learned they are not set in stone. They can be thwarted as long as the person in my premonition changes one thing."

"What do you mean?" asked Leo. He caught himself leaning forward, eager for new information. He'd not had premonitions before, but that didn't mean he never would.

"For example," began Val, "if I had a premonition about you and I saw you wearing exactly what you have on right now, I'd tell you to take off your shoes and throw them away. If you don't have those shoes, then what I saw won't happen." She smiled. "At least not in that exact way." Leo nodded. "So, now, tell me about this fight you picked with your ghosts."

"I didn't pick a fight with anyone," Leo grumbled. "They started beating me up for no good reason." Val smiled and nodded at him, and Leo found himself telling her everything he'd told Hattie not half an hour earlier. "They only stopped because Sid yelled at them."

Val leaned forward. "She yelled at them?"

Leo nodded.

"But she can't see them?"

Leo shook his head. "I pointed to where they were standing in front of me, and she stood there and yelled at them and told them to stop attacking me."

"And they did?" asked Val. When Leo nodded, she added a good, long "hmmm." Val contemplated him for a long moment and then turned to Hattie. The two women exchanged looks, and then Val said, "Haunting, don't you think?" Hattie nodded her agreement. Val scooted her chair back and stood up. "Well then, you'll need some protection. Follow me."

They went downstairs to Val's shop, and she removed a small, plastic container from under one of the jewelry counters. "Let's see what we have." Val rummaged around in the box, which was full of rocks. Some were shiny, some sparkly, but they were rocks nonetheless. She selected three and held them out to Leo on the palm of her hand. Pointing to each of them in turn, she said, "Shungite, jet stone, and amethyst." Two smooth black rocks and a jagged, sparkly, purple one. "This combination should prove useful. Together they provide protection against otherworldly beings, like ghosts, and against curses."

"Curses?!" Leo stepped back in surprise.

Val chuckled. "Highly unlikely," she assured him, "but best to be safe." She handed him the rocks, and Leo noted that they felt cold to the touch. Val closed the lid on her box. "Keep them in your pocket when you go to that golf course. Probably best to keep them with you at all times—in your pocket or by your bed at night—especially for the other one."

"Other one?" Leo glanced between Val and Hattie as his pulse began to race. "What other one?"

Hattie raised her eyebrows and crossed her arms over her chest. "Yeah, Val. What other one?"

Val sighed. "I had a premonition about our meeting." She leaned her elbows on the glass top of the jewelry case. "I knew you would be coming this morning. That's why I had the coffee and tostadas prepared. I didn't know what we would be talking about, but I saw you both arriving at my door with another." She frowned. "The third was in shadow."

Hattie grunted. "And when we arrived, did you see it? This third one?"

Val nodded. "It was behind you, maybe ten or twenty feet away. Just a shadow. But it vanished quickly."

"Any feelings? Any messages?" asked Hattie.

Val shook her head. "No, none. I think that's good. I don't sense danger, but . . ."

Hattie frowned. "But it's in shadow." Val nodded, and Hattie turned to Leo. "You keep those crystals with you, boy. And if you see or feel anythin' unusual, you come find me or Val. You hear me?"

Leo smirked. "More unusual than getting my butt kicked by two dead golfers?"

The two women laughed.

"Yes, boy. More unusual than that," Hattie said, wagging a finger at him. "Especially if it feels dangerous." She placed her hands on his shoulders and looked up at him. "But we are here to help. You have people who love you and care about you in the here and now. No matter what you encounter walkin' around in this life—whether it seems good or bad, innocent or dangerous—you don't have to be afraid. You hear me, Leo? You don't need to be afraid. Not of your ghosts or of anybody else's."

Leo nodded, less out of understanding and more out of embarrassment. Hattie's words about people loving him had his eyes pricking with tears, but her comments about trying not to be afraid of ghosts and other dangers had the short hairs on the back of his neck standing on end.

"One more thing, Leo," said Val over Hattie's shoulder. "Next time you see your golfing ghosts, I think you should speak to them."

Chapter Six

By midmorning, Sid was sitting in her office and staring across her desk at Tony Davis. Since her husband's untimely death, Tony had switched from the marine unit and was currently a detective in the major crimes unit. He had come by her office less than an hour after she'd made the call to him, bringing with him donuts and coffee, as was his habit whenever he stopped by to discuss one of her cases. He'd also brought his four-year-old son, Dante, whose dimpled smile always tugged at Sid's heart. Tony was on childcare duty while his wife, Naomi, worked a weekend shift as an emergency room nurse at Flagler Hospital. Sid and Tony talked while Dante played with his toy cars and his favorite stuffed bunny named Hopper, leaving an impressive dusting of donut crumbs all over Sid's floor as he did so.

"The car belongs to Cameron Chase," said Tony as he selected a donut for himself from the box on Sid's desk. "Know him?"

Sid shook her head. "No. Should I?"

Tony smiled. "Probably. Local boy makes good and all

that." Tony read from his notebook, "Cameron Chase. Twenty-four years old. Born and raised here in St. Augustine. Attended Saint Augustine High School, where he was captain of the golf team and ranked second in the state of Florida. Got a full ride to the University of Florida on a golf scholarship—"

Sid snorted. "That's an actual thing?"

Tony frowned. "Yes, Sid. Golf is an actual sport. They give college scholarships for it and everything. There's all kinds of tournaments, trophies, prize money. Even ugly blazers. The pros make serious bank, too."

"And this kid was one of these big-shot pros? At only twenty-four?" Sid shook her head. She'd never understood the game of golf, and even now that she'd landed a big, fancy golf club as a client, she still didn't want to.

Tony swallowed the rest of his donut. "Not yet, but he is on his way. You probably saw it on the news. Or were you too busy watching the coverage of you and the sheriff to notice anything else?" Sid chucked her wadded-up napkin at Tony's head, but he caught it with his free hand and tossed it into the trash can next to Sid's desk.

"Anyway," Tony continued, "Cameron Chase was the highest-ranked amateur in the nation two years ago when he graduated college. His first year on the PGA tour wasn't great, but he's kicked it up a notch this year. In fact, he's expected to do really well at the big PGA tournament in Savannah next week. It's the last big tour event of the season." He noticed Sid was staring blankly at him. "Happens every Labor Day weekend?" She continued to stare. "I take it you're not a sports fan then." Sid shrugged, and Tony shook his head. "It's a big deal. Big money. TV coverage, interviews. The kid's expected to do really well. If he finishes high enough on the leaderboard, it could mean lucrative endorsement deals. And if he wins it . . ." Tony blew out his cheeks. "That's next-level fame and fortune."

Sid slowly sipped her coffee as Tony reached for another donut. "But he hasn't made it big yet?" she asked. Tony shook his head and mumbled something with his mouth full. Sid frowned. "So, how is he able to afford a fancy sports car? Family money?"

Tony washed down his donut with a sip of coffee and checked his notebook. "Not that I can tell. He has an apartment over on Anastasia. One of those old-time, eight-unit deals. Rent is probably high but only because it's close to the beach, not because it's high-end luxury. His dad lives in that trailer park off of King Street. You know the one? It's over the railroad tracks and past the cemetery." Sid nodded because everyone knew about Paradise Trailer Park, the perfect mix of Old Florida nostalgia and modern meth labs. "Mom's not around. His parents divorced when he was around five. She left the area shortly after. No sign of her since."

Sid smiled at the detective. He was a big man, all towering height and bulging muscles that hadn't diminished much since his glory days playing college football at UF, and Sid was afraid the chair he was sitting in might collapse under his weight. It was only a discarded dining room chair from the local thrift store, after all. She really needed to get something sturdier if he was going to make it a habit of stopping by her office. "So, Detective Davis, you found out all of that information just by looking up the license plate I gave you?" She smirked and took a bite of her donut.

"Not exactly." Tony grinned and tossed his empty coffee cup into the trash can. "But when I learned the vehicle was a Maserati GranTurismo, I looked into it a little more. Made some calls." He sat back and checked his notes, Sid wincing as his chair groaned in protest. "It's leased from a dealership up in Jacksonville. A lease like that is over two grand a month, easy. Even if he got a good deal on it—local celebrity, good advertising for the dealership, that sort of thing—it would still have cost him more than he could probably afford. As far as I can tell, based on the recent news coverage, his tournament winnings last year were around forty thousand dollars, and he works part-time as a golf pro at Oakmire Golf and Country Club. Looks like he has some small endorsement deals, nothing major. Nothing that would give him the kind of cash flow needed for a Maserati."

Sid raised an eyebrow. "So, what are you saying?"

"I'm saying there's probably more to this kid than just being a good golfer." Tony closed his notebook. "Is he involved in a case you're working?"

Sid shook her head. "Not that I know of." She filled him in on the barest details about her newest client and the late-night callout of Deputies Tweedledee and Tweedledum. "Chase's car was still in the parking lot when we left. That was well after midnight. I doubt very seriously that he was still on the course taking practice shots . . . or whatever it is that golfers do."

Tony shook his head. "Probably not." He checked his watch, then stood and scooped Dante into his arms. The little boy laughed, showing the dimples in his cheeks.

Sid helped Tony pick up the toys and walked them out to Tony's car. After the detective strapped his son into his car seat, he turned and leveled a serious stare at the PI. "Take care of yourself, Sid. My gut tells me this Chase kid was probably involved in something." He shrugged. "Let's hope it's nothing to do with your case."

Sid grinned. "I'll be careful, Detective."

She waved goodbye to Dante and watched as they drove away. Then she returned to her office and did a quick online search for Cameron Chase. All she had to do was type in the young man's first name, and up popped his full name and a thumbnail photo. There were countless articles, photos, and videos chronicling the golfer's burgeoning career, not to mention numerous fan sites and online discussions. It only took a few clicks for Sid to understand what all the fuss was about. The golf world's newest rising star was a fit, trim, handsome young man with a shock of ginger curls.

At six o'clock that evening, Sid and Leo returned to the Oakmire Golf and Country Club for another stakeout. Sid had called her contact on the board, Jonathan Beedlemeyer, who was the current chairperson, and asked him to give her a tour of the golf course. Mr. Beedlemeyer had recently taken over from the previous chair, a man who had occupied the seat for seventeen consecutive years, from the early 2000s until he died in his sleep a few months back at the tender age of ninety-six.

Last night when she and Leo had arrived for their stakeout, they found that Beedlemeyer had already gone home for the evening despite having promised to be there to meet her, so the pro shop manager had shown them where to set up. When Sid called the chair earlier this morning, she demanded that he meet her at the club this evening. After some hemming and hawing about dinner plans, he'd finally agreed to give her a tour of the course, but Sid wasn't holding her breath.

Thus, she was more than a bit surprised and very relieved to see Jonathan Beedlemeyer waiting for them on the grand veranda of the clubhouse when they pulled into the parking lot. Beedlemeyer was a short skeleton of a man who looked like he could barely swing a club. He wore crisp, khaki slacks and a starched, white, long-sleeved, collared shirt that looked at least two sizes too big for his small frame. His fine wisps of white hair had broken free of their comb-over and were flapping about in the wind. Beedlemeyer raised his hand and waved at them but made no move to walk across the parking lot to help them with their equipment.

Sid and Leo took their time emerging from the car and unloading their bags, chairs, and cooler from the trunk. "That car's here again," said Leo, pointing to the sleek, black sports car.

"Or maybe it's still here," Sid muttered. "As in, it never left." The car was parked in the same spot that they'd seen it in last night. This evening, though, it was covered with a dusting of pollen and a smattering of fallen leaves from the nearby live oak. The car looked as if it hadn't been moved since yesterday. "It belongs to some hotshot professional golfer," she added. "Some local kid named Cameron Chase." Leo glanced sideways at her, and she shrugged. "I called Detective Davis this morning and asked him to run the plates."

Leo looked longingly at the shiny, black car. "Maybe I should take up golf."

They trudged across the parking lot and up the front steps to the veranda. Jonathan Beedlemeyer shook their hands. "We are in luck," said Beedlemeyer as he clasped his hands together and grinned at them. "The tournament is wrapping up a bit earlier than we expected. Come, we should be able to get started." He led the way first to his office, where they deposited their gear, and then out to the golf course.

"Tell me more about this tournament," Sid prompted.

On their way out of the clubhouse, they had to navigate through a swarm of golfers who had gathered both inside at the bar and outside on the back veranda, which overlooked the first and eighteenth holes. The golfers all smelled of sweat, bug spray, sunscreen, and alcohol. Most of them appeared well and truly drunk, and Sid wasn't sure whether that was from the open bar or the attractive cart girl who drove past them in a golf cart fully equipped with coolers that were no doubt empty of alcohol this late in the day. Most of the golfers were men, and almost none of them looked like athletes of any sort.

Leo noticed his two ghosts were hanging around a particularly boisterous cluster of seven men, all of whom were laughing hysterically at one of their crowd's animated reenactments of a failed golf swing. The ghosts seemed to be laughing right along with the men. Leo felt in his pocket for Val's three stones and then tugged the brim of his baseball cap. Fortunately, the ghosts didn't make a move toward him, seemingly content to party with the live golfers.

Beedlemeyer strode toward the first tee box, appearing to ignore the clamor and mayhem that dozens of drunk golfers were causing on the club's lovely veranda and lawn. "This is an annual charity event hosted by Tolbert, Nussbaum & Tate."

Both Sid and Leo knew the name. It was one of the largest, if not the largest, personal injury law firms in Florida, and it had managed to successfully expand into several other states in the Southeast over the last twenty years. The firm's managing partner, a short, slick-haired man with a chiseled jaw and a voice an octave higher than should be appropriate for a grown man, was famed for two things: the single largest class action judgment awarded by a jury in the last ten years and an interview in which he claimed that his firm's goal was world domination of the personal injury market.

TNT, as the law firm was commonly known, ran television and radio ads twenty-four hours a day, seven days a week on every available channel, and they made no apologies for aggressively marketing themselves as *the* law firm for the common man. The fact that they took up to 40 percent of any award in a plaintiff's case was not mentioned with as much prominence or frequency. The law firm's success translated into branch offices in just about every town in Florida, private jets for the big rainmakers, and carte blanche to misbehave at firm outings like this one. Sid turned her head just in time to see one of those high-flying lawyers take a very ungraceful tumble off the bottom two steps of the veranda and land on his ample backside to the laughter and cheers of the crowd. Someone shouted whether anyone knew a good lawyer, and Beedlemeyer visibly cringed.

"As I was saying," said Beedlemeyer, clearing his throat. "The firm hosts an annual shotgun tournament here on the weekend before Labor Day. We are very fortunate that they select Oakmire for this event every year."

Sid raised an eyebrow. "Why is that? Seems like they may be more trouble than they're worth."

Beedlemeyer cleared his throat again. "TNT spends a great deal of money on this event. We have to charge them a premium, given that they hold the tournament on one of our busiest Saturdays of the year." He paused before adding, "And two of our board members are senior partners in the firm."

"I see," said Sid, glancing back over her shoulder at the crowd of drunk lawyers. "Were they in the majority or minority of those who voted to hire me?" When Beedlemeyer hired Sid, he had explained that the decision to do so was not unanimous.

Beedlemeyer frowned. "Minority, I'm afraid."

"Names?" asked Sid.

She was aware that TNT got its start in Jacksonville as a small, family-run law firm back in the 1970s. Photos of that first tiny office and its founding members, all white men sporting long sideburns and wearing comically wide neckties and suit lapels, appeared in a number of their commercial ads. But TNT had found real success, monetarily speaking, when they threw their hat into the class-action lawsuit ring in the late 1980s. By the turn of the millennium, they'd begun opening offices in other states. The Jacksonville office was now their largest office in the country and occupied the top six floors of one of the downtown high-rises. It was logical that some of their bigwigs would live here at Oakmire, given its pomp and grandeur and proximity to TNT headquarters.

"Castiglione and Langston." The way Beedlemeyer said the names practically dripped with disdain, and he looked as if uttering them left a sour taste in his mouth.

Sid nodded. "Good to know." She pulled out her phone, typed the names into the Notes app, and then snapped a number of photos of the tableau on the veranda. "As I mentioned when I called this morning, it would be helpful to walk the course so that I can get a better understanding of where the poaching might be happening."

Beedlemeyer nodded. "Yes, of course. As I said, the tournament is almost over. I believe there are only a handful of foursomes still at play, and they are mostly on the back nine. If we begin here at the first hole, we shouldn't be interrupting anyone's game."

He led the way down the first fairway, pointing out various spots of interest: where the marsh was particularly shallow, where the course tended to flood during heavy rains at high tide, the best points of ingress from the river, and where alligators had been spotted on dry land. Much to Sid and Leo's surprise, the last of these was a surprisingly high number. Six alligator sightings in the past couple of months on the first hole alone. There were another four alligator hot spots on the second hole and a whopping ten on the third. Sid snapped photos of all of them.

When they got to the third hole's green, Beedlemeyer pointed to a spot near the wooden cart bridge leading to the fourth hole. "This is one of the possible spots where poachers may be landing. One of our members, the owner of that house over there?" Beedlemeyer paused to point to one of the mini mansions at the other end of the cart bridge next to the fourth hole's tee box. "He heard people talking out here one night and came out to investigate. He told me that he scared away three men in a small boat. They took off when they saw his flashlight."

Sid snapped photos of the green, the cart bridge, and the house in question. "When was this?"

"About a week ago," Beedlemeyer answered. "There have been other reports of trespassers along the first three holes as well as the seventeenth and eighteenth."

"And you think these trespassers might be poachers?" She typed more notes into her phone. "Couldn't they have been someone just trying to get in a little extra putting practice?"

The elderly man shook his head. "Doubtful. That sometimes happens on the other holes, four through sixteen, because they are surrounded by houses. Any home that is not located on a marsh lot is welcome to keep their lights on at night. We get more putting practice, as you say, on those holes, where there is a bit more visibility on the course." He made a sweeping gesture to the homes along the swamp. "These homes are not permitted to keep their backyard lights on at night. We have strict rules regarding that. As a result, the marsh holes are very dark. It's nearly impossible to see, and late-night putting practice is a rarity." He shook his head. "No, I believe the activity on the marsh holes is most likely poachers. I've gotten more calls from our members complaining about noises—voices, splashing, boat engines, that sort of thing—over the last month than I think we've had in the last ten years. Something is amiss." He shook his finger. "Someone is trying to poach our alligators."

Chapter Seven

Sid crossed her arms. "And poaching your alligators is a problem because . . . ?"

"Because it is illegal, for one!" Beedlemeyer's face began to redden. He huffed and puffed as if Sid had just blasphemed in church. "This marsh is their home. They were here before we were, and they should have every right to remain. They do not cause us any problems—"

Sid interrupted, "Crawling out of the swamp and sunbathing in the middle of the golf course isn't a problem?"

"We have an experienced groundskeeper who deals with any such interloper. He has been with us for years. Decades, in fact." Beedlemeyer smoothed down his flyaway hair, but it only popped back up again in the breeze. "He's our alligator whisperer, if you will. The man knows how to coax an alligator back into the marsh without causing it any distress. Such matters are handled expediently, of course, and play on the course is rarely held up for more than a few minutes." Beedlemeyer frowned and shook his head. "There has been only one alligator that needed to be removed from the premises in all the years I've lived here, which will be eighteen in December."

"Why?" asked Leo as he watched the marsh for any signs of movement, absently scratching at the mosquito bite on his neck.

"Well, the alligator in question had to be removed from someone's backyard pool." Beedlemeyer cleared his throat. "It tore a hole in the homeowner's screened pool cage; snatched the owner's toy poodle, who had been on the patio barking at the alligator; and dragged the poor dog into the pool."

Leo's eyes widened. "It killed the dog?!"

"I'm afraid so." Beedlemeyer blushed.

"Did it eat the dog?" whispered Leo, his stomach roiling at the thought.

Beedlemeyer nodded once. "It was not a very large alligator. Six feet or so, no more."

The kid barked out a laugh of disbelief. "Wait. That's not large?"

"Oh no, son. It was an adult, yes, but we have much larger adult alligators here." He smiled and cocked an eyebrow. "Perhaps you have heard of Big Boy?"

Sid chuckled. "Leo's new to town. I don't think he's acquainted with Big Boy."

"Ah, I see." Beedlemeyer nodded. "Big Boy is our resident celebrity. Been here for ages, and we are very proud to have him. He's a gorgeous twelve-footer. Likes this hole and the seventeenth the best, but he's been known to frequent the other marsh holes from time to time." Beedlemeyer held up a finger. "But Big Boy is very fickle. We don't see a lot of him, and when we do, it's usually at sunset once play has completed. He's never given us any trouble. In fact, he's rather gentle, so we just leave him be."

Leo shook his head. The man was talking about a twelve-foot gator as if it was a prize-winning show dog, not a monster from the deep that could cut you in half with one bite. "When was the last time you saw him?"

"Oh, a couple of weeks ago now." Beedlemeyer looked off to his left. "A Sunday, I think. Over there on the fairway." He pointed back down the third fairway. "Big Boy just sat there for a while and then returned to the marsh. Play was over for the day, but word got out that he was making an appearance. People tend to come out to take photos when he graces us with his presence. No one was in any danger, mind you. Everyone knows to stay well back. Big Boy posed for photographs and then left us." The man smiled at the apparently fond memory.

Sid and Leo exchanged glances. Leo rolled his eyes, and Sid made some more notes. "I'd like to talk to your alligator whisperer, if I may," she said.

Beedlemeyer nodded. "Of course. He's not here today. He usually works either Saturday or Sunday, alternating every other weekend, and usually half days during the week unless we have a big replanting or something like that. I can double-check his schedule, but he'll probably be in tomorrow."

The trio finished up on hole number three, skipped most of the landlocked holes, and jumped over to holes seventeen and eighteen. Beedlemeyer, checking his watch every five minutes, showed them another dozen alligator hot spots between the final two holes. As they walked back toward the clubhouse, Beedlemeyer pointed out the cart barn and the groundskeeper's shed. All was quiet at the shed, but the barn was a hive of activity. Several employees dressed in green golf shirts and khaki shorts were washing the carts and lining them up for the next day. Sid took a few photos of the workers in action.

One boy was unloading heavy golf bags from the carts, wiping down the clubs, and lining the bags up near the parking lot so they could be loaded into their owners' cars when the time was right. Sid watched the boy, who didn't look much older than Leo, as he hustled to and fro, sagging under the weight of the bags. "That's Noah Zimmerman," Beedlemeyer said, pointing at the boy. "He's a good worker."

"He doesn't look strong enough to be lugging those bags around," said Sid as she snapped a photo. "He's just a kid."

Beedlemeyer chuckled. "He's not, actually. Not a kid, nor too weak." The chairman nodded in Noah's direction. "He's twenty-two, if I'm not mistaken. Maybe even twenty-three now." The man shrugged. "Either way, he's been with us for years, and he's one of our best caddies. Some of our members like to have a caddy accompany them on their rounds, and Noah is one of their favorites. He makes good money in tips as I understand it." Sid frowned, seeming to think poor Noah looked like a good breeze might blow him over, as Beedlemeyer continued. "I'm told Noah's been playing golf since he could walk. Mind you, his talent isn't in swinging the club. That young man is a whiz at reading the greens. I've not seen him get it wrong yet." Beedlemeyer quirked an eyebrow. "That being said, not everyone can manage to hit the shot he tells them to hit, but if they do . . ." The chairman whistled low. "Well, it's something to see."

Sid watched Noah Zimmerman wipe down some clubs in a particularly gaudy red-and-white golf bag. "Good for him," she said, though she wondered just how much fun it was to carry someone else's golf bag around for hours while they ignored your advice or lacked the talent to follow through on it. No matter what kind of tips he was making, Sid was pretty sure it wasn't enough to make her put up with the kind of bullshit that young man likely had to endure at a place like Oakmire.

Back at the clubhouse, Beedlemeyer showed Sid and Leo to his office so they could retrieve their gear, and then he scampered off to avoid being late for his dinner reservation. The TNT afterparty was petering out, with those lawyers left behind having moved inside the clubhouse to be closer to the bar and away from the mosquitos. Sid and Leo skirted the crowd and carried their equipment outside. They stood on the veranda, and Sid stared at the sunset over the marsh, a glorious wash of crimson and orange fading into the dark, watery terrain of the swamp. Leo, on the other hand, was scanning the golf course.

"See 'em?" asked Sid, not bothering to look around herself.

"Nope." Leo shook his head. "I saw them earlier in the TNT crowd. They seemed to be enjoying the party, but I don't see them now."

"Good." Sid shifted her bag higher up on her shoulder. "Let's set up on the third hole. I think that's our best bet tonight."

"Great," Leo mumbled. "But if Big Boy shows up, I'm out of here."

Sid smiled. "You and me both, kid."

It was almost dark by the time Sid and Leo set up their temporary camp on the east side of the third hole's fairway, right where the land began to form a peninsula that jutted out into the marsh. They picked a spot under the cover of a giant live oak, and behind them was a thick, twenty-foot-long hedge of azalea bushes. On the other side of the azaleas stood a number of mini mansions on manicured lawns, all lined up like sentries around the fourth hole. Most of these homes already had their backyard lights turned off. From their stakeout position, Sid and Leo agreed they should be hidden from anyone approaching from the marsh along any part of the third hole's peninsula, especially the green.

The alligator chorus had not yet begun their evensong, and Leo shuddered at the memory of their concert the night before. He opened a bag of chips and a soda and waited as Sid surveyed the area through the long lens of her camera. A dog barked from somewhere to their right, and Sid swung her camera in that direction.

"Just a woman walking her dog on the wooden bridge by the green." She lowered her camera.

"Probably going to let him take a dump in the hole." Leo shook his head and popped a chip in his mouth.

The dog's barking, though, grew louder and more frantic. Sid picked up her camera and took another look. She could see the small, gray-haired woman was trying to pull the leash to keep the dog in check, but the dog was winning their game of tug-of-war. The dog dragged the poor woman across the bridge and over the green. The dog stopped at the edge of the green, and its barking reached an ear-piercing level. Sid watched through the camera lens as the woman's hands clutched at her chest. And then the woman let out a bloodcurdling scream.

Sid shot up, dropped the camera onto the seat of her camp chair, and took off at a sprint. Leo followed behind her, abandoning his soda and bag of chips. When they reached the woman, Sid and Leo understood what all the commotion was about.

Sid grabbed the woman by the shoulders. "Go home!" she ordered. "Take your dog and go back home. I'm going to call the police now." The woman stopped screaming, but her dog kept barking. "Did you hear me? Go home. I'll call the police. Now go!"

Sid pulled her phone from her pocket and snapped several photos of the woman trying to drag the dog back the way they came. The police would probably want to speak to her, but Sid wanted peace and quiet to be able to think clearly. Beedlemeyer could give the police the name and address of the woman by identifying her from the photos. Once the woman was on the other side of the bridge and the dog's barking had subsided, Sid turned to Leo, who was now white as a sheet.

"Go back and pack up our stuff. I'll call Burt to come pick you up."

Leo shook his head and glanced over his shoulder toward their encampment. "No." He looked at her. "The ghosts are over there."

Sid glanced down the fairway, momentarily forgetting that she wouldn't be able to see the two dead golfers, and placed her arm around his shoulders and turned him around. "Well, you can't stay here." She walked him across the green and onto the wooden bridge. "Is this okay? Can the ghosts reach you from here?"

Leo shrugged. "Ghosts and spirits don't like hanging around death, so this is probably okay."

Sid smirked. "Really? They don't like death?" Leo shook his head. "How ironic." She glanced back to where they'd been standing by the marsh and was satisfied that Leo could no longer see anything, so she told him to stay on the bridge and wait for her.

Sid walked back across the bridge and dialed 911. She turned around to check on Leo just in time to watch him retch over the side of the bridge. "Great," she muttered as the emergency operator picked up the call. Her first thought was that Burt was going to kill her as soon as he found out about what Leo had seen tonight. Her second thought was that this case had just gotten much more interesting.

Once she finished her conversation with the 911 operator, she called Detective Tony Davis. "You busy right now?" she asked when he finally answered after five or six rings.

Tony laughed. "Just trying to wrestle Dante into bed. What's up?"

Sid could hear the little boy's squeals in the background. She explained where she was, what had happened, and what she was looking at. "I just thought . . . I don't know. I thought you might want to know. Maybe come down here. I called 911, and I'm sure patrol officers are on the way, but this is . . . this is bad, Tony."

"How can you be sure, Sid?" asked Tony.

"I'm not sure of anything." Sid retreated to the middle of the green. Her stomach was turning somersaults and threatening to reject the burger and fries she'd eaten on the drive over. "But the car is still here, and it doesn't look like it's been moved."

"Yeah, but that doesn't mean—"

"And the hair is red."

There was silence for several seconds before Tony said, "I'll be right there."

Chapter Eight

While Leo waited on the cart bridge for Sid to finish her phone calls, he retched a few more times, but by the end it was mostly dry heaves. Fortunately, the pungent fragrance of swamp decay masked the smell of vomit. Leo leaned over the bridge railing, his head in his hands, wishing he'd brought his soda with him to settle his stomach. He turned his head and watched Sid pacing back and forth across the green while occasionally glancing in the direction of the marsh. After a few more minutes, she hung up the phone and joined him on the bridge.

"Word is going to spread," she said. "I doubt that woman will keep quiet about what she saw."

"Yeah." Leo stood and faced her. His stomach hurt, his throat burned, and he really wanted to go home and crawl into bed.

She leaned against the railing next to him. "How are you holding up?" He shrugged. "I called Burt. He's coming to get you."

Leo groaned. "Is he mad?"

Sid considered how to answer. "He's worried." That was probably the best word for it. "I'm sorry you had to see that."

"It's not your fault," Leo said.

"Maybe. Maybe not." Sid closed her eyes and pinched the bridge of her nose, but she couldn't erase the image from her mind. She knew Leo couldn't either. "I brought you out here tonight." She held up a hand when he began to protest. "Granted, none of us—not you, me, or Burt—had any idea that we'd find . . . well, that this would happen. But it did. And it happened on my watch." She managed a weak half smile for the boy. "Burt's not mad at you. He's mad at me. Mostly, he's mad that we can't seem to shield you from all these horrible things. Or, at least, I don't seem to be able to."

"But it's not your fault," Leo repeated.

"Thanks, kid." She punched him lightly on the arm. "But I think you're going to have to sit this one out."

"No!" Leo took a step away from her. "That's not fair. I haven't done anything wrong."

Sid held up her hands. "Calm down, Leo. I'm not saying you can't help me ever again. Just maybe not on this case."

"This sucks!" He kicked at the railing and began pacing back and forth. He had been sidelined from all except the least consequential of Sid's cases ever since they solved the mystery surrounding the death of her husband and daughter. He was tired of finding lost pets, and he feared she might decide that she didn't need his help after all. He wanted to help. He wanted to be wanted, to be needed. If Sid didn't need or want him around, then perhaps no one else would either.

"Hey, this will give you more time to spend with your girlfriend," Sid suggested. "That'll be nice, right? Ellie would probably like to see more of you."

Leo had developed a crush on Ellie Owen, a pretty, strawberry-blonde girl who worked in the N'Ice Day Ice Cream

Shop on St. George Street. Ellie and her sister, Ava, had helped Sid and Leo gather intel with their last big case. The two girls had no idea that they'd helped, and Sid felt a tinge of regret at having used them for information. But all's fair in love and investigation.

Leo slowed his pacing but didn't look over at Sid. "Not really," he grumbled.

Even in the dark, Sid could see the boy's posture slump as if he'd just been handed a defeat. "Oh? Why not? You two have a fight or something?"

"No," he mumbled. Sid waited for him to say something more, and after a full minute, he did. "She's busy with school now. She's involved in a lot of clubs and stuff, and she cut back her hours at the ice cream shop. So I don't think I'll be seeing her much."

Sid nodded in understanding. Ellie Owen was off doing typical teenage stuff: attending the local high school, playing a sport or marching in the band, running for student council, that sort of thing. Leo, on the other hand, was taking online classes via some homeschool program his mother had found for him. He had no afterschool clubs, no pep rallies, no built-in group of friends to hang out with.

"Have you heard from her?" Sid asked. "You guys talk on the phone? Or text or whatever it is you kids do now?" She rolled her eyes. Dating sounded so complicated these days. *Just pick up the phone*, she thought to herself.

"Not really."

"You should call her."

"No."

"Just do it."

"No."

"Then text her."

"I did."

"And?" Sid wanted to groan out loud. Sometimes a conversation with a fifteen-year-old boy was like pulling teeth.

"She hasn't responded."

Sid sighed, her heart squeezing a little for the kid. "I'm sure you'll hear from her. Maybe you should stop by the shop when she's working. Just to say hi, ask her how school's going. If nothing else, you two can at least be friends. Right?" Sid wanted to mention that Ellie was currently his only friend in St. Augustine—at least the only one who was his own age.

"I guess." Leo kicked the railing again and resumed his pacing.

Sid let that conversation die and waited in silence for a minute before asking, "Are the ghosts still here?"

Leo stopped and looked around. He'd forgotten about them during all the vomiting, and now he didn't see them anywhere. He shook his head. "Nope, but it looks like we have company."

Sid and Leo left the bridge, then walked around the green and about fifty feet down the fairway, where they stopped and waited. Three newcomers approached, sweeping their flashlights back and forth across the fairway. Less than fifteen minutes had passed since Sid and Tony had hung up, but here he was now with Deputies Adcock and Weber in tow.

"Sid. Leo." Tony nodded to each of them in turn, and then he stuck out his hand to Leo.

"Detective." Leo shook the big man's hand, smiling inwardly at the gesture of male bonding.

"I've called Burt. He's on his way," said Sid. "Maybe one of the deputies can escort Leo to the parking lot and wait with him?"

Leo blinked at Sid in surprise.

"Yeah, let's get you home." Tony clamped a hand down on his shoulder and pointed to Deputy Weber. "Weber, walk him out, and wait with him until his grandfather shows up to collect him."

Leo and Deputy Weber walked away, both of them sulking and dragging their feet, and Tony turned back to Sid. "Show me what you found."

Sid led Tony and Deputy Adcock across the green to the marsh's edge, where they stood and stared at the mutilated corpse that had washed ashore.

"Shit," whispered Deputy Adcock. "He's missing his face."

"And his arm," Sid added.

Tony blew out a seemingly nauseous breath. "And most of his innards." He swept his flashlight over the marsh to the left and right of the body and then turned to Adcock. "Call it in." She nodded and stepped away to make her phone calls.

"It's a male," said Sid. That much was plain to see from the torso, or what was left of it. Based on what Sid could see in the dark, the body looked to be that of a young man who was slim, with lean muscles and a head of ginger curls. There was no shirt left on the body, assuming there had even been one in the first place, and the dark shorts were shredded to pieces. The shoes might have been either sneakers or golf shoes, but Sid couldn't tell which, given that his feet were still mostly submerged. "It could be him."

Tony shook his head. "We don't know that. Not yet any way."

"No, we don't," Sid agreed, "but it would be an awfully big coincidence."

"And an awful damn shame," added Tony. He took Sid by the arm and led her a few yards away, up onto the green. They stood with their backs to the corpse. "So, a woman with a dog found him first?"

"Yeah." Sid nodded. "But she wasn't any closer than this." She went and stood about twenty feet away from the body.

"This is about where she was standing when she began screaming. I sent her home without bothering to get her name. She wasn't in any fit state to answer questions, and I didn't want her or her dog contaminating the area. I did snap a few photos of her, and I'm sure the chairman or someone else in the clubhouse can identify her for you if you need to talk to her."

Tony nodded. "Send me the pics." He swept the area with his flashlight beam again. "And this is where you heard the scream and the boat engine last night?"

"Yeah." Sid pointed to the back side of the green by the cart bridge. "I got a tour of the course earlier today from Jonathan Beedlemeyer. He's the chairman of the club. He said there's a spot right over there where he thinks boats have been landing. Someone in one of those houses saw some men in a boat right about there only a week ago."

"Okay." Tony ran a hand over his face, then pulled out his phone to call Naomi. "God, this is gonna be a long night."

Just as Deputy Adcock was rejoining them on the green, a cluster of flashlight beams came into view from between the two houses nearest the far end of the cart bridge. A crowd wielding their electric torches marched toward them, joined by a noisy chorus of yapping dogs.

"Great," Adcock muttered. "That's all we need."

She and Tony went to head off the approaching mob before it crossed the bridge while Sid stayed where she was. It was another ten minutes before Deputy Weber returned with patrol reinforcements. They quickly dispelled the mob of homeowners and sealed off the area, and it was another twenty minutes before more detectives and crime scene specialists arrived. Sid answered everyone's questions until she felt ready to pass out on her feet, and then Tony handed her off to Deputy Adcock and promised to call when he had any news.

The two women arrived back at Sid's car in the parking lot.

"You ever seen anything like that before?" asked Adcock.

"Never, thankfully." Sid shook her head. "And I hope I never do again."

"Yeah," agreed Adcock. "Poor bastard. Must have been an awful way to go."

Sid could only nod in agreement. She slid into the driver's seat and started the engine as Adcock waved goodbye and walked back toward the clubhouse. Sid cranked the air-conditioning on full blast and stared across the parking lot at the black Maserati GranTurismo, still parked in the same spot.

Chapter Nine

The banging downstairs woke Sid from a sound sleep. She glanced at her alarm clock, noting that less than four hours had passed since she had crawled into bed. The banging started up again, and she realized it was someone knocking on her office door. Knocking was a polite way of referring to what was happening because it sounded like someone was trying to break in using a battering ram. She rolled out of bed and rubbed her eyes.

"Sidney!"

Sid knew who it was without even looking. She also knew what was coming next.

"Get your ass down here!"

Yep. That was what she'd been expecting, except that she'd thought there'd be a few more expletives. She leaned over the banister of the metal staircase that connected her upstairs apartment to her office below. Burt Roberts was standing in the doorway, obviously having used his own key to get in, and was glaring at her with eyes that appeared ready to pop out of their sockets.

She rubbed her eyes again. "Burt, it's not even seven o'clock in the morning."

"We need to talk," he growled. "Now."

She held up her hands in surrender. "All right, I'm coming down. But I need coffee first."

"There's coffee in the kitchen. You've got five minutes." He turned and stormed off across the yard toward the house.

Sid sighed. Though she wasn't surprised by Burt's anger, she had been hoping to avoid this conversation until later in the day, or at least until a more civilized hour of the morning. She threw on some clothes that didn't reek of bug spray and trudged over to the house. Burt was waiting for her at the tiny kitchen table with two cups of coffee already poured. She slid onto the bench seat opposite him and took two large gulps of coffee, which burned her tongue and throat on the way down.

Burt leaned forward. "Sid," he began in a voice that was barely above a whisper but still filled with rage, "what the hell were you thinking?"

"How's Leo?" She wanted to know the answer to that question before she answered any of his.

Burt sat back. "He said he was fine, but what else was he gonna say?" He shook his head. "He didn't look fine. Looked green around the gills. Now, what happened, Sid? No bullshit this time."

"I'm not bullshitting you, Burt." Sid jabbed a finger in his direction. "What I told you last night is the truth. We took a lovely tour of the golf course, got set up for our stakeout, and some old lady with a dog stumbled upon a dead body. The lady started screaming; the dog started barking. It was crazy." Sid gripped her coffee cup with both hands. "Surreal." She shook her head, trying to clear the memory of the mutilated corpse. "I didn't know what was happening until it had already happened. I'm sorry Leo saw what he saw, but I'm pretty sure he sees worse than that on a daily basis around here, what with all the ghosts and spirits and all."

"I know." Burt ran a hand down his face. "Just wish he didn't have to see it live, so to speak."

"Me, too." Sid nodded. "I'll tell him he's off the case."

"No!" Leo burst into the kitchen, his chest heaving. "No! Don't take me off the case. Grandpa, please! It wasn't Sid's fault. It wasn't anyone's fault. And she's right: I do see worse than that. I see spirits that are all kinds of messed up. I'm used to it." He shuffled a couple of steps closer to them. "That body last night just caught me off guard, that's all. But I've seen worse, believe me." He glanced from his grandfather to Sid and back again. "Please don't make me stop doing the PI work."

Burt closed his eyes and groaned. "I don't know, Leo."

"Please!" begged Leo. "I can handle it. I swear I can."

Burt frowned at Sid, who sighed in return. "Okay, Leo," said Burt, and Leo's face lit up. "But," he held up a finger in warning as he added, "there are conditions."

Leo pressed his lips together, trying to hide his smile.

Burt crossed his arms and rested them on his belly. "Your homeschool classes start tomorrow, and you'll have all of your schoolwork done each day *before* you do any work for Sid."

"No problem." Leo nodded. He'd already agreed to this with his grandfather.

The two of them had sat together last week and gone through his homeschooling curriculum, the list of virtual classes he'd be taking, and the online school's calendar. It had taken nearly an hour for Leo to explain everything to Burt and to answer all of his questions.

Once Burt was satisfied, it had taken him only a few minutes to explain to Leo how it was going to be: Leo would attend his online school every day, finish all of his assignments on time, and not just pass but excel in all of his classes. If Leo failed to do so, he would cease working for Sid, and Burt would enroll him in the local high school.

The thought of having to attend a public high school in a place like St. Augustine terrified Leo. Not only would he be the awkward new kid in the thrifted clothes, but he would have to sit through class and appear like a normal student even as spirits popped up and wanted to talk to him. It happened every year. He'd been labeled a freak in elementary school because he'd slipped up one day and spoken to a spirit, not realizing it wasn't a real child. That stigma had followed him all through middle school and into high school back home in Norfolk. He really didn't want to repeat that experience here in Florida.

Sid chimed in, bringing Leo back from his horrid memories. "And if at any point I think you can't handle it, or if Burt thinks you can't handle it, then that's it. No ifs, ands, or buts. You're off this case once and for all. Got it?"

Leo nodded. "Got it." He smiled. "I promise, I've got this."

Sid smirked in response. "Okay. We're heading back out to Oakmire tonight. Be ready to go at six o'clock."

Leo smiled. "Got it, boss." He tore out of the kitchen and bounded up the stairs to his room.

Sid turned to face Burt. "I'll watch him closely, Burt, and I'll pull the plug if I think he's not handling it."

Burt got up from the table and poured his coffee down the sink. "He reminds me so much of his father. Gunner always said nothing was wrong, that the spirits didn't bother him, that he could handle it." Burt glanced over at Sid. "But I never really believed him. I wish I could have done more to help him, but what could I do?" He shook his head. "And look how it turned out for him."

Burt left the house, and Sid returned to her office. She sat at her desk and pulled a folder labeled "L. R." from the bottom drawer of one of her filing cabinets. She'd started the file the day Leo arrived in the Old City and Burt had announced that Leo would begin working for her. She removed the news clipping she'd printed from the local paper's website and read it over again.

The obituary was short and sparse in details:

Petty Officer First Class Gunner James Roberts, age 32, of Norfolk, VA, died at sea on the 7th of June. He was born in St. Augustine, FL, and graduated from Saint Augustine High School before enlisting in the United States Navy. Gunner was preceded in death by his father, James Dixon, and mother, Camille Roberts, and is survived by his wife, Trisha, son, Leo, and stepfather, Burton Roberts. A memorial service will be held on June 16 at 2:00 p.m. at Church of the Good Shepherd in Norfolk, VA. Donations to charities supporting military families are greatly appreciated.

Sid didn't know much more than that. Burt had told her that Gunner had died at sea. One minute he'd been on deck of the aircraft carrier, and the next he was gone. True, there'd been a storm, but Gunner was a seasoned sailor, with fourteen years in the navy and more tours at sea than Burt could count. Gunner had been good at his job, so said everyone. And, according to Burt, Gunner was most at peace when he was at sea, when the noise of the ship and the aircraft seemed to drown out the voices of the dead. He went overboard, and no one saw a thing. Search and rescue was impossible in the storm, and his body was never recovered.

Sid remembered the day Burt told her that Gunner died. He'd banged on her door, much like he'd done this morning, and announced that he'd be gone for a while. Sid stood by while he loaded his bags into his truck. Burt drove through the night to Norfolk so that he could comfort his grieving daughter-in-law and grandson. When he returned home, the man who had always been larger than life to Sid appeared shattered by his own grief. He shared with Sid his biggest fear—that Gunner had gone overboard on purpose. Burt had no proof of that, of course, but he suspected it nonetheless.

Sid knew Burt's biggest fear was that Leo would follow in his father's footsteps—and in his missteps. Burt felt responsible in part for Gunner's death. Granted, Burt wasn't on the aircraft carrier that night, but he also hadn't sought help for Gunner when his stepson lived at home. Everyone, including Gunner, tried to ignore his mediumistic talent. Burt said Gunner called it his curse. Though he often played it off as no big deal, Burt knew it plagued his waking life. When Gunner enlisted in the navy, Burt sent the young man on his way with his blessing, thinking that getting out of the Old City and going to sea would be the best thing for him. Apparently, it wasn't.

As Sid knew from Leo, the spirits of the dead were everywhere. So why wouldn't they also be on a giant ship in the middle of the ocean, one that had seen its fair share of military conflict? She leaned back in her squeaky desk chair and drummed her fingers against the obituary. It was now up to her and Burt to keep Leo from succumbing to the same fate as his father.

Chapter Ten

Sid received a call from Detective Tony Davis as she was checking her cameras and making sure everything she needed was packed and ready for tonight's stakeout. She answered the phone with a sinking feeling in her stomach. "'Afternoon, Detective. Any news?"

"It's not Cameron Chase." Tony didn't mince words, and Sid was grateful. She blew out a breath as Tony continued. "We've got an ID. One of the deputies on the scene last night recognized a tattoo on the arm. That got the ball rolling. The body also had several scars—shoulder, knee, wrist; all of that helped us narrow it down. The parents just came in and ID'd the body. Turns out, it was a kid named William Arthur Chase IV. Went by the nickname Dru."

Sid nodded to herself. "Short for 'quadruple,' right? Because he was the fourth in his family with the same name?"

"Yep," Tony answered.

Sid made a note. "How old was he?"

"Just turned twenty last week."

"Shit."

"Yep," said Tony again. "The deputy who gave us a preliminary ID last night was his cousin. Turns out Dru had a lot of cousins."

"Let me guess," offered Sid. "He was cousins with Cameron Chase, our elusive golfer with the fancy sports car."

"First cousins. Their fathers are brothers. All of them live over in Paradise Trailer Park. I went over there this morning. That place is such a dump." Tony paused, and Sid could just imagine him shaking his head at the memory of the dilapidated trailers, the rusted-out vehicles up on blocks, and the broken kids' toys strewn about like unloved lawn ornaments. "The father didn't want to talk to me, but the mother said Dru had gone out on Friday night with some friends. Claims she didn't know who those friends were, and I'm not so sure I believe her. She told me Dru hadn't come home yet. She thought he was on a bender or off with some girl. Apparently, there was no steady girlfriend that she knew of, but plenty of girls he saw casually."

Sid huffed. "Okay. So setting aside the fact that the kid was only twenty and not old enough to legally drink, his mom hadn't seen her son in a day and a half, and her immediate thought was that he was off somewhere getting drunk or getting laid?"

"That's about it," Tony replied. "When I told her we thought he was in the morgue, she didn't seem particularly shocked. Neither did his father. They agreed to come down and ID him for us, but they took their sweet time about it. I saw them around nine this morning, and they showed up here about four o'clock."

Sid pinched the bridge of her nose. Everyone grieves in different ways; she knew that better than anyone. When her daughter, Iris, died, Sid fell to pieces, and it took years before she was able to begin putting her life back together. There was no telling what Dru Chase's parents were going through at the moment, so Sid was trying not to judge them too harshly. But she couldn't imagine how they could wait so long to visit the morgue, knowing their son might be lying there all alone. Families. Sometimes, they really sucked. "Did his parents have any ideas about how he might have ended up washed up on a golf course, half eaten by alligators?"

"Nope. They clammed up once they ID'd the body," said Tony. "Neither of them cried. They simply walked out and refused to answer any more questions."

"Really?" Sid sat back in her old chair, which creaked and squealed as if begging to be oiled.

"Yeah, but the deputy who's Dru Chase's cousin told us where the kid worked." Tony paused before asking, "Wanna take a guess?"

"Oakmire?"

"Yep."

"Seriously?"

"Yep," Tony repeated. "He worked in the kitchen as a busboy. I'm heading over there now. Not sure who will be there on a Sunday evening, though."

Sid looked at her watch. It was nearly six o'clock. "They'll be shutting the course soon, but I think the restaurant stays open until nine or so. And the bar is open until ten or eleven. I doubt that any managers will be there, but you might find a board member or two in the restaurant." She picked up her backpack and slung it over her shoulder. "I'm heading over there now. Going to give this stakeout thing another try since my last two attempts have been a bust. I'll probably see you there."

"Sounds good," said Tony. "Just be careful, Sid. I don't want to get a phone call that some woman and her dog found *your* body half eaten by alligators."

Sid couldn't help but smile. "Me neither, Tony. That would be very bad for business."

By the time Sid and Leo arrived at the Oakmire Golf and Country Club for their third attempt at a nighttime stakeout, Detective Tony Davis was already there. Sid parked next to the detective's SUV, and she and Leo lugged their chairs and equipment into the clubhouse. Tony was nowhere in sight, and neither was Jonathan Beedlemeyer. The course marshal in the starter's shack informed them that two foursomes were still out on holes seventeen and eighteen but should be finishing play soon. At Sid's request, the marshal pointed Sid and Leo in the direction of the groundskeeper's shed, which was located behind the cart barn on the outskirts of the clubhouse parking lot.

The doors to the shed had been thrown wide open, and two box fans whirred away at full speed, but the shed was stifling. It smelled of gasoline and freshly mown grass. An elderly man was bent over a workbench, tinkering with some part of the riding lawnmower that lay disemboweled behind him. He was tall, with a potbelly and a wiry, gray ponytail, and he was wearing oil-stained overalls.

As Sid and Leo approached the shed, Sid quickly pulled out her phone and snapped a photo of the tableau. The pair stood in the doorway for a few moments, waiting for the man to look up, before Sid finally cleared her throat. "Hello?"

The man glanced their way and smiled. His face was tanned and creased like well-worn leather. "*Bonjour,*" he said with a musical, Cajun drawl. "*Comment ça va?*"

Sid and Leo glanced at one another. Leo shrugged. "Mr. Broussard?" asked Sid.

"Henri," said the man. He placed a hand on his chest. "Call me Henri. How may I assist you, *cher*?"

Sid smiled. "Okay, Henri. By any chance, are you the alligator whisperer that we've heard so much about?"

Henri laughed, his belly bouncing up and down in rhythm. "Don't know 'bout all that." He waved off the notion with a swipe of his big hand.

"Henri!" yelled a male voice. Sid and Leo turned to see Noah Zimmerman slide to a halt in front of the open doors. "Oh, hey." He looked back and forth between Sid and Leo.

"Hello, Noah," said Sid. She smiled at the young man, who blinked at her in surprise.

Noah quickly looked past them to Henri. "Sorry to interrupt, Henri, but the rake for the long trap on the left side of the seventh fairway is missing again. Just thought you'd want to know."

Henri patted the air in front of him, as if he'd heard this a thousand times before. "Okay, okay. *Merci*." Noah nodded and left the shed with a sideways glance at Sid and Leo.

When Sid and Leo turned back to face Henri, he shook his head. "That would be Casanova."

Sid and Leo both raised their eyebrows in surprise. Sid grinned. "You mean Noah?"

Henri laughed again. "*Non, non, non*. The dog. Casanova is a big, fat golden retriever." Henri blew out his cheeks and held his arms out by his sides, miming someone even larger than himself. "He lives in the house behind the sand trap on seven. Likes to steal the rakes. That old boy thinks they are giant sticks for him to play with." Henri shook his head, wiping the corner of one eye. "Noah? A Casanova?" He chuckled some more. "That's a good one, that."

Sid smiled again, indulging the man's joke, and explained

why she and Leo were there before asking if Henri had seen any poachers.

"*Non.*" Henri shook his head. "*Couillons!*" He crossed his arms and rested them on his belly. "Crazy bastards, they're goin' after Big Boy. You know that?" He shook his head again. "But they'll never catch 'im."

"Do you know who *they* are?" asked Sid.

"*Oui et non.* I don't know names." He shook his head. "But they are amateurs. For sure."

Sid ran a hand across the back of her neck, wiping away a sheen of sweat. "But why are they poaching the alligators? Is it for sport? For eating? For selling?"

Henri leaned forward, his eyes wide and his face reddening. "For golf!"

Sid and Leo exchanged glances. "I'm not sure I understand," Sid said. "I thought the alligators didn't disrupt play too much. And that's what you do. You coax them back into the marsh whenever they appear on the course."

"*Oui,* I do." Henri's lip curled in disgust. "But they want to get rid of our gators so that they can bring in the PGA." He gave a low growl that sounded to Sid and Leo a lot like sounds made by the alligator swamp chorus. "The PGA won't allow a big tournament here because they say there are too many of them. It's too dangerous. Bah! There are as many gators here as there are at any course in Louisiana or Mississippi or Georgia. They don't know what they're talking about." He shook his head. "But big tournaments mean big money. If they get rid of the gators, they get a big tournament. And you know what that means." He whistled and pointed his thick finger skyward. "Property values go through the roof. Everyone wants to come here. Lots of money to be made. Everyone wins, *oui?*" He barked out a laugh. "*Non!* No one wins. Traffic. Damage to the course. And all those gators killed for no reason other than to make some rich fools even richer."

Sid and Leo listened patiently as Henri Broussard ranted and raved for another five minutes, and then they left him to his blade sharpening and walked back to the starter's shack. The course marshal gave them the all-clear, and they wandered off to find a good place to set up camp on the eighteenth hole.

"So, how was school today?" asked Sid as they rucked their way over the golf course.

Leo shrugged. "Fine. Easy."

"Do you like taking classes online?"

"Yeah. It's fine."

"Are they interesting?"

"Yeah."

"Do you have a favorite yet? What's your best subject?"

Leo merely shrugged in response.

"That's it? That's all you've got to say about tenth grade?" Sid glanced sideways at him before mimicking his voice. "It's *fine.*"

"Yeah." Leo blinked at her, and she shook her head at him. He smirked and asked, "Are you going to interrogate me about school every day?"

Sid shook her head. "Nope. That's Burt's job." She sighed. "I was merely curious."

Leo was silent for a full minute before he said, "Science." Sid raised an eyebrow. "I like science best."

Sid opened her mouth to ask another question, but Leo turned his head away from her and looked out at the marsh. The conversation was apparently over, but Sid smiled and decided to take his sharing this small bit of information as a victory.

Like the third hole, number eighteen had a clear, shallow landing spot behind a sand trap just below the green. Directly across the fairway from that sand trap sat the largest live oak on the entire Oakmire campus. Its branches extended outward over forty feet from either side of its trunk. Behind this giant tree, a long row of azalea bushes formed a tidy border between the edge of the rough and the backyard of the nearest house. A number of other live oaks were lined up next to it, like soldiers in file along the eastern side of the eighteenth hole. Their canopies were so large and intertwined that they effectively blocked the views of the houses behind them, denying those homeowners views of the marsh and the Matanzas River beyond. From their vantage point under the largest oak, however, Sid and Leo had a clear view of the long par 5 from tee box to green. It was the prettiest hole on the entire course.

Leo dropped the gear under the beautiful oak and began setting up the camp chairs. It was quarter to seven in the evening, and though sunset wasn't scheduled for another forty-five minutes, the low sun was bathing everything in the warm gold of twilight. The air was hot and sticky with very little breeze to stir the leaves overhead.

A shiver ran up Leo's spine as he kneeled to wrestle with the legs of one of the chairs. He glanced over at Sid, who was typing away on her phone. Leo slowly reached one hand into his pocket and wrapped his fingers around the three stones. With the other, he tugged on the brim of his baseball cap. Then he stood and turned away from Sid, coming face to face with the two dead golfers. Leo wasn't sure what to do, and it was that split second of hesitation that got him into trouble.

Chapter Eleven

Leo felt the golf club come down on his shoulder like a frozen whip. The ghost wielding it was the burnt one, whom Leo had nicknamed Bacon. The other was Bucket, as in "kicked the bucket," since Leo wasn't certain of the man's exact cause of death. Leo reached into his pocket and closed his fingers around the three stones. So far, Val's assessment of the stones' effectiveness appeared to be woefully inaccurate. Leo widened his stance, squared his shoulders, and raised his head, all of which were hard to do given that both Bacon and Bucket were trying to beat him senseless. The cold lashes were particularly painful when they hit one of the bruises from the other night, but he had a plan. Rather, Hattie and Val had come up with a plan yesterday in Val's shop, and Leo had reluctantly agreed to give it a try.

"My name is Leo Roberts." Leo gritted his teeth against the lashing he was receiving and did his best to give these two ghosts a close-lipped smile. "This is my boss, Sidney Stone." He pointed to Sid, who had stopped typing and stared wide-eyed at the empty space that Leo was addressing. Leo glanced over at her and nodded.

"Hello," said Sid. She waved a hand at the empty space. "Nice to meet you . . . gentlemen." She looked to Leo for confirmation that she'd gotten it right, that they were in the presence of the two deranged, dead golfers who liked to beat people with their invisible golf clubs.

Leo nodded and smiled at her. As he did, he felt the beating stop. When Leo turned to look at the ghosts, both Bacon and Bucket were staring at Sid. Bacon wore a lopsided grin over the part of his face that wasn't burnt to a crisp, and Bucket had removed his sun visor and begun smoothing his hair.

Leo took a deep breath. "We are private investigators. Well, she is." Leo pointed to Sid again. "I'm her assistant. Sort of a PI in training." Sid raised an eyebrow at him but kept quiet. "We'd like to ask you for your help." This was the key part of the plan: engage the ghosts, ask them for help, get them on his side. It would show them that Leo was no threat to them and give them something else to focus on other than beating the shit out of him.

Bacon and Bucket glanced at Leo as he spoke, but their gaze kept sliding back to Sid. Fortunately, neither of them raised their golf clubs or made a move to hurt him. They simply waited. So far, so good, but Leo hadn't given much thought to what he'd say next. This was all Hattie and Val had suggested, and Leo hadn't bothered to try to come up with anything else since he had doubted the plan would work at all. He opened his mouth to say something but wasn't sure what.

Sid jumped in to fill the silence. "Gentlemen," she said again, moving to stand next to Leo. Leo nodded once in the direction of Bacon and once in the direction of Bucket, trying to show Sid where the ghosts were located so she would know where to look.

Sid followed suit and smiled into the emptiness. "We have been hired by the Oakmire board of directors to look into the illegal poaching that has been taking place on the golf course. It occurs to me that you two probably know more about this place than anyone else." She paused, and Leo nodded to signal she should continue. Both Bacon and Bucket were hanging on her every word.

Sid cleared her throat. "We found a dead body yesterday. Did you know about him?"

"*Yes.*"

The reply sounded in Leo's mind, their voices in unison. One bass, one tenor. Leo turned to Sid to translate, "They did."

"Good." Sid nodded. "I found out today that the man's name was William Arthur Chase IV, but his family and friends called him Dru. He was only twenty years old. His birthday was last week." Sid paused, unsure whether to ask the next question, though she decided to roll the dice. "Have you seen his spirit hanging around the course?"

"*No.*"

Leo shook his head for Sid's benefit and then asked a question of his own: "Do you know what happened to him?"

The images flooded into his mind as if two movies were playing on the same screen at the same time. Leo's hands flew to his head, and he squeezed his eyes shut. "Stop, please!" He exhaled with relief when the images stopped. "That's too much. I can't . . . I can't see what you're trying to show me." He looked to Bacon first. Based on the style of his attire, including the flared pant legs and impressive side-burns, he assumed this golfer had been haunting the golf course longer than his friend and therefore might expect deference to his seniority. "Can you show me first, please?" He looked over at Bucket. "And then you can show me. Is that okay?" The images returned, but this time there was only one movie playing on the screen inside his head.

Even though the sun was setting and the full length of the eighteenth hole was still visible in the fading light, Leo was plunged into the pitch black of night. In his mind, he was standing on the cart bridge at the far end of the third hole, watching a small, flat-bottomed boat row ashore on the back side of the green. There were three people in the boat—three men, based on their size and shape, dressed in black. One was large. The other two were smaller, thinner. The smallest of the three climbed out of the boat with a box. Leo drifted closer and came to stand next to him. Leo realized he was standing next to the young man whose dead body, torn and slashed to pieces, had washed up onshore just twenty-four hours ago. Leo felt his own stomach spasm at the realization that he was being shown Dru Chase's last moments on earth.

Leo watched Dru Chase open the insulated cooler he was holding and remove something, which he placed on the ground by his feet. He then took a few steps to his left and repeated the process, doing so again and again along the edge of the marsh. Upon closer inspection, Leo realized the items being placed on the grass were raw chicken parts. When the last chicken quarter was dropped into place, Dru emptied the cooler, spilling the liquid into the swamp. He returned the cooler to the boat, was handed a long pole with a round circle of wire at one end, and then walked back to the farthest pile of chicken parts. The largest of the men joined Dru onshore, standing next to the boat with a contraption that Leo recognized as a crossbow.

Leo drifted once again to stand beside Dru. In his mind, the scene jumped ahead, and Leo understood this to mean that some amount of time had passed. Dru still held the catchpole, but he swayed a little on his feet as his eyes drifted shut. There was a low rumble, almost imperceptible over the soft splashing of marsh waves along the bank of the third green, but Leo heard it. So did Dru Chase. The young man startled and looked around, only then noticing the alligator that was less than three feet away from him. The gator was big, probably eight feet or more, although it was difficult to tell; its hindquarters were still partially submerged. The gator began to open its mouth, and Dru thrust the catchpole toward it. The gator's massive jaws bit down on the wire ring at the end of the pole, and the gator jerked its head and shoulders to the side. The motion threw Dru off-balance, causing him to trip and fall forward. The pole slipped from his grip, and he moved to brace his fall with his arm.

Dru's arm hit the ground, and the gator's mouth clamped down on it. Leo saw Dru's face, just inches from the gator's, contort with fear and pain. His mouth opened wide, and he screamed. The sound was so much sharper, more terrifying, than it had been when Leo had heard it from a distance, sitting in the comfort of his camp chair next to Sid.

In the next second, Dru was struck in the neck by an arrow from his fellow poacher's crossbow. A bright light suddenly flooded the scene, and Leo watched in horror as the alligator shook his head, snapping Dru's arm. Blood poured from the arrow wound, and Dru ceased moving on his own. The big man bounded across the green, still holding the crossbow. The alligator began crawling back into the marsh, Dru's arm held tightly in his jaws. The man reached out to grab hold of Dru's other arm, but he hesitated. As Dru's body began to slide into the marsh, the poacher took hold of the arrow and yanked it from the body, stumbling backward as he did so. Dru Chase and the alligator disappeared into the dark swamp.

Leo sucked in a breath and blinked in the weakening light of sunset. He was back on the eighteenth hole, standing under the giant oak. Sid grabbed his arm, and Leo flinched before realizing she wasn't the alligator.

"Leo?" It was Sid's voice, not one of the ghosts', and she was standing right next to him. "Leo, what's happening?"

Before he could respond, he was back again on the third hole in the dead of night. He watched the scene play out again, this time from the cart bridge. He saw Dru Chase place bait along the marsh's edge. He saw Dru and the other poacher waiting with their weapons in hand. He saw the third man, still sitting in the boat and fiddling with rope and a long hook. Time jumped ahead again, and he watched as the alligator slowly emerged from the swamp without Dru noticing.

But the big man with the crossbow did see the gator's approach. He tracked the movement of the water. He kneeled slowly. He was steadying his aim when Dru fell and the gator grabbed the young man's arm. He fired, knowing he'd hit something. His run across the green had not been that of a man who was racing to rescue his friend. Rather, it was the long-strided sprint of a man who believed himself to be victorious. The big man's hesitation to help had been real. So had the stumble backward after pulling the arrow from the boy's body.

The third man had been the one to light up the gruesome tableau with a small spotlight, which Leo noticed was mounted on the boat. After Dru went under, the third man had leaped out of the boat with the empty cooler and gathered up the raw chicken parts. It was this third man who grabbed the big poacher by the collar of his shirt and dragged him back onto the boat.

Leo watched as the third man shoved the boat away from the shore, climbed in and gunned the engine. As the boat disappeared into the night, Leo turned to look down the fairway and saw two figures running toward him, their flashlight beams swinging wildly back and forth.

Leo's knees buckled, and the realization that he'd just seen himself running down the third fairway was enough to make him want to vomit. He sucked in deep breaths of hot, humid summer air, tainted with the scents of sun-dried, cut grass and that awful bug spray that smelled like cat piss.

Sid kneeled beside him and wrapped her arm around his shoulder. He leaned into her hug, grateful to be back with her under the giant oak. Technically, he'd been here the whole time, but his body was exhausted, and his mind was still reeling from the back-to-back evenings spent watching a man die by alligator bite and friendly crossbow fire. Leo let himself be helped over to one of the camp chairs, and Sid handed him a cold soda from the cooler. He chugged it, longing for the sugar and caffeine to kick in and steady his world as soon as possible.

Sid placed a hand on his arm. "What did you see, Leo? Can you tell me?"

He nodded and closed his eyes. "I saw Dru Chase. I know how he died."

Sid reached into her back and pulled out her bright pink notebook, the one she still used when there was too much information to simply type into her phone. Leo recounted the events to Sid, combining the two vignettes so that he only had to tell the story once. When he was done, they both sat back and stared across the fairway at the darkening marsh beyond.

Leo looked up at Bacon and Bucket. "Thank you both for showing me what happened."

"Yes, gentlemen, that was very helpful," Sid added. "I'm sorry all of you had to witness that tragedy."

Leo could feel waves of emotion coming from the two ghosts. It was common for him to feel such things from spirits, but it had never happened with a ghost. Granted, his interactions with ghosts before Bacon and Bucket had been limited, but they had always seemed much more guarded than his easy and effortless connection to spirits. (Much too easy, in his opinion.) The few ghosts that he'd encountered had all kept their distance—emotionally speaking, that is.

Here, though, under the oak, the emotions that Bacon and Bucket were sharing surprised him. He mostly felt sadness for the death of Dru Chase, but there was something else, something that seemed odd, given the waves of sorrow coming off the ghosts. Leo's eyes widened when he realized what he was feeling. He glanced between the ghosts and Sid.

"What?" asked Sid. "What's wrong?" She frowned at him. "Are you feeling okay? You look flushed."

Leo's hands flew to his blushing face. "No! N-nothing, I'm fine," he babbled. He took another large gulp of soda, hoping the waves of emotion would pass. He really didn't like experiencing these two dead golfers' longing for his boss. The feelings of love were bad enough, but the waves of lust were more than he could bear. He squeezed his eyes shut again and turned away from Sid.

As he did so, he heard the ghosts' voices in his head again. They weren't done with him, apparently. He heard one word.

"Others."

Chapter Twelve

The can slipped from Leo's grip, landing on an exposed tree root and splashing soda all over Sid's shoes. He shot to his feet, staring at the ghosts. "What do you mean?" he asked them.

The insistent word came again:

"Others."

Sid picked up the soda can and set it atop the cooler. "What are they saying?"

Leo swallowed. "Others. They're saying there are others."

Sid froze. "More dead bodies?"

Leo shrugged uneasily. "I guess."

"Okay," said Sid as she picked up her backpack, fished out the flashlight, and swung the bag up onto her shoulder. "You stay here."

Leo turned to her and smirked. "So you're going to go with them and have them show you where the bodies are? How's that gonna work?"

"Shit," Sid muttered under her breath. "Fine. You can come. But"—she poked him in the chest—"you do what I tell you. If I say stay back, you stay back. If I say leave, you leave. If I say run and get help, you do exactly that. Understand?" Leo nodded. "All right then. Ask them to show us."

Leo rolled his eyes. "They can hear you, Sid."

"Good." Sid squared her shoulders and cocked an eyebrow. Using another of her teacher voices—the one she used to order her kids to pay attention or stand in a straight line—she said, "Gentlemen, I understand that there is something else you wish to show us. I ask that you take us there. But before we do, I also want to ask you for a favor. Leo must be kept far enough away so as not to see the worst of it."

"Sid!" growled Leo in protest, but Sid held up her hand.

"Is that understood, gentlemen?" She waited for a response, unsure of exactly how that would come.

Leo felt the emotions coming in waves, making him blush again. He stared at his shoes, too embarrassed to look his boss in the face. "I think they understand."

"Good." Sid smiled. "Then please lead the way, gentlemen."

Leo blinked, and Bacon and Bucket were halfway down the fairway already. "Come on," he ordered. "They're moving fast."

The two investigators jogged down the eighteenth fairway toward the tee box. From the tee, they followed the ghosts along the cart path that snaked around some oaks and emerged next to the seventeenth fairway. The seventeenth hole was a short par 3 that ran from east to west, perpendicular to the island's natural shoreline. Jonathan Beedlemeyer had told them it was one of the course's most challenging spots.

In the daylight, the seventeenth hole emerged from a line of houses and jutted out into the marsh with a lovely view of the river beyond. Mangroves grew along the southern edge of the fairway and green, thicker than on any of the other water holes. About three-fourths of the way down the short fairway was a canal that sliced the hole in two, cutting off the green from the rest of the mainland. The green was accessed by a wooden cart bridge on the north edge of the fairway.

Between the canal and the green was a wide sand trap that ringed the green from about two o'clock to ten o'clock on the dial. The pin placement was usually far back at the twelve o'clock position, with very little ground between the hole and the marsh. Beedlemeyer had joked that the fortune lost on golf balls on this hole alone could probably pay for an annual club membership. He'd laughed as he said it. Sid had politely smiled while Leo had rolled his eyes.

Leo came to an abrupt stop on the near side of the wooden cart bridge, and Sid almost bumped into him. Bacon and Bucket stood on the bridge with their golf clubs raised, ready to strike. "Um, I think they want us to stop here."

"You mean this is where they want *you* to stop," said Sid. Leo frowned, and Sid patted his shoulder. "Thank you, gentlemen," she said into the darkening air. "Now, please be so kind as to point to the spot where I need to look."

Bacon stayed where he was with his golf club raised, but Bucket drifted to the middle of the green and pointed to the southern end of the sand trap, near the mangroves. Leo pointed in Bucket's direction. "Over there. Looks like, whatever it is, it's in the sand trap."

Sid nodded once and took a deep breath. "Stay here." She glanced sideways at Leo. "I mean it."

"I know," Leo grumbled. He leaned against the railing of the cart bridge as Sid walked across.

Sid shivered as she crossed the middle of the bridge. "Ghost," she whispered and shivered again with the realization that she'd just walked through one. She felt another sudden drop in temperature as she walked across the green. She tried to shake it off as she scanned the green with her flashlight. Nothing out of the ordinary. She stepped down into the sand trap at about six o'clock on the dial, shining her light all around her. Still nothing.

"All right, gentlemen, where is it? And what exactly am I looking for?" Sid felt something cold brush against her cheek and fought the urge to leap right out of her skin. "Show me," she whispered. She took two steps to the left, and the cold vanished. Two steps to the right, and it returned. More steps to the right. Still cold.

Sid reached the far end of the sand trap and stepped up onto the grass. The cold vanished, and the hot air returned. She stepped back down into the sand trap and walked over to the marsh's edge, peering down into the water. Something white appeared in her flashlight beam. Sid kneeled on the lip of the trap and peered into the mangrove thicket.

Tangled in the roots just below the water's surface was a piece of white fabric. Sid reached out, fishing her hand in between the roots, and touched it. When she tugged, the fabric began to come free from the roots. At least, that's what Sid thought was happening until an arm emerged from the dark water.

Sid faltered, teetering at the edge of the trap, and the flashlight slipped from her hand into the water. The beam still shone under the surface and illuminated what was clearly an arm and torso. The head, if there was one, was in the water, hidden from view by the mangrove roots.

Sid crab-walked backward across the sand until she felt the soft grass of the green under her palms. Even after a few deep breaths, her heart was still banging against her ribs. Gripping her phone with shaking hands, Sid called Detective Tony

Davis. She hoped he was still at Oakmire and hadn't quit for the evening.

He answered on the first ring. "Hey, Sid. Please don't tell me you found another dead body."

Sid remained silent.

"Shit," muttered Tony. "Where are you?"

"Sssss . . . eh . . ." Sid's voice was stuck in her throat. She swallowed to clear it and managed to whisper, "Seventeenth green." She wiped her free hand on her pant leg, trying to remove the sand and the feel of the water-logged fabric from her fingers. "Are you still here? At Oakmire?"

"No. Are you in danger?" asked Tony.

"No." She looked around, but she knew no one else was there. Just Leo and two dead golfers. "No, I'm fine. I'm safe." She was still whispering and told herself it was so that Leo wouldn't hear her, but that was not entirely true.

"On my way," said Tony, and Sid heard a car door slam through the phone. "I assume I don't have to remind you to stay back to preserve the scene."

He didn't. Sid nodded even though Tony couldn't see her. "No problem." She pocketed the phone and was suddenly bathed in light.

"Why are you sitting on the ground in the dark?"

Sid closed her eyes against the bright light and sighed. "And why don't you ever listen to me?"

"I saw your flashlight go into the water. And then there was nothing." Leo kneeled next to Sid and angled his flashlight downward. He could hear the panic in his voice, so he knew Sid could, too. "I thought you fell in. When you didn't scream or call for help, I thought maybe you hit your head or an alligator had dragged you under. I came . . ." He swallowed. "I came to see . . ."

She squeezed his shoulder. "I'm fine, kid. I didn't fall in.

No alligator got ahold of me. I'm totally fine. Now, help me up." Leo pulled her to her feet, and she brushed the sand off her pants. "We need to get off the green. Let's go back to the bridge."

Leo led the way with his flashlight. "Did you find something?"

"Yes."

"Another dead body?"

"Yes."

"Who?"

Sid sighed. "No idea. I called Detective Davis, and he's on his way. We'll wait for him here." She leaned back against the bridge railing while Leo paced back and forth. "Where are the —" She almost said "ghosts" but stopped herself. "Where are our two friends?"

Leo pointed to the end of the bridge about twenty feet away, and Sid nodded. They were quiet for several minutes as Sid waited for her heart rate to slow and Leo tried to wear a groove into the bridge's wooden planks.

Something Leo had said earlier was niggling at her. She really didn't want to ask the question, but since Tony was on his way, it was probably better that she find out now. "Hey, Leo. Stop pacing for a second." When he came to a halt in front of her, she asked, "Is there another one?"

"Another what? Dead body?" His eyes widened in surprise.

Sid nodded. "You told me that our friends said there were others. Plural. As in more than one."

"Oh." Leo bit his lip and glanced over at the ghosts. "I guess I'll ask."

Bacon and Bucket were standing on the fairway just off the bridge. "Excuse me, sirs," Leo began. He felt silly being so formal, but it seemed to work for Sid. These ghosts had responded to her respectful manner and tone, so he might as well give it a try himself. "You mentioned earlier that there were others. Does that mean that there are more? Are there more dead bodies here?"

"*No.*"

Leo shook his head. That was not the response he'd been expecting. "But you said 'others.' Plural. As in not just one, but two or more. Are you saying that the body my boss just found is the only other? There are no other dead to be found here?"

"*No.*"

Leo ground his teeth and clenched his fists to stop himself from yelling at them. He took a steadying breath and mustered as much politeness as he could. "I'm sorry, but I don't understand. What did you mean? If there are no more bodies to find, then what else is there? What is the *other* that you want to show us?"

With that, a series of images flashed in his head. They came fast, making him feel dizzy and disoriented. Leo staggered to his left as the sequence of images repeated from a slightly different angle, and he realized that the ghosts had taken turns showing him what they wanted him to see. "Okay, okay, stop! Please!" Leo begged. He turned back toward the bridge, stumbled to the edge of the canal, and dropped to his knees, where he promptly vomited into the water.

"Leo!" Sid charged across the bridge, kneeled next to him, and placed a hand on his back. "What the hell happened?"

Leo coughed, spat into the canal, and wiped his mouth with the hem of his T-shirt. "There isn't another dead body for us to find." He let her help him up and grabbed the bridge railing to steady himself. "They weren't referring to another body."

Sid held on to his shoulders. "Then why were you depositing your dinner in the canal?"

Leo smirked. "Better there than on the golf course. Henri wouldn't be very pleased if I hurled all over his pretty grass."

"Leo," Sid growled in warning.

"They showed me some things . . . sort of like photos, I guess." He closed his eyes. The images were still in his mind, except now he could sift through them slowly and without the nausea. "It was me. They showed me images of me."

When Sid tightened her grip on his shoulders, Leo explained, "They were pictures of me here at Oakmire these last few days. At the clubhouse, in the parking lot, on the golf course. I didn't even know that they, that our friends were watching me all that time, but I guess they were."

"I don't understand." Sid let her hands fall to her sides and stepped back from him. "So they just showed you images of yourself? So what?"

"Sort of." Leo wiped his mouth again. "When they do that, when I see myself from their viewpoint, it makes me sick to my stomach. And when there are a lot of those images and they come really fast, it makes me throw up." When Sid nodded her understanding, he continued. "But they weren't just images of me. There was someone else."

"Me?" offered Sid.

Leo smiled. "Well, yes. Sometimes you were there, too, but no, there was someone else. At least I think it's a someone." Leo shoved his hands in his pockets. "There's a shadow following me. That's what they were trying to show me. It's been around me this entire time."

"What do you mean a shadow is following you? What does that even mean?" Sid's voice had taken on a shrill quality.

"I don't know." He shrugged. "Val said she had a premonition about a shadow following me. I guess it's the same one. I don't know what it is or who it is or what they want, but it looks like it's been around a lot."

"Have you seen it yourself?" asked Sid.

Leo shook his head. "No."

Sid sighed. "Okay, kid. You and I are going to have a very long talk tomorrow morning about everything you saw, all the images that these . . . these guys showed you. You're also going to tell me who this Val person is, and we are going to figure all of this out." Leo nodded once. "Because if we can't figure this out, you are going to have to stop coming on this job with me."

"No!" whined Leo.

Sid flung her arms out wide. "All of this started when we came here. The ghosts and the dead bodies and now some kind of shadow haunting you. It all kicked off here. So if we don't find a solution, then you are not coming back here. Do you hear me?"

"Sid!" pleaded Leo.

Sid crossed her arms and used her teacher voice. "Do you understand me?"

Leo gaped, his mouth open in protest for a moment or two. When she proved unswerving, he finally mumbled, "Yeah," in surrender. He turned away from her, kicked at the post, and spent the next ten minutes pouting and trying to ignore her.

Bacon and Bucket joined him on the bridge, and Leo noted that their feelings had changed to something like sympathy and annoyance. He was oddly comforted, both for their solidarity with him in being angry at Sid and for not having to endure their waves of lust. The presence of the ghosts also meant that the temperature around him cooled significantly, a welcome break from the summer heat. It lasted for about ten minutes, and then Tony Davis showed up.

Chapter Thirteen

Detective Davis came marching down the cart path toward the bridge leading to the seventeenth green. Behind him were a couple of uniformed deputies. Sid was almost disappointed that they weren't Deputies Adcock and Weber—the twins, as she had come to think of them—because that meant she'd have more explaining to do. At least Adcock and Weber knew her and why she was on the golf course at night.

"Sidney, Leo." Tony nodded to each of them. He didn't bother to introduce the deputies. "Show me." Sid and Leo turned to lead the way across the bridge and onto the green, but Tony held Leo back. "Just Sid. You need to wait here, Leo." His voice was low but far from soft.

Leo frowned but didn't bother whining in protest. He didn't think the big detective would yield to his pleas any more than Sid had, so he decided to save his breath. He did as he was ordered and stayed behind on the bridge while the adults traipsed across the green to the mangroves on the far side.

He felt Bacon and Bucket join him on the bridge before he

saw them. The two ghosts weren't watching what was happening on the green, though. Instead, they were focused on the cart path that wove through the trees and shrubs toward the eighteenth hole. Leo turned to see what had captured their attention, but there was nothing. At least, nothing more unusual than darkness and the serenade of the alligator chorus. Leo was becoming immune to their song, and he almost chuckled at the realization that their growls had nearly caused him to pee his pants a few nights ago.

And then he saw it, a shadow within the blackness of night. A figure standing among the trees, darker than the space around it. It was person-shaped, but Leo wasn't sure it was a person. Nor could he swear that it was a spirit or ghost. He'd never seen anything like it in his limited experiences. Whatever the shadow was, it had Bacon and Bucket rattled. They huddled so near to him that Leo felt his flesh prickle with goose bumps, and he wrapped his arms around himself for warmth. Neither he, the ghosts, nor the shadow moved for several minutes. Leo felt as if he were in a showdown, like some sort of paranormal *Wild West* movie.

One of the deputies walked past him on the bridge, and the spell Leo had been under was broken. The shadow vanished. Leo blinked several times as the deputy marched along the cart path and vanished from view on his way toward the eighteenth hole, walking right over the spot where the shadow had been.

Leo shook his head, trying to clear it. "I must be seeing things." He looked again, but nothing seemed amiss. "Do you think I'm going crazy?" Leo heard laughter in his head and glanced at the ghosts on either side of him. He grinned. "Don't answer that."

Another ninety minutes passed before the body tangled in the mangroves was able to be pulled from the water. At first, only a handful of additional patrol deputies and someone from the medical examiner's office arrived to secure the scene and recover the body from the marsh. All that changed once Tony Davis put in a call to his supervisor, waking the man out of a sound sleep.

"Well, I haven't taken fingerprints or checked any dental records, Harry, but I'm pretty sure, yes," said Tony. He listened to his boss for another minute before hanging up. He pinched the bridge of his nose and turned to Sid. "We're gonna have to crawl all over this place."

"Oh, I bet the board of directors is going to love that." Sid smirked. "Whatever will they do if they can't play golf?"

Sid and Tony stared down at the bloated and mangled body of Cameron Chase. The once-handsome young golfer was missing one arm, the other hand and one leg below the knee. While there were wounds to the back of his head, his face was surprisingly intact, even after being submerged in the water for some length of time. His ginger curls, which in online photos were usually worn shoulder-length and tucked behind his ears, had recently been shorn. Cameron Chase's new haircut was short on the sides and longer on top, and Sid presumed this was the young man's attempt to look older and more respectable now that he'd risen to the heights of golf superstardom. Dru Chase had worn his curly red hair to his shoulders, just like his cousin, which was why Sid had thought yesterday's body might be the famous golfer. Two boys from the same extended family, both of them meeting the same fate.

Tony shook his head. "Damn shame."

"It certainly is," said Sid. "His family's going to be devastated." Tony merely grunted, and Sid frowned at him. "You don't think so?"

Tony sighed. "They'll miss the money, that's for sure. His dad is a grade A piece of shit."

"You don't mince words, do you, Tony?" Sid turned away from the dead body. "Poor kid." She shook her head. "Because that's what he was. He was still just a kid."

"Yeah." Tony ran his hand down his face. "He was just a kid."

―――

Leo caught a glimpse of the body when they pulled it out of the water. How could he not? The portable lights the deputies erected on the green lit up the area like it was the middle of the day. The body was in horrible shape, bloated and missing limbs, and the sight of it made his stomach clench. Fortunately, he'd already thrown up enough for one night, so he didn't have to worry about embarrassing himself in front of Tony and the other sheriff's deputies. Once the body was on dry land and had been photographed from every possible angle, it was placed in a black body bag. After that, Sid and Tony joined him on the bridge, and Tony said they should go home and get some sleep and that he would be in touch tomorrow.

Leo waited until they were back at their stakeout site under the big oak on the eighteenth hole before he finally asked, "So, who was it?"

"There's no official ID yet," said Sid in a low voice, "but it looks like it's Cameron Chase."

Leo's eyes went wide. "The guy with the Maserati?"

"I'm afraid so," she replied. "He was only twenty-four."

Leo heard the sadness in her voice and decided to remain silent. Sid grabbed the cooler and let Leo take the two camp chairs. When they reached the parking lot, the police were in the process of loading Cameron Chase's fancy sports car onto a tow truck.

Leo slid into the passenger seat of Sid's car and fastened his seat belt. "Do you think an alligator got him?"

Sid sighed. "Yep. I'm pretty sure he had all of his limbs before he went into the water."

Leo glanced over at his boss. "Think he was poaching?"

She started the engine and began to pull out of the parking lot, dodging the various sheriff's vehicles. "I don't see why he would have been messing around with alligator poaching. The guy was just beginning to make it big as a professional golfer. He had money and fame coming his way. Tournaments and endorsement deals. Now, if you had that"—she pointed to the Maserati now sitting on the tow truck bed—"would you be sitting in a little boat in the middle of the swamp in the dead of night, trying to poach alligators?"

"No." Leo shook his head. The ghosts had shown him what had happened to the redheaded poacher who died the other night, the one who was accidently shot by his friend and finished off by the alligator. "Not for all the Maseratis in the world."

Chapter Fourteen

The next morning, Sid sat at the kitchen table waiting for Leo to wake up and come downstairs for breakfast. They'd gotten home around midnight from Oakmire, and she knew Leo would be sleeping late as a result. She, however, had set her alarm, started Burt's coffee maker, and been waiting for the man in his kitchen when he lumbered downstairs before dawn. Sid explained what had happened the night before: how the ghosts had told Leo there was another body, how she had kept Leo back so he wouldn't see anything, how the cops had shown up to take care of things, and who it was they had pulled from the marsh.

Burt took a sip of coffee and frowned. "You're telling me he didn't see anything?"

"I don't believe so, no." Sid shook her head. "Both Detective Davis and I told him to stay far away from the scene, and he actually listened to us this time."

Burt nodded. "And this isn't related to your case?"

"I don't see how it can be. The kid was a professional golfer. Rising star, apparently. I can't see any reason why he'd be trying to poach alligators in the middle of the night, not when all that golf money was starting to flow his way." Sid sipped her coffee and waited while Burt mulled it all over.

After a couple of minutes of silence, he rubbed his eyes and sighed. "All right. Leo can keep going." He stood, filled his travel mug with coffee, and headed for the door. He turned back to Sid before leaving the kitchen. "Be careful. Both of you."

Sid nodded, and Burt left the house for his renovation job at La Señora.

Once she heard his car crank to life on the driveway, Sid breathed an audible sigh of relief. She'd feared another telling-off, but Burt had been surprisingly calm about the whole thing. He might not have been so calm, however, if Sid had told him the whole truth. She was fairly certain that Leo had seen something of the body when it was finally freed from the mangroves and placed on the grass. There were too many lights shining on it for him not to have seen something, but she had made sure that he was far enough away not to have to witness the worst of it.

Sid had also left out the part about the mysterious shadow that was following Leo. In truth, she didn't know enough about this shadow thing to be able to tell Burt what it was or what it even meant. Until she knew everything, Burt wouldn't know everything either.

Sid felt bad about lying to him, but was it lying, though? It was more like omitting some minor details. Crucial ones, perhaps, but overall, they were probably not enough to have made a significant difference in how he processed the situation. At least that's what she would continue telling herself, she decided. She poured herself a bowl of cereal and waited for Leo to wake up.

She didn't have to wait long. Within the hour, Leo clomped

down the stairs and shuffled into the kitchen in search of food. Sid could tell he was still half asleep, so she let him pour a bowl of cereal and pop some frozen waffles in the toaster without saying anything to him. She simply sipped her coffee and waited. When he was almost finished with his breakfast and looking more alert, she set her cup on the table and sat back. "Leo, we have some things we need to take care of this morning."

"'Kay," he mumbled through a mouthful of syrup-drenched waffle.

"We're going to go visit your friend Val." Leo stopped chewing and stared at her. Sid raised an eyebrow at him. "When you're finished eating, clean up and go get dressed. I'll meet you in the office." She got up from the table, placed her mug in the dishwasher, and left Leo sitting in the kitchen, still wide-eyed and frozen in his seat.

At half past nine, Sid and Leo stood on Cuna Street in front of Muy Local. Sid had been to the shop before, several times in fact, but had never bought anything. Though she liked the idea of supporting local artists, most of the stuff in the shop hadn't interested her. The few pieces that had caught her eye—a painting or two, some pieces of jewelry—were all priced well above what she was willing to spend, especially given that she'd had more debt than income these past several years. Sid frowned at the flamingo-pink trim, thinking how out of touch it was with the surrounding aesthetic of old Spanish Florida combined with sun-bleached ramshackle. "So, Val lives here?"

"There's an apartment upstairs. She runs the shop." Leo was staring at the cobblestones as he traced their outline with the toe of his sneaker. "She's not open 'til eleven."

Sid crossed her arms and turned to face him. "How did you meet this woman?" When the boy hesitated, Sid used her teacher voice. "Leo, answer me."

He answered without looking at her, "Miss Hattie took me to see her."

Sid rolled her eyes. "And who the hell is Miss Hattie?" Again, he hesitated. "Leo!"

He threw up his hands. "She's a woman I met in the park. You know, the one by the cathedral, the one with all the cannons and stuff."

"I know the park, Leo." Sid was losing her patience. "Who is Miss Hattie?!"

"She's a woman who can see spirits. She's . . . she's been helping me." His voice was so quiet that Sid almost didn't hear him.

"Fine. Let's go." Sid turned on her heels and marched up Cuna Street, turning left on St. George. "You're going to introduce me to her," she called over her shoulder. Leo had to jog to keep up with her as they made their way to the Plaza de la Constitución.

When they reached the park, Sid let Leo take the lead and was surprised when he walked around it and crossed onto Aviles Street. "Where are we going, kid?"

"We have a stop to make first," Leo replied. "Two stops, actually."

Fifteen minutes later, they walked back to the Plaza de la Constitución and followed the sidewalk toward one of the giant oaks. Leo stopped in front of an old woman who was wearing a billowing maxi sundress and seated cross-legged on a folded blanket. She was leaning back against the tree trunk with her broad, straw hat pulled down over her face. Sid stood next to him, holding the two cups of coffee they'd purchased at Pirate Joe's.

Leo cleared his throat and shifted back and forth on his feet. "Miss Hattie."

The woman sat forward and tilted her hat back on her head. She looked up at him from behind her oversize sunglasses and smiled her largely toothless grin. "Good mornin', Leo." She swung her gaze to Sid. "And you must be Sidney Stone."

"I am, yes." Sid nodded.

"How . . . how did you know?" Leo stuttered and glanced between Hattie and Sid.

Hattie chuckled. "Well, she's famous, isn't she? All over the news 'cause of that business with the sheriff." She shook her head. "Never liked him." Then she shrugged. "And Eli's mentioned you a time or two."

"Eli Williams?" Sid raised an eyebrow. "Burt Roberts's friend?" She was thinking of the large, Black man with the booming laugh who was the lead singer of the band, Recent Geezer. Burt was the Geezers' bass guitarist, and the band practiced at Burt's house almost every Sunday.

"The very one." Hattie nodded. "Eli's my cousin. His mama and my mama were sisters. Didn't see each other all that much when we were kids. His mama moved him to New Orleans when he was real little. Worked on the shrimp boats there when he was a kid, then came back here after servin' in the army for a while. Took up shrimpin' again. Eventually bought his own boat." She nodded approvingly. "Really made somethin' of himself, that boy."

Sid smiled. That "boy" had turned seventy last spring. Sid remembered the Geezers' celebrating his birthday during their Sunday jam session. The party went late into the night and had included a fancy birthday cake baked by the band's most loyal groupie—Burt's neighbor, Kitty Lonigan. Sid had been the one to finally break up the festivities when several of the neighbors threatened to call the cops because the band wouldn't stop playing.

"Eli's a very nice man," said Sid, and Hattie nodded in agreement. Sid held out a coffee cup, the one with the most cream and sugar. "This is for you."

"Well, aren't you sweet," said Hattie. She took the cup, removed the lid, and inhaled deeply. "Pirate Joe's. Just the way I like it." She nodded toward Leo. "I told this boy that he didn't need to bring me coffee no more."

Leo blushed. "It's no big deal."

"Sit, sit." Hattie patted the ground in front of her. "Are you here for a social call? Or is this business?"

Sid sat on the ground in front of Hattie. "Honestly, I'm not sure."

Leo sat and took one of the datil-pepper-glazed donuts from the bag he was holding. He held out the bag to Sid, who declined it with a wave of her hand and then passed it to Hattie. She removed one of the two remaining donuts and gave the bag back to him.

Leo sighed. "Sid wants to talk to Val." He glanced sideways at Sid, who was still staring at Hattie. "She knows about the shadow."

Hattie nodded and balanced her donut on her knee, bits of the glaze flaking off onto her sundress as she did so. "Have you seen it, Leo?"

He nodded. "Last night."

Sid whipped her head around toward him. "You did? When? You told me last night that you hadn't seen it, not in person."

Leo nodded. "I saw it when you were with Detective Davis and . . . and the body."

Hattie raised an eyebrow. "Body? Another one?" Leo

nodded. Hattie frowned. "Awful lot of death over at that fancy Oakmire club." She turned to Sid. "But death itself isn't always what we need to be afraid of. Sometimes the living are much, much worse."

"True." Sid removed the lid of her own cup to let the coffee cool a bit. "But when this kid's vomiting and shaking and being beaten with invisible golf clubs, I think maybe it's time to be a little afraid. Don't you?"

Hattie pursed her lips, nodded once, and turned to Leo. "Tell me what happened." She wagged a crooked finger at him. "Leave nothing out."

Leo swallowed the last bite of his donut, wiped his mouth on one of the paper napkins, and began his tale. He told her about the ghosts responding to Sid's polite requests and leading them to the body on the seventeenth hole. He described the images that Bacon and Bucket had shown him, at least those he could remember, where the shadow had been present. Finally, he admitted to seeing the shadow in the trees, how the ghosts had reacted, and how it disappeared when one of the deputies walked by.

"I didn't feel anything," said Leo. "Nothing good or bad. The ghosts were on alert, but they didn't seem to know more than I did."

Hattie nodded. "Well, something has taken an interest in you, boy. Not sure what, but I don't think we need to assume it's all bad."

"Really?" Sid squirmed on the ground. Whether it was due to sitting in the grass or listening to Leo talk about seeing ghosts and shadows, she couldn't seem to get comfortable. "Some weird shadow thing is following him, and we don't need to be worried?"

"Not everything dark and unknown is a monster," said

Hattie. "Sometimes the real monsters are the ones who smile sweetly and look all innocent." The old woman tapped her temple with a crooked finger. "The real trick is knowing which one to be afraid of."

Sid sighed. "Did he pick up this shadow at Oakmire? Is that where all of this started?"

Hattie shrugged. "I've got no idea. You best ask Val 'bout that."

Thirty minutes later, Sid, Leo, and Hattie were crowded around Val's kitchen table, enjoying Cuban coffee. "I'm afraid I can't tell you much more than I did last time, Leo," said Val as she added sugar to her cup. "Whoever this is, he or she is keeping watch. Do you still have the stones?" Leo nodded and pulled them from his pocket. "Good, good. They should help."

"But is it dangerous? And did it come from Oakmire?" Sid's annoyance was growing, as was her trepidation. Why couldn't these women give her some answers?

Val took a sip and set her cup back down. "I don't know the answer to either of those questions." Sid almost growled in frustration, a point Val seemed to notice, as she smiled and continued. "I know that is not what you want to hear. I don't know if the shadow came from Oakmire, but it is not limited to Oakmire. It appears elsewhere. It follows him. I've had no visions of him being in harm's way, but that being said, it is always best not to go courting danger." She raised an eyebrow at Sid. "Perhaps taking him someplace where dead bodies keep appearing is not exactly staying away from danger."

Sid took a slow breath, her nostrils flaring, before she responded. "And yet walking down St. George Street surrounded by ghosts of long-dead pirates is better, is it?"

Val shrugged one shoulder. "Those long-dead pirates don't seem to be following him around."

Hattie interrupted, "Do you see the shadow now, Leo?"

Leo glanced around the room and shook his head.

"On the street," said Val. She nodded toward the window and took a sip of her coffee.

The other three stood up and hovered in the window, scanning the street below.

"There," said Leo. "That courtyard area." He pointed across the street and to the left, toward the river. There stood a one-story clapboard house that had been turned into a fine-dining tapas restaurant. In front of the entrance there was a small courtyard, decorated with blooming plants that had withered in the unforgiving summer sun.

"Yes," said Hattie, nodding in agreement.

"Where?" asked Sid, pressing her forehead into the glass and straining to see something, anything.

"Next to the palm," said Leo. "There's a shadow that's darker than the rest."

But Sid could see nothing. "So, how do we get rid of it? Do we need a séance or an exorcism or something?" The three mediums turned toward her with various looks on their faces, ranging from humor to annoyance to hope.

"Would that work?" asked Leo.

Hattie chuckled. "Probably not a séance or an exorcism, but I have an idea." She pushed past the others, then thumped downstairs and out the front door of the shop, the others hot on her heels. Hattie motioned for them to stay on the porch while she approached the restaurant's courtyard.

She stood in the middle of Cuna Street, saying nothing and staring at the empty courtyard. A few tourists were forced to walk around her, shaking their heads at the old woman as they did so, but Hattie stood stock-still.

Leo watched the shadow in the courtyard. It stayed put as Hattie stood facing it in the middle of the street. After a minute or so of nothing happening, Hattie began to walk toward it, and the shadow vanished.

Hattie returned to the porch and shook her head. "It wouldn't talk." She turned to Leo. "Keep your wits about you, boy. I don't know what it wants, but it has its sights set on you."

Chapter Fifteen

After a fair bit of arguing, which lasted through lunch, Sid finally caved and agreed that Leo could accompany her back to Oakmire that evening. She wanted him to steer clear of the place and was, in fact, beginning to regret involving him in her PI business at all. Spirits, ghosts, a scary shadow figure, and two dead bodies—how much more could a fifteen-year-old boy take?

But Leo had argued that, for him, all of those things (minus the two dead bodies) existed everywhere and were around him all the time. It didn't matter whether he was at Oakmire helping her, down at La Señora helping his grandfather, or sitting at home playing games on his laptop. For a boy like him, it simply didn't matter. She might as well put him to good use and teach him how to be a private investigator so that he could do it full-time one day. Sid had rolled her eyes at that last part of his argument.

Later that evening, the two of them waited in the car as the Oakmire security guard opened the front gate, the one meant to keep the neighborhood safe and secluded. While the front gate seemed to succeed at the latter of those two tasks, it had recently failed to achieve the former, at least with respect to Cameron and Dru Chase.

Despite all of Sid's misgivings, she was actually glad Leo was there with her. She wasn't looking forward to the tasks at hand this evening, and she hoped his presence would encourage everyone to behave well. He was a good kid, after all, and adults seemed to like having him around. Sid hoped that worked in her favor today.

Shortly before six o'clock, Sid parked the car on the street in front of a stately mini mansion of red brick, with tall, white columns. A woman answered the door dressed in a pale-gray maid's uniform, and Sid fought against the urge to roll her eyes. After she announced their reason for being there, she and Leo were shown into a formal living room decorated in reds and golds, with velvet sofas, crystal lamps, and a Persian rug that probably cost as much as the house itself. Sid strode across it and plopped down on the scarlet sofa, running her hand over the soft velvet. Leo stood awkwardly in the doorway.

"Sit down, Leo." She patted the sofa next to her. He shook his head and shoved his hands into his pockets. Sid sighed. "Just sit. It's fine. You're not going to mess anything up." He frowned and slowly crossed the ornate rug to sit next to her, perching on the edge and hoping his thrift-store shorts didn't leave a mark on the fancy fabric.

They waited a solid twenty minutes before anyone came to find them. The man who finally did stormed into the room as if he were a Broadway actor arriving onstage for his showstopping number. "Herbert Langston," he bellowed, and Sid wondered if he was about to break into song. "How may I help you?"

As Langston held out his hand to Sid, she did her best to surreptitiously look him up and down.

Herbert Langston was one of two TNT lawyers on the

Oakmire board of directors. He was a small, round man with a small, round face. His complexion was ruddy, marking him as no stranger to strong drink, and he had the fiery red hair of a stereotypical Scotsman in some period Highland drama. The red hair reminded Sid of Cameron and Dru Chase, although Langston's locks were lighter.

"Nice to meet you, Mr. Langston." Sid shook his hand, which felt small and round in her own. Sid noticed his fingers looked like swollen sausages. "I'm Sidney Stone. I'm the private investigator who's looking into the possible poaching activity here on the property. This is Leo Roberts, my assistant."

Langston shook Leo's hand and motioned for them to sit back down on the sofa. He took a gold damask-covered armchair for himself, and Sid noted how it allowed him to sit taller than his guests. The better to look down his nose at them, she presumed. Langston steepled his fingers in front of him. "So, what have you found?"

Sid arched a brow. "Well, two dead bodies for a start."

Langston coughed and sputtered, caught off guard by Sid's candor. "Yes, well, that is unfortunate. It's certainly not going to help property values around here."

"Yes, that is my primary concern as well," Sid replied. She held Langston's gaze, refusing to look away. "I understand that you voted against hiring a private investigator to look into the suspected poaching."

"Nothing personal, Ms. Stone. I assure you." He smiled, revealing small, slightly crooked, overly white teeth. "But I saw it as a waste of the club's money."

Sid returned his smile. "You don't think the poaching is happening?"

He shrugged. "Can't say either way. I just don't think we need to pay someone a ton of money to find out."

"I can assure you that I am not getting paid a ton, although that is an interesting way to calculate my rate schedule. I'll have to give that further thought," said Sid, keeping her smile in place. "But you're not bothered that people may be trespassing onto club property and illegally poaching alligators? I would think something like that wouldn't exactly help your property values."

Langston chuckled and shook his head. "My dear Ms. Stone, the alligators around here are a menace. If someone wants to surreptitiously remove them for us, then I don't see why we need to stand in their way." He held out his hands, palms up, as if he were pleading his case to the jury. "And while I'm sure you are very good at your job, if there is illegal activity taking place on club property, I'm sure the authorities will handle it." The corner of his mouth quirked upward. "That is, assuming the sheriff's office has stopped reeling from their recent scandal." His lips slid into a full-blown smirk. "Brought about by you, if I'm not mistaken."

"I'm afraid you are mistaken." Sid didn't miss a beat, nor did she shift her gaze or let her smile drop. "The department's scandal was brought about by Sheriff Colquitt, not me. I merely stumbled upon it." She tilted her head slightly to the left. "You have a lovely home here, Mr. Langston. There must be some spectacular views of the river and the eighteenth hole."

Langston sat up a bit straighter. "Yes, there are."

"Ever find an alligator in your pool?" asked Sid.

"No." He chuckled. "That's never happened to me, thankfully."

"Do you play golf?"

"Of course."

"Ever had a round of golf interrupted by an alligator on the course?"

"More than once."

Sid paused. "I understand there is a debate among club

members about whether to lobby the PGA to allow Oakmire to host one of its prestigious tournaments." She tilted her head a little farther to the left. "I'm curious which side of that debate you're on, Mr. Langston."

Langston's nostrils flared and his ruddy complexion grew even more flushed. Sid continued to smile at him.

She had learned a lot about that ongoing debate in the last twenty-four hours. After her conversation with Henri Broussard, she had called Jonathan Beedlemeyer and done some further digging on her own. Beedlemeyer had filled her in on the heated arguments among board members as well as the ongoing disputes among property owners. The club had lobbied the PGA a number of times over the years, but their proposals were always rejected, citing the alligator nuisance and consequent danger to the players, staff, and fans. The club's last proposal was made and rejected nine years ago.

Beedlemeyer was soundly opposed to Oakmire becoming a PGA host course, but the last decade had seen a dramatic decline in the club's old guard. Many of its long-standing members were either dying or moving to active-adult and assisted-living communities. New people had moved to Oakmire, younger members with lots of money, and they were pressing hard for Oakmire to court the PGA. Prestigious tournaments meant revenue for the club and skyrocketing home values for its members, but bringing a tournament to Oakmire meant getting rid of its alligators.

The arguments within the Oakmire community were vitriolic, pitting neighbor against neighbor, golfing buddy against golfing buddy, and according to the news coverage, the wider community of St. Johns County had been ensnared by the controversy. Environmental groups had weighed in, as had local businesses and community leaders. This dispute had been simmering for decades, but the influx of new homeowners with money, power, and influence had turned up the heat over the past few years.

"Mr. Langston?" Sid prompted. "What are your thoughts on the PGA tournament debate?"

"I find it to be an interesting proposition," said Langston.

Sid wanted to roll her eyes at his typical lawyer response. "That's it? Just an interesting proposition?"

He nodded once. "It makes no difference to me whether we host a tournament or not."

Sid raised her eyebrows in mock surprise. "But it might make a difference to your property values. Surely, if you are concerned that two dead bodies will harm the value of your home, then it seems you would take a keen interest in an opportunity like a PGA tournament, which could cause your property value to go through the roof." She smiled. "No pun intended."

Langston pressed his lips together and exhaled loudly through his nose before responding. "Ms. Stone, though I am enjoying this conversation immensely, I'm afraid I'm going to have to bring it to a close. I have another meeting beginning soon, and I'm going to have to jump online to attend." He stood and extended his arm toward the door. "I'll show you out."

As Sid and Leo walked down the driveway toward Sid's car, Leo looked back over his shoulder, half expecting Herbert Langston to be peering at them through a curtained window. "He's lying. He wants a PGA tournament to come here."

"Of course he's lying." Sid slid into the driver's seat and started the engine, cranking up the air-conditioning to full blast. "He's been one of the ringleaders of the movement to get the PGA to bring a tournament here. I found him quoted in several news articles, and there's a video of him online being interviewed by some kid reporter from Channel 7's News at Night." Sid put the car in drive and headed to their next stop.

"Langston's champing at the bit to bring a major tournament here. He wants the revenue and the prestige and the windfall he'll get on the value of his house." She glanced over at Leo. "But as far as people who might have hired the poachers, Herbert Langston isn't the only one at the top of that list."

"Really?" His eyes went wide. "Who else?"

Sid pulled in front of another mini mansion, this one even grander than the last. "Well, let's see if he's home."

Chapter Sixteen

Leo amused himself by kicking at one of the brick pavers that ringed a large stone fountain in the front yard, trying to see if he could loosen the brick. "No one's home," he called out. Sid checked her watch and rang the doorbell for the third time. He shook his head and sighed. "Let's just come back later. I'm getting hungry."

As if on cue, a red Porsche pulled into the drive, causing Leo to stop kicking the paver and Sid to step away from the front door. The driver cut the engine and climbed out, hooking his suit jacket with one finger and tossing it over his shoulder. He removed a black leather briefcase from behind the front seat and asked, "Can I help you?"

"Mr. Castiglione?" asked Sid, even though she recognized him from photos she'd seen online.

"That depends," answered the man. He was bald, slightly built, and no taller than Sid herself. His clothes were impeccably tailored, his shoes shiny, and his movements smooth and deliberate. "Who are you?"

Sid took a few steps toward him. "I'm Sidney Stone." He

walked toward her, scanning her from head to toe. She raised her chin slightly and continued. "I've been hired by the—"

"I know who you are," said the man. "I just wanted to see if you'd tell me the truth."

He brushed past Sid and walked to the front door, turning his back on her and Leo. Sid exchanged a glance with her assistant and then asked, "So, are you?"

"Am I what?" asked the man, not bothering to turn around.

"Are you Mr. Castiglione?"

"I am." He opened the front door and crossed the threshold, finally turning back to face Sid. "And I have no interest in speaking with you. Now get off my property." With that, he shut the door in her face.

Sid didn't flinch as the man slammed the door. She'd done her homework on Rocco Castiglione as well. From what she'd read about him online, Castiglione, like his fellow board member Herbert Langston, was a successful trial attorney with the TNT law firm. Castiglione was prone to fiery speeches and childish outbursts in the courtroom. One opinion piece in the *Miami Herald* insinuated TNT had a rule that Rocco Castiglione was to be assigned only to those cases which lacked enough substance to win on their own merits and, therefore, needed a flashy magician with a knack for smoke-and-mirrors showmanship. Sid originally thought the article was a bit harsh, but now that she'd met the man, she thought the author's scathing comments were probably too kind.

Leo came to stand next to her, both of them staring at the closed front door. "Yeah, he did it."

Sid smiled. "He's quite the charmer, isn't he?"

"He's an asshole," said Leo.

"Watch the language, kid," she said, though she had been thinking the exact same thing herself.

Sid and Leo drove to the clubhouse and were shown to a table in the restaurant, where they ordered hamburgers that cost more than Sid's weekly grocery bill. She pulled her bright pink notebook out of her bag and began to make some notes, including a reminder to add the cost of tonight's dinner to Beedlemeyer's bill. She filled Leo in on what she knew about the rift between the old guard and the new—those who wanted Oakmire to remain a little-known, alligator-infested haven for the golf enthusiast and those who wanted Oakmire to be a bright, shiny destination for highly-paid professional golfers, their obsessed fans, and sports television camera crews. Sid also shared what she knew about Herbert Langston, Rocco Castiglione, and the TNT law firm.

"And you think those two guys hired the poachers to clear out the alligators?" asked Leo.

"One or both of them, or maybe even another club member." Sid shrugged. "Whoever it was, I'm pretty sure they live here at Oakmire and that they are part of this movement to woo the PGA."

The food came, and the two of them ate in companionable silence. Sid continued to make notes regarding her conversations with Langston and Castiglione while Leo scrolled away on his phone.

"Have you heard from your mother lately?" Sid finally put her pen down, took another bite of her burger, and waited for Leo to answer.

Leo nodded. His mom had texted him back yesterday—only one day after he'd reached out to her—but she hadn't called him. Leo checked her text and said, "She's on her way to Nashville. They'll stay there for a couple of days and then go to Chattanooga. Then they'll go to Atlanta for something called

Dragon Con." His heart squeezed a little in his chest. He'd looked it up, and Dragon Con was something he would have liked to see. His mom would be going there without him. "It's a cosplay thing, apparently."

Sid frowned. "Is your mom into that kind of thing? Dressing up as cartoon characters and stuff?"

Leo rolled his eyes. Educating her on the width and depth of cosplay would take more time, energy, and patience than either of them had at the moment, so he simply said, "No." The fact of the matter was that he had no idea why his mother would be going to a cosplay convention. She hated that stuff. He could only guess that it would make for interesting photos and possibly widen her audience on social media. He shoved the final bite of his burger into his mouth so he wouldn't have to say anything further.

"Huh," Sid muttered, and they resumed eating in silence.

As Leo was polishing off the last of his French fries, the waitress placed the bill face-down on the table. Sid judged her to be about eighteen or so, probably just out of high school. She was short and curvy with long, straight, dyed-blonde hair that was pulled back in a low ponytail. She wore only a smattering of makeup, trying but failing to cover some acne on her cheeks and dark circles under her eyes. Sid smiled up at the young woman and tried to recall the name she'd given them when they sat down at her table. "Angela, is it?"

The young woman nodded. "Yes, ma'am."

Sid pulled cash from her pocket, checked the amount on the bill, and handed the money to the waitress. She'd included a generous tip for the girl. "Angela, by any chance, do you know Dru Chase?"

Leo stopped chewing and looked up at their waitress.

Angela's eyes darted between the two of them, and she bit

down hard on her lower lip. Sid was afraid she might draw blood. The young woman nodded again but said nothing.

"Is there somewhere we can talk?" asked Sid.

Angela stared at her for a moment, looked down at the cash in her hand, and then nodded a third time. "Behind the kitchen, by the cart barn. I have a break in about fifteen minutes." The young woman hurried away from their table.

Leo flashed Sid a quizzical look, and Sid grinned. "Just a hunch."

They left the restaurant and walked out of the clubhouse, across the veranda, and over toward the cart barn. On their way, a golf cart came flying past, causing Sid and Leo to jump out of the way. Noah Zimmerman pulled the cart up to the barn, hopped out, and began unfastening the two bags that were strapped on the back. Sid tugged on Leo's arm as she headed for the cart barn.

"Hey, Noah," said Sid, flashing a smile. "We meet again."

The young man looked up at her, his brow creasing. "Hey." He took one of the bags down from the cart and placed it in front of him. He then removed the other bag and placed it next to the first, effectively creating a barrier between himself and Sid.

Sid noticed that Noah was taller than she had originally thought, but not much taller than herself. Though he was skinny, he had that wiry look of a marathon runner—all lean, well-defined muscle, and no body fat anywhere. His hair was light brown and shorn close to his head, from what little Sid could see under his sunhat. Though his head was covered and he was probably wearing sunscreen, he had that tell-tale sign of someone who spent their days outdoors: his face, neck, forearms, and lower legs were tanned a dark reddish-brown, but when Noah lifted his arms, Sid could see the skin underneath his shirt was as pale as could be.

"I'm Sidney, and this is Leo." She pointed to Leo, who nodded once at Noah. "I was wondering if you could help me."

Noah's brow remained furrowed. "With what?" It was the same sort of scowl that Sid had just seen on Rocco Castiglione's face.

So much for friendliness, she thought. "Do you know Dru Chase?"

Noah didn't so much as blink. "Yeah, he worked in the kitchen." He snatched a towel from inside the door of the cart barn and began wiping the heads of the golf clubs. Bits of grass fell to the ground like confetti.

Sid pointed to the clubs. "I guess they spent a lot of time in the rough." Noah looked down at the grass that had fallen at his feet. When he looked back up at her, he had a smile on his face. Apparently talking about golf was the way to get this kid to loosen up. Golfers, it seemed, were all the same in that regard.

"Yeah. These two always do," Noah replied. "They make a good pair. They spend more time searching for their balls in the hazards than they do hitting from the fairway. And they spend even more time on the greens trying to sink their putts." He shook his head slightly, still smiling.

"Was he a friend of yours?" asked Leo. "Dru Chase, I mean. Not the bad golfers."

Noah shrugged. "Sort of. Not really." He kept wiping, going over the same clubs for a second time. "I knew him. He was behind me at school. I knew some of his family, but I wouldn't say that he and I were friends." He shrugged again. "Friendly, but not exactly friends. Know what I mean?"

Leo nodded.

"When was the last time you saw him?" asked Sid.

Noah narrowed his eyes. "Why?"

Sid smiled, trying to keep it light. "Just asking."

"Dunno. A few days ago, maybe." Noah stuffed a corner of the towel into his back pocket. "Last week sometime, I guess. I don't exactly eat in the restaurant." He motioned to the grass stains on his shorts and the sweat rings under his armpits. "And Dru was never out on the course, so our paths didn't really cross. I might have seen him in the parking lot, showing up for work or leaving at the end of his shift, but I can't remember." He lifted one of the bags and slid it onto his shoulder in a fluid motion. "Sorry, but I've got to get back to work."

"Thanks for your time," said Sid. She and Leo watched as Noah slid the second bag onto his other shoulder and waddled off toward the parking lot. "Come on," said Sid, tugging Leo's arm again.

They walked around the side of the cart barn and found the back door to the club's restaurant and kitchen. A few stone benches had been placed under a big oak, and there were two cigarette disposals discreetly hidden among the bushes. No one was occupying the makeshift smokers' lounge at the moment, so Sid and Leo took a seat and waited.

Twenty minutes later, Angela emerged from the kitchen with a soda and an order of fries. She sat on the bench opposite Sid and Leo, setting her food and drink down next to her. She dropped her gaze and pressed her hands together between her knees and rocked back and forth.

"Angela," began Sid, but she was quickly interrupted.

"Angie." The young woman's voice was barely more than a whisper. "It's Angie. The club wants me to use Angela because they say it's more professional, but my name is Angie."

Sid nodded. "I'm Sid, and this is Leo." Leo gave Angie a little wave when she finally looked up at him.

Angie met Sid's gaze. "Why did you ask me about Dru?"

Sid leaned forward, resting her elbows on her knees.

"Because we were the ones who found him." The girl inhaled sharply. "I'm sorry for your loss, Angie."

The young woman's chin began to tremble, and a tear escaped down her cheek. "How . . . how did you—"

"How did I know that you and Dru were friends?" asked Sid. Angie nodded, and Sid smiled at her. "I didn't. It was just a guess."

"He was my boyfriend." Another tear ran down her cheek. "We'd been flirting with each other for a while, and he finally asked me out." She exhaled a ragged breath. "We'd only been dating a couple of months. But I thought maybe . . ." She hiccupped in an effort to suppress a sob. "I thought he might ask me to marry him."

"I'm so sorry," said Sid. She fished around in her purse for a packet of tissues and handed it over to Angie, who removed two and passed the packet back. Sid knew what had happened to Dru Chase because Leo had told her about the images the ghosts had shared with him. She knew she needed to tread lightly, but she also needed answers. "Angie, I need to ask you some questions. I know this is a bad time. In fact, there's never going to be a good time, but I need your help."

After Angie took another ragged breath and nodded, Sid continued. "We know he was out on the water last Friday night. We know he was with two other men. Poachers. We know they came ashore on the golf course and that something must have gone horribly wrong." Leo glanced over at her, his eyes wide, but Sid kept her gaze fixed on Angie. "Who were the other men, Angie? Do you know them?"

Angie looked around to make sure no one was listening. "I only know one of them." She bit her lip. "Actually, I'm not even sure about that, but Dru said his uncle had a job for him. Said he could make a hundred bucks for a couple of hours' work. He didn't say what it was at first, but I guessed." Her shoulders slumped as if telling the story was causing her to deflate inside. "I caught him watching videos of guys in the swamp poaching alligators, and I'd heard the rumors going around the club that someone was trying to kill Big Boy." She shrugged. "I guessed that was what his uncle wanted him to do. I told him it was a stupid idea. Dru didn't know anything about alligators. We'd been to the alligator farm, but that's as close as he ever got to one." She shook her head. "He didn't listen to me. He told me not to worry, that everything would be okay." She dropped her gaze, and tears ran down her face, leaving wet spots on her apron.

Leo cleared his throat. "Is he a big man?" Angie looked up at him, and Leo mimed broad shoulders and a broad chest, with muscle-bound arms. "Dru's uncle. Is he a big man? Military haircut?" Leo hadn't been able to see much detail, given that the events the ghosts showed him had taken place in the dark, but he thought he'd be able to recognize the big man if he saw him again. As for the third man in the boat, Leo wouldn't have been able to pick him out of a lineup.

Angie nodded. "Yeah. How did you know?"

Leo shot Sid a quick look. "Just a hunch."

"What is Dru's uncle's name?" asked Sid.

"Declan." Angie lowered her gaze again. "Declan Chase."

Sid pressed her hand to her mouth, holding back the expletives she wanted to utter. "Okay, Angie." She picked up her bag and nudged Leo's shoulder. "We appreciate your time. Thanks for helping us. We're very sorry for your loss."

With that, the girl burst into tears again.

Sid handed her the half empty pack of tissues, gently rubbed her shoulder, and then herded Leo toward the parking lot.

"Who is Declan Chase?" asked Leo once they were far enough away from Angie to be out of earshot.

Sid sighed. "He's Cameron Chase's father." Leo's eyes went wide, and Sid nodded. "Yep, he's the father of dead body number two."

Chapter Seventeen

For the next three days, Sid spoke with everyone she could at the Oakmire Golf and Country Club—members, staff, even delivery people—but no one knew who the poachers were nor who had hired them. Everyone had heard about poor Cameron Chase, that rising star of the golf world who was struck down before he had a chance to make it big and, in the trickle-down theory of fame and fortune, bring notoriety to his home course at Oakmire.

News of Cameron's death broke on Tuesday morning, and the coverage was relentless. TV news vans were parked at the front gate of the club and along busy A1A, the main road running through Anastasia Island. That evening, Cameron's father, Declan Chase, gave an interview with the local anchor for Channel 7's News at Night. Declan lauded his son's accomplishments and waxed poetic about everything the boy could have achieved if he'd lived. But the man turned angry, pounding his fist on the table, when he was asked by the spray-tanned anchorwoman if he regretted getting his son involved with the sport of golf, given that the young man met his death on a golf course. The interview was terminated shortly thereafter.

By the next morning, Declan Chase was giving interviews to anyone who stuck a microphone in his face. Sid had watched the videos and scrolled through the articles with a sick feeling in her stomach. Declan Chase, for all his talk about how much he loved his son, seemed much more in love with the spotlight and the sound of his own voice. After all, this was the man Leo had seen in the ghosts' visions from last Friday night. This was the man who'd led the poaching team ashore on the third hole at Oakmire. And this was the man who'd shot a twenty-year-old in the neck with a crossbow. Funnily enough, Declan Chase never once mentioned his dearly departed nephew Dru.

Gossip around the club was running rampant, spinning tales of Cameron Chase's demise at the hands of a jealous competitor, a loan shark, and a jealous girlfriend. Sid made notes on everyone's theories. Some seemed more valid than others, but the prevailing rumor was that Big Boy had gotten him. This certainly did not bode well for the twelve-foot celebrity alligator. People were calling for his head—or rather his hide—to be mounted on a stake. Henri Broussard argued that Big Boy was a gentle giant incapable of harming poor Cameron Chase, or anyone else for that matter, but Sid thought any alligator who had lived long enough to grow to twelve feet in length was certainly capable of being an expert killing machine when it wanted to be.

She noted with an aching heart that Dru Chase was mentioned only by the Oakmire kitchen personnel and waitstaff. None of the club members or course rangers knew much about him, nor had they developed as many fanciful theories about his death. Other than Dru's girlfriend, Angie, anyone who did register an opinion on the young man's demise echoed the same sentiment: Dru Chase was a poacher who had gotten what was coming to him. Basically, no one felt much pity for anyone stupid enough to try to wrestle alligators in a swamp at night.

As to the broader subject of alligator poaching, the membership of the Oakmire Golf and Country Club seemed equally divided. Half of the people Sid talked to felt the alligators were integral to Oakmire's charm, uniqueness, and exclusivity. After all, not everyone was willing to put up with so many prehistoric-looking beasts wandering through their property. Oakmire homeowners, therefore, were made of stern stuff.

On the other hand, the rest of the membership seemed to want the odious monsters gone. They lauded the heroes who had been shrewd enough to hire poachers to quietly eliminate the problem. Exactly how it was being done was of no concern to them. All they wanted was their beloved marsh cleared of the impediment that stood—or rather crawled—between Oakmire and a major PGA tournament. The knock-on effects of rising home values and club revenue were simply an added bonus.

Sid arrived home around six o'clock on Thursday evening with a pounding headache and a general dislike for the Oakmire Golf and Country Club community. Some individuals had been pleasant enough, but most of the people she spoke with were loud, opinionated, and rude, quite the opposite of the sleepy community of genteel Southern homeowners and golf lovers that they tried so hard to portray to the public.

Sid had no sooner walked into her office and dumped her bag on the desk than Leo came barging through the door. "Did you solve the case without me?" He grinned at her, looking noticeably less haggard than he had when she'd last seen him on Monday evening. Apparently, a few days off from PI business, ghost hauntings, and dead bodies did wonders for him.

"Not yet." She smiled. She opened the mini fridge and pulled out two sodas, tossing one to him. "How's school?"

"The same as the last time you asked me." Leo rolled his eyes. "It's fine."

Sid held up her hands in surrender. "Just asking, geez."

Leo popped the top on his soda can. "Are we doing a stakeout tonight?"

Sid shook her head and winced in pain. "Nope. Declan Chase is still on his media tour, so I doubt he'll be resuming his poaching business anytime soon." She opened the bomb-shelter-size bottle of extra-strength ibuprofen that she kept next to the mini fridge and swallowed two tablets. "Maybe tomorrow or Saturday if the reporters and news vans decide to stop camping out at the gate."

"Good," said Leo, bouncing on the balls of his feet. "The Geezers are playing at Granny Oak's tonight, and Grandpa said I could be their roadie." Sid smiled at him as he stood there, fidgeting. "Are you gonna come? I can save you a seat."

Sid nodded. "Sure, kid. I'll come by." She took another sip of her soda. "Let me close my eyes for a bit and try to get rid of this headache, and then I'll meet you down there." She really hoped the ibuprofen kicked in soon. Otherwise, a concert at Granny Oak's Music Park would be the last thing her poor head needed.

He nodded. "Great! Want me to order you some fried shrimp, like usual?"

That had become their routine of late. Leo and Sid would eat fried shrimp and hush puppies ordered from the takeout window at Old City Seafood Company while watching Recent Geezer rock out at Granny Oak's. Sid was touched that this fifteen-year-old boy wanted to sit with her and eat takeout rather than run off to do whatever it was that teenage boys did these days. Even so, the thought of fried food at that moment had her stomach twisting and turning.

She smiled at him. "No, thanks, Leo. I'll eat something here." She headed for the narrow, metal staircase that spiraled up to the apartment on the second floor of the garage. "You better get going. Recent Geezer's best roadie can't be late to the show."

"Okay, boss." He gave her a salute and left the office, slamming the door shut behind him as he ran back to the house. Sid winced at the sound, climbed the stairs, and fell face down onto her bed. She was asleep as soon as her head hit the pillow.

Sid entered the music park to the pitch-perfect stylings of Recent Geezer. Tonight's set included "Take It Easy" by The Eagles, always a crowd pleaser. For a Thursday night, Granny Oak's was hopping. Of course, it usually was whenever the Geezers played. Burt was smiling away, playing bass guitar. The others—Eli Williams on lead vocals and guitar, Cesar Hernandez on lead guitar, and Guppy Goodwin on drums—looked like they were having the time of their lives, and Sid suspected they were.

Recent Geezer was one of the most popular bands, if not *the* most popular, to regularly play at Granny Oak's. All of the members were technically senior citizens (with Eli the oldest at seventy and Guppy the youngest at sixty), but they were rocking out like they were teenagers. In fact, Cesar Hernandez was smiling and winking at his usual bevy of groupies. Tonight, there were three provocatively dressed middle-aged women flanking his side of the stage.

Sid snaked her way through the crowd and joined Leo near the front. "They're in good form tonight." She had to practically shout in his ear in order to be heard. Leo nodded, although Sid wasn't sure if it was in agreement or simply in time to the music. When the song ended, Eli Williams thanked the crowd and told everyone they'd be taking a short break. He was met with a mixture of applause, groans, and even a few catcalls.

Most of the band exited stage right, congregating near the tiki bar on that side of the venue. Cesar, however, exited stage left to say hello to his fans. Leo hustled over to Burt and the others to see if the band members needed any help. Sid watched him go, chuckling to herself at his sense of urgent responsibility.

"What's so funny?" The voice came from her right.

Sid turned, startled to see Tony Davis standing next to her. He had Dante on his hip, and the little boy was dripping ice cream all down his daddy's T-shirt.

"Well, hello there!" she said. Dante giggled and licked his ice cream, then held out the cone for Sid to taste. "Oh, no, thank you, Dante. That's all for you." Dante nodded and kept licking. Sid pointed to Leo, who was passing out towels to the band. "Ever the dutiful roadie."

Tony looked over at Leo and smiled. "Nice gig. Bet it helps him with the ladies, too." He winked at Sid, who rolled her eyes at him in return. "You got a minute?"

Sid nodded and followed Tony through the crowd, about half of whom were now congregating in lines at the two tiki bars. Once they exited Granny Oak's, they huddled next to the six-foot concrete wall, painted the color of fresh honeycomb, that separated the music park from the bustle of St. George Street.

"What's up?" asked Sid.

Tony pulled a wad of napkins from his pocket and wiped Dante's mouth, chin, and neck, and the front of his own shirt.

Then he set the little boy down on a nearby stone bench. "Sit right there and eat your ice cream. Okay, little man?"

Dante nodded and took another big lick, dribbling ice cream down his chin.

Tony took one large step away from the bench, turned to Sid, and lowered his voice. "Thought you might want an update." Sid nodded, and Tony continued. "We confirmed the second body was Cameron Chase."

Sid smirked. "Gathered as much from the news coverage."

Tony huffed. "Didn't take long for Declan Chase to get his ugly mug on TV, did it?" He shook his head in disgust. "Anyway, preliminary autopsy reports on both bodies show wounds consistent with, well, an alligator. Interestingly, Dru Chase's cause of death wasn't drowning, so he was dead before he was dragged under by a gator. The boy had a wound to the neck that severed the carotid artery and spinal cord. No theories yet on exactly what happened, but we're working on it."

"Huh," Sid muttered. She bit her lip, trying to convince herself not to say anything, but it was no use. "Shot, maybe?" Tony raised an eyebrow, and Sid shrugged one shoulder. "Maybe a crossbow?"

Tony's brow creased, and his eyes narrowed. "What do you know?"

"Nothing." Sid shook her head.

"Sid, if you're withholding evidence—"

"I'm not!" She held up her hands in surrender. "Really, I'm not. It's just a guess. They use crossbows when hunting alligators, right? Poachers, I mean. They use crossbows. I've watched enough videos of these idiots to know that much."

"We don't know for sure that he was poaching," Tony warned.

Sid rolled her eyes. "Not for sure, no, but it's a pretty good guess. And what if he was shot? Accidently, perhaps. By an idiot who can't aim for shit. Maybe you should have the medical examiner take another look. And maybe you should check to see who in the area owns a crossbow."

"Oh, really? Is that what I should do?" Tony's voice grew loud and harsh enough that Dante stopped licking and stared up at his father with wide eyes.

"Don't get mad at me," Sid retorted. "It's just a suggestion."

Tony crossed his arms over his broad chest and widened his stance. "Well, how about Cameron Chase? Anything you don't know about his death but would like to share anyway? Any suggestions on how I can do my job better?"

Sid folded her arms and mimicked his stance. "No," she grumbled.

Tony pursed his lips and took a deep breath, releasing it slowly. "On the other hand, Cameron Chase's cause of death *was* drowning. He had water in his lungs, so he was alive when he went in the water, though not for long. He was likely dead by the time the gators got him."

Sid frowned. "So knocked out on land and then, what? Pushed into the water while he was unconscious?"

Tony's shoulders sagged. "Seems likely." Sid thought he looked tired. He'd probably been pulling long shifts lately. He sighed and added, "That's the latest theory anyway. Cameron's body doesn't have the same sort of bite marks that Dru's has, so the medical examiner doesn't think the gators had to drag Cameron into the water. He thinks Cameron was already in the marsh. Made the gators' job a lot easier."

"Right." Sid shuddered at the thought. "What does his dad say?"

"Pretty much the same thing he's been saying all over TV. That he loved his kid. That Cameron was destined for greatness. Etcetera, etcetera." He frowned. "And he claims to have an alibi for that night. Says he was sitting in Bootleggers getting drunk until after midnight."

Sid knew the bar. It was a hole-in-the-wall on the west side of town that was known for its sparse furnishings, sticky floors, and late-night callouts to the sheriff's office. Not a week went by without a Bootleggers' customer getting arrested for a drunken brawl or slashing another patron's tires.

"We're having trouble confirming that, though," added Tony. "Found a couple people who swear he was there, but apparently the owner gives a different account. I haven't been out there myself, but I sent some deputies back out there tonight to take more statements. Chase says he doesn't remember how he got home but that he likely walked since he lives just up the road. Thinks he might have gone home with a . . . let's call her a date." He shrugged. "Again, we haven't been able to confirm that."

Sid smirked, understanding his meaning. "Is Cameron's dad really a suspect?"

"Everyone's a suspect until they're not."

Dante began fidgeting on the bench, scooting to the edge and attempting to climb down without dropping his ice cream. Tony scooped him up and tried to wipe his mouth, but the four-year-old squirmed in protest.

"Oh, and we checked out Cameron's car after we towed it," Tony added. "Turns out his golf bag was in the trunk, along with his wallet and keys, but his golf clubs were missing."

"No clubs?" Sid frowned. "None?"

Tony shook his head. "Nope. We checked his apartment, and they're not there either." Dante began fussing even more, and his father finally gave in. "We better get going. It's past someone's bedtime."

Sid bid them good night and headed back into Granny Oak's. Mercifully, her headache had subsided enough that she thought she'd be able to survive the second half of Recent Geezer's set, but her mind was elsewhere. She was already planning tomorrow's trip to Oakmire. She would definitely need Leo's help for the next round of interviews.

After Recent Geezer broke for their intermission, Leo left Sid on her own and ran over to see if his grandfather or any of the other band members needed anything. He liked playing roadie, even enjoyed lugging the heavy drum kit to and from Guppy's van. It felt good to be useful, and it didn't hurt that the bartenders in the tiki bars gave him free sodas while he helped set up and break down the equipment.

The Geezers were standing around by the side of the stage, sipping beers and wiping the sweat from their faces, when Leo felt a tap on his shoulder. He turned to find Hattie grinning at him. She was wearing a billowy, navy sundress and her signature sunglasses. Her dreadlocks were pulled back at the nape of her neck, and even at this hour of the night, she stilled smelled like coconut sunscreen. "I see they put you to work."

Leo smiled. "Yeah, they let me roadie for them. They don't pay me, but I get free soda. And Grandpa buys me dinner."

Hattie chuckled. "They gonna let you play with 'em?" She pointed to the guitars in their stands, waiting to be picked up and plugged in again.

"Doubt it, especially since I don't know how." Leo looked longingly at the guitars.

"Eli!" bellowed Hattie.

Eli had been standing over at the tiki bar, getting a second beer, when he heard his name being called. He strode over to them. "How you doin', coz?" He leaned down and kissed Hattie's cheek, and she plucked the beer from his hand.

"Better now, thank ya kindly." She took a sip and smiled. Eli simply shook his head. "You need to give this boy some lessons. Teach him to play." She poked Eli in the arm and then pointed at Leo. "You ain't payin' him for his services, so you should be givin' him some free lessons."

Eli rubbed his chin and studied Leo. "You wanna learn to play, Leo?"

"Um." Leo looked from Eli to Hattie and back again. "I, uh . . . I guess so." The truth was that Leo had never thought about it before. He'd never had the opportunity to play any sort of instrument, either in school or just for fun. His parents weren't musical, at least as far as he knew, and there'd never been any money for lessons. If it was ever something Leo had wanted to do, that dream had been fleeting and had vanished years ago. "Maybe," he added and looked over at the guitars again.

"You ever play anything before?" asked Eli. Leo shook his head. "Got an instrument in mind that you'd like to learn?" Leo shook his head again. Eli placed his big hand on Leo's shoulder. "Well then, you be at the house on Sunday for band practice, and we'll get started."

Leo's eyes lit up. "Okay, Eli. I'll be there."

Eli chuckled, nodded to Hattie, and walked back to the tiki bar for another beer.

"Thank you," Leo whispered to Hattie.

She waved off the sentiment. "Now, tell me how you been gettin' along with those ghosts of yours."

Leo shook his head. "I haven't seen them. I haven't been out to Oakmire since Monday night, and I didn't see them then. They stayed away for some reason."

"Hmmm." Hattie took another sip of beer. "What about your shadow? Seen it again?"

Leo shook his head again. "No, ma'am."

"That's good. That's real good." Hattie looked around the venue. "Don't see it now, do you?"

"No, ma'am."

She nodded. "And you haven't seen it since you been stayin' away from Oakmire?"

"That's right."

Hattie turned back to him and smiled. "Looks like you found a solution. Stay away from Oakmire, and the shadow stays away from you. Seems simple enough."

"But I can't stay away," Leo protested. "Sid needs my help. We have a case. They've hired us to solve the case."

Hattie simply shrugged. "If I were you, I'd stay away. That shadow might not mean you any harm now, but it could change its mind at any time." She poked Leo in the chest. "Don't go givin' it a reason to." With that, she turned and walked off into the crowd.

When the band resumed playing, Leo and Sid were forced to stand off to the side of the stage for the rest of the set, having lost their seats during intermission.

"Hey, Leo." Sid had to practically shout to be heard over the music. "I'm going to need your help tomorrow."

"Okay," Leo yelled back. "With what?"

She leaned closer to him so he could hear her. "We need to talk to a couple of people. We're going back out to Oakmire."

Leo felt his stomach flip at the word *Oakmire*, and he looked over at Sid, who was nodding along to the Geezers' cover of Van Morrison's "Wild Night." Leo remembered Hattie's warning about not courting danger, and at that moment he wished Sid had asked for his help with almost anything else.

Chapter Eighteen

Sid slept in a little the next morning. She'd stayed up late after getting home from the concert, doing some research into Cameron and Dru Chase and their relatives. Theirs was a large extended family, with its St. Augustine roots going back to the late nineteenth century. It seemed like many of the Chase family members were skilled tradesmen—carpenters, fishermen, farmers—but there were also quite a few branches of that family tree that seemed to spend their time entangled with law enforcement. Cameron Chase's branch was one of those.

Cameron's father, Declan, had been arrested several times, mostly on minor offenses, and his grandfather had spent time in state prison for setting fire to his brother-in-law's shrimp boat. Curiously, Dru Chase's father appeared to have stayed out of trouble. Either that, or he just hadn't been caught yet. Regardless of the sins of their forefathers, neither Cameron nor Dru deserved to end up eaten by alligators and washed ashore on the banks of a swanky golf course.

Sid had finally gone to bed around two o'clock after making notes on the Oakmire case and starting a new file on Cameron

Chase. Technically, she wasn't working Cameron's death, but she now had a niggling sense that the two cases were somehow related. Printed copies of news articles and arrest reports, her hand-drawn Chase family tree, and lists of family members living in the area went into both files.

The last thing she did before turning in was watch a replay of a late-night sports show that featured a summary of the day's round of play in the major PGA tournament that was meant to be Cameron Chase's debut on the international stage. The sportscaster lamented Cameron's passing, made his prediction for who would win it all on Sunday, and then quickly moved on to Major League Baseball.

When Sid finally awoke the next morning, she discovered that she was out of coffee, cereal, bread, milk, and almost everything else. Such was the life of a hired private investigator. She grabbed the last snack pack of crackers and the last can of soda from the makeshift kitchen in her office and added both to her grocery list. As she locked the garage and walked to her car, she heard Leo calling her name. She looked up to find him standing half in, half out of the kitchen doorway with a bowl of cereal in his hand.

"Are you heading to Oakmire now?" he called.

Sid nodded and unlocked her car. "You ready?"

"Be right there!" He ducked back into the house.

Sid slid into the car, swearing as the backs of her bare legs hit the hot seat, and cranked up the air-conditioning, waiting for Leo to arrive. It was just after ten o'clock in the morning, and already the heat and humidity were merciless. September had just begun, and yet St. Augustine was unlikely to feel any seasonal relief until late November.

Leo came bursting out of the house a few minutes later and jogged over to the car. "Can we stop by the grocery store when we're done? Grandpa wants me to pick up milk."

"Okay," said Sid, liking how well that plan aligned with her existing ones. "Buckle up." Twenty minutes later they were pulling into the parking lot of the Oakmire Golf and Country Club.

This morning, they traipsed around the side of the club, past the cart barn, and over to the starter's shack. The elderly course ranger was so engrossed in watching the PGA tournament on his phone that he jumped when Sid knocked on the wooden frame of the little kiosk.

"Good morning!" The ranger quickly stashed his phone in his pocket. "Are you investigating again today, Ms. Stone?" he asked with a chuckle. "Plan on turning up any more dead bodies?"

"Let's hope not," said Sid, giving him her best smile. "But I need to take some photos of a couple of the holes. The only ones I have are of the course at night, and they aren't very helpful. Wanted to get a few shots during the day. You don't mind, do you? We won't be long."

He removed his sun hat and smoothed down his few remaining strands of gray hair. "Naw, that's fine. Just stick to the cart paths when you can, and don't interrupt the golfers. We've got play underway on all the holes this morning. It's going to be a busy one. Friday before Labor Day always is." The ranger shook his head, growing somber. "Was looking forward to watching young Cameron play this weekend." He tutted and put his hat back on his head. "Damn shame about that kid. I really thought he had a shot at making it big. The kid was such a talent. Always drove it long and straight. Could sink a putt from anywhere. And his finesse in the traps could just about make you weep." He shook his head again. "Damn shame."

"Yes, it is," Sid echoed. "So, you knew him well?"

The ranger chuckled. "I'd say so. The boy started coming

here for lessons when he was only ten." He rubbed the back of his neck. "Honestly, I don't know how his dad afforded it. Mind you, I couldn't afford lessons at this place." He smiled and winked at Sid. "But they must have worked out some kind of deal. The kid was a natural. Everyone could see it. He started working in the cart barn when he turned fifteen. That got him free access to the driving range and putting greens, and they'd let him go out on the course and play for free at the end of the day, after all the other golfers had finished and before it got too dark. He still does that." The ranger paused, and the smile slid right off his face. "Well, he doesn't anymore, I guess, but he would come out here to practice whenever he wasn't on tour. He was practicing out here that night they think he went missing." The ranger shook his head again. "It's a damn shame. I'm gonna miss watching him play. He was really something."

"When was that exactly?" asked Sid. "The last time he played here, I mean."

The ranger nodded. "Last Friday. He checked in with me around five o'clock that day. We still had play on. It was busy, but I let him start on one and follow the last foursome to tee off."

"And that was the last time you saw him? When he teed off on the first hole?"

The ranger nodded. "That drive was a beauty. Right down the middle. Perfect position. Boy, that lad could swing a club." He rubbed the back of his neck again. "Cameron never checked in with me at the end. Never saw him when he finished up, but that wasn't unusual. That boy would stay out on the course until it was too dark to see your hand in front of your face. I heard he was found on seventeen." The ranger sighed. "Makes sense, I guess. That was his favorite hole. Always liked to work the sand traps on that one. They are wicked, those traps."

"And you didn't see anything else?" asked Sid. She was

itching to scratch some notes in her notebook or type them into her phone, but she didn't want to disrupt the man's flow. "Didn't see anything out of the ordinary? Anyone around that shouldn't have been here?"

"Nope. Nothing." The ranger shrugged. "I almost took a cart out onto the course to look for him at the end of my shift. Just to say good luck, you know? Wish him luck for the big tournament. Tell him not to forget all us little folks when he made it big." The ranger stared off in the direction of the eighteenth hole. "But my wife called and told me I needed to hurry up home. She had supper waiting, so I didn't go look for him." He sighed. "Now I wish I had."

"I doubt that it would have made a difference," Sid offered.

"Maybe not," said the ranger, "but maybe we would have found him faster."

"I'm sorry for your loss," said Leo. He'd stayed out of the conversation up to this point, but he suddenly felt the need to offer this man at least a small amount of comfort.

"Thanks, kid," said the ranger, trying to muster a smile for the boy. "But it's really a loss for all of us, isn't it?" Leo nodded, not sure what else to do. The ranger cleared his throat as a foursome came off the eighteenth green, waved goodbye to him, and walked toward the clubhouse. "Well, you two go ahead and take your photos. Just mind the golfers and steer clear of play. Wouldn't want you getting brained by an errant shot."

Sid thanked him and guided Leo away from the shack. "Do you see them?"

"Who?" asked Leo.

"Your friends," she whispered. "The ghosts."

He nodded and pointed. The two ghosts were standing near the tee box on the first hole, golf bags at the ready, waiting to tee off. They'd been there this entire time, not bothering to approach Leo. He thought it likely that they didn't want to give up their spot in line, however futile it was to think they would be teeing off any time soon.

Sid placed a hand on Leo's shoulder. "I want you to ask them about Cameron Chase's death." Leo's eyes grew wide. He opened his mouth to protest, but Sid cut him off. "I know, I know. I promised Burt that we wouldn't do this again, but I want you to ask them if Cameron was involved in the poaching. That's all. Just that one question."

"Why?" Leo glanced over at the ghosts. He really didn't want to witness another death through the ghosts' eyes.

"Because I want to know if the two deaths are linked in some way," Sid muttered. Leo frowned, and Sid squeezed his shoulder. "Please, Leo. Just ask if he was involved with the poachers."

"Fine," Leo replied. He checked to make sure Val's three stones were still in his pocket and then began walking over to the first tee box. The ghosts met him before he'd made it halfway there.

"We need to talk to you," mumbled Leo. He glanced around, but there were too many people in the area to have a conversation with two invisible golfers. "Meet me over by the cart barn." He began to walk away but realized the ghosts weren't following. "Please. It's really important. My boss wants to ask you a question." The mere mention of Sid had the two ghosts racing past him in an icy breeze.

Sid and Leo found the ghosts waiting for them in the makeshift smokers' lounge near the cart barn. "They're here," Leo whispered. He sat on one of the benches, and Sid took a seat next to him. The ghosts sat on the bench opposite the investigators, both golfers smiling at Sid like lovesick teenagers. Leo nodded to Sid, indicating that everyone was present and accounted for.

"Gentlemen," began Sid. She crossed her long legs, a move

that did not go unappreciated by the ghosts. "I am hoping you can help us again. You led us to the body of Cameron Chase. He was a professional golfer, and I understand that he was here a lot. That he spent long hours playing golf on the course and taking lessons, and he used to work here as well." She pointed to the barn behind her. "Did you know him before he died?"

"Yes."

Leo heard both voices in his head, one high and one low. He nodded at Sid.

"Good," she replied and then took a deep breath to steady her nerves. "I want to ask you another question. But before I do, I need you to promise me that you will not show Leo too much. Only what is necessary, the bare minimum. Please." She looked over at Leo and put a hand on his shoulder. "He doesn't need to see everything, especially if it's . . . graphic." She turned back to face the empty bench, feeling a little silly talking to people no one except Leo could see. "Do you understand?"

"Yes."

Again, both voices sounded in Leo's head. "They said yes," he whispered to Sid. "Do you think this will work?"

"Let's hope so," she whispered back. Then she uncrossed her legs and recrossed them the opposite way. The ghosts smiled in appreciation. "Now, gentlemen," she said in a louder voice, "can you tell us whether Cameron Chase was involved with the poachers? Either with the same group as the other boy who was killed or a perhaps a different group of poachers. Do you know if the two deaths are connected?"

Images began to flood Leo's mind as both ghosts tried to show him scenes at the same time. "Wait, wait!" he cried, pressing his fingers to his temples. "One at a time. I can't understand it if you are both trying to do it together." The images stopped. Leo nodded and pointed to Bacon. "You first." He then pointed to Bucket. "And then you." The ghosts stared at him, so he added some politeness. "Please. If you don't mind."

The images returned, this time from only one viewpoint, and they came slower and with more clarity. Leo saw Cameron Chase standing on the tee box of the seventeenth hole. Bacon must have been standing directly behind the young man, so the view was of the back of Cameron as he looked down the fairway to the green and the marsh beyond. Cameron hit six balls off the tee, and each of them landed in the sand trap that circled the green. Watching Cameron work, Leo realized that each ball was being intentionally hit into the trap. The golfer was hitting them to spots he had specifically picked out, spaced out at seemingly even intervals.

Leo saw a flash of Cameron walking down the short fairway with his golf bag on his shoulder, and then another of the golfer stepping into the sand trap with a club in his hand. Leo watched as Cameron hit three of the balls up onto the green, moving clockwise around the green, with each ball landing no more than two feet from the hole. One ball landed two inches from the hole and rolled in. The ranger had been correct, Leo realized. Cameron Chase was a sight to behold. Even Leo, who knew nothing about the game of golf, knew enough to recognize that this young man had talent. The image in Leo's head changed yet again, and suddenly Leo saw Cameron Chase face down in the swamp.

Leo frowned. "Huh," he muttered. Clearly, Bacon had taken Sid's request seriously. Leo looked over at Bucket and nodded to the ghost. Now, Bucket's images began to appear in his head. Bucket must have been closer to the green when Cameron hit his six tee shots because Leo watched each ball land in the trap with a little spray of sand. Then he watched again as Cameron began to hit each ball out of the trap and onto the green. So far, both sets of images told the same story: Cameron Chase was an excellent golfer.

In Leo's head, he watched Cameron hit his third ball, the one that rolled into the hole, and then move clockwise around the sand trap to the fourth ball, but then the two versions of the story began to differ. Bucket began to show Leo some events that his otherworldly compatriot had not.

Leo watched as the two ghosts took turns hitting their own shots out of the same sand trap as Cameron. Bucket must have been in the middle, with Bacon in front of him and Cameron behind him. Bacon's ball rolled up onto the green, then Bucket's own ball followed, and then Cameron's. They repeated the same sequence—Bacon, then Bucket, and then Cameron. The two ghosts continued to hit balls out of the trap and onto the green while Cameron Chase grabbed the rake and began to smooth out the divots and footprints he'd made in the sand. Once again, Cameron worked clockwise around the green passing directly through both Bacon and Bucket in turn. Bacon shouted at him for disrupting his swing, but Cameron ignored what he could neither see nor hear. Leo did notice the young man shiver. Twice.

Once Cameron disappeared behind Bucket to continue his raking, both ghosts climbed out of the sand trap and walked across the green to inspect all three golfers' shots. Cameron's golf balls were easily distinguished as they were the only real ones. Bacon and Bucket's golf balls were interspersed with Cameron's, and the two ghosts soon began arguing over whose ball was whose. They were facing the marsh with their backs to the sand trap and pointing fingers at the various balls, some of which had landed rather far afield.

Their discussion became rather heated, with the language

growing more and more vulgar. Fortunately, or perhaps unfortunately, Leo was growing used to these expletive-filled exchanges between the two dead golfers. In the background, however, there were other sounds. Leo couldn't be sure, but he thought there were two distinct voices, one higher than the other. Unfortunately, Bacon and Bucket's quarrel was so loud and acrimonious that the other voices were nothing but background noise, with no specific words coming through clearly. By Leo's estimation, the two conversations—one between two living people, the other between two dead ones—continued for several minutes before the background noise ceased. The ghosts, however, continued their shouting and swearing.

Bacon abruptly stopped his ranting and took a step back. His mouth hung open, but no sound came out. Bucket ceased his bellowing and turned around to see what had caused his ghostly companion to grow silent, but there was nothing. Bacon flew to the edge of the green, and Bucket followed his fellow ghost. The next image in Leo's mind was the same one that he'd seen moments before from Bacon—that of Cameron Chase lying face down in the swamp.

The ghosts must have stood frozen, staring at the body, because it was several moments before Bucket finally turned his head. The last image the ghost shared with Leo was that of someone running off into the woods with Cameron Chase's golf bag.

Chapter Nineteen

"I'm telling you I didn't see who it was," Leo groaned. "And by that, I mean that the ghosts didn't see who it was."

"You're sure?" asked Sid.

"Yes!" This was probably the tenth time he'd said the exact same words to Sid since they finished their conversation with Bacon and Bucket in the makeshift smokers' lounge at Oakmire, but she kept asking him the same questions hoping he'd remember something else. Anything else.

They were in Sid's car and heading home, but for the moment they were stuck on the Bridge of Lions as the drawbridge opened for a sailboat. Rookie move, thought Sid. She'd lived in the Old City long enough to know not to try to cross the bridge on the hour and half hour when the drawbridge was raised, but she'd been too busy listening to Leo and not paying attention to the time.

"Well, tell me again what you did see," Sid pleaded. There had to be something there, something she was missing.

So Leo recounted the events as the ghosts had shown him—the six tee shots, the shots out of the sand trap, the ghosts hitting their own shots, the raking of the sand, the ghosts' argument, the background noise, the body in the water, and the mysterious person running away. "And that's it. The person looked smaller than Cameron Chase. Not as broad. Skinny like me and kinda short. Like you."

"First, I'm not short. I'm average height," Sid replied. "And second, you said *he?*"

"Or she," said Leo. "I told you I couldn't tell. The person, whoever *they* were," he said, his irritation shining through in his emphasis, "was smaller than Cameron. I could tell by the way they were carrying the golf bag. It was like it was weighing them down. They had it slung over their shoulders with this harness thing, and they were trying to run away, but it was slowing them down."

"And the ghosts didn't go after . . . *them?*" She matched Leo's irritation with her own. "They didn't chase this person down, try to find out what happened?"

"No." Leo stared out the window as the sailboat's mast disappeared behind the raised drawbridge. "They just stared at the body for a while. They didn't chase the other guy . . . or person . . . or whoever. Which is kinda weird, now that I think about it. Spirits don't like being around death. I've always assumed ghosts don't either, but those two stayed by Cameron's body." Leo frowned. "I guess Cameron meant something to them. Guess they'd been watching him for a while. Maybe they were like, I dunno, like his guardian angels or something."

"So much for guarding him," Sid muttered. "They were too busy working on their golf game to even notice that the boy had been killed." She ran her hand through her ponytail, twisting her hair around her fingers, when a thought struck her. "What happened to the golf balls?"

"Huh?" asked Leo. "What golf balls?"

"Cameron's." Sid turned to look at him. "You said he hit six balls out of the sand trap and onto the green. What happened to them? Did the person who took the golf bag pick up the balls and take them as well? Or were they left behind?"

Leo shrugged. "Dunno."

"Think, Leo," said Sid with a sigh. "What did the ghosts show you? Were the balls still there?"

Leo closed his eyes and replayed the scene of the mystery person running off with Cameron Chase's golf bag. His eyes flew open. "They were still on the green."

"Interesting," Sid murmured. "Wonder what happened to them." She turned all of the information over in her head for a solid minute, trying to imagine the scene as Leo described it. "And there was no scream?"

"No," Leo answered. "At least not that they showed me. If there was one, I would've thought they'd notice." He shrugged. "They were arguing really loudly themselves, though."

"Well, that's just great," she muttered under her breath as she banged her hand against the steering wheel, annoyed with everything—the traffic, the drawbridge, and most especially those two ghosts who couldn't stop arguing long enough to actually witness Cameron Chase's murder. "Either that person who ran away watched Cameron go into the marsh, or they were responsible for pushing him into it."

"So they're either a witness or a murderer," said Leo.

"Looks that way." Sid stared out at the water. With Cameron Chase, there was no scream, but that wasn't the case with his cousin. Dru Chase had screamed.

Sid and Leo watched the sailboat emerge on the other side of the bridge and sail toward the municipal marina while the drawbridge took its own sweet time lowering itself back down. Twenty minutes later, Sid pulled into the parking lot of the grocery store. At this point, she was so hungry and in need of caffeine that she was in danger of biting someone's head off.

Inside the store, Sid grabbed a cart, and Leo sauntered away from her. She hadn't even cleared the first aisle before Leo came to find her, lugging three gallons of whole milk. "Is that all?" She marveled at how much the boy could eat.

Leo nodded as he placed the jugs in the cart. "For this week, yeah." He turned on his heels and began to walk away, but Sid called him back. "Hey, kid. Why don't you go and order us a couple of Pub Subs from the deli. My treat."

"Sure." He grinned broadly. "What do you want?"

"Turkey, cheese, all the fixings," Sid replied.

"Got it!" Leo took off at a jog, heading toward the deli counter.

Sid completed the rest of her shopping and then made her way over to the deli. There must have been a long line because Leo was just now stepping up to the counter. Sid parked her cart and wandered through the bakery section, picking up a box of donuts and a container of chocolate chip cookies and enjoying the lovely scents of baked bread and vanilla. She looked up and saw a mother pushing a shopping cart with two small girls sitting in the basket. The woman pulled up in front of the brightly lit glass case featuring colorful cakes and pastries, and the little girls squealed with delight.

A bakery employee, whom Sid recognized from a family photo that had recently flashed across the news coverage, reached into the case and pulled out two sugar cookies topped with candy sprinkles, handing one to each of the girls. Sid watched the scene, suddenly developing a hankering for something special.

When the mother and her daughters moved on from the bakery case, Sid strolled up to the counter and greeted the same employee.

"I'd like to order a cake," said Sid.

"Right." The woman heaved a sigh and pulled an order pad

from her apron. Sid noticed the dark purple bags under her eyes. She wore no makeup, and though her hair was pulled tightly back from her face and covered with a hairnet, Sid could tell it was in need of washing. The woman leaned against the case, shoulders sagging and looking like she barely had enough energy to hold on to her pen. "What do you need?"

Sid ordered the smallest chocolate cake she could and asked that it be decorated with flowers and the word "Congratulations." There was nothing to celebrate, but she had to say something. The woman wrote up the order and handed Sid her copy. As Sid reached out for the piece of paper, she whispered, "I'm very sorry for your loss, Mrs. Chase."

The woman blinked in surprise. "How . . . how did you—do I know you?"

"No, ma'am," said Sid. "We've never met. My name is Sidney Stone. I'm a private investigator. I'm . . . I'm . . ." Sid stuttered, trying to find the most tactful way to say what she had to say, but Mrs. Chase interrupted her.

"You found my son, didn't you?" The woman was blinking hard now, trying to fight back tears.

Sid nodded. "Yes, ma'am. I'm so very sorry for your loss."

Mrs. Chase swiped at her cheeks, and Sid reached into her bag, pulled out a packet of tissues, and handed them over. She was glad she'd replenished her supply after her recent chat with Angie in the Oakmire's outdoor smokers' lounge. Sid felt immense sympathy for the woman standing before her. Grief was aging this woman rapidly, but Sid still recognized her from the photo she'd seen on the news. She cleared her throat. "I lost my child, too." Mrs. Chase simply stared at her. "Iris was five years old. She and my husband, Wes, were killed in a car accident."

The light went on behind Mrs. Chase's eyes. "You're that PI. The one who brought down the sheriff."

Sid nodded. The papers had outlined Sheriff Travis Colquitt's suspected involvement in the deaths of Wes and Iris, although the sheriff had yet to be charged with anything related to that matter. Sid had shared information with Carleigh Sutton, the attorney who represented Emmaline Colquitt in her divorce from the sheriff. Sid assumed it was Carleigh who had leaked the information to the press in order to help Emmaline achieve a swift and tidy divorce settlement. Sid knew Emmaline wouldn't have liked the information getting out, but the woman would have hated staying married to the sheriff even more.

"So, you know?" asked Mrs. Chase. "You know what it feels like to lose your baby."

"I do." She placed a hand on Mrs. Chase's arm, though only for a moment.

Mrs. Chase dabbed at her eyes. "Are you investigating his death?"

"Sort of," Sid admitted.

Mrs. Chase stood up straight, as straight as she could manage given the heavy grief she was carrying. "I get off at four. Meet me at The Sea Dog, and I'll tell you everything I know." With that, she turned and disappeared behind a partition separating the front of the bakery from the ovens in the back.

It was Sid's turn to blink in surprise. She hadn't meant to shake down Mrs. Chase for information. She had only intended to extend her sympathies to a fellow grieving mother, but now it looked like she was going to have to interview the woman. Sid bit her lip, knowing she'd need to tread carefully, and turned around to retrieve her cart.

Leo approached with two large subs wrapped in butcher paper. Sid had forgotten to tell him she only wanted a half, but she was pretty sure the boy would be happy to finish the other half for her if she offered it to him.

"Who was that?" he asked as he placed the subs in the cart.

Sid pushed the cart toward the checkout lines. "Mrs. Chase. She's going to meet me later to talk about what she knows about her son's death."

Leo's eyebrows shot up. "Does she know you found him?"

"Yes, she does."

"Are you going to tell her what you know?"

"Of course not." Sid frowned. "She doesn't need to know such details."

At four o'clock that afternoon, Sid pulled into the small parking lot of The Sea Dog, the Old City's only permanent hot dog stand. The place was empty save for two boys who looked like they were probably students at nearby Flagler College. Sid sat down at a picnic bench under a giant magnolia and waited. Fifteen minutes later, Mrs. Chase pulled into the parking lot in an old, beat-up hatchback that looked like it might not start up again once it stopped, let alone get its driver all the way home.

Sid waved, and Mrs. Chase shuffled over to the picnic table, still in her bakery uniform. "Are you hungry? Can I get you anything?"

Mrs. Chase looked around. "Diet soda. Large." Sid got up from the table, and on her way to the counter to place her order, Sid heard the woman murmur, "Thanks."

Sid placed the large soda in front of Mrs. Chase and sat down opposite the woman with a drink of her own. She'd also purchased a large order of fries, which she placed in the center of the table. "Help yourself," she said, pointing to the fries. "So you wanted to talk about your son?"

Mrs. Chase took a sip of her diet soda. "My son didn't know what he was getting himself into. He was such a trusting boy. Always believed everything everyone said. I knew it would get him in real trouble someday." She hung her head. "But I never thought... I never thought this would happen."

"Mrs. Chase," began Sid, trying her best to tread carefully.

"Kim. Call me Kim."

"All right, Kim." Sid nodded once. "Do you have any idea what might have happened to your son?"

Kim Chase looked up at Sid and blinked. Two tears spilled down her cheeks. In that same instant, her expression hardened.

"I know exactly what happened," she hissed. "They killed him!"

Chapter Twenty

"Who?" asked Sid, leaning forward. "Who killed Dru?" Kim's nostrils flared. "Declan and his buddy. I don't know his name, but I've seen him around. Skinny little guy. Runs a local loan-sharking business out of Bootleggers." She squeezed her eyes shut. "His own uncle, that piece of shit." Another tear rolled down her cheek, and Sid was pretty sure this one derived more from anger than grief.

"How did Declan kill your son, Kim?" Sid swallowed audibly, wondering exactly how much this woman knew.

"He convinced Dru to help him with a job. Poaching alligators, if you can believe it. How stupid do you have to be?" Kim shook her head and glanced at the road, watching the cars whiz past. "Declan didn't know anything about alligators, let alone poaching them. He watched a couple of YouTube videos." She threw up her hands, almost toppling her soda. "Big fuckin' deal!"

Kim huffed, took a sip of her drink, and then added, "Declan convinced Dru that it was no big deal. Easy peasy. In and out. Bag 'em and run." She jabbed the top of the picnic table with her finger. "He had a son of his own he could have recruited, but oh nooooo!" She held up her hands and feigned a shocked expression. "Declan couldn't possibly ask Cam. No, not Cam the golfer. Not Cam the golden child. Not Cam the superstar. No, Declan had to take my son. My boy!" She slammed her fists down on the table, causing the sodas and the basket of fries to jump. "That asshole took my baby out on the water looking for alligators and then he . . . he . . ." She choked on the words.

"He what, Kim?" whispered Sid. "What did he do?"

"He left him there!" shouted Kim. Her chin hit her chest, and her shoulders shook. "An alli . . . an alligator got him." She was trying to get the words out between sobs. "Declan, he just . . . left him out there." She hiccupped but continued. "He didn't call anyone. He didn't try to get help." She let out a wail that had the two college boys scurrying away. "He didn't even tell me or Trey."

Sid knew that Trey—or more specifically, William Arthur Chase III—was Dru's father and Declan's brother. She reached across the table and placed her hand over Kim's. "How did you find out about Dru? Who told you?"

Kim squeezed Sid's hand with both of hers, as though to steady herself. "Sheriff's deputies came by the house. Said they thought it was Dru. Asked us to come down and take a look at the body." She released one hand from Sid's, wiped her nose with the back of it, wiped her hand on her uniform skirt, and then returned to holding Sid's hand.

Sid did her best not to flinch. "Did you ask Declan about it? What did Declan say?"

Kim snarled. "He said he knew nothing about it. Hadn't seen Dru. Didn't know how he ended up dead and washed up on that golf course." She hiccupped again. "But Dru told me that he was doing a job with his uncle Declan that Friday night. He came home from his job at Oakmire." She paused and looked Sid in the eye. "He was a busboy at the restaurant there. He wanted to take a bartending course so he could get a job in the bar there rather than clearing tables and washing dishes. He was saving up for the course. Dru was a good boy."

Sid nodded. "He sounds like it."

Kim sighed and wiped her nose again. "He told me that his uncle asked him to help out on a job. He said Declan was going to pay him a hundred dollars for a couple of hours of work. All he had to do was ride along in the boat and help out while his uncle and that buddy of his did the dangerous stuff. He just had to help haul the alligator into the boat once they killed it." Kim shook her head. "I told Dru not to go. I told him that Declan was no good and he shouldn't trust him, even if the man was his uncle. But Dru trusted everyone, especially Declan and Cam." She rolled her eyes. "Lord, he practically worshipped Cam. Was tagging along after him from the time he could walk. And Declan, well . . ."

Her voice trailed off, and she heaved a sigh, pulling her hands back and placing them in her lap. "I told the police all of this. Trey doesn't know I talked to them. He didn't want me telling them anything about our family's business. But Dru's dead, and I'm done keeping my mouth shut." She huffed and shook her head. "I guess the police are trying to find evidence that Declan was out on the water that night and that Dru was with him. So far, I've heard nothing." She stared out at the passing cars. "I doubt they'll ever find anything. Declan is really good at covering up his crimes. Been doin' it for as long as I've known him."

Sid frowned and placed her hands in her lap, mimicking Kim's posture. What she really wanted to do was grab the hand sanitizer from her bag, but that would have to wait. "What do you mean, Kim? What sorts of crimes?"

"He only ever got caught on the small-time stuff, but Declan is a bully. That's his special talent," she sneered, "and no one ever wanted to cross him." She held Sid's gaze. "He beat his wife. Did you know that? That's why she left all those years ago. She tried to take Cam, too. Tried to run off with him in the middle of the night, but Declan tracked her down. Beat her within an inch of her life, so I heard. Then he dragged Cam back here with him." She shifted her gaze back to the traffic. "Used to beat Cam, too. Not as bad as his wife and only where no one could see the bruises, but still. We all knew he did it, but no one wanted to end up like Cam's mother." She pressed her lips together and shook her head.

Sid leaned forward. "Do you think Declan had something to do with Cameron's death?"

Kim blinked in surprise. "I . . . I thought Cam was killed by an alligator. While he was golfing. At Oakmire. That's . . . that's what I heard."

Sid held up her hands. "That may be exactly what happened. I'm just asking. If it wasn't an alligator, is it possible Declan had something to do with it?"

Kim bit her lip and shook her head. "I don't think so. At least not directly. Maybe Declan got mixed up in something, and it could have blown back on Cam." She paused and shook her head again. "But I don't think so. In fact, Declan was thrilled with Cam's success. Walked around crowing about it all the time. Once word got out that Cam was good—and I mean really good—well, Declan backed off. He started treating Cam better." She stared out at the road once more. "But I think that's why Cam worked so hard at golf. It was his ticket out of that hell. Out from under his father's grip. I don't think Declan hit Cam once he began taking lessons out at Oakmire. Declan threatened to hit him, of course, but I don't think he actually did it again. Why would he? Cam was his golden goose."

Kim looked over at Sid. "And you don't kill your golden goose."

―――

Sid walked into Burt's kitchen to find Leo making himself a sandwich. "Here you go, kid." She dropped the bag of fries on the kitchen table. Neither she nor Kim Chase had touched them, so she had decided to bring them home. Leo, the bottomless pit, would no doubt make quick work of them.

"Thanks!" Leo tore open the bag and shoved three huge fries in his mouth.

Sid frowned. "Don't you want to warm them up? They have to be cold by now."

"They're fine," answered Leo through a mouth full of food. He finished making his sandwich and sat down at the table.

"How can you still be hungry?" Sid poured herself a glass of water from the tap. "You had a giant sub, plus half of mine, just a few hours ago."

"Yeah, almost five hours ago." Leo huffed. "Now I'm starving."

"You're not starving," Sid mumbled.

"Hey, Sid." Burt strolled into the kitchen. "Are you joining us tonight?" When Sid's brow furrowed in confusion, he added, "Granny Oak's. There's a band up from Gainesville playing tonight. I want to check them out. Heard good things about 'em."

"No, thanks," said Sid, "but I need to talk to you both for a minute."

After Kim Chase had left The Sea Dog, Sid had sat on the bench and finished her soda. A knot had developed in her stomach during their conversation, and she couldn't seem to loosen it, at least not until she'd reached a decision. So here she was now, standing in Burt's kitchen, dreading what would happen next.

"What I'm about to do isn't—well, I shouldn't be doing it. I shouldn't be talking about the details of a case, but I need to do it. And I need you both to promise that you won't say anything to anyone ever." She stared them both down.

Burt and Leo answered her, talking over each other. "Yeah. Sure. Fine. Promise."

"Okay." Sid took a deep breath and resisted the urge to start pacing back and forth in the small kitchen. "I met with Mrs. Chase this afternoon. She's Dru Chase's mom. He's the boy we found at Oakmire. Well, the first one, that is." Burt and Leo nodded, and Sid went on to recount what Kim Chase had told her.

"Sounds like an asshole," said Leo. He'd put down his sandwich and left the fries alone as Sid talked.

"Doesn't he?" Sid nodded. "But the reality is that he is somehow involved in this. We know he's involved with Dru's death." Sid skirted around the details of that involvement, hoping to avoid sharing the goriest bits with Burt. "And he's Cameron's father. Who knows how he's connected to his own son's death, but I've got to believe he doesn't have clean hands in that case either."

Burt shifted in his seat. "So what are you saying, Sid?"

Sid could tell by his face that he already knew. "I'm saying that I think Leo shouldn't work this case with me anymore."

Leo's jaw nearly hit the table.

"I agree." Burt turned to his grandson. "It's not safe. A man like that is dangerous, and if he thinks he's in danger of being caught, he's likely to strike. I don't want you anywhere near him."

"But I won't be near him! Why would I be?" Leo's eyes were wild, like a trapped animal's.

Sid crossed her arms, trying to hold herself in place so she wouldn't start pacing. "Because I have to finish investigating the case, and that may lead me into Declan Chase's path."

"Maybe you should drop it," Burt suggested. "It's not safe for you either."

Sid nodded. "Believe me, I will if I think it's too much. But I owe it to the client to try to finish the job." She held up her hands as Burt opened his mouth to protest. "I won't take any unnecessary risks. At least, I'll try not to. But I can't promise that Leo will be safe if he continues with me."

"This isn't fair!" Leo shot up from the table. "It's not fair! Don't take me off the case, Sid. I can do this." He turned to his grandfather. "Grandpa, please. Let me do this. I'll be careful, I promise."

"I know you'd be careful, son," said Burt. "That's not what we're concerned about. It's Declan Chase or whoever he's working with. They don't care anything about your safety. They're only interested in self-preservation, and they'll do anything and hurt anybody they need to in order to stay safe themselves."

Leo's eyes darted between Burt and Sid. "Please!" he begged.

Sid's heart squeezed. Here was a boy wanting very much to be taken seriously, to be considered an adult. As much as she wanted to treat him as such, she wanted even more to keep him safe. "I'm sorry, Leo," said Sid. "You can work my other cases with me. Just not this one."

Burt nodded. "You need to sit this one out, Leo."

Leo's nostrils flared, and the color that had been creeping up his neck to his cheeks was now bright red. Tears spilled from his eyes, and he stormed out of the room. "I hate you both!" he yelled as he stomped up the stairs and slammed his bedroom door.

Sid slumped down into the seat vacated by Leo. "That went well."

"He'll get over it." Burt sighed. "Eventually."

Sid winced. "That was the right thing to do, right?"

"Absolutely." Burt sat forward, resting his forearms on the table. "Keeping that kid safe is priority number one. Keeping him happy has to be secondary."

Sid nodded. That knot in her stomach had loosened, but her heart ached. "I feel like shit."

"Well, you don't look great either." Burt smiled at her, and Sid rolled her eyes. "Get some sleep, Sid. Take a day off. If you're tired and stressed, you might do something stupid. And the stakes are too high for you to be stupid." He got up from the table and left the kitchen.

Sid pushed Leo's half eaten sandwich aside and rested her forehead on the table's cool surface. She really did feel terrible. Working with Leo had brought the boy out of his shell. His outburst minutes ago aside, Leo was a much happier kid now than when he had arrived on Burt's doorstep six weeks ago. Sid's decision today had probably set him back, erased all that good progress he'd made, but she wasn't about to put the boy in harm's way. At least not any more than she had already.

Sid dragged herself up, out of the house and back to her office. After grabbing the essentials, she loaded the car and drove to Oakmire. She wasn't going to risk Leo's safety. But hers? Well, she didn't have much to lose anymore.

Sid pulled into the Oakmire club parking lot and walked past the clubhouse to the groundskeeper's shed. Henri Broussard was just locking up for the day.

"Henri!" she called, jogging over to him. "Got a minute?"

But Henri Broussard hadn't even needed a full minute to tell Sid what she wanted to know.

She bid the Cajun groundskeeper a good night and walked to the starter's shack to check in. The course ranger on duty was not one Sid recognized, so she had to explain why she was there and what she needed to know. As the ranger was checking his logs to confirm how many golfers were still on the course, she watched a group of five finish up on the eighteenth hole. It took a few moments for Sid to realize that she was actually watching a foursome plus one caddy. That caddy was Noah Zimmerman. The young man was pointing to the flag and to various spots on the finely manicured grass, but only one of the golfers was paying close attention: Rocco Castiglione. Sid snapped a photo of the scene.

The foursome took their turns sinking their putts, two of them requiring more than one attempt at it, and then each plucked their ball from the hole when their turn was finished. The other three golfers climbed into the two waiting golf carts and drove them past the clubhouse to the cart barn.

Rocco Castiglione strolled leisurely toward the clubhouse, tugging off his golf glove finger by finger as if he were a burlesque performer. He tossed the glove over his shoulder, and Noah caught it with one hand, clearly used to this type of stunt by the lawyer. At the clubhouse, Rocco reached into his pocket, pulled out some cash, and tipped Noah, patting him on the shoulder. Sid snapped a photo of both men: Rocco with his smug smile, Noah with his timid one. The lawyer then sauntered up the veranda steps and disappeared inside the clubhouse while Noah shuffled off to the cart barn with Rocco's heavy golf bag.

The course ranger poked his head out of the starter's shack and told Sid that there were still two more foursomes out on the course. They were probably on the seventeenth and eighteenth holes, but she was free to roam the course when they finished their rounds. Sid thanked him and waited under one of the giant oaks near the eighteenth green, out of sight of the clubhouse and any chance of being seen by Rocco Castiglione.

Chapter Twenty-One

Leo heard the other members of Recent Geezer arrive at the house, one by one. His grandfather tried one final time to convince Leo to join the men at Granny Oak's Music Park to hear the new band from Gainesville, but Leo ignored Burt's knocks at his bedroom door. The Geezers finally left the house, and Leo waited a full ten minutes to ensure they weren't coming back. Then he picked up his phone and called his mom.

He hadn't scrolled through her social media feed yet today, so he wasn't sure where she was now. Probably Atlanta, but who knew. It seemed her schedule was always changing, her plans were never set in stone, and he couldn't rely on her to be where she said she'd be. It was so unlike the mom he had known back in Norfolk. When they lived there, Paizley Roberts ran a tight ship—never late, never forgetting things, never going back on her word. The Paizley Roberts who was currently driving around the United States, sleeping in a tiny trailer and blogging about her travels, was someone else entirely. But right this moment, Leo really hoped his old mom, the one from Norfolk, would answer his call.

"Hey, Leo!" Her voice was bright and happy, and Leo nearly fell off his bed when he heard it.

"Mom?"

Paizley Roberts laughed. "Did you mean to call me, or is this a butt dial?"

"No, I . . . no, I meant to call." Leo sat up and hugged his pillow to his chest. "I . . . I just . . ."

"Leo? Can you speak up? I can barely hear you." The noise of traffic was so loud that Paizley was shouting into the phone just to be heard. "We've got the top down on the jeep, and we're on I-75 at the moment, so it's really loud. You'll need to speak up."

Leo squeezed his eyes shut and began rocking back and forth. "Mom, I don't want to stay here anymore. I want to go with you. When are you coming to pick me up?"

There was silence on the other end, or at least as much silence as there could be while speeding down the interstate in an open-air jeep. In fact, Leo would have sworn they'd been disconnected except for the noise coming through the line. After several long moments, Paizley answered him. "What's happened, Leo?"

"Mom, I just want you to come get me," Leo pleaded. "I want to go with you."

"Put your grandfather on the line, Leo." Her voice had lost its bright, happy quality.

Leo sighed. "He's not here. He's down at Granny Oak's with the band."

"He left you home alone?!"

Leo almost rolled his eyes. Being left home alone for a few hours was certainly not any worse than being abandoned on someone else's doorstep. "He asked me to go with him, but I didn't feel like it. He'll be back in a couple of hours."

"So, what's the problem then?" shouted Paizley. Leo knew she was yelling to be heard, but he also thought that maybe she was yelling because she was angry.

"I hate it here." He didn't want to tell her why—that Sid and Burt had conspired to keep him from doing the one thing that made any sense to him these days, the one thing that he was pretty good at. "When are you coming to St. Augustine?"

Leo heard her sigh, so it must have been loud. And her loud sighs always meant she was exasperated with him. "Not for another couple of weeks at least."

"Please come soon, Mom. Just change your plans and come here next. Please!" At this point, Leo was not above begging.

Another sigh. Leo clearly heard it. She was probably commiserating with her friend Brooklyn and rolling her eyes for the benefit of Brooklyn's stupid little dog, Jezebel. "I don't think we can, Leo."

Leo's jaw clenched so hard he was afraid he'd crack a tooth or two. His mom had said *we*. Not I, not me. *We*. "Please, Mom," Leo whispered. He didn't bother to yell this time. He knew it wouldn't make any difference.

"Leo," said Paizley, and then she paused for another one of her sighs. "I'll take a look at our plans. If we can rearrange them, I'll let you know. In the meantime, just do your homework and stay out of trouble. And mind your grandfather, even if he's getting on your nerves. He's a good man, and he'll take good care of you." She paused, and Leo would have sworn she'd hung up save for the background noise. "I'll call you tomorrow once we get settled in Atlanta and it's not so noisy. We can talk then."

Leo heaved a sigh of his own. "Fine."

"Okay, Leo. I gotta go. Love ya tons!" And she hung up.

Leo held the phone to his ear for a full minute before finally lowering it to his lap. He wanted to throw it across the room, but he was pretty sure his grandfather wouldn't buy him a replacement if he broke this one. He flopped back on the bed and stared at the ceiling, letting the tears run down his temples and into his hair. He let himself wallow for several minutes before getting up, splashing some cold water on his face, and heading downstairs. He locked the front door behind him and headed for St. George Street.

Less than ten minutes later, Leo was standing under the faded green awning of the N'Ice Day Ice Cream Shop. Through the window, he could see Ellie Owen working behind the counter. Her long, blonde hair was tied back in a ponytail, and she was wearing the vintage tee he'd given her. Leo could just make out the tongue-and-lips logo of the Rolling Stones peeking over the top of her shop apron. He smiled. Ellie Owen was so pretty. Out of his league, if he was being honest with himself. She'd allowed him to kiss her the night before school started, and he was pretty sure he'd fallen head over heels in love at that very moment.

It was an amazing kiss. His first real kiss, too, if you didn't count Shelley Gregson in second grade. Shelley had kissed him on the playground, announced that they were now boyfriend and girlfriend, and then never talked to him again for the rest of the year. Her family moved right before the start of third grade, so he never saw her again. Given the short shelf life of that relationship, Leo didn't think Shelley Gregson's kiss really counted. Ellie was his first as far as he was concerned.

But Ellie had been ghosting him for the last two weeks. She'd made it clear that, once school started, she wouldn't be around much. School was too important, she was involved in too many things, and she was cutting back on her work hours. Between homework, babysitting gigs, and everything else, there would be very little time to hang out. Leo had smiled, said he understood, and told her that he'd be in the same boat. But he wasn't. He was managing his schoolwork just fine. Granted, Sid had him doing some late-night stakeouts recently, but that wasn't every night. He'd made the effort to text Ellie six times since that kiss. She'd responded to only two of them, and both times it was to tell him she was busy and would text him later. She never did, though.

So here he stood, waiting for the crowd in the ice cream shop to disperse so he could talk to her. He waited like that for twenty minutes before the shop emptied and the manager ducked into the back, leaving Ellie alone at the counter.

"Hey," said Leo as he stepped through the door. He gave her a little wave.

"Hey." Ellie gave him one of her near-perfect smiles, showing that one incisor that slightly overlapped its neighbor. Leo felt the tempo of his heartbeat kick up a notch.

He approached the counter, and Ellie grabbed a kid's cone from the stack behind her and placed a large scoop of salted caramel ice cream on top. "Let's go outside," she whispered, "so my manager doesn't see me giving you this for free." She winked.

They stepped out into the warm night, and Leo was grateful for the slight breeze blowing in from the bay. "How are you?" asked Ellie. "How's homeschool?" One corner of her mouth quirked up, and Leo knew she was teasing him.

"It's good. Fine. Good." Leo nodded. Ellie had teased him about homeschooling, but when he'd shown her his curriculum, assignments, and schedule, she'd blinked in surprise. It didn't stop her from nagging him to enroll in the local public high school, the same one she went to, but she'd stopped making jokes about homeschooling being for babies.

"So it's good?" She gave a full smile, and Leo knew the teasing had changed back to their usual playful banter.

He grinned. "Yeah. How about you? I haven't seen you around, and you haven't texted me back."

Ellie nodded and dropped her gaze to the ground. She began tracing a crack in the sidewalk with the toe of her beat-up Chuck Taylors. "Yeah, it's okay. I've been busy. Taking a lot of honors classes this year. And lots of clubs and stuff." She shrugged. "Sorry I haven't been able to hang out."

Leo waited for her to look up at him, but she didn't. She just kept tracing the sidewalk crack with the toe of her shoe. "Well, we could hang out tonight," he offered. "There's a new band playing at Granny Oak's. Grandpa says they're real good. He and the Geezers are there now, checking them out. Wanna go?" He bit his lower lip, hoping that she'd say yes. Hoping she'd just look at him.

"I can't, Leo." She lifted her gaze but didn't meet his eyes. Instead, she stared at the smiley face logo on his Nirvana T-shirt.

The shirt had belonged to his dad, so it was faded and well worn, but Burt had saved it and all the other concert tees for Leo. The shirts were all vintage now, and Leo thought they made him just a little bit cooler than he otherwise would have been—which was not cool at all. "Well, maybe when you get off work, if they're still playing—"

"I can't." She turned around and paused in the doorway. "I work until nine, and then I have to get home to finish my homework. I'll text you tomorrow. Enjoy the ice cream." Ellie walked back inside and disappeared into the back of the shop.

Leo had forgotten all about the ice cream cone in his hand. The frozen dessert had begun melting down the sides of the cone, making his fingers sticky. He tossed the cone in the first trash can he saw and stomped down St. George Street. He stopped outside Granny Oak's, pausing just long enough to catch the last refrain of a song that the Gainesville band was belting out. Burt was right. They were good.

Leo kept walking, heading toward the northern end of St. George Street and the original gate of the Old City. The City Gate was in remarkable shape, given that it was built just after the turn of the nineteenth century. The gate was actually two tall pillars made of coquina stone—hard-packed bricks made of coquina shells—with a short wall extending out on either side made of the same material. There had been a wooden drawbridge, according to the local history, but it was long gone now. Leo passed through the gate and came to a halt on the sidewalk, looking across Castillo Drive to the old fort. Leo waited for a lull in traffic and then darted across the empty four-lane road to reach the vast expanse of lawn on the other side.

If he was smart, he would turn back now. He should go back to Granny Oak's. Better still, he should go home, crawl into bed, and pull the covers up over his head.

This was the last place he should be. The sudden drop in temperature told him as much.

Chapter Twenty-Two

Leo could see them. Soldiers in various uniforms, too many to count. There were others as well—Native Americans, a few pirates, and civilians dressed in clothes from a bygone era. Or maybe more than one era. He hadn't studied Florida history, so what did he know? There were also several children. This place was crawling with spirits.

Castillo de San Marcos was in remarkably good shape for being the oldest masonry fort in the continental United States. Leo remembered very little from the tour he'd been on when he was seven years old, but he remembered that the fort was very old and that it was made of coquina stone, a miraculous form of building material that simply absorbed cannon fire. The coquina stone was the reason the fort was still standing over three hundred years after it was initially completed.

Lots of people had died here. St. Augustine had changed hands several times in its long, turbulent, mosquito-infested history. This was a location of many battles, on land and at sea, which was why the presence of so many spirits was confusing to Leo. In his experience, spirits seemed to want to be where there was life, not where there was death, but the close proximity of Castillo de San Marcos to the tourist-filled historic downtown district of the Old City—not more than spitting distance away, if you wanted to get technical—had to be an enormous draw for these spirits. The fort itself occupied a lovely piece of real estate, right on Matanzas Bay. Location, location, location, as they say.

Leo tugged the brim of his baseball cap down a little farther and repeated the words Hattie had given him. Curiously, it seemed to be working. In fact, it seemed to be working too well. The spirits of soldiers and pirates and Native Americans turned to stare at him and parted to make way as he walked across the vast, green lawn surrounding the fort. No one approached him. No one spoke to him. No one clambered for his attention. They all stayed back, giving him plenty of room, and it unnerved Leo. It was almost more unsettling than being bombarded by them.

He made his way to the high seawall behind the fort and climbed up on top of it. The concrete-and-coquina wall was wide on top, but its sides sloped gently outward like a trapezoid. Leo stood on the wall and stared out at the bay. There was a nice breeze, which kept the mosquitos away, and the dozen or so sailboats that were moored there bobbed lazily in the water. Leo wrapped his arms around himself, trying to keep warm. Even though the spirits were staying back, the sheer number of them made the temperature around him drop significantly.

"Fuck!" hissed Leo. He shut his eyes tight and inhaled the salty evening air, trying to calm himself.

Everyone in his life had rejected him, and all in the span of less than an hour. Sid and Burt ganged up on him to pull him off the Oakmire case, so he was now relegated to handling the odd lost pet case. How was he supposed to become a private investigator if all he did was search for people's missing iguanas?

And he did want to be a private investigator. It was the only thing he'd ever done that made sense, that made him feel like he wasn't a useless freak of nature. His ability to see and talk to dead people was actually an asset, so why wasn't he being allowed to help? He admitted that Declan Chase was one scary dude, but Sid was in danger, too. She wasn't quitting, so why did he have to?

And if being benched by Sid and his grandfather wasn't bad enough, his mom had dismissed him. She hadn't even tried to listen to him, hadn't even given him a chance to tell her what had happened. She never had time for him anymore, and Leo felt like maybe she was happier without him in her life. She'd gotten pregnant at such a young age. Maybe she didn't even want him. Maybe she was perfectly happy to leave him with Burt forever and never come back. Leo choked back a sob and squeezed his eyelids shut even tighter against the hot sting of tears.

And then there was Ellie. He liked her so much, and he had thought she felt the same way, but it was clear now that she didn't. She was back at school with all her friends and her clubs and her homework. She probably had lots of boyfriends, and he was nothing more than a brief summer fling; someone to hang out with for a couple of weeks before moving on to someone better, someone normal. Maybe she preferred guys who were athletic or brainy or rich. He wouldn't blame her. Who would want a skinny boy with a dead father and an absentee mother, one who wore nothing but thrift store clothes, lived with his grandfather, and worked for some lady who lived in their garage apartment and got paid to spy on cheating spouses? No one would. Certainly not pretty Ellie Owen.

Leo's knees grew weak, so he crouched, placed his hands on the cool, rough stone and sucked in huge gulps of sea air.

"*Leo.*"

It was nothing more than the faintest whisper in his head, but he'd heard it. Even over the waves lapping at the seawall and the din from the bars and restaurants across the street, Leo had heard it. He leaped up and spun around—and promptly lost his balance.

As Leo fell backward toward the dark water below, he saw it. It was right behind him, and it was the reason all the other spirits were keeping their distance. The shadow, darker than the surrounding night, had been right behind him.

"*Leo.*"

It was barely a whisper. And then Leo hit the water.

Sid sat cross-legged on the cart path that ran alongside the third hole. Henri Broussard had told her that the best location for poaching was the green on the third hole. It was Big Boy's favorite hangout and had the best landing spot for a jon boat out of any of the other water holes, so Sid had doused herself with bug spray, pulled out her camera, and waited.

Henri had also informed her that someone from his groundskeeping crew had found a bunch of golf balls on the seventeenth green the morning after Cameron Chase went missing, although no one had known he was missing at the time. Apparently, it wasn't unusual to find balls abandoned on the course. Usually, they were discovered in the bushes or the long, rough grass or even in the shallow water along the marsh-side holes. Every once in a while, a ball would be found still sitting in the hole, abandoned by a golfer after they'd sunk the put. Most of the time, Henri paid little attention. But six balls abandoned on a green? That was out of the ordinary. Henri had assumed the reason for the abandonment had been innocent enough: The golfers lost sight of their balls in the dark. They got distracted or simply decided to quit their round early. They were chased off the green by an alligator. That sort of thing.

Regardless, Henri instructed the groundskeeper who found the balls to drop them off at the driving range. Thus, Cameron Chase's own golf balls—the last ones he'd hit before his life was cut tragically short—were sitting in a giant bin of beat-up range balls, waiting to be struck by golfers who would never come close to his level of skill or fame.

Sid hadn't brought a chair or a cooler, thinking she didn't want to be weighed down by them if she had to make a quick getaway, but now she regretted leaving them behind. The cart path was far from comfortable, and she was hungry. There was only one bottle of water in her bag, and she was rationing it with the hope that it would last her all night. She hadn't prepared very well because she'd been in such a hurry, but she was here now. And she had a job to do.

It was just past ten o'clock when she heard the boat engine. Sid moved off the cart path and stood behind one of the big oak trees that separated the third hole from the tidy row of mini mansions. It was the same one she and Leo had camped out under the night they found Dru Chase, if she wasn't mistaken.

Sid was grateful that she'd inherited her former boss's camera equipment when he folded up his PI practice and retired to the Keys. Trip Murdock had loved his cameras. The one she held had an effective night vision setting and a tele-photo lens. It was her most expensive and most effective piece of equipment. Even her computer didn't cost as much as this camera.

Sid snapped away, capturing in a sequence of shots the boat approaching from the marsh and coming ashore at the same place as last time. Two men were in the boat, both of them tall and scrawny. Neither of them was Declan Chase.

"Shit," Sid muttered. She was really hoping to catch Declan in the act, but his absence probably explained why these two men had used the motor on arrival instead of rowing ashore. It was easy to cut corners and be lazy when the boss wasn't watching.

Her photos captured the men baiting the edge of the green with colorless blobs of something. Leo had told her he'd seen the poachers use raw chicken parts in his visions. The thought made Sid's stomach turn sour. The two men moved to the middle of the green and stood back to back, one holding a rifle and the other holding a crossbow. Sid continued to shoot the scene. The men stood that way for nearly half an hour before they finally moved, both of them turning toward the boat. Something must have stirred in the water, although Sid couldn't see what it was from where she was standing. She was at least a hundred yards away and unable to hear subtle splashes in the water or make out anything the men were saying. They both raised their weapons, waiting to shoot whatever was about to emerge from the marsh. Sid photographed the scene.

And then her phone rang. The sound pierced the night as if it had been blasted from a loudspeaker.

Seconds later, a bullet hit a tree about fifteen feet away from where Sid was standing. Sid heard the shot and hit the ground, landing on her side so as to cradle the camera in her arms. Her shoulder hit a tree root, but she managed to swallow the scream of pain before it erupted. Sid rolled on to her belly and raised her camera, snapping away as the man with the rifle fired another shot. This bullet hit a little farther away, striking the metal post of a screened pool cage belonging to one of the houses behind her. The man with the crossbow grabbed his partner by the collar and dragged him over to the boat. The two men pushed off, cranked the engine, and sped away into the dark swamp. Sid caught it all on camera.

She counted to ten, watching through her telephoto lens and waiting until the sound of the engine had faded from earshot. Then she picked up her bag and ran in the opposite direction. Her legs and lungs burned as she reached the parking lot and slid into the relative safety of her car. She squeezed the steering wheel and released the sound that she had kept bottled up for the last few minutes, a combination of a scream and a sob. Her limbs were shaking with adrenaline, and a tear rolled down her cheek, but she continued to hold the steering wheel in a death grip because she needed to feel in control of something—anything—in order to avoid losing it completely.

Her phone rang again, and Sid jumped in her seat. In the pandemonium of being shot at and running for her life, Sid had forgotten it was her phone that had given away her position. Why hadn't she silenced it? Such a rookie move. She should know better by now, but that's what happens when you rush into things without keeping a cool head.

It took some effort to uncurl her fingers from around the steering wheel and reach for the phone in her bag. Her hands shook as she swiped at the call and held the phone to her ear. "Sidney Stone," she croaked, her voice breaking like she was a teenage boy in the throes of puberty.

"Sidney?" The voice was female.

Sid cleared her throat. "Yes. This is Sidney."

"Sid, it's Naomi Davis. Tony's wife."

Sid should have recognized the voice. If she hadn't had so

much adrenaline pumping through her body that her ears were ringing, then she probably would have. "Naomi, hi. What's up?"

"Sid, I'm here at the hospital."

At this, Sid sat up, her mind clearing. "What's wrong? What's happened? Who's hurt?"

"It's all right, Sid. Don't panic." Naomi's voice was soothing, but Sid was too charged with electricity to calm down.

"It's Leo," said Naomi. "Can you come to the emergency room?"

Chapter Twenty-Three

Sid didn't hear anything after Naomi Davis uttered the phrase "emergency room." She'd hung up, thrown the car into drive, and squealed out of the parking lot, leaving tire tracks in her wake. The drive took her less than ten minutes, but Sid didn't remember any of it. She'd burst through the emergency room doors and marched straight up to the receptionist, demanding to see Leo Roberts.

When the receptionist, an elderly woman with cottony-white hair and oversize bifocals, asked if she was family, Sid blurted out "stepmom" without even thinking. The receptionist told her to have a seat, but Sid flatly refused.

All the emergency room televisions were tuned to the local news, and the sports reporter was talking about the PGA tournament in Savannah. Cameron Chase's name was mentioned over and over again, and Sid thought she might lose her mind. In fact, she was just about to start shouting when Naomi came through the doors and motioned for her to come back.

"He's all right, Sid," said Naomi, putting an arm around her shoulder. "We couldn't get a hold of Burt. He wasn't answering his phone."

Sid nodded. "He's at Granny Oak's. Probably didn't hear it ringing."

Naomi squeezed her shoulder. "Well, I'm glad you picked up." Sid flinched at Naomi's words, remembering that it was her own phone's ringtone that caused the poachers to shoot at her. "He's in here."

The two women stepped into a tiny room just off the main hallway to find Leo sitting on the examination table, staring at them.

Sid's breath caught in her throat. "What the hell happened?!"

"I fell in the river."

Sid blinked in surprise. That was not the answer she'd been expecting. "What do you mean you fell in the river?" Leo's arms were bandaged from his hands to his elbows. He had gauze wrapped around the shin of one leg, the thigh of the other. He wasn't wearing a shirt, and Sid saw large gauze pads taped to several places on his back. Sid pointed to the bandages. "How does this happen by falling into water?"

Leo merely shrugged and hung his head. He was holding his T-shirt in his lap. His dad's Nirvana concert tee was ruined, the back of it sliced to shreds and stained with blood. It would have to be thrown away now. That thought, more than the pain from the cuts or the antiseptic, made him want to cry. He tried to hunch over, curling in on himself, but the movement pulled at the bandages on his back and forced him to sit up straight. He couldn't answer Sid, not without crying or saying a lot more than was prudent in front of Naomi.

Naomi raised an eyebrow. "Two men brought him in. One of them was in a dingy, returning to his sailboat, where it was moored in the bay right off the old fort. He happened to see Leo fall in and raced over to help him. When he saw Leo was bleeding, he sped back to the marina and had a friend drive them to the hospital."

"Did you break anything?" Sid wanted to grab hold of him, run her hands over his limbs feeling for broken bones, but she folded her arms and clenched her fists instead.

Leo shook his head. "No. I just got cut up. There are all these really sharp shells on the bottom. The water wasn't deep where I fell. Maybe five feet or so, but I landed on my back on the shells. And when I tried to push myself up, I sliced my hands and stuff." He picked at one of the rips in the T-shirt. "It really hurt."

"I bet it did," said Sid. The seabed around the fort was covered with oyster shells. Sid knew firsthand how sharp those shells could be. It must have felt like falling on a bed of razor blades.

"We cleaned and debrided the wounds," said Naomi. "No stitches. We don't want to trap any bacteria inside. He'll need to keep everything clean and change the bandages regularly, and we'll send him home with a prescription for doxycycline. He'll need to take it." She raised an eyebrow at Leo. "All of it." Leo nodded but continued to stare at his hands. "He was very lucky it wasn't worse." Naomi patted his knee and turned to Sid. "Let me go get his prescription and paperwork, and then you can take him home."

Sid nodded and waited for Naomi to leave the room before turning to Leo and hissing, "What the hell happened?"

Leo glanced up at the doorway and shook his head slightly. "Not here," he whispered.

Sid's eyes grew wide, and she refrained from saying anything more until they were back in her car. On the drive home, Leo told her what had happened at the fort—how the spirits stayed away, how he heard his name being called, how he saw the shadow right behind him, and how he toppled backward off the seawall into the water below. He left out the part about being angry at her, being dismissed by his mother, and being rejected by Ellie.

"Did you recognize the voice?" asked Sid.

"No." Leo shook his head. "It was just a whisper. I couldn't even tell if it was male or female."

"And the shadow," began Sid.

"It was just a shadow. A dark outline. Darker than the darkness around it. Person-shaped, but that's it." He shrugged. "I have no idea who it is or what it wants."

They pulled into the driveway, and Sid accompanied Leo inside. The Geezers were sitting in the living room, drinking beer and discussing the Gainesville band's set. They fell silent when Leo and Sid walked into the room. Leo was still shirtless, carrying his damp, torn, and bloody T-shirt in his hand.

"What the hell happened?!" exclaimed Burt.

"Why does everyone keep asking that?" muttered Leo. His shoulders sagged, and he looked to Sid for help.

"He had a little accident," Sid explained. "He fell off the seawall at the old fort. One of the sailors in the harbor picked him up and drove him to the hospital." She placed a hand on his shoulder. "Just some cuts. They cleaned him up and sent him home with this." She handed the prescription and paperwork over to Burt. "He has to keep the wounds clean and take all of the antibiotic. The instructions are in those pages." Sid carefully slid her arm around Leo's shoulder and gave him a light squeeze. "He's fine. Just needs some sleep, right?"

Leo nodded.

Burt studied Sid's face. She gave him a small nod, and he sighed. "Okay, Leo. Go on up to bed. We'll head over to the pharmacy in the morning and get your medicine."

Burt opened his arms, and Leo leaned in for a hug. He wanted to cry on his grandfather's shoulder, but he blinked back the tears. "Sorry I missed the concert," he whispered.

"It's okay, son. There'll be plenty of others." Burt ruffled the boy's hair. "Go get some sleep."

Leo trudged upstairs to his room. Everyone else waited to hear the click of his bedroom door before whispering all at once, "What the hell?! Shit! Fuck!" and so on.

Burt's voice was the loudest, "What was he doing on the seawall at night?"

"Sulking, I expect," Sid answered. "He was furious with us earlier this evening, or don't you remember?"

Burt sighed. "Why did they call you and not me?" He patted the pockets of his cargo shorts and frowned. "Where's my phone?"

"They tried calling you, but you didn't pick up, so they called me." She flopped down in the chair next to Cesar, who handed her his newly opened beer. She accepted it and took a long swig. "And in case you're wondering, I think we made the right decision taking Leo off the Oakmire job."

"Oh?" said Burt, who was now distractedly looking for his phone.

"Yeah." Sid took another sip. "I got shot at tonight."

Thus began another round of colorful language from the Geezers.

"What happened?" Burt demanded, so Sid recounted her adventures that evening on the golf course.

"You got those pictures?" asked Cesar. Sid nodded, and Cesar held out his hand. "Lemme see."

Sid fished her camera out of her bag, scrolled back to the first photo from that evening, and handed it over to Cesar. The other Geezers gathered around him, studying the photos of the poachers landing, setting out their bait, shooting at Sid, and fleeing the scene.

"I know them fellas," said Guppy. "Well, one of 'em, at least." Cesar handed him the camera, and Guppy scrolled back to a shot of both men standing in the middle of the green. "The one with the crossbow. He works for me." Everyone in the room stared at him. "He came up from Miami a few months ago. His cousin has worked for me for several years now. Good workers, both of 'em. I hired this one,"—he tapped the screen on the camera—"because his cousin vouched for him." He shrugged. "He hasn't given me any trouble, but I'll be firing his ass tomorrow, that's for damn sure. Right after I beat the shit out of him."

"Don't do that!" blurted Sid. "I don't want him tipped off. Let me talk to Detective Davis first. You can fire him once the police come calling."

"You sure?" Guppy frowned. She nodded, and he handed the camera back to Sid.

The Geezers said their goodbyes, and Sid and Burt retired to the kitchen. Burt pulled a carton of ice cream out of the freezer and two spoons from the drawer, and then he sat down opposite Sid at the table. "Now, you wanna tell me what really happened?" asked Burt, fishing a giant chocolate chip out of the ice cream.

Sid scooped out her own spoonful. "With me or with Leo?" Burt merely raised an eyebrow, and Sid smirked. "He's got this shadow following him. He doesn't know what it is or what it wants with him. I've talked to two women in town who usually know about these things, but they don't know anything about it either."

Burt slammed his spoon down on the table. "How long has this been going on?"

Sid shrugged. "Off and on. Maybe a week now." Burt opened his mouth to say more, but Sid cut him off. "Nothing has happened. This shadow thing has kept its distance. These women, Hattie and Val—"

"Hattie? As in Eli's cousin Hattie?" interrupted Burt. Sid nodded, and Burt sat back in his seat. "I didn't know she had the gift, too. Eli's never said anything."

Sid shrugged. "Apparently she's helped Leo before. Given him some advice. He likes her, trusts her." She scooped up some more ice cream. "For what it's worth, I trust her, too. And Val seems okay as well. She runs Muy Local, that shop over on Cuna Street. Know the one I'm talking about? I think Hattie and Val are only trying to help. When I spoke with them on Monday, they weren't overly concerned, but I think it may be time to ask them for some more help."

Burt's nostrils flared. "You think this shadow pushed Leo off the seawall?"

"No, I don't think that's what happened." Sid twirled her spoon in her fingers. "I think it was just trying to get his attention. Maybe scare him. But I don't think it pushed Leo. He said he turned around real fast and lost his balance. I think falling in the water was an accident."

Burt was quiet for several moments. "So, what do we do now?"

Sid swallowed. "You take care of Leo. Get his prescription filled, change his bandages, all that good stuff. I'll find Hattie and try to convince her to intervene. Maybe she can talk to this shadow thing and get it to stop . . . whatever it is it's doing."

"And what about you? What are you going to do about what happened on the golf course tonight?" Burt fished out another chunk of chocolate.

"I'm going to try to find a connection between tonight's poachers and Declan Chase," answered Sid. "Because arresting those two idiots won't stop the poaching. It may delay things a bit while more idiots are recruited, but neither of those two geniuses is the brains behind this operation. This is Declan Chase's game."

Burt shook his head. "You have any idea what the rules of the game are?"

"That's just it," said Sid. "I don't think there are any rules anymore."

Chapter Twenty-Four

Detective Tony Davis arrived bright and early, pounding on her office door. She'd texted him last night before going to bed, asking if she could speak to him in the morning. She'd mentioned that she had photos of some of the poachers, caught in the act, and that they'd shot at her without success. Sid knew that would get his attention, so she had set an early alarm. It was not even seven o'clock, and she'd barely gotten dressed and brushed her teeth when she heard the banging.

"Good morning, Detective." Sid gave him a bright smile as she opened the door and waved him inside.

"Where do I even begin?" Tony punctuated his question with a shake of his head. "My God, woman. Are you trying to get yourself killed?"

"Hardly." Sid shrugged. "Just doing my job."

"Cut the crap, Sid, and tell me what's going on?" He stomped into the room and stood in a wide stance with his arms crossed, biceps bulging.

"Can I put on some coffee first?" She started the coffee brewing, standing over the little makeshift kitchen in her office and wishing Tony had brought donuts like last time. "Please tell Naomi thanks again for last night."

"Yeah, she told me what happened to the kid." Tony took a seat in one of the guest chairs, the wood groaning in protest. "Sounds like you both had quite a night."

"Leo ended up worse than me." Sid sat down at her desk.

Tony smirked. "You could have ended up dead."

"True." Sid swung her monitor around so that Tony could see it. She'd loaded up her photos last night after she'd texted him, and now she flipped through them one by one. "Guppy told me last night that this guy"—she tapped the screen—"works for him."

Tony took his notebook out of his back pocket and began scratching notes. "You got a name for him?"

"Nope, sorry." Sid ran a search on her phone, pulling up the website for Guppy's landscaping business. He ran a large outfit that catered mostly to commercial properties—hotels, office buildings, some government facilities—and some high-end residential customers. "Here, this is Guppy's info." She passed her phone over to him so he could scroll through the website. "If you want, I'll call him. I'm sure we can go over there this morning and talk to him."

Tony looked up from the phone. "We?"

"Yes, *we*." She rolled her eyes. "We need to tie these guys"—she tapped the screen again—"to Declan Chase."

"Agreed, but that's not your job, Sid." He passed the phone back to her. "It's mine. And so is arresting these two assholes." He pulled his own phone from his pocket. "You can go with me to Oakmire to show me where you were when you were shot at. Maybe we can find the bullet casings, pull the bullet from that tree you said they hit, take some photos in the daylight, but that's it. You need to leave this alone now."

"Tony, I—"

"Sid!" he interrupted. "Leave it alone."

"Fine," she grumbled. Sid poured some coffee in a travel mug, grabbed a granola bar, and they headed out before most of the other residents on Saragossa Street had even gotten out of bed.

They arrived at the Oakmire clubhouse in record time, given that the streets of St. Augustine were blessedly quiet at that time of the morning. A couple of patrol vehicles were already parked in the lot.

"You called in reinforcements?" asked Sid, pointing to the department vehicles.

"I did. Last night, after I got your text." Tony parked and got out. "They've cordoned off the third hole for us."

While the streets of the Old City had been peaceful, the scene at the starter's shack was another story. Tony flashed his badge to the course ranger, who responded with, "Finally!" and shooed them off in the direction of the third hole. He agreed to hold all of the golfers at the first tee until Tony gave him the all-clear signal.

Sid and Tony walked side by side along the cart path past the first and second holes. Tony greeted the deputies as he and Sid passed the third tee box and continued down the path alongside the fairway. Sid directed him to the spot where she'd been sitting the night before. Tony pulled out his phone and shot photos of the relevant locations as Sid pointed them out. They couldn't find the tree that had absorbed the first bullet, but they did find the second bullet in the bottom of a homeowner's swimming pool.

The homeowner gladly fished out the bullet with his skimmer net and proceeded to talk Tony's ear off about University of Florida football, seemingly more concerned about his favorite team's chances this season than he was about someone shooting a hole in his pool cage during the night. A walk around the edge of the third green revealed a few bits of raw chicken that still littered the grass near the marsh. Tony took more photos and dismissed the deputies, and then he and Sid returned to the clubhouse.

As they approached the starter's shack, Tony waved to the course ranger, and the line of golfers waiting to tee off cheered in relief. A few of them uttered expletives of frustration. When Tony changed direction, veering away from the clubhouse and toward the waiting golfers, the disgruntled cries immediately ceased. He stopped, removed his sunglasses, and stood with his hands on his hips, letting the golfers take in the sheer size of him. He scanned the crowd, meeting the eyes of the few who dared to look directly at him, but no one said anything further. He slowly replaced his sunglasses and strode back over to where Sid was standing.

"Nice trick," she whispered as they climbed the stairs to the veranda, which Tony took three at a time. "I bet that comes in handy."

"It does. Too bad I have to use it more often than I'd like," he answered.

Jonathan Beedlemeyer's office was dark. They found a teenager working the register in the pro shop, watching the streaming coverage of the PGA tournament in Savannah. The kid looked up from his phone just long enough to admit to not having seen Beedlemeyer yet that morning. Tony left his card with the kid with a request that Beedlemeyer get in touch as soon as possible. On their way out of the clubhouse, Sid spotted a familiar landscaping company's van parked off to the far side of the lot, close to the path leading to the groundskeeper's shed.

"Come with me," Sid urged. She tried tugging on Tony's forearm, but it was like trying to wrap her hand around a steel beam. "There's someone you should talk to."

Sid led the way along the path, past the outdoor smokers'

lounge and cart barn to the groundskeeper's shed. Once again, the doors to the shed were wide open, and laughter could be heard inside. "Gentlemen," said Sid as she and Tony stepped through the door. The two men turned, and their mouths fell open.

Henri whistled. "You're a big 'un, ain't you?"

Guppy stepped forward, holding out his hand and grinning from ear to ear. "Detective Davis." Tony shook his hand. Guppy glanced over his shoulder at the other man and asked, "You know who this is, Henri?" When Henri shook his head, Guppy made the introduction. "This here is Antonio Davis, one of the all-time greatest tight ends to ever play college ball."

Henri narrowed his eyes, studying Tony. "I remember you." He nodded slowly. "I also remember what you did to my LSU Tigers that year in the conference semifinals." Henri's gaze dropped to Tony's leg. "Damn shame 'bout your leg. But it looks like you're doin' a'right." He nudged Guppy in the ribs. "Did I hear you call him detective?"

Tony reached out and shook Henri's hand. "That's right. And my condolences on your Tigers' loss."

Henri chuckled. "I doubt you mean that."

Tony smiled in return. "I surely don't."

Sid sighed. She was tired of listening to football chatter and wondered if this is what Tony had to deal with everywhere he went. "I was just showing Detective Davis where the poachers were last night when they shot at me."

Henri leaped up from his stool, a movement that was surprisingly quick and agile for a man with such a big belly. "Someone fired at you? On my course?"

Sid recounted the details of her run-in, and Tony held up his phone to show the men a photo of the two poachers. "Recognize either of these two men?" Both men nodded.

"That one works for me," said Guppy. He pointed to the poacher with the crossbow.

Henri pointed to the other poacher. "And he is on my groundskeeping crew."

Tony put his phone away and took out his notebook. "I'll need their names, addresses, and any other details you can give me."

Guppy put his arm around Sid's shoulder. "You gonna arrest those bastards for shootin' at our girl, Detective?"

"That's the plan." Tony held up his pen, poised to take down details. Guppy pulled out his phone, and Henri pulled some papers from an old file cabinet he kept in the corner of his shed. Tony wrote down everything the two men shared with him. "Any chance these guys are working here today?"

Both men spoke at once. "Yep. Yes, sir. I'll call him." They reached for their phones.

Tony held up a finger. "Give me a minute to call for backup just in case they decide to run. I don't chase down suspects anymore if I can help it." He flexed his knee, and both men nodded solemnly. Tony took Sid by the arm and escorted her out of the shed. "I want you to head home. I don't want you anywhere near here when we make these arrests. If they know it was you they shot at, that it's you who's pointing the finger, you could be in danger."

"They probably already know it," said Sid. "I'm pretty sure Declan Chase is their ringleader, and I'm pretty sure I know who hired Declan Chase." Tony raised an eyebrow, and Sid continued. "Two of the club's board members were adamantly opposed to hiring me to investigate the poaching. They are also very wealthy and very much in favor of securing a major PGA tournament, which won't happen if the alligators are still in residence here." Tony pulled out his notebook again, and Sid gave him the names and addresses of Herbert Langston and Rocco Castiglione.

"All right," said Tony. "You've done enough here today. I want you to make yourself scarce. Let us bring these guys in, squeeze 'em a bit. Maybe we can get them to name Declan Chase and admit that it was someone from Oakmire who hired them."

Sid grinned. "That's hoping they're as stupid as they look."

Chapter Twenty-Five

Sid drove back to the house, parked outside her garage apartment, and immediately took off on foot for the Old City's historic downtown district a few blocks away. Her first stop was Aviles Street. She picked up donuts at Fire in the Hole and then went next door to Pirate Joe's. The coffee shop was busy on this sunny Saturday morning, and Sid waited in line to place her order. As the two cups of coffee were finally set down on the counter, Sid heard her name being called.

"Sidney? Sidney Stone?" Sid looked around to find a pair of women seated at a two-top table by the window; one of the women had her hand raised to attract Sid's attention.

Sid recognized the woman immediately, even though she'd only ever spoken with her by phone. Carleigh Sutton looked exactly like her photo on her law firm's website—hair cut in a severe, shoulder-length bob and died a rich chestnut brown with reddish-gold highlights, eyes that were such a pale blue they looked almost silver, and teeth so white that you needed sunglasses to take in her smile. Carleigh was tall, over six feet, and most of that was legs. She had a reputation for being a highly effective family law attorney, as most recently evidenced by the mindboggling speed and efficiency with which she'd handled Emmaline Colquitt's divorce.

Sid waved to Carleigh, picked up her coffees, and walked over. Carleigh moved an empty chair over to her table and motioned for Sid to sit down. "Hi, Carleigh. I'm afraid I can't stay."

"This will only take a moment," said Carleigh, patting the seat of the empty chair. "Promise." Sid sat down, placing the coffees on the table and the bag of donuts in her lap. "This is my sister, Lorelai." Carleigh gestured to her companion.

"Half sister," Lorelai muttered. "Same father, different mothers." She looked up from her phone, barely glancing at Sid before dropping her gaze back to her screen.

"Right. Forgive me for forgetting that." Carleigh rolled her eyes and turned her attention back to Sid. "It's lucky, running into you like this, Sidney, because I was going to call to see if we could make an appointment with you. Lorelai is, well, she's having a bit of trouble. And I'd like to engage you, put you on retainer so to speak, in case we need you to look into things for her."

Sid narrowed her eyes, glancing between the two sisters. They were remarkably similar in looks and mannerisms. The biggest differences were their eyes (Lorelai's were a darker blue), the length of their hair (Lorelai's was down to her waist), and their ages (there appeared to be at least a ten-year gap between the two, with Lorelai only in her early to mid-twenties at most). But they had the same posture, the same long legs, the same high cheekbones.

Sid lowered her voice. "What exactly is the trouble?"

Lorelai slapped her phone face down on the table and looked up at Sid. Without lowering her voice, she said, "My boyfriend died, and the police think I had something to do with it." A few other customers glanced in her direction.

Carleigh leaned forward and whispered. "Her *ex-boyfriend*, emphasis on the '*ex*' part"—she added air quotes to drive home her point—"was somewhat of a public figure."

"He was famous," Lorelai corrected, sweeping her long hair off her shoulder. "You probably know him, everyone does. His name is Cameron Chase." She crossed her arms and raised an eyebrow, as if challenging Sid to deny his celebrity status.

Sid held Lorelai's gaze for a few moments, giving nothing away, and then glanced over at Carleigh. "I'm free Monday morning. We can meet at my office."

Carleigh grimaced, sucking in air between her teeth. "Any chance we could meet tomorrow? I know it's Sunday, but I have a jam-packed schedule next week. Could we meet at noon?" asked Carleigh. "I'll bring lunch." Lorelai huffed at the suggestion and picked up her phone.

Sid heaved a sigh. That was the life of a private investigator. Never a day off unless there was no work at all. "Tomorrow's fine. I'll see you then." Sid stood, picked up her coffees, and nodded at Carleigh.

The lawyer smiled at her and mouthed the words, "Thank you."

Sid left the Sutton sisters and walked out of Pirate Joe's and over to Plaza de la Constitución. As Sid had hoped, Hattie was sitting under the same tree as the last time they'd met. Once again, the old woman was cross-legged on her blanket, leaning back against the trunk of the giant oak.

Sid cleared her throat. "Good morning, Hattie. Mind if we have a chat?"

Hattie smiled her toothless grin. "I see you come bearin' gifts. You know I told the boy that he didn't need to do that no more. It was my way of testin' him the first time. Seein' if he was serious 'bout askin' for help and takin' my advice."

"I know. He told me." Sid smiled and sat down on the grass in front of Hattie. "Honestly, I was craving coffee and donuts myself this morning, and it's always nice to have a little company."

"You butterin' me up, girl?" Hattie chuckled as she took the proffered cup.

"Yes," Sid admitted, "because I need your help. *Leo* needs your help." While the old woman ate her donut, Sid told Hattie what had happened to Leo the night before. "You should see him. He's a mess." Sid shook her head and pried the lid off her own to-go cup. "He said that shadow thing whispered to him. It knew his name."

"I see," said Hattie. She stared past Sid toward the sparkling waters of Matanzas Bay.

"What do you think it means?" Sid took a sip of her own coffee. "Is it bad? It's bad, right?"

"Probably ain't good." Hattie shrugged. "But we won't know 'til we talk to it."

"Talk?" Sid almost spilled her coffee in her lap. "What do you mean talk to it? Leo could have broken his neck last night after talking to it."

Hattie shook her head. "No, that was the shadow trying to talk to Leo, not Leo talking to it. *We* need to talk *to it*." She pointed a crooked finger at Sid. "But we need to do it carefully. Safely." She stared out at the water again, running her few teeth back and forth over her bottom lip. Sid sipped her coffee and waited. It was a good two or three minutes before Hattie spoke again. "We'll do it tonight at your house." She nodded to Sid and took a bite of her donut, as if that were the end of the discussion.

Sid gawped at the woman. "Do what? And I don't have a house. I live in Leo's grandfather's garage apartment."

"Fine. Burt's house then."

Sid blinked as her mind raced to connect Hattie and Burt, finally remembering that Hattie was Eli Williams's cousin and Eli was bandmates with Burt. "Right, okay. I'll have to check with him."

"Go on then," said Hattie, waving her arthritic hand at Sid.

Sid pulled out her phone and dialed Burt. He picked up on the second ring. "Hey, Burt, I'm here with Hattie. She's Eli's cousin, remember?" Sid smiled at the woman. "Any chance we can use your house for a, uh, séance this evening?"

Hattie clucked her tongue. "I ain't talkin' 'bout no séance, girl." She shook her head in disgust. "It's just a readin'. Just a conversation."

"Right, sorry, not a séance." At this point, Sid wasn't sure who she was apologizing to, Burt or Hattie. "Hattie wants to do a reading. She wants to try to have a conversation with Leo's shadow thing to see if we can get to the bottom of what's going on." Sid nodded along as Burt chatted away on the other end of the line, and then she covered the phone with her hand and said to Hattie, "Burt wants to do it tomorrow night. He says Leo's not going to be up to it tonight. Tomorrow night would be better. You can come by in the evening. He's having the Geezers over for band practice in the afternoon, and then he's barbecuing after that. He says you're welcome any time after six o'clock."

Hattie nodded. "That's fine."

Sid relayed Hattie's assent to Burt and hung up. "Do you know where the house is?" Hattie nodded, and Sid put the lid back on her coffee. "Anything you need us to do to get ready? Anything you need? Candles or tarot cards or anything?"

Hattie clucked her tongue again. "Child, you really don't know nothin' 'bout this stuff, do you?"

"Sorry, no." Sid shook her head.

"Well, it's a good thing the boy's got me then," Hattie muttered under her breath. It was loud enough for Sid to hear, which Sid thought was probably intentional. "I don't need nothin'. You just be ready."

Sid rose to her feet and offered Hattie the bag with the remaining donuts, but Hattie waved her off. "Ready for what exactly?" asked Sid.

"Your guess is as good as mine." Hattie tipped her head back, leaning against the tree again. "Because even if that shadow means the boy no harm, that don't mean it ain't dangerous."

Chapter Twenty-Six

At twelve thirty on Sunday afternoon, Sid sat at her desk, swearing under her breath. Carleigh Sutton and her sister Lorelai were a no-show. Sid had risen early, showered, blow-dried her hair, and even put on a little makeup. She'd also donned one of the two new sundresses she'd bought with her recent earnings, a little gift to herself and a much-needed boost to her wardrobe, which was otherwise full of shorts and yoga pants. She wasn't sure why she was going through so much trouble for these two women, especially given how hot it was outside and the fact they'd made this appointment for a Sunday of all days.

On Saturday afternoon, Sid had spent several hours doing a deep dive into Lorelai Sutton, the twenty-four-year-old self-appointed influencer and wannabe social media darling. According to her multiple pages and channels, Lorelai had recently graduated magna cum laude from the University of Florida with a dual degree in finance and public relations. She belonged to a sorority, volunteered at an animal shelter, and enjoyed cake decorating, all of which produced a bounty of colorful photos and videos for her several thousand followers. Over the past year, her posts had shifted to more fashion and lifestyle content as well as travel photos and videos. She was promoting small-time clothing labels, beauty brands, jewelry lines, and meal-prep kits.

Lorelai Sutton was posting up to five times a day, each and every day. Sid wondered where the young woman found the time to do anything else. Perhaps that was the point, thought Sid. It was clear that Lorelai was trying hard to make a living by being online. She was hocking wares and reviewing products in an almost frantic effort to look rich and chic and relevant.

It all left a sour taste in Sid's mouth, one she couldn't seem to wash away even with the two bowls of sugary cereal she'd had for dinner last night. Sid scrolled and clicked her way through years' worth of posts before finally calling it quits. By the end, her eyes burned, her head throbbed, and she failed to see the appeal of any of it.

Sid herself went out of her way to avoid social media. She'd never had a Facebook page or an Instagram account or posted anything anywhere online. She liked being anonymous. No one needed to know what she was eating or wearing, where she was vacationing, or what she thought about anything—not unless they were sitting next to her and enjoying an actual, real-life conversation.

The only aspect of Lorelai's life that Sid found even remotely interesting was her relationship with Cameron Chase. From what Sid could piece together, the two young lovers began dating in high school. She'd been a cheerleader, he'd been a golf prodigy, and they'd been crowned prom king and queen before they both enrolled at the University of Florida. Cameron found glory on the golf course while Lorelai excelled in her studies and honed her skills as a social media expert. Throughout all of this, their relationship appeared to be a rocky one. For every dozen or so of Lorelai's photos and videos depicting them as blissfully happy, all of it being self-professed evidence of their true and everlasting love for each other, there was another post of her crying over their recent breakup or vowing never to take him back. This roller coaster had lasted the entirety of their four years at UF and the three years after graduation.

A little over two weeks ago, Lorelai had posted her most damning video yet. In it, she declared that Cameron Chase had broken her heart for the very last time. With the wind blowing through her hair and dark mascara and eyeliner running down her face, Lorelai Sutton outlined a litany of complaints against her once-again ex-boyfriend: he was controlling; he was indifferent to her needs; he was self-centered, self-absorbed, self-obsessed; and he was a much better golfer than he was a lover. Lorelai also alleged that Cameron had borrowed money from her to cover significant gambling debts and had yet to pay it back. She was threatening to sue if he didn't pay up.

Sid couldn't imagine that any of this sat well with Cameron or his corporate sponsors. Lorelai Sutton was a loose cannon, someone whose unpredictability on social media could be a serious liability to the rising golf star. What had Cameron's reaction been, she wondered. So far, she'd found no direct response from him on any of Lorelai's pages, nor had he posted any retort on his own social media accounts.

After posting the video, Lorelai went radio silent about Cameron Chase. Then, the evening he died, she posted a series of six photographs, all of them action shots of Cameron on the Oakmire golf course. Sid studied the photos, recognizing some of their locations. The final two photos had been taken from the little bridge leading to the seventeenth green. In them, Cameron stood on the velvety green grass, looking tanned and handsome and very much alive, as the sun set over the marsh behind him.

At 12:35, there was a knock on Sid's office door. It was opened immediately, before Sid could even stand up from her chair, and Carleigh Sutton poked her head inside. "Hi! So sorry we're late. Are you still free to meet with us?"

Sid forced herself to smile. "Sure. Come on in."

Carleigh entered, carrying a large paper bag with the logo of a swanky, oceanfront restaurant on Vilano Beach that Sid had never had sufficient cashflow to visit. Sid moved her files aside to make room for the bag. Lorelai lagged behind her sister, carrying a cardboard tray filled with drinks in one hand and scrolling through her phone with the other.

Carleigh began unpacking the food. "I am so sorry we're late. Someone had an impromptu photoshoot this morning." She tilted her head in the direction of her sister and frowned. "So, instead of coming with me to church services, I had to go all the way back to Vilano Beach to pick her up. That's the reason for the delay." She passed her hand over the food as if modeling it for a game show. "And since I was over on the island, I picked up salads for us. I wasn't sure what you'd like, so I got you their Cobb salad. I thought you could just pick off anything you don't want, but it's really delicious." She smiled and eyed the two guest chairs.

Sid pointed to the Queen Anne dining chair, the one Detective Davis always sat in. It was the sturdier and more comfortable of the two. Sid plucked the empty bag from her desk and dropped it on the floor behind her. "Please have a seat, Lorelai."

At this, the young woman finally looked up. The disgusted look on her face as she took in Sid's office, with its metal file cabinets, mismatched chairs, scratched desk, and side table stained with water rings, evaporated any sympathy Sid had felt toward her after scrolling through her social media accounts. Sid smiled, took the drinks carrier from her, and pointed to the second guest chair. Lorelai wrinkled her nose and sat down without touching the chair with her hands. Sid was secretly glad that she hadn't replaced the chair with something better. It was a sick sort of satisfaction, seeing this social media starlet sink so low into the old chair's sagging seat that she was below the eye level of the other two women.

"What can I do for you?" asked Sid, turning to Carleigh.

"Well," began Carleigh, though she interrupted herself to pass out the drinks. "Unsweetened iced tea. Hope that's okay?" Sid nodded, secretly wishing it was sweet tea, and Carleigh continued. "The thing is, Lorelai has been interviewed by the police regarding Cameron Chase's death. We haven't been told how he died other than what's been reported in the news, that he was found in the marsh and"—she shot a quick glance at Lorelai, who remained stone-faced—"that there were alligators involved." Carleigh reached for the arugula, beet, and goat cheese salad on the desk.

"I don't think they've made any statement other than that they are investigating," said Sid. "And I think that's because they don't know how he died exactly."

Carleigh nodded. "Yes, but we both know that they wouldn't be interviewing people if it were clearly an accident. So there must be something suspicious."

"That's a reasonable assumption"—Sid shrugged—"but I haven't heard anything."

Carleigh bit her lip and looked at her sister. When she spoke, it was with much the same effort as one would use when crossing a plane of thin ice. "The thing is, well, Lorelai posted several photos of Cameron on the day that he is believed to have—I mean, the day he went missing. And apparently, one of the places in those photos was the location where his body was found. So . . . I can see why the police would want to question her."

Sid nodded and speared a grape tomato with her fork. "Did you take those photos, Lorelai?"

"Of course." She raised her chin, looking affronted that there might be any doubt in Sid's mind. "I'm an excellent photographer. We had great lighting that day, and the weather really cooperated. I had him shoot some photos of me, too, which he was not happy about doing, and they came out awful. I deleted them immediately."

"I'm sure they weren't that bad," said Sid. "When were they taken?"

"That Monday," said Lorelai. "The Monday before Cam died."

Sid noticed the young woman was still holding her chin up, trying to maintain eye contact, so she returned her gaze. "Were you playing golf with Cameron that day?"

Lorelai snorted a laugh. "I don't play golf. Never have. I don't really even like it, if I'm honest. I don't mind being out on the course and watching Cam play, but it does get a little boring after several hours." She rolled her eyes. "It's the slowest game in the world, and it just takes forever for them to line up their shots and whatever. God, it's mind-numbing sometimes." She picked up her phone and began scrolling.

Sid smirked, secretly agreeing with Lorelai's assessment of the game of golf. "So you saw Cameron on Monday at Oakmire?" Lorelai nodded, and Sid asked, "What about the rest of the week? Did you see him again?"

Lorelai sighed and looked up again. "I was busy on Tuesday and Wednesday, so I couldn't meet him then. We planned to meet up again on Thursday afternoon, but by then we were fighting, so it didn't happen. It took me all week to get around to editing the photos and posting them. That's why they didn't go up until Friday."

Sid made some notes in her file. "So, the last time you saw Cameron was on Monday at the golf course?"

"Well, no." Lorelai smiled. "I spent Monday night with him. Technically, the last time I saw him was Tuesday morning when I left his apartment."

Sid nodded. "Sounds like the two of you got back together then. I saw your video about your breakup a couple of weeks ago. Seemed like you'd ended things for good. What changed?"

Lorelai scratched at her glittery phone case with her thumbnail and shrugged one shoulder. "It's always like that with Cam. We've been on-again, off-again since we were teenagers. When we're broken up, we both try to date other people, but it isn't much fun. Neither of us ever found anyone better, I guess. I know I didn't, and I thought he felt the same way." She shifted in her seat and crossed her long legs. "That Monday—the day I took those photos—he texted and asked if we could meet up. Just to talk, you know? But he was practicing a lot, getting ready for his big tournament, so I met him out at Oakmire. I'd done that plenty of times before. Walked the course with them, taken photos of Cam, hung out with them in the clubhouse."

"Sorry," Sid interrupted, "but you said *them*?"

Lorelai nodded. "Yeah, Cam and Noah."

Sid blinked. "Noah Zimmerman?"

"Yeah." Lorelai frowned and glanced quickly at her sister. "He's Cam's best friend. Noah was a year behind us in school, but he and Cam grew up on the golf course. They took lessons together, were on the golf team together. They were pretty inseparable." She raised an eyebrow. "You know he was Cam's caddy on tour, right?"

Sid tried to still her face. "No, I didn't."

Lorelai nodded. "Apparently, Noah's a much better caddy than he is a golfer, although I wouldn't have any idea about that. Cam always said so. When Cam was first out on tour, Noah went with him. Just tagged along for moral support. But then Noah started caddying for Cam, and Cam's game really improved. He started winning, started really moving up in the rankings. And then Cam won that big tournament a little while back, and that got him a spot in the major." She sat up. "In fact, it's this weekend, isn't it?" She scrolled through her phone and nodded. "I totally forgot with everything . . . with Cam . . . I haven't been watching it." She bit her lip and stared at her phone for a long moment. "Poor Cam."

Sid watched the young woman. This was the most emotion, the most empathy, that she'd exhibited since Sid had known her. "So if I understand the sequence of events correctly: Cameron texted you on Monday and asked if you could hang out. You met him at Oakmire. You and Noah walked the course with Cameron while he practiced for his tournament. You left with Cameron and spent Monday night with him at his apartment. You said goodbye to each other on Tuesday morning, and by Thursday, you were fighting again so you didn't see each other that day or Friday. And you were busy all week, so you didn't get around to posting Monday's photos until Friday evening. Yes?"

"Correct," said Lorelai, straightening her posture. "I posted the pics right before I went out. My friend Mandy got a bartending gig at a new restaurant up in Jax Beach, so me and two of our other friends went up there to support her. I took some photos and posted them online that night."

Sid made some more notes. She'd seen the photos of Lorelai and her friends at the bar. They'd been posted around midnight. "When did you head up there? And when did you get home?"

Lorelai squinted and tilted her head to one side. "I think we headed out around seven. We had dinner at the restaurant. The food was okay, but it's too pricey for what you get." She drummed her fingers on the arm of the chair. "Anyway, I think we left there around midnight. I edited the photos in the car on the way home and posted them. Probably shouldn't have done that." She held up her finger. "You should never post drunk. Cardinal rule of influencing."

"Good to know," said Sid, resisting the urge to roll her eyes as she made some more notes. "Why were you and Cam fighting?" She looked up from her file when Lorelai didn't answer right away.

The young woman was biting her lip, her brows drawn down. There was silence for a few moments before she spoke. "He . . . he told me that he didn't want to get back together. That he wanted to be a free agent." She let out a laugh. "He actually said that. *Free agent*. He said he was going to have a chance to meet models and other famous people and that he was leaving his old life behind. I was his high school girlfriend, that's all. He'd outgrown me." She huffed. "*Outgrown me.* That's what he said. Despite the fact that he'd texted me for a booty call on Monday." She bit her lip again and looked away.

"So he broke up with you on Thursday," said Sid, watching Lorelai visibly flinch at the remark, "and yet you still posted photos of him on Friday. Why is that?"

Lorelai shrugged. "They were good photos."

Sid ate a forkful of salad, stared at the young woman, and waited for Lorelai to continue speaking. Her sister opened her mouth to try to fill the silence, but Sid held up a hand.

Lorelai finally sighed and glanced back at Sid. "Because I didn't think it was really over. Or, I mean, I didn't *want* it to be over." She lowered her gaze. "It wasn't the first time he'd broken up with me only to call me again a few days later begging to get back together. I figured he'd do the same thing again this time, except..." Her voice trailed off and her brow creased.

"Except what?" prompted Sid.

"Except he'd never been so mean before." Lorelai shrugged. "I thought if I posted the photos, then everyone would think we were still together. Any girl he might hook up with would see them and think he had a girlfriend. It would be his word against mine. And who would you be more likely to believe? Me or the guy trying to cheat on his girlfriend?"

"I see," said Sid. She exchanged a glance with Carleigh and then asked, "Have you talked to Noah or Cameron's father?"

Lorelai shook her head. "No. I don't like to be around Declan. Cam did a really good job of making sure I was never alone with him. I never went to Cam's house in high school. He always came to mine. In college, it was fine. We could see each other all the time in Gainesville, but when we came home for breaks, I never went over there. He always came to see me. Then Cam finally got a place of his own after we graduated, and that was fine. Declan hardly ever came around to Cam's apartment."

"Why did you avoid Declan?" Sid was pretty sure she already knew the answer.

Lorelai crossed her arms in front of her. "Because he was mean. When I did meet him, he always made snide comments about me, even with me standing right there. He called me a gold digger once. To my face, if you can believe it. And he once grabbed my ass in high school."

Carleigh blanched at this. "You never told me that."

Lorelai shrugged. "I was in high school. If it happened now, I'd know how to deal with it a lot better, but back then I was young and stupid. I thought maybe I'd done something. That I'd led him on without knowing it." She shook her head. "We were at a football game. I was in my cheerleading uniform, talking to Cam before the game, and Declan came over. I think Cam went to get food or something. I don't really remember now. But he was gone for a few minutes, and Declan put his hand up my skirt and grabbed my ass."

Carleigh reached out and squeezed her sister's arm. "I wish you'd told me."

"It's okay." Lorelai shrugged again. "Besides, you were in law school at the time. You were pretty busy."

"Lor," murmured Carleigh. "I am never too busy for you."

Lorelai rolled her eyes. "Whatever."

Carleigh frowned and slumped back in her chair.

Sid cleared her throat, looking for a way to diffuse the situation. "What about Noah? Have you talked to him?"

Lorelai shook her head again. "I texted him on Tuesday when I saw the news, but he never responded. He was probably as mad at Cam as I was." She twisted a strand of hair around her finger. "And maybe he feels kind of bad about that now, too. It's . . . it's complicated. Loving someone and hating him, too."

"Why would Noah have been angry with Cameron?" asked Sid.

Lorelai frowned. "Because Cam broke up with Noah, too. Didn't you know that?" Sid shook her head. "Yeah, when Cam and I had it out about him outgrowing me so that he could run off and date famous models, he told me that he'd sacked Noah, too. Cam said he hired another caddy. Some famous guy who'd been on the tour a really long time. Cam told me he was moving up in the world, so he needed to shed the dead weight." She barked out another laugh. "He called me and Noah dead weight." She scowled and shook her head. "Asshole."

This was the version of Lorelai that Sid had seen in the breakup video rant—hurt, frustrated, and royally pissed-off. "How much money did Cameron owe you?" asked Sid.

Carleigh's eyebrows shot up as she turned to look at her sister, but Lorelai didn't miss a beat. "Five thousand dollars." She held Sid's gaze even as Carleigh's mouth dropped open.

"That's a lot of money," said Sid.

"It is." Lorelai nodded. "He said it was to pay off his gambling debts."

Sid placed her elbows on the desk and leaned forward. "Was it?"

Lorelai shrugged. "I don't know. I guess it could have been, but Cam had never been a gambler. That was all Declan. Cam always told me that he worked too hard for his money just to throw it all away by gambling. His father was the one who gambled, but I don't think he ever won or lost very big. At least Cam never said anything like that. He just said that his dad would piss away his paychecks on beer and poker, that there was never enough to eat in the house, and the money always ran out before his dad's next payday." Lorelai twirled her hair around her finger again. "So when he asked for the money to pay off gambling debts, I assumed it was really for Declan and Cam was just too embarrassed to admit it."

"Did Cameron ever pay you back?" asked Sid.

"No," Lorelai answered with a scowl. "That night we slept together he told me he'd pay me back from the purse he won at the tournament." She recrossed her legs, fidgeting in her seat. "But then the bastard had to go and die without paying me, and now I'm out five grand." She turned her head away. "Asshole," she muttered again, under her breath, but Sid saw her try to surreptitiously swipe at her cheek to wipe away a tear.

"Okay," said Sid. She turned to Carleigh. "What do you want me to do?"

Carleigh blinked, trying to process everything her sister had just confessed. "I, um . . . I guess I would like to put you on retainer. I'd like you to try to find out what the police know about Cameron's death, make sure Lorelai isn't a suspect or a person of interest. Or let us know if they say she is one. They haven't told us either way." She glanced at her sister. "And if she is, then I'd like you to investigate separately from the police. Lorelai has an alibi for the night Cam . . . for that night, but the police may still think she's involved somehow. If they do think that, we'd like to know so we can be prepared." Carleigh opened her purse and pulled out a check. "I wrote this out for a retainer. If it's not enough, let me know, and I'll have another one delivered tomorrow."

Sid glanced at the check and swallowed hard. It was more money than she'd seen in quite a long time. She pulled a form from a desk drawer and filled in a few of the blanks, then slid it across the table to Carleigh. "This is my engagement letter. Standard stuff. And you should note that Lorelai would be my client." Sid tapped the page, pointing to the young woman's name printed at the top. "Lorelai can pay me however she likes, including having you foot the bill for her, but she will be my client." Carleigh bit her lip and looked at her sister, who still had her head turned away. Carleigh gathered up the pages and began reading, and Sid ate her salad in silence. After a few minutes, Carleigh nodded. "Fine. This looks fine." She plucked a pen from Sid's desk and handed it to her sister. "Sign here, Lor."

Lorelai did as she was told and looked up at Sid. "Are we done then?"

Sid forced a smile. "I'll need your phone number, address, and email as well." Lorelai scratched the information on the back of the engagement letter and placed the paperwork on the desk. Sid nodded. "I'll be in touch when I learn something."

Lorelai stood, picked up her iced tea, and stormed out of the office.

"Thank you," said Carleigh after the door slammed shut.

"She really is upset about Cam and, well, all of this. I'm afraid she tends to get ornery when she's upset."

Sid raised an eyebrow. "She must be really upset then."

Carleigh snorted. "Yeah, but I've seen worse. Once when she was little, our dad had to cancel a trip to Disney World during summer vacation, and Lorelai tore her room apart and refused to speak to anyone for a week. So this"—she pointed to the door—"is not too bad, all things considered."

That was exactly what Sid considered as she sat at her desk, eating the rest of her salad after the Sutton sisters departed. Lorelai was prone to fits of rage when she was hurt and disappointed. If the young woman hadn't spent her entire evening in the company of friends at a crowded bar in Jax Beach, an hour north of the Oakmire Golf and Country Club, then Sid would have sworn Lorelai Sutton was the prime suspect in Cameron Chase's murder.

Chapter Twenty-Seven

Later that Sunday afternoon, the members of Recent Geezer set up their instruments in Burt's living room and commenced their jam session with gusto. They were scheduled to play Granny Oak's Music Park the following Thursday and were working out some new set material. Their most loyal groupie, Kitty Lonigan, was in attendance. Kitty was well into her eighties, although she was quite cagey about her exact age, and lived across the street in a yellow house with a porch swing and a front yard filled with rosebushes.

Kitty sat on the sofa and listened to the band, her pink cardigan pulled tight over her narrow, bony shoulders due to the chill in the air around her. That chill was caused by her deceased husband, who stood right behind her, dressed in the light gray seersucker suit and pink bowtie that he'd been buried in. Mr. Lonigan was smiling and bobbing his head to the music while his wife clapped along.

Leo sat with Kitty on the sofa, as far from the spirit of Kitty's dead husband as he could get. He studied the Geezers and their instruments while they played. He had no idea what instrument he might want to try, but he'd secretly like to have a crack at all of them. Maybe he'd have a hidden talent, and the Geezers would help him discover it. Leo crossed and uncrossed his fingers for luck.

After a couple of hours of practice time, the band took a break. Burt went out back to fire up the grill, and Kitty went to busy herself in the kitchen. The rest of the Geezers took turns introducing Leo to their respective instruments. Eli stepped in for Burt on bass guitar, which turned out to be the instrument that Leo took to best. He was hopeless on drums, unable to move his hands and feet at the same time, and though the guitar was fun and something to aspire to play one day, it was the bass guitar that seemed to make the most sense to Leo that afternoon. After their respective turns with Leo, Cesar Hernandez and Guppy Goodwin left the living room, collecting beers from the refrigerator on their way outside to join Burt at the grill. This left Leo alone with Eli Williams.

The big man sat next to Leo on the sofa, giving him basic instructions and helping him with finger placements. After about half an hour, Eli called a halt to the lesson. "I think it's best if we keep it short. Don't want to open up any of those cuts." He took the guitar from Leo and placed it in Burt's stand. "How you feelin'?"

"Fine." Leo gingerly poked at the bandages on his hands and wrists. "Still a little sore."

"I imagine they'll be sore for a while." Eli nodded and took a seat in one of the chairs opposite Leo. "I understand Hattie's comin' by this evenin'." Leo bit his lip and nodded, looking at the big man to see if he was going to say more. Eli smiled. "She told me 'bout your gift. I haven't said anythin' to the others. It ain't my place." He shook his head. "But I think they'd understand. They've seen and done a lot of crazy stuff in their lives.

Learnin' that you see ghosts probably ain't the most shockin' thing they've ever heard."

Leo laughed. "You're probably right."

Eli smiled at the boy. "Anyway, just wanted you to know that I am here to help you in any way I can. I don't have the gift that you and Hattie have, but you can talk to me 'bout it any time you like. I ain't no stranger to the supernatural. My family's been communin' with the dead for generations." He nodded slowly. "When I was a kid, I wished I could do what Hattie can do, wished I could see what she can see, but as I got older, I came to know that it's not always a good thing. In fact, a lot of the time, it ain't no fun at all."

Leo nodded. "It can be pretty scary sometimes."

"I bet it is," said Eli. His deep baritone voice was so kind and soothing that it made Leo almost want to cry. Eli cleared his throat. "Well, I just wanted to tell you that. How 'bout we go check on your grandpa and see if he needs any help with them steaks?"

Leo nodded and entered the kitchen behind Eli when the doorbell rang. "I'll get it," he said, leaving Eli to join the others in the backyard while Kitty hummed away, preparing an enormous bowl of potato salad.

Leo opened the door to find Hattie standing on the front porch. She was wearing another billowing sundress, this one a dark green with large, white flowers, as well as her signature sunglasses. She had a large, canvas tote bag slung over one shoulder. "Hello, Leo."

"Hi, Miss Hattie. Come in." He stepped back and let her enter the house. Hattie looked around the living room, scanning it slowly, and then she turned to Leo with a soft smile. "How you doin'?" She pointed to his bandages. "I understand that you went for a swim."

Leo grinned. "Sort of." He rocked back and forth on his

heels. It felt odd to have her here, standing in his grandfather's living room. This was the strange woman who sat under the tree in the park, the one who saw spirits like he did. Until this moment, Hattie had only ever existed out there—one of the eccentricities of the Old City, and now he felt unsure of what to say or do next.

"Well, we'll see what we can find out." Hattie nodded once and then opened her tote bag, removing two large Tupperware containers. "My grandma's famous cornbread." She grinned. "It's Eli's favorite."

"Awesome!" said Leo, his mouth watering at the sight of the cornbread. He took the containers from her. "I'll put these in the kitchen. Grandpa's grilling steaks right now. I imagine we'll be ready to eat soon." He moved toward the kitchen. "Do you want to come outside with everyone?"

Hattie shook her head. "I think I'll just sit here for a bit. Get a feel for what's here."

Leo's eyebrows shot up. "Oh, okay." He looked around. He'd only ever seen the spirit of Kitty Lonigan's husband in the house, and that only happened when Kitty visited. The spirit only ever arrived with her, and it left when she did. "Um, can I get you something to drink?"

"Sweet tea, if you got it. If not, then never mind." Hattie dropped her tote bag next to the sofa and sat down, her back ramrod straight. She remained quiet and perfectly still, and Leo wondered if her eyes were closed. He couldn't tell because she still wore her sunglasses.

Leo quietly headed for the kitchen. He deposited the cornbread with Kitty, who sampled it and declared it delicious, and then poured Hattie a glass of sweet tea from the pitcher in the fridge. When he returned to the living room, Hattie was nowhere in sight. Her bag sat where she'd dropped it, so Leo knew the old woman couldn't have gone far. He set the glass down on the coffee table and was about to go looking for her when Sid entered the room from the kitchen.

"Hey, kid. I brought that cake I ordered from Dru Chase's mom the other day at the grocery store, but I don't think we'll need it. Have you seen what Kitty made for dessert?" She smiled at him, and Leo took in the light blue dress, sleeveless and belted, with a skirt that fell below her knees. She was also wearing tan sandals with small, blue and white stones embedded in the straps.

Leo frowned. He'd grown so used to seeing her in shorts and T-shirts lately that it was weird to see her like this. "Why are you all dressed up?"

She looked down at her dress. "Oh, I had a meeting earlier." She brushed the memory of it away with a wave of her hand. "I'll tell you about it later. Burt says dinner's almost ready, and he wants you to set the table."

Leo smirked. "Did he really say that?"

Sid placed her hands on her hips and cocked an eyebrow. Leo thought this was probably what she looked like as a teacher, and he bit his lip to suppress his grin. "Yeah, Leo, he really did say that. You want to go ask him yourself?"

Leo shook his head. "No." He trudged past her toward the kitchen. "By the way, Miss Hattie's here." He pointed to her bag. "But I'm not sure where she went."

"I'll find her," said Sid. Leo left to gather plates and napkins, and Sid went in search of their missing guest.

She found Hattie upstairs in Leo's room, sitting cross-legged on the floor. Sid leaned against the doorframe and cleared her throat. "Dinner's ready."

Hattie didn't move for several seconds, and when she did it was to look out the window, not at Sid. "This should be very interestin'," said the old woman. Her voice was more somber than it had been when Sid spoke with her yesterday in the park.

"What do you mean?" Sid stepped into the room. "Dinner? Or... or what's going to happen after?"

"After." Hattie turned to face Sid and grinned. "Although dinner should be interestin', too. Always is when the Geezers get together."

Sid chuckled and helped Hattie to her feet.

They went downstairs and joined the festivities. Dinner was a long, leisurely affair filled with laughter, raunchy stories of the band members' exploits, and plenty of second and third helpings of food. Hattie's cornbread didn't last long. Between Eli and Leo, it was polished off quickly. Kitty had made brownies for dessert. They were dark, decadent treats filled with extra chocolate chips. Leo ate three.

After about two hours, when all the food was gone and plenty of beer had been drunk, Hattie nodded to Sid, who stood up and began clearing the plates. Kitty moved to join her, but Sid waved her off.

She nudged Burt with her elbow, and Burt stood as well. "Thanks for coming, everyone," he said, "but I'm afraid we'll have to call it a night." The others looked around.

Cesar's beer bottle was frozen halfway to his lips. "You kickin' us out, Burt?"

Burt nodded. "I'm afraid so, guys. Leo and I have something to take care of this evening."

It was Eli who finally got everyone moving. He stood and lowered his voice to an even deeper timbre than usual. "It's time to go."

That was all he needed to say. The Geezers hopped up from the table, packed away their instruments, and said their goodbyes. Kitty collected her containers from the kitchen, gave both Burt and Leo a peck on the cheek, and headed home with the spirit of her dead husband trailing behind her. Sid, Burt, and Leo cleared the table. While all this was happening, Hattie sat by herself in the living room.

After the other guests departed, Sid got to work loading the dishwasher, and Burt took out the trash and cleaned up the grill. Leo returned to the living room and found Hattie walking around it with a tightly bound bundle of smoking sticks in one hand. The smell was earthy and pungent.

"What are you doing?" he asked as he pulled his T-shirt up over his nose and mouth. "That smells awful."

"It's called smudging," explained Hattie. "My mamma and aunties taught me how to do it. They'd learned it from their mamma and aunties and from other friends and neighbors, folks who can do what you and I do." She winked at him. "Every one of 'em had their own unique way of doin' it, had their own mix of plants they liked to use."

She passed her free hand back and forth through the smoke, fanning it up toward the ceiling and into the corners of the room. "I took what they taught me and did some experimentin' of my own. Took lots of practice before I got it right, but this"—she waggled the smoking bundle—"works best for me. It's my own special blend: sage, rosemary, lavender, mint, basil and cedar. And I grow all of it in my own backyard."

Leo blinked in surprise. He had never thought of Hattie living in a house or having a garden. He'd only ever seen her in residence under her favorite tree in the Plaza de la Constitución.

Hattie kept fanning the smoke. "Doin' this cleans the energy of a space. Rids it of bad energy. Helps clear the mind. Makes it easier and safer to speak with the other side."

Leo lowered his T-shirt and continued to watch her work the smoke.

"Here, come try it yourself." Hattie waved him over, placed

the bundle in one hand, and showed him what to do with his other. "Now, you go around the room doin' just what I did."

He followed her instructions, waving the smoke toward the ceiling, into the corners, and around the windows and doorways. At the beginning, he coughed and sputtered, but he eventually became used to the smell and was able to take deeper breaths.

Hattie watched him from her perch on the sofa. Leo continued walking around the living room until Sid and Burt returned. He handed the bundle back to Hattie, who pulled a large abalone shell from her tote bag. She placed the bundle in the shell and set the shell on the coffee table. There was very little smoke still wafting up from the bundle, its embers slowly dying out.

"Have a seat." Hattie motioned to the chairs across from her and then patted the sofa cushion next to her. "Leo, come sit by me." Everyone did as they were told.

It was dark now, the sun having set almost an hour ago, and the world outside the house seemed unusually quiet. No cars were rolling up and down the street; there was no breeze blowing through the trees, no frogs or crickets singing their nighttime tunes. Inside the house, it was just as quiet. Hattie had dimmed the lights, leaving on only a couple of lamps on either side of the room. Leo squirmed in his seat while Burt and Sid shot nervous glances at each other.

For the first time since Leo had met Hattie, the old woman took off her sunglasses. She shifted on the sofa so that she could stare directly at him. He held her gaze, marveling at the color of her irises. The left one was a golden amber, the right a golden green.

Hattie reached out and placed her hand over his. "It's here. You know that, right?" Leo blinked in surprise. She nodded in the direction of the staircase, visible through the living room doors. Toward the top of the stairs, almost out of Leo's view, was a darkness that was blacker than the surrounding shadows. His fingers closed around Hattie's, and she gave him a squeeze in return. "It's all right. I'm gonna call it down."

She closed her eyes but continued to hold Leo's hand. Leo watched as the shadow slowly descended the stairs and came to a stop in the living room doorway. Burt and Sid glanced back and forth between the staircase, Hattie and Leo, and each other.

"What are we lookin' at?" whispered Burt. Sid shrugged. The others said nothing.

Hattie tilted her head to the side. "Hmmmm." She opened her eyes and glanced around the room, ignoring the shadow standing in the doorway. Her gaze landed on some photos arranged on an old upright piano in the corner of the room. The piano had belonged to Burt's wife, Camille, Leo's grandmother. It hadn't been played since her death years ago and now served as a repository for family photos and mementos. Hattie pointed to the photos and then turned to Burt. "That your boy?"

Burt squinted up at the photos. A gold-framed photo in the front row showed a boy, a few years younger than Leo, standing next to Burt and holding his bass guitar. The boy was smiling at the camera. Burt pointed to the photo. "Yes, that's Gunner. That's Leo's father."

Hattie nodded and turned to Leo. "Well, he's your shadow."

Less than ten minutes later, it was all over. Hattie's reading didn't reveal much more than the identity of the shadow that had been following Leo for the past two weeks. She had no answers for Leo as to why Gunner Roberts was haunting him, but everyone in the room, including Hattie, agreed that what was happening was undeniably a haunting.

Leo lay in his bed that night, long after Hattie left, the others had gone to bed, and the spirit of his father had vanished. Tears streamed from his eyes, soaking his pillowcase.

Gunner had revealed himself to Hattie and only to Hattie. Leo asked—no, he'd begged—for his father to appear before him, to show him his true form. But he'd refused.

According to Hattie, Gunner had stood in the doorway of the living room in his working naval uniform, the one he'd been wearing on the flight deck the night he went overboard. He was soaking wet, dripping a puddle onto Burt's hardwood floors, but that was all Hattie would reveal about his appearance.

Gunner had said nothing to Hattie, no matter how hard she tried to get him to communicate. And, she'd said the emotions she felt coming from the spirit were hard to decipher. Hattie's best guess was anger and fear, but it was hard for her to determine who Gunner was mad at or why he was afraid.

Hattie had ended the reading abruptly, saying the emotions felt too dark and dangerous to continue safely. She'd ordered Gunner to leave, which had actually worked, and then she'd salted all the doorways and the corners of every room. While she'd been busy, Leo had cried on his grandfather's shoulder, and Sid had paced back and forth across the living room. Hattie gave Sid two more bundles of her special mix of dried sticks, the abalone shell, and instructions for how to smudge the house. As soon as Hattie left, Leo ran upstairs to his room, slammed his door, and dove under the covers.

All Leo wanted in the world was to see his dad again. Gunner had left on deployment nearly six months before his death, and that tour was almost at an end. He was due to come home for shore leave, and they'd made plans as a family to take a vacation in St. Augustine to see Burt, go to the beach, and enjoy the sights. But Gunner Roberts never came home. He went overboard into the water on that stormy night, and he'd left Leo and Paizley with a huge hole in their lives and an even bigger one in their hearts.

Leo didn't understand why his dad would be haunting him. Gunner had always been somewhat distant, never able to relax, never comfortable just being at home. He'd always wanted to be at sea, on the flight deck, among the chaos and noise. Because that was the only place in the world where Gunner Roberts had ever found peace and quiet. It was his sole refuge from the constant barrage of spirits that had plagued him his entire life.

Gunner had never learned to control his gift, and he'd only ever taught Leo two things about it. The first was that blasting music as loud as possible helped a little to drown out the voices, and the second was that the dead were something to be feared. His and Leo's ability to see and talk to spirits was no gift at all. In fact, it was a curse. That's what Gunner had always believed.

So that night, Leo sobbed into his pillow. He cried because his father wouldn't reveal himself. He cried because his father was haunting him, refusing to communicate even with Hattie. And he cried because it was evident that Gunner Roberts hadn't found peace even in death. He was still angry, still fearful, still cursed.

Chapter Twenty-Eight

Sid spent Monday morning doing a deep dive into Noah Zimmerman's social media accounts. She learned that he had turned twenty-three this past July, that he was a die-hard Jacksonville Jaguars fan, and that his favorite food was tacos. Hardly scintillating stuff. What was most surprising was that, for a skinny, awkward young man, Noah Zimmerman had a surprising amount of charisma on camera.

Most of his social media posts—close to 90 percent of them, by Sid's rough estimation—were related to golf. The other 10 percent were photos of food and commentary about Jags games. Noah had dedicated his social media accounts to the promotion of his love for and expertise in the game of golf. There were plenty of photos and videos of his best friend, Cameron Chase: his drives, his putts, his bunker shots out of the sand traps. For each of them, Noah would comment about the efficiency of the swing, the alignment of the ball, and other technical details and strategies, most of which made no sense at all to Sid.

When not featuring Cameron Chase, Noah's posts were

aimed at demonstrating his own skills. There were countless videos starring Noah demonstrating some swing or technique, giving lessons on how to read the green, providing instructions for club selection based on course conditions and wind speed, and so on. The clear message in all of his efforts across his various channels was that Noah Zimmerman was a talented professional who really knew his stuff. He was someone you could learn from. He was someone you wanted by your side, whispering in your ear, helping you become a world-class player. The confident image portrayed in these posts was so at odds with the quiet, shrinking kid, struggling under the weight of heavy golf bags, Sid had met at the club.

When Sid arrived at Oakmire shortly after eleven o'clock that morning, she found Noah sitting by himself in the outdoor smoking area near the cart barn. He was wiping his face with a towel and scrolling through his phone.

"Good morning, Noah." She took a seat across from him.

Noah barely glanced up. "Morning."

"Do you have a few minutes to chat?" Sid put her bag down next to her and crossed her legs. "I'd like to talk to you about Cameron Chase."

Noah glanced at his watch. "Can't. I have to caddy for someone." He stood, shoved his towel into the back pocket of his shorts, and walked off toward the starter's shack.

Sid followed after him. "I'm very sorry for your loss, Noah. It must have been quite a shock to learn about Cameron's death."

"Yeah, it was." Noah kept his head down, continuing to scroll on his phone.

Sid quickened her step to keep up. For as short and slight as he was, Noah was a remarkably fast walker. "Why didn't you mention that you were friends with Cameron when we spoke the other day?"

"You didn't ask about Cam," replied Noah. "You asked about Dru."

"That's true." Sid nodded. "But Cameron was your best friend, and yet you don't seem very upset about his death."

Noah stopped so suddenly that Sid almost blew right past him. "Of course I'm upset." His lips were tight, his voice terse. "Just because I'm not bawling my eyes out doesn't mean that I'm not upset. Now, if you'll excuse me, some of us have work to do." He tried to storm off, but Sid held out a hand to stop him.

"Why did he fire you?" she asked.

"What?" Noah blinked rapidly. "What are you talking about?"

"Cameron Chase fired you." Sid moved to stand in front of him. "You were his caddy, and he sacked you. He hired someone else just in time for the big tournament."

Noah turned his head away from Sid, nostrils flaring. "So?"

"So that must have been a shock," she said. "Couldn't have felt very good, not after all those times you'd caddied for him before. And right on the eve of a major PGA tournament."

Noah shook his head, still staring off into the distance. "It was a smart move. Cam wanted to go to the next level, and Jimbo could help him get there."

Sid frowned. "Jimbo?"

"Yeah, Jimbo Rollins." Noah turned back to look at Sid, his brow furrowing. "He's the caddy Cam hired. Jimbo's been on the tour, gosh, maybe twenty . . . twenty-five years now. The last couple of guys he caddied for moved up to the senior tour, so Jimbo's been looking for a younger golfer to bring him back down to the tour. Get back to the majors, you know." Noah stared at his feet, kicking at the concrete cart path with the toe of his shoe. "He's good. Great, even. He would have been good for Cam."

"Better than you?" asked Sid.

Noah looked up but couldn't meet Sid's eyes. "Probably." He pursed his lips and swallowed hard. "Yeah."

Sid studied the young man's face. It was awash with emotions that he seemed to be struggling to control. "So, is Jimbo Rollins here? When did he start working with Cameron?"

Noah shook his head. "No, he's in California. He was going to fly in for the tournament." Noah huffed. "Jimbo couldn't even be bothered to show up early so they could get to know each other a little. The first time Cam would step foot on a golf course with Jimbo was going to be the morning of the first day of play." He shook his head again. "It was insane."

"Sounds like it." Sid nodded in agreement. "Since Jimbo wasn't going to be around, did Cameron ask you to help him prepare? To help him practice or whatever before the tournament?"

Noah barked out a laugh. "Yeah. He fired me by text. I'd spent the whole afternoon with him, working with him and helping him get ready, and he never said a word. No, he just texted me out of the blue that same night."

Sid itched to pull out her phone and take notes, but she wanted to keep the young man talking. "When was this, Noah?"

"The Wednesday before he died." Noah swallowed hard again. "He just texted me. He couldn't even call me to tell me I was fired, let alone do it face to face. And then he had the nerve to text me the very next day and ask if I'd work out with him. As if nothing had happened. As if he hadn't just cut me loose and told me to go—"

"To go . . . where?" asked Sid.

Noah held Sid's gaze and sighed. "He told me to go fuck myself."

Sid frowned. "Some friend."

Noah nodded as his shoulders slumped. "Yeah, some friend."

"I take it you didn't meet him to practice."

"No."

"So you didn't see him on Friday, the day he died?"

"No." Noah shook his head. "But maybe if I had . . . maybe if I had met him, then maybe he wouldn't have died." The hitch in his voice made it sound more like a question than a statement.

"Maybe," said Sid. "Or maybe you would have met the same fate."

Noah's eyes grew wide, and he nodded once, as if that thought hadn't occurred to him until Sid mentioned it. "I . . . I gotta go. I have a tee time." He pointed to a foursome gathering by the starter's shack.

Sid nodded. "Thanks for your time, Noah." The young man walked off to meet his waiting golfers, and Sid walked back to the parking lot. She pulled out her phone and called Detective Davis.

Tony answered on the first ring. "You must be psychic, Sid. I was just getting ready to swing by your office. You there?"

"No, I'm at Oakmire. Wanna grab lunch?" Sid's stomach was growling, and she realized that she'd poured a bowl of cereal for herself that morning but never eaten it. She'd been distracted by Noah's social media videos, so the cereal was probably a soggy mess still sitting on her kitchen counter.

"Sure," answered Tony. "Stay there. I'll come to you."

Sid waited on the front porch of the Oakmire clubhouse, enjoying a rocking chair in the shade. She made notes on her conversation with Noah and double-checked the young man's social media channels. Unlike Lorelai Sutton, Noah didn't appear to have an alibi for Friday night, but Tony could probably tell her whether that was the case or not.

She'd been waiting about fifteen minutes when a large pickup truck pulled into the parking lot. Shiny and black with oversize wheels, the truck looked brand-new. The driver parked catawampus across two spots and got out. Declan Chase stood next to his truck, checked his hair in the side mirror, and strode across the hot asphalt toward the clubhouse. Sid jumped up from her rocking chair and walked toward the porch steps before her better judgment could talk her out of it.

"Mr. Chase, may I have a word?"

Declan Chase slowed his approach, his eyes roaming over her bare legs, and Sid wished she'd chosen to wear long pants today instead of shorts.

She held out her hand. "My name is Sidney Stone." A slow grin spread across Declan's face as he shook Sid's hand. Sid tried to remove her hand from the big man's grip, but Declan held firm. "I'm very sorry for your loss, Mr. Chase."

"Call me Declan. All my friends do." He brushed his index finger over the inside of Sid's wrist, and Sid had to fight the urge to flinch.

"Declan," Sid began, tugging against Declan's grip before he finally relented and released her hand. "I was very sorry to hear about your son, Cameron."

Declan nodded. "He was a good boy. A real talent. He could have been number one."

"That's what I hear." Sid gave him a mild smile. "You must be devastated."

Declan nodded again. "What parent isn't devastated when they lose a child, especially one as special as Cam?"

Sid pressed her lips firmly together before responding. "That's very true. I lost my daughter several years ago, so I know what you're going through."

"I doubt it." Declan's grin never wavered. "Cam was special."

"I'm sure he was." Sid fought hard to keep her own smile in place. "I understand he was expected to do well in that big tournament this past weekend."

"To win it, you mean." Declan slid a half step closer to Sid. "My son would have won the whole thing."

"Even though he'd never worked with his new caddy before?" Sid slid back half a step, bumping into the porch railing. "Seems like quite a leap of faith."

Declan's hand slammed into the column next to Sid, a move so quick she didn't register what was happening until he was leaning closer toward her. "See, the thing you don't know about golf is that caddies are irrelevant. They're simply there to carry your bag, pass you the clubs, and take the flag in and out of the hole. All that nonsense about them calling the shots and reading the greens, it's all bullshit. The golfer is the star of the show. His caddy is nothing but a glorified errand boy in shorts and a bib."

Sid noted Declan's use of the words "his" and "boy" as if golfers and caddies weren't also women. "So it wouldn't have mattered who Cameron had as his caddy, whether it was Jimbo Rollins or Noah Zimmerman?"

Declan turned his head away and snorted with laughter. "That little punk? The only reason Noah ever carried my son's bag was because his daddy paid me for it." Declan grinned. "But to answer your question, no. It wouldn't have mattered whether it had been Noah or Jimbo or little Red Riding Hood. My son was the real talent. He would have won the whole damn thing, even if he'd been carrying his own bag."

Sid worked to keep her expression neutral. "Did you know that Cameron had fired Noah and hired Jimbo?"

Declan shrugged one shoulder. "Doesn't matter."

"But you said Noah's father paid you to let Noah caddy for your son." Sid raised an eyebrow. "Did he ask for his money back?"

Declan merely licked his lips and ran his gaze all over Sid.

Sid tasted bile in the back of her throat, and she leaned away from him. She pointed over her shoulder toward the parking lot. "Did you spend Noah's daddy's money on that shiny, new truck?"

Declan's other hand shot out and gripped the porch railing next to Sid, effectively caging her in. She could smell Declan's breath, a sour mix of coffee and cigarettes. "Why are you asking so many questions?"

Sid ignored him. "I'm sorry about your nephew, Dru, too." Sid saw a small twitch in the man's left eye, the only movement in his otherwise stony expression. "To lose two young family members at the same time and under such terrible circumstances, it must be an ordeal for your whole family."

"It is," Declan growled.

Sid waited for him to say something about Dru Chase's death, but Declan remained silent. "I'm sure Dru's death was an accident," she said. She paused, noting the muscles flexing in Declan's jaw. "Wasn't it?"

"How would I know?" His nostrils flared.

Sid gave him another smile. "I understand you were there."

Another twitch of his eyelid. "You don't know what you're talking about," Declan snarled.

"The alligator bit Dru," began Sid, trying to keep her voice steady, "but instead of trying to help your nephew, you shot him with a crossbow."

It happened so fast that Sid was powerless to react. One moment, Declan was glaring at her, his face so close that she could smell his breath, and the next moment his hands were around her throat.

"Shut up!" Declan bellowed.

Sid couldn't breathe. Declan was squeezing her throat and lifting her up so that her toes barely touched the wooden planks under her feet. She tried to pry his fingers away from her throat, but the man's grip was like a vice.

He leaned in close and growled, "I was aiming for the gator." He chuckled and then pressed his lips to the shell of Sid's ear. "No great loss, though."

Sid reached out, scratching Declan's face and drawing blood. She tried to go for his eyes, but he straightened his long arms. The move pushed her away from him, bending her even farther back over the railing, but at least her feet were now flat on the floor. She tried to kick out, but Declan pressed his knees against her legs. Sid scratched at his arms, drawing more blood.

"Let her go! Now!"

Declan released his hold and stepped back in one quick movement. Sid's legs gave way beneath her, and she collapsed to the ground, gasping for air and sputtering with the effort. Tears stung her eyes and rolled down her cheeks as she brought a trembling hand to her throat. It hurt to swallow, to breathe.

All the while she was gasping for air, lying in a heap on the veranda, Declan's whispered words played over and over again in her head: *No great loss, though.*

Chapter Twenty-Nine

"What the hell were you thinking?!" shouted Tony as he stood in front of Sid. His arms were crossed, feet wide apart, and nostrils flaring. "Are you trying to get yourself killed? Is that it?"

Sid sat on the porch steps of the Oakmire clubhouse and watched Deputies Adcock and Weber load a handcuffed Declan Chase into the back of their patrol vehicle. It was Tony who had arrived in time to see Declan strangling Sid. It was Tony who had drawn his gun and ordered Declan to stop. And it was Tony who had handcuffed Declan, read him his rights, and called for backup. Sid had missed all of it. She'd been too busy having the life choked out of her and then lying on the ground, struggling to catch her breath. By the time she'd stopped crying and shaking and was breathing with any sort of regularity, the additional deputies had arrived.

Tony held out a hand to her. "Come on, let's go."

"Where?" croaked Sid.

"To the hospital." When Sid shook her head at him, he

lifted her to her feet and led her to his car. "Get in. This isn't up for discussion."

Sid sat in the passenger seat, staring out the window and trying not to swallow too much. They drove in silence for a few minutes until Tony finally blurted out, "What the hell, Sid?"

Sid sighed and then cringed when that simple act caused spikes of pain. When she spoke, her voice barely worked. "He admitted to killing Dru."

"I know," Tony replied. Sid swung her head to face him, wincing in pain. Tony nodded. "Jonathan Beedlemeyer heard Declan say that he was aiming for the gator. The old man was beating on Declan, trying to get him to let go of you, when I arrived."

Sid stared out the front window. Beedlemeyer? How had she not seen him trying to help her? "I didn't know he was there."

"Well, you were a little busy being strangled to notice much." Tony glanced sideways at her and smirked. "And you'll be glad to know that I called a friend at Channel 7, and I gave Adcock and Weber strict instructions not to take Chase out of the car and walk him into the building until the cameras started rolling."

Sid smiled. "Thanks."

Tony nodded. "You're welcome. And you'll also be happy to know that we arrested the two poachers you caught on camera. The one who works as a groundskeeper at Oakmire is Dru Chase's mother's brother. Not a blood relative of Declan, but still a member of the family. The man's a junkie who's been in and out of jail since he was a teenager. He told us that Declan agreed to pay him a thousand dollars if he poached Big Boy. You know the one? That big alligator out there?"

"Yeah, I know about Big Boy." Sid squinted into the sun. "Dru's mom told me that Declan only offered Dru a hundred dollars." She shook her head. "When Declan was strangling me, he said that Dru's death was no great loss. Can you believe it? His own nephew. Did Beedlemeyer hear that part?"

"I don't think so." Tony heaved a sigh. "Declan Chase is a real piece of work, isn't he?"

Sid gently touched her neck. "He certainly is."

———

It was dinnertime when Sid arrived back home, and she was starving. Burt and Leo met her in the driveway and ushered her into the house, where she joined them at the kitchen table. They ate barbecued chicken that Burt had cooked on the grill while Sid dug into a carton of ice cream, picking out the chocolate chips and leaving them in a small pile. She could barely swallow ice cream, so chewing anything was beyond her ability at that moment.

Using as few words as possible, Sid told Burt and Leo about her run in with Declan, his arrest and her visit with Naomi Davis in the emergency room. "Nothing broken. Just bruised. Swelling."

"So, what happens now?" asked Leo, wiping barbecue sauce off his chin.

Sid shrugged, then said hoarsely, "Right now, I'm going to take some painkillers and go to bed." The cold of the ice cream had helped. She put her spoon in the sink and the empty ice cream carton in the trash.

"I meant with the case," said Leo. "What happens now that Declan confessed to shooting Dru with the crossbow?"

"I'll talk to Beedlemeyer and see if he wants us to continue. With Declan and two of his poachers in jail, I doubt that they'll be back on the job any time soon. But that doesn't mean that whoever was funding them won't take their business elsewhere." Sid opened the door and stood in the doorway. "Frankly, I'll be happy to be done with this case."

"I'll go with you when you talk to Beedlemeyer," announced Leo.

"Absolutely not!" blurted Sid and Burt in unison.

Sid touched her throat and winced. "You'll stay far away from it."

"But you took me off the case because Declan Chase was dangerous." Leo held out his hands, pleading his case. "Now, he's in jail. What's the danger?"

Sid glanced at Burt who gave the slightest shake of his head. "Sorry, kid, but the danger's not over," she replied. "Whoever hired Declan did so because Declan is a brute and would do the job by whatever means were necessary. There's no telling who'll they'll try to hire next."

Sid left Leo sulking in the kitchen and made her way back to the garage and upstairs to her little apartment. She downed the pain meds Naomi had given her at the hospital and curled up in bed.

No great loss, though. Those words played over and over in her head until she finally succumbed to sleep.

Sid left messages for Jonathan Beedlemeyer for the next two days, but the chairman of the board never returned her call. By Thursday afternoon, Sid was tired of waiting. She drove to the Oakmire Golf and Country Club. Beedlemeyer was not in his office, nor in the clubhouse, and he wasn't answering his cell phone.

The course ranger in the starter's shack confirmed that the chairman was out on the course, so Sid sat on the back veranda and waited. A foursome of golfers finished up on the eighteenth hole, left their golf carts and bags on the cart path, and made their way into the clubhouse. Unfortunately, Beedlemeyer wasn't among them.

Noah Zimmerman arrived to drive one of the carts back to the barn and take care of the bags. Sid abandoned her rocking chair on the veranda and walked over to the second golf cart. When Noah returned for that second cart, he found Sid sitting behind the wheel.

"Hop in," she said. "I'll drive."

Noah climbed in, scowling. "You're not supposed to be driving the carts. Not unless you're a member or a guest of a member."

"I'm a guest of a member," replied Sid, navigating her way to the cart barn.

Noah crossed his arms. "Who?"

Sid smiled at him. "Jonathan Beedlemeyer."

"Oh," said Noah. He sat up straighter. "I didn't know. Sorry."

"That's quite all right." Sid waved the matter away with a flick of her wrist. "You had no reason to know. Just like I had no reason to know that your father paid Declan Chase money so that you could caddy for Cameron."

Noah spun around so fast that he had to grip the top of the cart to keep from toppling out. "H-how . . . that's not . . . it wasn't like that," Noah sputtered, his eyes growing wide.

Sid came to a halt under the shade of an old oak. She engaged the parking brake and turned to look at the young man. "Then tell me what it was like, Noah."

Noah seemed to deflate before her eyes. He slumped down in the seat, his arms going slack by his sides and his gaze drifting to the azaleas next to the cart. "I caddied for Cam because I'm good at it." He turned pleading eyes to Sid. "I really am."

Sid smiled. "I believe you. I've seen your videos."

"Really?" A slight smile curved Noah's lip. "I am good. And Cam knew it. He started winning when I was on the course with him." But Noah's face fell again, and he stared straight ahead. "I know my stepdad paid Declan money. He thought he had to do it so that Cam would hire me as his caddy, but that wasn't the case. Cam would have hired me anyway. But Declan needed the money, and my stepdad has loads to spare, so Cam and I kept our mouths shut. We let our fathers think they were brokering some sort of deal for us, but the reality was that it didn't matter. I got to caddy for Cam. Cam started winning. Declan got paid. And my stepdad felt like the big man he thinks he is." Noah shrugged. "Everybody wins."

"Until Cam fired you," noted Sid.

Noah nodded. "Yeah, until he fired me."

"That wasn't part of the plan, was it?" asked Sid.

"No." Noah sighed and squinted into the sun. "When Cam got word that he was going to play in the major, my stepdad paid Declan a bonus to ensure that I would caddy for him. But Cam had other plans. He fired me and hired Jimbo Rollins. By then, Declan had already spent the money, and Cam couldn't ask for it back, so he tried to pay my stepdad back himself."

Sid shifted in her seat. "How much did he owe your stepdad?"

"Ten grand." Sid raised an eyebrow, and Noah nodded, adding, "I know. Nice bonus, huh?"

Sid recalled Declan's shiny, new pickup truck. The bonus had probably served as the down payment. "Did Cameron have that kind of money?"

"He had half of it." Noah scratched at a grass stain on his khaki shorts. "But he had to borrow the other half."

Sid nodded. She now had an answer as to where Lorelai

Sutton's five thousand dollars had gone. "How did your stepdad respond?"

Noah shrugged. "Fine, I guess. I wasn't home when Cam came by to drop off the money. By then, I'd already been fired, and my stepdad knew all about it." He squinted into the sun again. "He blamed me, of course. My stepdad." Noah shook his head once. "Told me that I blew my big chance to make something of myself. Blah blah blah. You know, all the usual stuff. My stepdad's only ever been proud of my caddying ability. Until he realized that I was good at it, he thought I was a waste of time and space." He scratched at the grass stain again. "He's always reminding me of how he made his fortune through grit and hard work and whatever. Told me I had to do the same. And I'm trying. I really am." He shook his head again and looked away. "But it's not enough. It's never enough for him."

"I'm sorry," Sid murmured. And she was. Noah Zimmerman was still just a kid, one who had a talent but would still never measure up in his father's eyes.

"I need to get back to work," said Noah with a sniffle.

Sid got out, and Noah slid across the seat to take her place behind the wheel. "Hey," she called, "when did Cameron give the money to your dad?"

"Friday morning." Noah released the parking brake. "And Rocco's not my dad. He's my stepdad."

"Wait!" Sid grabbed Noah's arm before he could drive away. "Rocco Castiglione is your stepfather?"

Noah Zimmerman nodded. "Yeah. You know him?"

Chapter Thirty

Leo had been sulking for the last three days, and his grandfather had finally had enough. That's how Leo found himself once again playing roadie for Recent Geezer at Granny Oak's Music Park on Thursday night, but unlike all the other times, his heart just wasn't in it.

The injuries from his recent swim in Matanzas Bay had healed well enough that he was able to help lug the equipment from Guppy's van to the venue, assist the band with setup, and fetch them drinks. When they were busy chatting among themselves, Leo slipped out of the park and jogged down St. George Street to the N'Ice Day Ice Cream Shop to see if Ellie was working.

He came to a halt outside the shop, staring through the big window under the faded green awning. Ellie was indeed working, and his heart gave a little flutter. It was crowded in the shop. At least a dozen teenagers, most of them large, tall boys, were standing around the cases of ice cream. A few of the boys wore Saint Augustine High School Football T-shirts. One of the boys, the tallest of the bunch, was leaning on the counter, chatting with Ellie. He reached out and wrapped his fingers around the end of her ponytail, tugging it gently. Ellie giggled.

Leo blinked hard, as if to clear his vision. She giggled? Is that really what just happened? And who was that tall kid with his hands in Ellie's hair? Leo watched as Ellie playfully pushed him away but then immediately leaned toward him, smiling and flirting. That's it, thought Leo, suddenly realizing exactly what he was seeing. Ellie Owen was flirting. And she was doing it with someone other than himself.

Leo turned around and walked back to Granny Oak's. It was at this moment that Leo finally understood his boss's obsession with running. Sid didn't seem to love the sport, but she did it often and told Leo that it helped her clear her head. Right then, that was exactly what he wanted. He wanted to clear his head of what he'd just witnessed. Ellie—his Ellie—had been fawning over some football player who went to her high school. Leo wanted to burst into a run, legs pumping and lungs burning, anything to take his mind off her.

But he didn't. He simply shuffled along St. George Street, following the music back to Granny Oak's. He didn't run because, first of all, he was wearing flip-flops, and the last thing he wanted was to trip and face-plant in front of all the tourists. Second, he didn't have any idea where he would go. The last time he had ventured off in the night by himself, he'd ended up in the Matanzas Bay, which had led to a trip to the emergency room. And lastly, he didn't really know how to run. He could sprint a little, that was easy enough, but for the kind of mental and emotional therapy he needed, a fifty-yard dash wasn't going to cut it. Perhaps he'd ask Sid to teach him, help him train. Knowing how to run for long distances might come in handy in the future—for both mental clear-outs and private investigation.

Leo stopped at the entrance to Granny Oak's and listened

to the Geezers play. If he remembered the set list correctly, they'd just begun their second song, "Free Fallin'" by Tom Petty. How fitting, thought Leo. It was like they'd chosen the song with him in mind. Perhaps they had. Leo smirked at the idea.

His phone buzzed in his pocket, showing a series of texts from his mom:

> Hey Leo
>
> In GA mountains
>
> Up for a quick call?

Leo's heart raced as he dialed his mom's number. "Mom!" he shouted when she answered his call. "How are you? You're still in Georgia? I thought you were coming to Florida. You were supposed to be coming here." He knew he was acting a bit manic; he could hear it in his voice.

"I know, kiddo, but we changed our plans. We were in Athens and this woman at a diner near our campsite told us we needed to go check out Dahlonega and Helen, so we did. We're up in a place called Unicoi State Park. It's really pretty. Bet it will be even prettier in another month or so when the leaves start changing."

Leo had wandered away from Granny Oak's toward the north end of St. George Street and emerged by the City Gate. This time, he turned away from the old fort and crossed Orange Street to a small patch of grass in front of a four-foot-tall stone wall. "Sounds nice, but when are you coming back?"

"Soon, Leo," said Paizley. "Maybe in a couple of weeks. Shouldn't be too long, though. We're heading south after this." Leo could tell his mom was tired because her voice had a vocal fry that was only present when she was bone-weary. He'd heard it often as a kid when she was working two jobs.

"You okay, Mom?" Leo leaned back against the wall, careful to avoid the still-healing cuts, and stared at the tourists walking past.

"I'm fine, kiddo. Just tired." As if on cue, Paizley yawned. Leo also heard the little dog Jezebel in the background, her high-pitched yapping making his head hurt. This was followed immediately by Brooklyn scolding the poor creature, although the precise words she used were mercifully muffled by the weak cell phone connection.

"Mom, can I ask you something?" Leo bit his lip for a moment, unsure how to phrase what he wanted to say. "Was Dad ever . . . was he . . ." Leo sighed before trying again. "Why was Dad mad at me?"

"Mad at you?" Paizley sounded startled by the question. "What are you talking about? Why would you think that? Did Burt say something? Put him on the phone!"

Leo smiled. It felt good to have her sticking up for him. He hadn't been so sure that she wanted him anymore, not after leaving him on Burt's doorstep, but he could hear in her voice that she still cared. "No, Mom. Grandpa didn't say anything. It's, well, it's just a sense I have. I thought maybe Dad was mad at me for some reason."

There was silence on the other end of the line for a few moments, and Leo wondered whether they'd been disconnected. "When you say 'sense,' do you mean what I think you mean?" asked Paizley, her words coming out low and clipped.

"No. Sort of . . . not really," Leo stuttered. "It's not what you think. I just sort of . . . I don't know. I think maybe I feel him a little. Sense him." He couldn't tell his mom that Gunner Roberts was haunting him, appearing as a dark shadow and scaring him into tumbling off a wall into the bay. "It's not a big deal. Nothing bad has happened." Leo stared at the cuts on his arm, wrist, and hand. They were healing well. Even the deeper ones were starting to scab over.

"Leo," said Paizley, her voice more soothing now but still fried with exhaustion. "Your father loved you very much. He was a good dad."

"I know." Leo jabbed at the patchy grass under his feet with the toe of his flip-flop.

"He wasn't mad at you. He was never mad at you. Not even when you were being a pain in the ass." Paizley chuckled, and Leo smiled at the sound. He missed it so much. "If anything, he felt guilty."

At this, Leo pushed away from the wall and stood up straight. "What do you mean, Mom?"

"Well, you know." Even though Leo couldn't see her, he knew that she had just shrugged. That was always her response whenever this topic came up. Paizley cleared her throat. "He felt guilty that he passed his curse on to you. It just tore him up inside. 'Cause, Leo, you know how much he struggled with it. He couldn't control it, and so he couldn't teach you how to control it either. He always felt so bad about that."

"Oh," Leo replied, his shoulders slumping. "Yeah, I know he struggled with it." He looked up at the bright streetlights of St. Augustine and thought of Sid and Hattie and Val, all of them trying to help him these past couple of weeks. For the first time in a long time, Leo didn't feel so afraid. "But it's not a curse, Mom. It's really not. I've met some people here who can do what I do, and they can control it. They're teaching me how. And it's working. It's really helping."

"Who are these people, Leo?!" Paizley's voice went up almost a full octave. "Does Burt know? Has he met them? You haven't given them any money, have you?!" Leo could hear the notes of panic in her tone.

"It's okay, Mom. Grandpa knows one of them. She's the

cousin of one of his bandmates. We had dinner with her the other night. She's being really helpful." He heard her start to protest but cut her off. "And no, I haven't given anyone any money. They're not con artists. They're mediums." He smiled, even though his mom couldn't see it. "Like me."

He hung up with his mom a couple of minutes later, when Brooklyn cranked up her blender to make margaritas. He slipped the phone in his pocket and turned around, leaning on the stone wall with his elbows and taking in the view beyond. Headstones of various shapes and sizes dotted the quiet space on the other side of the wall known as the Huguenot Cemetery. Leo took in a huge breath of warm night air and smiled. There were no spirits here, no icy temperatures, just peace and tranquility. He'd always liked cemeteries and graveyards. Spirits stayed away from them. They liked crowds and parties, anyplace where the living were doing just that—living.

Leo closed his eyes and let the warm breeze off the bay wrap around him, making soft music in the branches overhead. And then he felt it. An icy grip on his upper left arm.

"No!" yelled Leo. He yanked his arm away from the invisible hand and stumbled backward, his heel catching on an exposed tree root. He landed hard on his backside.

"Whoa there!" exclaimed a voice behind him. "You okay there, matey?"

Leo felt two strong hands grip him under his arms and haul him to his feet. Spinning around, he came face to face with a pirate. Leo blinked in surprise.

The pirate, who was dressed in an over-the-top ensemble of a frilly, white shirt, baggy pantaloons, and a red, suede vest embroidered with gold thread, smiled at him. The man had wiry, gray hair pulled back in a low ponytail and a thick, full gray beard. A large, black tricorn hat sat atop his head. The pirate was taller than Leo by a good three or four inches and was easily twice as wide, with broad shoulders and a sizeable gut. His nametag read, "Pirate Gregg."

"Did ya see somethin', matey?" Pirate Gregg practically growled the question, squinting one eye for added effect. "A ghost perhaps?"

"Um . . . uh," Leo stammered. He looked around and only then noticed a group of about a dozen people standing behind Pirate Gregg. They were all ages and sizes, including an elderly man with a cane and a young couple pushing a sleeping toddler, and all of them were staring at him. He shrugged. "Sort of."

That was all the encouragement that Pirate Gregg and his ghost tour group needed. They pushed past Leo and pressed themselves against the stone wall surrounding the cemetery.

A chorus of questions rang out from the tour group: "Where?" "What did it look like?" "Did it say anything?" "I don't see it, do you?" "What are we looking for?" "Is that it?" "Where?"

One woman, a buxom, bottle-dyed blonde who Leo would have guessed was a little younger than his grandfather, swung back around to face him. Pointing her finger at him, she demanded, "What did you see? Where was it? Tell us right now, young man."

"No," Leo replied with a sneer. "No. Find it yourself." The woman gawped at him, clearly not expecting to be denied her ghost sighting. Leo had no time for her or anyone else who thought it was their right to demand that spirits and ghosts and any other mysteries of the universe be revealed to them simply because they wanted it. He turned on his heels and left the blonde woman, Pirate Gregg, and the rest of the ghost tour to their hunt.

Glancing over his shoulder, Leo saw the dark shadow standing not more than ten feet from the blonde woman. She was oblivious to it. Leo stopped walking and watched as the shadow drifted closer to the woman. In the blink of an eye, the shadow enveloped the woman, and she yelped. Leo assumed her outburst was the result of feeling the shadow's stinging cold presence. The woman spun around, flailing her arms. The shadow stepped away for a few seconds and then swooped in again, causing the woman to yelp and jump and flap about.

Leo, watching this strange dance between the blonde woman and the shadow, couldn't help but laugh. Perhaps his dad was having a bit of fun. Leo certainly hoped that was the case. The woman wasn't hurt, just frightened. "Serves you right," he muttered to himself. "Thanks, Dad."

The shadow stopped tormenting the woman and floated away, coming to a stop on the sidewalk across the street from where Leo was standing. Leo turned and ran down St. George Street as fast as he could in his flip-flops, ducking into the relative safety of Granny Oak's Music Park just as Recent Geezer began to play the first few chords of King Harvest's "Dancing in the Moonlight."

Leo fought his way through the crowd to the side of the stage where the band's instrument cases were stacked up. His lungs hurt from sprinting, and he made a mental note to really talk to Sid about taking up running. Leo bent over, hands on his knees, and took in great gulps of the warm, beer-tinged night air. When he finally looked up, he had to bite his lower lip to keep from screaming.

The shadow stood in front of the stage, right in the middle of the dozen or so people who were dancing to the beat. The dancers seemed not to notice, and Leo sensed that the shadow was watching both him and the band.

Recent Geezer finished their set, packed up their instruments, and headed home. When Guppy dropped off Burt and Leo at their house on Saragossa Street, the shadow was waiting for them in the backyard. When Burt and Leo entered the house through the kitchen door, the shadow remained where it was. And when Leo finally turned out the lights to crawl into bed, he peeked out his bedroom window and saw the dark shadow—his father, still waiting for him in the backyard.

Chapter Thirty-One

Early on Friday morning, Sid met Detective Tony Davis at the St. Johns County sheriff's office off of US Highway 1, a few miles north of the Old City's historic downtown district. She brought with her two cups of coffee and two dozen donuts from Fire in the Hole.

"Why do I get the feeling you're going to ask for something big?" asked Tony as he took the boxes of donuts from Sid and ushered her down the hall to his desk. He shared a two-person workstation with another officer, who hadn't arrived yet, so Sid took the other chair and spun to face Tony.

"I need to ask a favor." She smiled. "Well, a couple of favors."

Tony removed the lid on his coffee to allow it to cool a bit and removed a donut from the top box. "I'm not gonna like this, am I?"

"Probably not." Sid shook her head. "I need to know whether you're looking at Lorelai Sutton as a suspect or a person of interest."

Tony raised an eyebrow. "Why?"

Sid sat back, the chair squeaking in much the same manner as her own desk chair back in her office. "Lorelai and her sister came to see me. Do you know Carleigh Sutton?"

Tony nodded. "Lawyer. Practices family law mostly, if I'm not mistaken. She does some pro bono work for the guardian ad litem office, so I've seen her in court a few times."

Sid shuddered. If Tony saw Carleigh Sutton in court where she was appointed as guardian ad litem, then the case likely involved child abuse, neglect, or abandonment. It was necessary and admirable work, and Sid marveled that Carleigh would volunteer her time to help the children in such cases.

"Well, Carleigh brought Lorelai to see me, and they've hired me to help them find out whether Lorelai is being treated as somehow involved in Cameron Chase's death." Sid gave Tony a weak half smile. "Care to help a girl out with that?"

Tony blew out his cheeks. "You met the girlfriend. What do you think?"

Sid had been hoping that Tony wouldn't ask her that question, but here it was. "Ex-girlfriend, technically speaking. And I don't know," she answered honestly. "Her personality seems a bit volatile, but I also think that she loved him, or at least cared about him."

"Lots of crimes are committed in the name of love, Sid." Tony took a bite of his donut and waited for her response.

She thought carefully before speaking again. "Lorelai has a solid alibi for that night." Tony nodded his agreement, and Sid continued. "She had an on-again, off-again relationship with Cameron for years. In fact, they were both on and off that very week he died." Tony nodded again. "But I don't think she would resort to killing him or even hiring someone to kill him. Lorelai Sutton could do a lot more harm to Cameron just by using social media." Sid grabbed her phone and began scrolling. "She posted a video a couple of weeks ago bashing Cameron in about a dozen different ways. It got tens of thousands of likes." Sid found the video and held it up for Tony to see. "If she really wanted to hurt Cameron Chase, she just had to make another video. Or lots of videos. He was becoming famous, so people would take notice if his longtime girlfriend began telling the world he was a jackass. It might have distracted him, compromised his golf game and his winnings. He might have lost sponsorships over it. She could have done a lot of damage this way."

"I've seen the video." Tony took a sip of coffee. "And I agree with you. I don't think she killed him." He held up a finger as Sid began to breathe a sigh of relief. "However, we are still looking into whether she had any connection to whoever did kill him." He shrugged one shoulder. "But I don't think she did it herself."

Sid smirked. "So you're saying it's official then? It wasn't death by alligator?"

Tony shook his head. "Technically, he drowned, but the contributing factor was death by golf club. The injury to his skull is consistent with being struck with a golf club. Most likely an iron. And the blow would have knocked him out. Someone pushed him into the water, and he drowned. The alligators got him later." He took another sip of coffee while Sid digested that bit of gruesome news.

"Then the blow to his head must have been done with a lot of force," Sid proposed.

Tony nodded. "Whoever hit him was likely either someone really strong, who used sheer brute force, or someone with an understanding of how to swing a club. Someone who appreciated what kind of speed and range of motion were needed in order to effectively strike that kind of killing blow."

Sid folded her arms. "That rules out Lorelai Sutton. She didn't play golf, and I doubt she had the strength to muscle it out."

"Agreed," said Tony, holding up a finger again. "But for the actual murder. It doesn't rule her out for a possible conspiracy to commit murder."

"Right." Sid chewed on her bottom lip, thinking she'd like to see Lorelai's cell phone records, bank statements, emails, and social media comments, anything that might implicate her in the planning or arranging of her ex-boyfriend's murder. "That's helpful, Tony. Thanks."

"Unfortunately," added the detective, "it doesn't rule out everyone else who had access to the golf course that day—residents, guests, employees, contractors, you name it. The murder took place on a golf course. Lots of people there knew how to swing a club."

Sid snorted. "Are you sure about that? I've seen some of those so-called golfers. There are quite a few of them who can't even find the fairway despite the fact that it's stretched out in front of them." Tony chuckled, and Sid smiled at the detective. "Now, for the other favor."

"Ugh," Tony moaned, brushing donut glaze and crumbs off his fingers.

Sid crossed one leg over the other. "I want to talk to Declan Chase."

Tony stilled, his coffee cup halfway to his mouth. "Oh, sure, because that went so well for you the last time you two had a little chat."

Sid continued, "And I'd like you to come with me."

"So, I can pull him off of you when he tries to strangle you again?" Tony put his cup back down on his desk. "Sid, I don't—"

"He won't try to kill me this time." Sid shook her head. "I want to offer him a deal."

"A deal?"

"Yes."

"What kind of deal?"

"I'm going to offer not to press charges if he tells me everything he knows about the poaching operation: who approached him, who paid him, how much money was involved, who else he hired to help, where he took the alligators, who bought them from him, everyone he talked to, all of it." Sid batted her lashes. "I just need you there as backup."

Tony shook his head. "That might be the dumbest idea I've ever heard. He's been charged with battery, Sid. He could get prison time. Not a lot, but some is better than none."

Sid shook her head. "No, I need him to tell me who hired him. Besides, if I don't want to press charges, then that's that."

Tony chuckled. "Sorry, Sid. But the state attorney doesn't actually need you to testify. They have two other witnesses: Jonathan Beedlemeyer and me." He jabbed his sternum with his index finger. "I'm their witness. I saw him strangling you. I was present when it happened."

Sid groaned in frustration. "If Declan agrees to cut a deal, to name names and all that jazz, then you and the state attorney can wrap up a poaching ring, including some rich bigwigs who are financing it all." Tony ran a hand down his face, but Sid pressed on. "As I understand it, alligator poaching is a third-degree felony. If Declan agrees to the deal, then you're right. He won't go to prison on the battery charge. But other folks—and some pretty important ones at that—could go away for quite a while."

Tony took a deep breath, considering her argument. "The state attorney would have to agree."

Sid grabbed the second box of donuts. "Then let's go ask her."

Chapter Thirty-Two

Tessa Barnes, the state attorney for St. Johns County, plucked a datil-pepper-glazed donut from the box, sat back in her chair, and closed her eyes. Sid and Tony remained silent as Tessa savored her first bite. She swallowed, opened her eyes, and glared at the two of them. "You've got two minutes. Make 'em count."

"Got it," said Sid, sitting forward in her chair. "I want you to offer Declan Chase a deal."

"Why on earth would I do that?" Tessa picked a bit of glaze off her donut and placed it on her tongue.

"Because it would incentivize him to roll over on an alligator poaching ring," Sid offered. "Declan Chase was hired by someone at the Oakmire Golf and Country Club—someone with money—to do some illegal poaching. This person, or maybe there's more than one, wants to rid the property of alligators so that the PGA will accept the club's bid to bring a major golf tournament to Oakmire."

Tessa frowned. "And you know this is happening because?"

"Because the board of directors hired me to find evidence

of poaching so they could put a stop to it." Sid pulled out her phone and began scrolling through her photos.

"We arrested two men who were poaching in the marsh at the Oakmire golf course. One of them shot at Sid," Tony added.

"Right. We charged them with the shooting." Tessa nodded. "But we didn't charge them with poaching."

Tony shook his head. "Not yet."

Sid held out her phone to Tessa. As the state attorney scrolled through the photos of the two poachers, Sid explained, "I don't think these guys know much more than who hired them, and that was Declan Chase." Sid returned her phone to her bag when Tessa finished. "Declan's the go-between. He's the one who can point the finger at the money man—or woman or . . . or whoever—and maybe even the people downstream, the ones who buy the alligators once they're caught and killed."

Tessa swiveled in her chair and stared out her window. "He'd have to give up everything to make it worth my time—I don't like the idea of letting him off easy. That guy has a long list of near misses, and I'd love to finally see him spend some time in prison." She swung back around to them. "Besides, I hate seeing his ugly face on my television. I don't care if his son did just die, that man gets on my last nerve."

"Agreed." Sid smiled at Tessa and then at Tony. "So, how do we go about this?"

Sid had been hoping that the plan would involve her wearing a wire or something equally clandestine, but Tessa and Tony had nixed all of her suggestions and taken a much more pragmatic approach. Subtlety be damned, apparently.

Tony had Declan Chase brought over from the St. Johns County jail, where he was awaiting trial. The judge had denied bail at his arraignment, so Declan's media tour had been cut short by his residency at the county's main detention center. When he arrived at the sheriff's office, he was placed in a tiny room and left there to stew by himself for almost two hours. Watching on the monitor, Sid was fairly certain that Declan had fallen asleep with his head on the table. She, on the other hand, was pacing back and forth and driving Tony crazy.

Finally, at a little before five o'clock, Tessa Barnes joined them. She sat down in front of the monitor and crossed her legs. "Let's hurry this along. I have plans for happy hour."

Sid palmed the door handle and took a deep breath. Now that she was here, she regretted insisting that she be the one to talk to Declan and offer him the deal. They'd all agreed that she was the one with the most knowledge about the poaching case, but Sid knew nothing about interviewing suspects or playing cop—either good or bad. What seemed like a good plan a few hours ago now seemed like a folly. Perhaps Tony was right. Maybe this was her dumbest idea ever.

Sid opened the door and stepped inside the room. Declan Chase, his face turned away from the door, didn't even bother to raise his head from the table. "Good afternoon, Mr. Chase. Remember me?"

Declan grunted but didn't bother to look up. Sid took the seat opposite him at the table and folded her arms. They sat that way for a full minute before Declan finally sat back, blinked hard, and glared at Sid. "What are you doin' here? Came back so I can finish the job, eh?"

Sid smirked when she saw the scratches she'd given him were still visible on his face and arms. "Wow. That's a whole new level of stupid that I haven't seen before. Threatening to kill me. In a police station."

"Sheriff's office."

"Whatever."

"Maybe I was talking about sex." Declan grinned. "Some people consider choking to be a form of foreplay." He winked at her, leaning forward on the table. "Do you, Sidney Stone?"

Every word out of his mouth made Sid want to turn to the side and retch all over the floor. "Can't say that I do. But I'm not surprised at all that you would." Declan licked his lips while Sid's lip curled in disgust. "I have a proposal for you."

"Marriage? Already? Well, ain't you an impatient little minx." Declan sat back grinning wide. "Sorry, sweetheart. You're not really my type."

Sid took a breath, letting the anger and repulsion settle for a moment, before saying, "I convinced the state attorney to offer you a deal. She will drop the battery charge altogether on the condition that you tell me everything about your little poaching enterprise at Oakmire."

Declan licked his lips again. "Now, why would I do a stupid thing like that?"

Sid frowned. Why did everyone think this idea was stupid? Then again, she'd thought it was asinine just moments ago as well. "Because without the deal you'll get up to five years in prison on the felony battery charge. No way you're walking away with a sheriff's detective as the primary witness to the crime." She shrugged. "If you take the deal, though, the charges will be dropped. There'll be no trial, no conviction, no prison time for strangling me. You'll give up everyone else in your poaching ring—the people who hired you, the people you hired, the people you sold the gators to, all of it—and you'll get off scot-free for the poaching at Oakmire as well."

"I'm not tellin' you shit," snarled Declan. He dropped his smile, his face contorting into an expression that Sid had seen up close only a few days ago.

"Then you're going to prison." Sid stood up. "Thanks for your time." Sid walked slowly to the door, expecting Declan to call her back, but he didn't. She left the room and paced back and forth in the hallway, swearing under her breath.

Tony poked his head out of the monitor room and motioned for her to join him. "Nice job," he said. "Maybe you should consider police work."

"But I blew it," Sid whined. "He didn't take the deal."

"We'll see." Tony pointed at the monitor.

Sid watched Declan Chase fidgeting in his seat. It was the most agitated she'd seen him since he had had his hands around her throat. After a few minutes, he pounded on the table asking for the "bitch" to come back in.

Tony smiled. "Looks like you're being hailed."

Sid reentered the room, and Declan motioned to the seat across from him. As she sat, he pointed a finger at her. "I'll give you the names of the guys I hired and the guy I sell to, but that's it."

"The guy you sell to is a good start. But the guys you hired? Two are already in jail and one is dead. That leaves . . . one?" Sid shook her head. "Not good enough. You have to give us everyone in the chain. That means your contact, the money man . . . everyone."

Declan shook his head and folded his arms. "Not doin' that."

"All right then. Thanks again for your time." Sid left the room and rejoined Tony at the monitor. It was another ten minutes before Declan banged on the table again to summon her.

She entered the room for the third time but didn't bother to sit down. "Declan, it's getting late. Everyone wants to go home. People have happy hour plans." She hooked a thumb over her shoulder. "They're getting ready to take you back to your cell and put you to bed for the weekend, so if you don't mind . . ."

"I'll take the deal." Declan placed his forearms on the table, clasped his hands, and hung his head.

Sid sat down and listened. When Declan was through sharing everything he knew about his poaching operation, he said, "I want police protection, too. I'm gonna need protection. Those folks . . . they know people. They got people everywhere."

Sid stood and walked to the door. "First of all, you should have negotiated protection before you spilled your guts. That's lesson 101 of basic plea-deal bargaining. And two, I don't think anyone is going to be able to get to you for a very long time. You're going to prison for, what? Ten to thirty, I expect."

Declan shot to his feet, sending his chair scooting across the floor and landing on its side. "You said you were dropping the charges!"

"I said the state attorney agreed to drop the battery charge for strangling me and to not charge you with any poaching offenses, so you won't be going to prison for any of that," Sid explained, her hand firmly on the door handle in case she needed to escape quickly. "But, you see, the state attorney also told me that the detectives searched your trailer and found that arrow you hid underneath it in the underbelly. The same arrow you shot with a crossbow into your nephew's neck. They told you they found it, right?"

Declan's nostrils flared as he breathed hard in and out, spittle flying from his mouth.

"Oh dear. I guess I have to be the one to break the news to you." She clucked her tongue at him. "You will have the dubious honor of being prosecuted for manslaughter in the death of Dru Chase."

Sid tilted her head and said, "Guess you must have been in a big hurry to hide that arrow. You didn't manage to clean off all of the blood." She sighed. "What I don't understand is why you didn't just chuck that arrow into the Matanzas River when you had a chance. Too afraid it might wash up onshore somewhere? Or were you just not thinking clearly at the time and forgot to get rid of it in your rush to get away?"

The man stood there, eyes bulging and chest heaving, but he said nothing. No denial, no protest, nothing.

His silence angered Sid. "You shot that arrow into your own nephew's neck. Maybe you didn't intend to shoot him. Maybe you were aiming for the alligator and missed. It doesn't really matter." She shook her head slowly. "What does matter is that you pulled the arrow out of that boy's neck and left him there for the gators to get him. You didn't try to help him. You didn't take his body with you when you ran away. You didn't call the police to report what had happened. You didn't even bother to tell his parents, your own brother and sister-in-law, what had happened to him. No, you played dumb—not a big stretch for you, by the way—and you said nothing. You really are a heartless bastard, aren't you?"

For a fraction of a second, she saw his face falter, saw a hint of something flash in his eyes. Was it sadness? Remorse? She didn't really care.

"Declan Chase, you're going to go to prison for a very long time." Sid shrugged a shoulder. "No great loss, though."

Chapter Thirty-Three

Sid bought Tony a slice of pizza on St. George Street while they waited for Tessa Barnes's phone call. Actually, she bought him two slices, both of which were the size of her head. "Do you think the judge will sign the search warrant?" asked Sid, wiping grease off her fingers with a flimsy paper napkin.

Tony nodded. "Tessa can be pretty persuasive."

Tessa Barnes was meeting a local judge who had been her legal writing professor during her first year of law school at the University of Florida. The man had been on the bench a long time and was currently well into his third consecutive six-year term. On Tessa's instructions, Tony had begun preparing the search warrant before Sid's conversation with Declan Chase had ended. Now, all they needed was for the judge to sign it.

Tony's phone rang before they'd finished eating. Sid tossed what was left of her slice in the trash, but Tony grabbed his second slice to go and finished it before they reached the fancy tapas restaurant, the one across from Muy Local, where Tessa and her judge friend were having drinks at an outdoor table. When Sid and Tony arrived, Tessa walked over to them and handed Tony the signed warrant. "Let me know what you find. It would be really nice to nail all those bastards." She smiled at them and sauntered back to her table.

Sid and Tony waited in the parking lot of Bootleggers until the squad car arrived and parked down the street. Tony wanted backup just in case things got rough, as was known to happen at this particular bar, and backup on a Friday night apparently consisted of Deputies Adcock and Weber.

"Them?" asked Sid, once the twins were in place about fifty yards down the street from the bar.

"They'll do," Tony replied. He gave the deputies some instructions and then escorted Sid into the bar.

Bootleggers was exactly as Sid had imagined it would be: dirty windows that let in little outside light, the thick fug of stale beer in the air, country music playing too softly from the ceiling speakers for the words to be distinguishable, and floors so sticky they might as well have been coated with flypaper. The place was only half full, and all of the patrons looked like they'd been sent from central casting to fill the roles of hardened drinkers and poor souls down on their luck. Just like in the movies, the din of conversation dropped as soon as the two of them walked through the door. Sid was pretty sure that it had less to do with them not being regular customers and much more to do with the sheer size and mass of Detective Tony Davis. Tony removed his sunglasses and surveyed the room for several long, awkward moments.

A short, stooped, elderly man shuffled over from his position at the end of the long bar. He wore a T-shirt with the bar's logo on it and faded, baggy jeans that were held up by a cracked leather belt cinched tightly around his narrow waist. The few wisps of hair around the sides of his head were pure white, as was the stubble on his cheeks. "You're that football star I saw on the TV, aren't you? The one who got his leg all busted up?"

Tony nodded. "Yes, sir. I'm Antonio Davis." He held out his big hand.

The elderly man smiled and placed his small, bony hand in Tony's. "Pleasure to meet you, young man. I'm Ed. Welcome to Bootleggers. What are you drinkin'? It's on me."

Tony smiled and leaned in closer, lowering his voice. "How about I buy you a drink, and then you can tell me where I can find the manager?"

Ed chuckled. "I'll do you one better, Antonio. I'll introduce you to the owner." Ed stuck out his bony hand again. "Ed Stubbin. I'm the owner of this here drinking establishment. How may I be of service?" Ed winked at Sid as the two men shook hands once again. "Now, drinks are on me. What'll you have, pretty lady?"

They stood at the bar while Ed called the bartender over and ordered three pints of an IPA from Ghost City Brewery, a local microbrewery over on Anastasia Island. Sid found it difficult to understand how this polite, jovial old man could be the owner of a bar known for its late-night brawls. While they waited for their beers, Tony placed the search warrant on the bar, pushed it toward Ed, and explained what they needed.

Ed pushed the warrant back toward Tony. "You needn't have bothered with all that, Antonio. Come with me. You, too, miss." He crooked a finger, urging them to follow him. "Bring your beers."

They did as Ed instructed and followed him to an office in the back. It was filled to the brim with boxes of booze, paper towels, and toilet paper. "I installed a new security system last year," explained Ed as he sat down at his desk and pushed aside a pile of receipts and invoices. "Had a bartender who was stealing from me, so I made a small investment. And now"—he threw up his hands—"no more stealing. Just like that." He grinned and slowly pecked at his desktop computer. "I've got twelve cameras: four covering the outside of the building, two covering the back parking lot, and six inside the bar. Oh, and I back up everything to the cloud. Digital storage is so cheap these days." He smiled as he shook his head. "Technology is amazing, isn't it? What a time to be alive."

Ed moved his mouse and typed on his keyboard for another minute before standing up and motioning for Sid to take his seat. "I've got it all queued up for you, my dear, starting with the day before just to be safe. Whatever it is you're looking for should be on there. If not, then it didn't happen." Ed patted Tony on the arm as he passed by on his way out the door. "I'll be in the bar. Holler if you need a refill!"

Tony moved some boxes off a wooden stool in the corner and pulled it up next to Sid. On the desk sat two twenty-seven-inch monitors, which showed the footage from all twelve security cameras. The colors were muted, but the clarity was nothing short of high definition. Sid started the footage rolling, increased the speed of the playback, and sat back in awe. She studied one monitor while Tony studied the other. Bootleggers opened at eleven o'clock in the morning, and nothing of note happened until almost ten o'clock that night.

"Look!" Sid slowed the playback and tapped the screen, where a large, black pickup had just parked in the lot. Sid recognized the driver.

They watched Declan Chase emerge from the truck and stride into the bar, where he ordered a beer and took it to a booth in the back. Declan sat alone, sipping his beer, for not more than five minutes before a short, skinny man in a dark T-shirt, dark jeans, and a dark baseball cap slid into the booth across from him. Tony and Sid watched the recorded exchange between the two men, which quickly turned heated. Declan lunged for the man and, a split second later, was hauled out of the booth and escorted from the building into the parking lot by two men who were even bigger than he was. They took turns punching him in the gut until Declan fell to his knees, writhing in the gravel. The two hulks left Declan where he lay and went back inside, taking up their positions at the far end of the bar nearest the restrooms. The skinny man with the ball cap joined them, removed his cap, ran his hand through his thinning, red hair, and placed the cap back on his head.

Sid rewound the video, pausing it when the skinny man's face was in full view of the camera. She snapped a photo and stood up. "Keep going. I'll be right back."

She left Tony in front of the monitors and went to find Ed Stubbin. The elderly man was sitting on a stool at the corner of the bar nearest the door, and Sid hopped up onto the seat next to him. "Ed, do you know this man?" she asked, careful to keep her voice low. She placed her phone on the bar, the photo of the skinny man in the baseball cap featuring brightly on the screen.

Ed nodded and whispered. "That's Irish Mike."

Sid turned her phone face down on the bar to hide the photo. "So he's from Ireland?"

"No, no, no." Ed shook his head and chuckled. "I don't think he's got a drop of Irish blood in him. His parents are Russian, but he was born right here in St. Augustine. Local boy, don't you know. They call him Irish Mike because of his red hair."

Sid rolled her eyes. "And what does Irish Mike do?"

"Bit of this, bit of that," Ed muttered, "but I believe his primary source of employment is loan-sharking."

"Okay," said Sid. "And do you know Declan Chase?"

"Everybody knows Declan." Ed scowled and took a sip of his beer. "I kicked him out last week and barred him from coming back until he pays his tab. I'm sick and tired of that man running up a big tab and forcing his son to come in here and pay it off." Ed shook his head. "Always felt sorry for young Cameron. He was paying his father's bar tab even as a teenager. He'd come in with wads of singles that he made in tips out at that fancy golf club, and he'd have to spend all of his earnings to pay for his no-good father's drinking habit." He sighed and ran a crooked finger up the side of his glass, wiping away the condensation. "I was glad to see that boy was finally going to make it out of here." He shook his head again. "Damn shame he died before he got to rub his father's nose in it." He held up his glass. "To Cameron. May he finally find some peace." Ed took a drink and placed his glass down on the bar.

Sid stayed quiet for a moment out of respect. When Ed turned to look at her, she asked, "Do you know if Declan owed money to Irish Mike, too?"

"Yeah, he did." Ed nodded. "And I know exactly how much."

"Oh, really?" said Sid. "Do tell."

Ed held up one finger. "One way I know how much Declan owed is because of the kind of talking-to Irish Mike's boys gave Declan in the parking lot a few weeks ago."

"I think they used more than just their words," Sid muttered. Ed nodded in agreement. "And how much do you have to owe Irish Mike to get a talking-to?"

Ed shrugged. "Less than five thousand. If it was over five, they would have broken his arm. Over ten, and they break a leg." He raised his glass to his lips. "You get the idea."

Sid nodded to signal that she did. "And what's the second way?"

"Ah." Ed winked and tapped his ear. Sid noticed the flesh-colored hearing aid nestled snugly inside. "I can hear everything that goes on in this bar. These babies are worth every penny."

Sid smiled. "So how much did he owe?"

"Four thousand six hundred and change." Ed took another sip of his beer and then tapped his ear again. "Told you. I hear everything."

Sid thanked him, slid off the stool, and returned to the office to find Tony, now seated in the desk chair and staring intently at the monitors.

"Come look at this, Sid." He patted the stool next to him and then rewound the video. "This is from the next day." The date and time stamp indicated that it was ten minutes to noon. There were only five people in the bar: Ed, the bartender, two old men seated at the bar with their newspapers, and Declan Chase. "It's just as Declan said. He was telling the truth. Watch." Tony pressed play.

Sid watched as two familiar figures walked into the bar and joined Declan in his booth, the same one he'd occupied the previous night. The conversation took no more than ten minutes. During that time, the shorter of the two men passed a brown, #10-size envelope across the table to Declan. After the two men left and Declan was alone in the booth once again, he opened the envelope and counted the cash inside.

"I've run this back several times. Based on the thickness of the envelope and the time it takes him to count, and assuming, of course, that those are hundred-dollar bills, my best guess is two to three thousand dollars." Tony rubbed his eyes. "Nothing much happens after that. He stays for about an hour, buys a round for the bar. Big spender." He smirked. "And then he left, drove off in the direction of home."

Sid nodded, remembering that the Paradise Trailer Park where Declan lived was within walking distance of the bar. "Well, I suggest that we ask Ed if he heard any of that conversation. Apparently, he has bionic hearing thanks to some high-tech hearing aids. Says he can hear everything that happens in his bar. Maybe we'll get lucky." She then brought up the photo she'd just shared with Ed. "He told me that this little guy is a loan shark called Irish Mike."

Tony nodded. "I've heard of him."

"Based on the lack of broken bones, and the fact that Ed has bionic hearing, Ed told me Declan owed Irish Mike over forty-six hundred dollars." Sid took a sip of her beer. "I bet if we keep watching, we'll find Declan paying off Irish Mike with the money from that envelope."

They spent the next thirty minutes scanning video footage, and just as Sid predicted, two days later Declan walked into Bootleggers with Dru Chase on his heels. Dru veered off, heading for a rickety pinball machine in the corner near the front door while Declan met with Irish Mike at the far end of the bar. Declan handed over the familiar brown envelope. Payment was received with a frown by Irish Mike, who gripped the back of Declan's neck and pulled him down so that their faces were mere inches apart. The two men spoke for several minutes and then left the bar together, Dru Chase once again trailing behind Declan.

"That's one week before Dru Chase was killed," said Sid. "What do you think's happening?"

Tony sighed. "If I had to guess, I'd say that Declan's payment fell short, and they worked out some sort of deal."

Sid nodded. "Declan said his buddy Mike Somebody was one of the poachers he hired."

Tony smirked. "Mike Morozov. I remembered the name. Sounds Russian."

"That's Irish Mike!" Sid swatted Tony's arm. "Ed told me that Irish Mike's family is from Russia. They just call him Irish Mike because he has red hair." She pointed at the screen, where they'd paused the video showing the three men climbing into Declan's truck. "I think Irish Mike made Declan cut him in on the poaching job as a way to pay off his debt."

Tony frowned. "But why would a loan shark risk going out into the swamp to poach some alligators just to get a payoff?"

"Adrenaline junkie?" suggested Sid. "Or maybe he thought it was the only way to keep Declan honest and ensure that he got paid. I mean, I wouldn't trust Declan as far as I could throw him, and I've only met him a few times. I'm willing to bet Irish Mike knew Declan a whole lot better."

"You're probably right." Tony fast-forwarded through the next week, spotting Declan and Dru collecting Irish Mike from the bar on three more occasions.

"This is the night that Dru Chase died," said Sid, pointing to the date and time stamp on the screen.

They watched Declan and Dru arrive at the bar shortly after eight o'clock to pick up Irish Mike. The three men left Bootleggers less than ten minutes later. Five hours after that, only Declan and Irish Mike returned to the bar, which was packed with people. The crowd at the bar parted to let Irish Mike through, and the redhaired man immediately ordered drinks. The bartender placed two shot glasses down on the bar and poured a dark liquid into them. Irish Mike's hand shot out and yanked the bottle out of the bartender's hand. With a flick of his wrist, Irish Mike ordered the bartender to make himself scarce.

Sid and Tony watched Declan and Irish Mike down shot after shot until most of the bottle was gone. Irish Mike kept one hand on Declan's shoulder the entire time, occasionally whispering in his ear. At two o'clock, Declan could barely pick his head up off the bar, and Irish Mike made a phone call. Twenty minutes later, Irish Mike's two goons arrived, picked up a visibly drunk Declan, and poured him into his truck. One of the goons drove Declan's truck out of the parking lot while the other goon chauffeured Irish Mike in a dark SUV, trailing closely behind.

Tony reached out and paused the video. Next, he pulled a couple of thumb drives from his pocket, slipped one into the computer's USB port, and began downloading the video footage. He sat back, shaking his head. "That looked to me like an impromptu wake for Dru Chase."

"I agree," said Sid. Goose bumps covered her body. "And I think we just watched Declan Chase drink himself stupid an hour after he killed his nephew."

Chapter Thirty-Four

Sid got a late start the next morning. She liked to do her Saturday run at dawn, before the temperatures soared and the tourists came out in droves, but she'd stayed up late after finishing her beer with Tony at Bootleggers. She'd opened another beer when she got back to her office and drank it while she made notes in her Oakmire case file.

Tony had insisted that she do nothing further on the case until the sheriff's office had the opportunity to arrest some of the participants in Declan Chase's poaching ring. These included Irish Mike and the two downstream buyers to whom Declan had sold half a dozen alligator carcasses. Those arrests were expected to happen today. After that, Tony would bring Sid in for the arrests of the money men.

To Sid's relief, Declan had admitted to not being able to poach Big Boy. The elusive reptilian monster was still at large. Jonathan Beedlemeyer and Henri Broussard would be happy to hear that bit of news, but they would have to wait to be told until after all the arrests were made. Tony didn't want anyone accidently tipping off the gentlemen at the top of the poaching scheme.

All this meant Sid now had time to kill while she waited for Tony's call, so at around ten o'clock, she laced up her running shoes, slathered on some sunscreen, and stuffed her ID and some cash in her pocket. When she opened the door to her office, she found Leo standing on the threshold, hand raised as if ready to knock.

"Oh! Leo," said Sid, slipping on her sunglasses. "What's up?"

"Can I go running with you?" he asked.

Sid smiled at the boy. "You want to go running?" He nodded, and she grinned even wider. "I thought you only did that when you were being chased."

"Yeah, well." He rubbed the back of his neck. "I thought it might help . . . clear my head . . . or whatever."

Sid's smile faltered a little. With everything happening in the Oakmire case recently, she'd forgotten that this teenage boy was being haunted by a dark shadow that seemed to be his dead father. Sid reached out and rubbed his arm. "Of course you can run with me." She stepped back and studied his attire. "That will work for now, but if you really want to run, we'll need to get you some proper running shoes. And maybe some shirts and shorts that are more moisture wicking. But this"—she waved her hand up and down—"will work for today."

Leo stared down at his clothes. He'd donned the one pair of gym shorts that he owned, which he often slept in because they were soft and comfortable, and his father's old Tom Petty and the Heartbreakers concert tee, which was speckled with yellow paint. On his feet were the nearly new sneakers that Sid had found for him at a thrift store when Leo first arrived in town.

"Come on, kid. We better get going before we melt out here." Sid walked him over to the shade of the neighbor's giant oak whose thick branches spread out over Burt's backyard. She took him through a series of stretches before leading him across the lawn to the sidewalk. "Okay, we're gonna make our way over to San Marco Avenue and then run down it to where it intersects A1A, leading to the bridge over to Vilano Beach, but we won't go down to the bridge. We'll just go up to A1A and back, and we'll alternate running and walking so you can get a feel for it. If you feel like you can run more, let me know and we'll keep going. Sound okay?"

Leo nodded and followed Sid as they walked down Saragossa Street toward the historic downtown district. At the end of the street, they broke into a slow jog. They zigzagged their way north past the City Gate and the Huguenot Cemetery and continued on San Marco Avenue. Leo managed to keep pace with Sid until they reached the intersection with A1A.

They started with thirty seconds of running and one minute of walking and then increased it to one minute of each, alternating back and forth. By the time they reached A1A, they were up to three minutes of running at a time. When they crossed San Marco Avenue for their return home, Sid suggested they run until Leo felt he couldn't go any farther. He made it half a mile before he had to tug on her arm to get her to stop.

"Nice job, kid." Sid slowed to a walk and patted Leo on the back. "How do you feel?"

"Like I'm getting a blister," said Leo, taking in big gulps of air and wiping his face with the hem of his T-shirt.

"That's easy to remedy," Sid replied. "But how do you feel otherwise?"

Leo thought for a moment, taking a mental survey of his body. He felt tired but strong, fatigued but alive. And miraculously, his mind felt clear. They'd passed several spirits on their run, but none had approached Leo to ask for his help. The cherry on top was the dark shadow of his father was nowhere to be seen.

Leo smiled. "Good. I feel really good."

"Well, then I think we should celebrate." She stopped in front of a small, one-story, Florida-cracker-style house that was painted bright white. It had dozens of pots and flower boxes, all of them spilling over with a riot of colorful blooms, strategically placed along the porch and around the various café tables and chairs in the paved front garden. Hanging from the porch eves and from the branches of the magnolia trees in the garden were strings of nautical flags. The big sign over the porch read, "Smooth Sailing," in bright blue letters. In smaller print underneath were the words, "Smoothie Bar and Brunch Café."

Leo's mouth watered as he read the sign and inhaled the sweet, buttery scents coming from the café.

Sid smiled as she watched Leo's face light up. "Grab us a table, kid. I'll be right back."

Leo did as he was told, snagging a two-top near the sidewalk under one of the giant magnolias. He wiped his face again with his T-shirt and was tempted to take off his shoe to study the blister on his foot, but he resisted, fearing what he would find once he did.

By the time Sid returned, Leo's breathing had returned to normal, and his sweaty hair and shirt were beginning to dry in the warm breeze. Sid placed a tray down on the table, loaded up with two bottles of water, two large smoothie cups, and an enormous blueberry muffin. She handed him a bottle of water, which he downed in just a few gulps.

"Wasn't sure what you'd want, so you can pick between the Strawberry-Mango-Kiwi-Sunrise-Something-or-Other and the Banana-Chocolate-Peanut Butter-Decadence-Whatever-You-Wanna-Call-It." She held up the two smoothie cups, and Leo reached for the chocolate-and-peanut butter concoction. She smiled, knowing that was exactly the one he would choose, and moved the muffin closer to him. "And that's yours, too."

Leo nodded, his cheeks caving in from sucking the thick smoothie through the straw. After he swallowed, he smiled at her. "Thanks!" He tore the muffin's paper wrapper off and took a huge bite. Sid sat back, took the lid off her cup, and began tackling her own smoothie with a spoon. They ate in silence for a couple of minutes before the swish of a long, dark ponytail caught Sid's attention.

"Lorelai!" Sid waved at the young woman who was walking past them on the sidewalk.

"Oh, hey." Lorelai Sutton walked over to her table and pushed her designer sunglasses up on top of her head. She smiled down at Leo, whose mouth was full of blueberry muffin. He gave her a closed-lip grin and a small wave.

Sid pulled over a vacant chair from a nearby table, and Lorelai sat down, placing her handbag on her lap. Sid gestured toward Leo. "This is my assistant, Leo." The two young people exchanged nods of greeting, and Sid continued. "I wanted to let you know that I spoke with a sheriff's detective yesterday, and he confirmed that you are not a suspect."

Lorelai nodded. "That's good to know."

"But they haven't ruled you out as still possibly involved," said Sid. "It would be helpful if you could prepare some information. Bank statements for the past couple of months. Screenshots of any social media comments you made or online conversations you had about Cameron. The detectives may ask for this kind of stuff. They will want to see if there is any indication that you talked to anyone else about Cameron, insinuated that you wanted him harmed, enlisted anyone's help to get back at him. That sort of thing. I wouldn't try to hide anything because they'll find out everything eventually. If there is anything bad, it's best to be prepared with an explanation." She held up her hands. "I don't need to see any of it, at least not yet, but you might want to start preparing for that line of inquiry from the sheriff's office. I fear it might be coming soon. Your sister can help you, I'm sure. She's a lawyer, so she'll be able to give you some good advice."

Lorelai looked down at her fingers, which she'd been twisting into knots while Sid was talking. Sid noticed her nails had been bitten down to the quick.

"Okay." Lorelai nodded. "I'll talk to Carleigh and ask her to help me." She glanced at her watch. "I'm sorry, but I have to go. I have a tattoo appointment in a few minutes." She plucked her sunglasses off her head.

"Tattoo?" Sid smiled. "Sounds fun." Personally, Sid didn't think it sounded fun at all. She couldn't imagine voluntarily paying someone to stick needles in her skin for the purpose of scarring her body forever. "What are you having done?"

Lorelai fished around in her bag and pulled out a golf ball. She handed it to Sid. Someone had drawn on the ball in black permanent marker. It was a little stick figure, posed like it was running with its arms and legs akimbo.

"Cute," said Sid. She held up the ball so Leo could see the tiny drawing.

Lorelai's brow furrowed. "It was Cameron's mark." Sid and Leo both stared at the young woman as Lorelai took the golf ball back from Sid. She ran her thumb over the drawing. "He drew this on all his balls and on the grips of his clubs. It's a little runner. He said it was perfect for him since his last name is Chase." She tried to smile but couldn't seem to manage it. "I told him it was stupid, but he'd been drawing this little guy on every piece of golf gear he owned since he was a little kid. Like, maybe nine or ten years old. He said it was his trademark. Said it brought him luck." She sighed. "I'm going to have it tattooed on my ankle. That way he'll always be with me. Maybe it will bring me luck, too."

"That's a nice way to remember him," Sid offered.

Lorelai nodded. "You know, Cam gave me this ball after his last big win, the one that got him into the major in Savannah." She ran her thumb over the drawing of the little runner again. "I thought it was his way of telling me he was ready to get serious. He was on the verge of making it big, and I thought maybe he was ready to settle down. Maybe get married." She held up the ball, turning it this way and that. "He'd never done that before—given me one of his winning golf balls—and I thought it was meant to be this grand gesture." She huffed and dropped the ball into her purse. "Now, I realize it was probably his way of telling me goodbye. But neither of us has ever been very good at saying goodbye."

Lorelai stood abruptly to leave. Sid stood as well, and Leo followed an awkward moment later. "Good luck with the tattoo. I'm sure it will turn out great," said Sid. "I'll be in touch as soon as I know anything further."

Sid and Leo watched Lorelai Sutton square her shoulders, pull herself up to her full height, and stride to the colorfully painted building next door. The chimes on the front door rang out as Lorelai disappeared inside the Dark Mark Tattoo Palace. The building was less of a palace and more of a square, squat stucco building with a flat roof and few windows. Its only impressive aspect of note was the exterior paint job; colorful, graffiti-style murals wrapped around the building, covering every square inch from foundation to eaves.

"Do you have any tattoos?" asked Leo. He went back to slurping his smoothie as he studied the Dark Mark's exterior artwork.

"No." Sid raised an eyebrow. "You?"

Leo snorted a laugh. "No, but I want to." His brow

furrowed as he thought about his response. "Or at least I used to."

"Not sure anymore?" Sid downed the last of her water.

"My dad had a tattoo on his arm." Leo pointed to the outer part of his upper arm, so skinny and pale under the ratty T-shirt. "It was a bass guitar with a skull and crossbones where the sound hole would be. And a rose vine wrapped around it." He picked at the last of the crumbs from his muffin. "I always thought it was cool. He got it when he turned eighteen, right before he enlisted and left home. The bass was for Grandpa. The rose was for Grandma. Dad said he wanted a camelia flower because her name was Camille, but the guy who did the tattoo didn't know what that looked like. So he got a rose instead."

"And the skull and crossbones?" asked Sid.

Leo frowned. "For the spirits who'd haunted him all his life."

Chapter Thirty-Five

Early Sunday morning, Sid and Leo sat in the car in the parking lot of the Oakmire Golf and Country Club. On their way to the club, Sid had received two texts from Detective Tony Davis. The first stated that he and his team were on surveillance as planned, but that there was a delay of about half an hour. The second text ordered her to wait in the parking lot until he arrived.

Thus, Sid sat in the driver's seat, playing solitaire on her phone, while Leo doodled in a notebook that he'd brought with him in his backpack. Sid had managed to convince Burt to let Leo tag along this morning; there was a good chance the Oakmire case would be closed today. Burt had consented only when Sid mentioned to him that Detective Davis would be with them.

"What are you drawing?" asked Sid as she watched Leo sketching in his notebook. He was hunched over, his tongue poking out from between his teeth.

Leo quickly covered the drawing with his hand. "Nothing."

He twirled his pencil between the fingers of his other hand. "Just something I was thinking about."

"All right," said Sid, glancing away from him and looking out her side window.

A few moments passed, before Leo piped up again. "I can show you if you want." Sid turned back to look at him, and Leo ran his teeth over his lower lip as he slowly removed his hand from the page. "It's not finished. It's just . . . it's just an idea I had."

Sid leaned over and studied the drawing. It was an upright acoustic guitar positioned on a pile of rocks with an anchor leaning against it. The pick guard on the body of the guitar was a flowery teardrop shape, and where the hole would be in the center of the guitar, there was a skull and crossbones. The drawing was remarkably good.

"That's really cool, Leo. What's it for?"

"My tattoo," he answered in a whisper. "When I turn eighteen." He pointed to the various parts of the drawing, explaining each one in turn. "The guitar for Grandpa. The paisley for Mom. The anchor for my dad, and the skull and crossbones for the spirits. And for St. Augustine." He shrugged.

"And that?" Sid tapped the pile of rocks on which the guitar sat.

Leo kept his eyes on the page. "Stones." He swallowed audibly and then whispered, "For Sidney Stone."

Sid had to blink rapidly to fight the sharp prick of tears that stung at her eyes. She reached out and squeezed his arm. "It's beautiful, Leo. It really is." She had to turn her head quickly and feign tucking her hair behind her ear in order to swipe at an errant tear that managed to escape. "But it's a good thing you have to wait a few years to get that tattooed on your body." She turned back and smiled at him, trying to lighten the mood. "By then you may not like me so much."

Leo looked up at her with a cheeky grin. "Who says I like you now?" He tapped the pile of stones in his drawing. "That's why you're at the bottom."

Sid gave him a playful shove just as her phone rang. "Detective, please tell me you're on your way."

"Right behind you." Tony hung up and got out of his car, which he'd parked directly behind Sid's. Neither she nor Leo had noticed him pull up, being so engrossed in their poignant conversation about the tattoo drawing. Tony strode toward them and held out his hand. "Leo, how's it going?"

"Good," Leo answered, trying to suppress a smile as he shook the big detective's hand. Sid suppressed a smile of her own at the exchange.

"All right, here's what I need from the two of you." Tony proceeded to outline his plan. Sid had heard all about Tony's plan the night before, when he called to let her know they'd picked up Irish Mike and the two downstream buyers, but she knew this second recitation was for Leo's benefit.

When Tony finished reciting his instructions, he walked off in the direction of the cart barn and groundskeeper's shed while Sid and Leo strolled straight through the clubhouse and out the back, down the veranda steps, and over to the starter's shack. They recognized the course ranger, who checked his list and answered their questions. Sid and Leo thanked him for his help and marched down the cart path that ran along the eighteenth hole. They stopped their progress when any of the golfers on eighteen took a shot, and eventually they found themselves in the wooded area between the seventeenth and eighteenth holes.

Sid and Leo ducked behind the trunks of a couple of large oaks and waited while a foursome arrived at the seventeenth hole and began to tee off. Leo looked around and saw two groundskeepers near the seventeenth tee box. They were kneeling, appearing to replace a sprinkler head positioned among some azaleas. "Is that them?" he asked, nodding in the direction of the two groundskeepers.

"I guess so," Sid answered.

She didn't recognize either undercover deputy—one man and one woman, both of them lean and muscled, wearing khaki slacks and dark green golf shirts that resembled the uniform they'd seen Henri Broussard and his staff wearing on the course. Sid was grateful that the deputies were there, and she knew that Tony would not be far away either.

Tony had selected this hole because of its isolation. There were few houses nearby, the green was surrounded by water, and there was nowhere to run. Sid stared across the green to the spot where she'd stood and looked down at Cameron Chase's body tangled among the mangrove roots. A chill ran up her spine, and she shivered at the memory. When the cold persisted, she knew she was not alone.

"They're here, aren't they?" she asked.

Leo nodded, both to signal Sid and to greet Bacon and Bucket. The two ghosts stood on either side of her, gazing at her with rapt appreciation.

Sid smiled, not sure exactly the direction she should face, and said, "Gentlemen, so glad you could join us."

Leo grinned. "They're happy to be here."

Sid didn't ask how he knew that. "Leo, are you okay with me asking them a few questions?" When he nodded, she asked, "Gentlemen, do you remember the night that Cameron Chase died?"

"Yes."

Both voices came through in unison, one tenor and one bass. Leo relayed the message to Sid with a nod.

Sid fished out her phone. "Can you remember any more details about the person you saw running away after Cameron's body went into the marsh?"

The image that flashed in Leo's head was the same one he'd seen before: someone who was shorter than he was, rather skinny, laboring to run away with the heavy golf bag. Leo shook his head. "I see the same thing as before."

Sid nodded. "Did the person have red hair?"

Silence.

Sid brought up the photo of Irish Mike on her phone. She knew it was unlikely to be him based on when he had arrived at Bootleggers to meet Declan and Dru for their poaching gig that night. The timing wouldn't have worked out, but still she had to check. "Could it have been this man?"

Silence.

Sid scrolled through social media and brought up another photo. "Was this the person?"

Silence.

Sid nodded. She had already ruled out Lorelai Sutton, given that the young woman had an alibi and was too tall to fit Leo's description of the person he saw in the images shared by the ghosts. Lorelai was six feet, if not taller. The person Leo saw was shorter, her own height or less.

Sid scrolled again. "How about this?" She held out her phone, showing a photo she had snapped more than a week ago. She angled the screen away from Leo, hoping he wouldn't be influenced by the photo. She wanted the answer to come from the ghosts, not from Leo.

Leo frowned. "I don't know what's happening." He shook his head, trying to clear the flood of images. "None of them made much sense."

"Which one?" asked Sid. There were two men in the photo. "Ask them if it's either of these people."

Leo felt waves of feelings coming from the ghosts. "I'm not sure." He closed his eyes, trying to make sense of what he was thinking and feeling. "I don't think they know. I just keep seeing the same image as before: someone running away. But I feel"—he paused, trying to find words to match the ghosts' feelings—"sorrow. No, pity. Yeah, I think it's pity." He squeezed his eyes shut tighter. "And anger. Maybe frustration. Or, I don't know, something else?"

"Disgust?" offered Sid. "Contempt?"

"Yes."

Leo nodded. "Yes, that's it. One of those. Or both. Maybe both."

Sid waggled the phone out in front of her, still angling it away from Leo. "And do they feel that way because of what happened to Cameron? Or are those feelings from things that happened before?"

"Before."

Leo opened his eyes in surprise. "Before," he repeated.

"Okay, kid. That's enough." Sid put the phone away. "Thank you, gentlemen. I appreciate your help."

Leo smirked. "They say you're welcome." He rolled his eyes and shook his head.

"What?" asked Sid. "What are they doing?"

"Trust me," he replied. "You don't want to know."

The foursome on the seventeenth hole finished up, left the green, and trekked through the woods toward the final hole. Sid and Leo, still standing behind the oaks, nodded to the golfers as they passed.

A new group of six appeared on the seventeenth hole, five

golfers and one caddy. Sid recognized them immediately. The entire board of directors of the Oakmire Golf and Country Club pulled drivers from their golf bags and took a few practice swings while Noah Zimmerman raced around the tee box, picking up stray magnolia leaves. Noah helped Jonathan Beedlemeyer line up his tee shot while the others waited patiently for their turns. The undercover officers continued to pretend to fix the sprinkler head in the azaleas. Sid scanned the area for any sign of Tony but couldn't see him.

"Get ready, kid," whispered Sid as they watched four of the five golfers land their tee shots on the fairway, short of the water that surrounded the green. One of the golfers hooked their tee shot into the mangroves. Sid and Leo could hear the swearing from their hiding places and shared a silent smile behind the oaks.

Sid watched as the directors got back in their carts and drove the short distance down the cart path, parking by the wooden bridge leading to the green. Sid noticed the fake groundskeepers collect their tools and walk down the fairway, stopping occasionally to pretend to check other sprinkler heads. Eventually, all of the golfers chipped onto the green with varying degrees of success—and with a fair bit of colorful language coming from the one director having a particularly bad day on the course.

Once all five of the golfers plus their caddy had crossed the bridge and made their way onto the green to study their putts, Sid and Leo emerged from the woods. Sid set her phone to record and tucked it into the side pocket of her backpack. On a whim, Sid detoured around the carts, plucked a golf club from one of the bags, and took it with her.

"Good morning, gentlemen," said Sid, flashing her brightest smile. The six men on the green turned toward her, all of them wearing looks that ranged from surprise to outright fury.

"We are in the middle of play!" Herbert Langston was red-faced and sweaty, and Sid wondered if he was on the verge of having a heart attack.

Sid held her smile in place. "I can see that. And doing quite well, I'm sure. Who's winning?"

"That's irrelevant!" Langston blurted.

Sid gave him a wink. "So not you, then."

"Ms. Stone, I really don't think now is the appropriate time to have a conversation," said Jonathan Beedlemeyer. "Herbert is correct. We are in the middle of play."

"Don't worry," said Sid with a swipe of her hand. "This won't take long." She took a few steps forward, signaling for Leo to stay where he was at the edge of the green. Sid felt the familiar chill of the ghosts and was oddly comforted by their support. "I wanted to inform all of you that I have wrapped up my investigation. I can report that there was poaching activity on the course late at night, and that six alligators were taken by the poachers." When Beedlemeyer opened his mouth to speak, Sid held up her hand. "Big Boy was not among them. He is safe and sound and lurking out there . . . somewhere." She waved her hand at the marsh.

"Well, that is a relief," said Beedlemeyer, his hand reaching up to cover his heart. "At least Big Boy is safe. And we thank you for your efforts, Ms. Stone."

"You're welcome," said Sid with a smile. "But there's more." She held up a finger. "There were five poachers in all. Four of them are in jail. And one of them, sadly, is dead." Sid scanned the men's faces. "I'm sure you all heard about Dru Chase. He used to work as a busboy in the club's restaurant. Perhaps some of you knew him." All of the directors remained silent while Noah Zimmerman nodded his head.

"Well," continued Sid, "arrests were also made of two downstream buyers. They were the ones who purchased the alligators who were killed here on the course." At the mention of killing, the men's faces all took on a sour look, as if they'd all sucked on a lemon in unison. "And I'm told the police will be arresting the two men who hired the poachers." Sid looked at her watch. "That should be happening any minute now."

"Really?" Beedlemeyer perked up. "So, you know who paid these men? These poachers?" Sid nodded. "Were they club members?" Beedlemeyer's gaze narrowed, and a sly smile crossed his lips. "I bet anything they were."

"You would be correct, Mr. Chairman," Sid answered. "Not only are they club members, but they are also board members."

There was a long beat of silence before Herbert Langston bellowed, "This is preposterous! I don't have to stand here and listen to this nonsense!" He began to storm toward Sid, his complexion turning the color of cooked beets, but after taking only four or five steps, Langston abruptly halted.

Sid noticed the other men were also frozen in place, eyes growing wide and color draining from their faces. Sid glanced over her shoulder and saw Detective Tony Davis standing with one hand on Leo's shoulder and the other on the handgun holstered to his hip. Likewise, the two undercover officers had swapped their groundskeeping tools for their own firearms. Tony nodded for Sid to continue.

"As I was saying"—she turned back to face the golfers and their caddy—"we have CCTV footage of Herbert Langston and Rocco Castiglione meeting with Declan Chase at a bar called Bootleggers, which is where they hired him and paid him money to poach alligators here at Oakmire."

"Nonsense!" shouted Langston. "That is utter nonsense!"

Sid shook her head. "It's high definition, actually. Quite impressive."

Langston huffed and stuttered in response.

"Even if you do have video evidence of such a meeting," Rocco Castiglione replied, his voice even and cool, "you have no proof of what was said or the actual reasons for any money possibly changing hands. Video evidence is not enough." He crossed his arms and widened his stance.

Sid nodded. "True, but we also have Declan Chase's sworn statement."

Rocco shrugged. "His word against ours."

"And someone else overheard you." Sid tapped her ear and winked. "You should have paid closer attention to your surroundings." She smiled when Rocco's smug grin faltered a little.

"What you don't know, Ms. Stone, is that I have been paying Declan Chase money on a regular basis." Rocco glanced sideways at Noah, who seemed to shrink under the knowledge of what was about to be revealed. "For the past couple of years, I have paid Declan a steady sum of money so that his son, Cameron, would hire my stepson, Noah, to caddy for him at tournaments." Rocco flicked his hand in Noah's direction.

Sid nodded and leaned on the golf club she was holding, using it like a cane. "Oh, I know all about that. Declan told us. He even shared his bank records with us." She smiled. "You did pay Declan Chase pretty regularly. It started with five hundred dollars, but the payments grew larger and larger as time went on. Ten thousand was the last one." Sid whistled. "That Declan, he is one greedy bastard, isn't he?"

The other members turned and stared at Rocco, some of them wide-eyed with surprise and others frowning with derision. Sid was grateful that none of them were sparing a glance for Noah, who looked ready to take a flying leap into the marsh.

"You paid Declan all of those amounts by digital wallet. There's a trail, all nice and neat. Guess you thought it wouldn't matter if anyone found out. Big man that you are, what do you care if anyone finds out you were paying to help your kid?" Sid shrugged. "And it shouldn't matter." Sid winked at Noah and then swung her gaze back to Rocco. "But you paid cash that night in Bootleggers. Three thousand dollars to hire Declan Chase to commit illegal alligator poaching."

At this, a visibly distressed Herbert Langston began to spill his guts and jabbed a sausage finger in Rocco's direction. "That money was not mine! None of it! It was all his! I only accompanied him to that hellhole of a bar because I thought we were going out for drinks. I had no idea that any such conversation would take place. I was completely against it! I never participated in any such solicitation." Langston's blustery rant went on for several minutes, after which he began a verbal assault on his good friend and partner in crime, Rocco Castiglione. Rocco, for his part, remained silent. The undercover officers handcuffed them both.

"One more thing," said Sid. She picked up the golf club she'd been leaning on and held it out in front of her in both hands, palms open to the sky, presenting the club as reverently as if it were Excalibur. "You've been playing today's round with Cameron Chase's golf clubs."

There was nothing but silence in the moments that followed. No birdsong. No crickets chirping. No frogs singing from their perches in the swamp. No one said a word.

And then everyone began talking at once. Everyone, that is, except Rocco Castiglione and his stepson, Noah Zimmerman.

Chapter Thirty-Six

An ear-piercing whistle silenced the crowd. All heads swung toward Detective Davis. "Let the lady finish, please." He drummed his fingers on his holster. "Go ahead, Sid."

"Thank you, Detective." Sid grabbed the metal shaft of the club in one hand and righted it so that it was perpendicular to the ground. "This is Cameron Chase's golf club." She waggled the club for effect. "I know it's Cameron's because of this bit here." She pointed to the rubberized handle. "What do you call it?"

"The grip," said Jonathan Beedlemeyer with an encouraging nod.

"Yes, that's it, the grip." She tapped the grip, which featured a black-and-white chevron pattern. Toward the narrow base of the grip was a small white band, about half an inch wide, in which appeared the brand name in black letters: Sun-Dry.

"Those are common grips. Everyone has them," said Rocco.

He maintained his wide stance, chest puffed out and chin held high, despite his arms being handcuffed behind his back. "They're aftermarket. You can have them put on right here at the club."

"That's very true, Mr. Castiglione." Sid nodded. "But you see, Cameron Chase was a bit superstitious. He had this trademark, a signature of sorts, that he drew on everything. He'd been doing it since he was a little kid." She cast a glance at Noah. "Surely, you remember what it was?"

Noah nodded, his face now white as a sheet even in the blistering Florida sun. "Runner," he whispered. He cleared his throat and tried again, louder this time. "A runner."

"That's right. A runner." Sid smiled at Noah. "He put it on everything, didn't he? He put it on all of his golf balls." Sid turned the club around and pointed to the white band on the back side of the grip. "And on all of his golf clubs."

Rocco's nostrils flared, and his lips pressed together in a thin line. While he continued to fix his stare on Sid, she could see him struggling to keep his emotions in check and fighting against the urge to turn his head.

And in that moment, Sid's stomach felt like it always did on the first drop of a steep roller coaster. Because that's the moment she knew for sure.

Sid glanced down at the ground and shook her head once. She didn't want to continue, didn't want to say what needed to be said next. When she looked up, her eyes met the pair staring back at her.

Steeling herself, she flipped the club upside down and pointed to the head. "Sand wedge," she said. "This is what you used to kill him, isn't it?"

All heads turned to follow her gaze, and she continued. "This is the club Cameron was using when you approached him. He was hitting balls out of that sand trap." She pointed to the trap nearby. "Practicing his bunker shot for the big tournament. He laid it down when he picked up the rake to smooth the sand in the trap. You and Cameron argued. You picked up the sand wedge. And you struck him over the head with it."

She mimed the strike, hating herself as she did it. "He fell, and then you pushed his body into the marsh." She lowered the golf club. "But what you may not realize is that Cameron didn't die from the blow to his head. No, he died from drowning. That young man was still alive when he went into the water." Sid took a breath. She'd recited all of it exactly as Leo had explained it to her, filling in the gaps that the ghosts had missed.

She shook her head, still holding the man's gaze. "It was the money, wasn't it? Cameron Chase was taking money, too, just like his father, Declan. Isn't that right?"

A single nod in response. And that was all it took.

She wanted to vomit. She wanted to rush to the edge of the green and retch into the swamp. She wanted very much to drop the murder weapon and spend the rest of the day scrubbing the feel of the club from her hand.

Detective Tony Davis walked over and placed a hand on the man's shoulder. "We are also arresting you for the murder of Cameron Chase."

Noah's knees gave out from under him, and he began to fall. Tony caught him around the waist and held him up. With the help of the undercover officer, Tony began to half walk, half carry, Noah off the green toward the golf carts. Tony took the sand wedge from Sid as he passed her.

"I didn't mean to!" Noah wailed.

"Shut up!" screamed Rocco. "Shut the fuck up!" The second undercover officer shoved Rocco forward, causing him to stumble, and then forcibly removed him as well.

The rest of the group stood in stunned silence as the officers loaded Herbert Langston, Rocco Castiglione, and Noah Zimmerman into separate golf carts and drove off toward the clubhouse.

"They're taking my cart," said Jonathan Beedlemeyer. Sid wasn't sure the man had blinked in the last several minutes, nor was he fully processing what was happening. "They took my clubs." He pointed to the spot where the carts had disappeared into the woods.

"I'm sure you'll get them back, Mr. Beedlemeyer," offered Sid, "and I want to thank you for your business. I'll deliver my final, itemized bill to you in the morning. I would appreciate payment by the end of the week."

Sid walked over to Leo, put her arm around his shoulders, and spun him around. The two of them crossed the wooden bridge and followed the cart path back to the clubhouse, leaving the other three directors standing on the green of the seventeenth hole with their mouths hanging open.

"How did you know it was Noah?" asked Leo as he shoveled a tortilla chip loaded with shredded chicken, cheese, and guacamole into his mouth.

They were sitting at one of the rooftop tables of Don Pedro's Cantina. It was one of two Mexican restaurants on Avenida Menendez, the street that formed the eastern edge of the Old City's historic downtown district. Don Pedro's was the cheaper of the two restaurants and had beautiful views of the Matanzas Bay, the Castillo de San Marcos, the Bridge of Lions leading to Anastasia Island, and the Plaza de la Constitución.

Sid lifted a portion of their loaded nachos onto her little plate. "Honestly, I didn't." She laughed when Leo stopped chewing in surprise. "I knew it was either Rocco or Noah, but I wasn't sure until I was standing there looking at them both."

"How did you figure it out?" Leo took a sip of his soda and shoveled in another mouthful.

"Process of elimination." She sat back, squinting in the bright sunlight. "When I showed your ghost friends—"

"Bacon and Bucket," muttered Leo.

"What?"

"That's what I call them. Bacon and Bucket."

"Why?!"

"You don't want to know."

Sid frowned at the teenage boy sitting across from her, devouring their plate of nachos. He was right, she thought. She probably didn't want to know. "Anyway, I showed them those photos on my phone. At least I think I was showing them." She raised an eyebrow, and Leo nodded to signal confirmation. "Good, well. The first photo was Irish Mike, the loan shark that Declan owed money to. I thought maybe Irish Mike decided to get his money directly from Cameron since Declan was such a deadbeat. But the timing wasn't right, so I was pretty sure he couldn't have done it."

Sid swirled the ice around in her soda. "The next photo was Lorelai Sutton, Cameron's girlfriend. Cameron still owed her five thousand dollars and had dumped her yet again, saying some pretty mean things. But Lorelai had a solid alibi." Sid shrugged. "Besides, she was too tall to fit the description of the person you saw in your ghost visions."

Leo nodded, his mouth full once again, and Sid continued. "Then I showed your ghosts—I mean, I showed Bacon and Bucket the photo I took of Rocco and Noah that day I saw them finishing up a round of golf. They seemed to know each other pretty well, and then I found out that Rocco was Noah's stepdad." She sighed heavily.

"Noah told me about Rocco paying Declan money, thinking he was buying Noah a position as Cameron's caddy."

Leo wiped his mouth with his napkin. "Wasn't he?"

Sid shrugged. "Noah said it wasn't necessary. He thought Cameron hired him because they were friends and because Noah was good enough to help Cameron win. He claimed the payoffs were a farce between Rocco and Declan. Declan got money. Rocco got to feel like a big shot. Whatever the truth, it all came apart at the seams when Cameron fired Noah and hired another caddy."

"So Noah killed Cameron because Cameron replaced him with someone else," Leo suggested.

"Not quite." Sid shook her head. "Noah was upset about being fired, yes, but he was more upset by what his stepfather said to him about being fired. Apparently, Rocco can be really cruel when he wants to be."

Leo grunted. "And I bet that's most of the time."

"Probably." Sid smiled at Leo as the boy shook his head and went back to eating. "What Noah didn't know was that Cameron was taking bribes as well. I think Rocco told Noah that he'd been paying Cameron, too. For years, Noah thought his friend was hiring him because he was a good caddy, but thanks to Rocco, I think Noah realized that it was all a lie."

Leo wiped his hands on his napkin. "How did you know Cameron was taking bribes from Rocco?"

"Cameron's financial records." Sid took a sip of her drink. "Tony got a hold of Declan's records, and Declan identified all the digital wallet transfers from Rocco. Interestingly, the same transfers—same amounts on the same dates—appeared in Cameron's records, too. I'm sure once Rocco's financial records are subpoenaed, they'll be able to prove that he sent the money to both of them."

"Is that how Cameron was able to afford the Maserati?" asked Leo.

Sid smiled. "I don't know. I hadn't thought of that, but you may be right."

Leo grinned from ear to ear and then went back to stuffing his face with nachos.

Sid sighed and added, "When I pointed out Cameron's little drawing on the golf club handle, that's when I knew who'd done it. Up until that point, Rocco was very stoic. Very calm, cool, and collected." Sid smirked. "When I showed him Cameron's trademark, he got angry. I could see it in his face. That was the moment Rocco realized he'd screwed up. And that's the moment I knew it was Noah, not Rocco."

Sid continued to swirl the ice in her cup. "I think Noah found Cameron on the seventeenth hole and confronted him about the bribes from Rocco. I'm sure they argued, and Noah lost it. He lashed out. For him, I think it was the worst kind of betrayal." She took a sip and returned her glass to the table. "After it happened, I think Noah panicked and ran off with the bag. Rocco found out, or maybe Noah confessed. Who knows? But I think they removed the clubs from the bag because they probably all had blood on them at that point, not just the sand wedge, and they hid everything else in the trunk of Cameron's fancy sports car. Unfortunately, the car was towed away before they could clean the clubs and sneak them back into the bag." Sid shrugged again. "They were stuck with the clubs. And what better place to hide them than in plain sight—in Rocco's own golf bag?"

Sid smiled, picking at her nachos. "When I saw how badly Rocco was playing, hitting his ball into the marsh and swearing like a sailor, I suspected that he was probably playing with Cameron's clubs. Who would know the difference? Most people would assume they were his usual clubs, and if not, he could always say he got a new set. The man had money to burn, so no one would bat an eye."

Leo nodded. "And that's why you took the club from his bag. To check for the runner on the handle."

"Bingo." Sid took a bite, noting that there was barely anything remaining on the platter now.

Leo stared out at the water for a few moments, brow creased in concentration. "But how could Noah do it?" He looked back at Sid, and the honest disbelief on his face made her want to wrap him up in a tight hug. "How could Noah hit Cameron over the head with a golf club? I mean, he hit him hard enough to knock him out. And then he rolled Cameron's body into the swamp and let him drown and then be eaten by alligators?" His lip curled in disgust. "How can you do that to your best friend?"

Sid shrugged. "Remember what Miss Hattie said?" Leo tilted his head to the side and frowned. "Sometimes the real monsters don't look like monsters at all. Sometimes they're the ones who look the most innocent."

"Yeah, I remember." Leo nodded. "Can't say I like that idea, though."

"Me neither, kid." Sid raised her glass. "Here's to another case solved, to getting paid, and to hoping we don't run into any more monsters for a while."

"To no more monsters," Leo echoed. He reached for his glass but ended up slamming his hand into it and splashing his soda all over Sid.

"Whoa!" exclaimed Sid, sliding her chair back and standing up. Ice cubes and sticky-sweet soda slid down her legs and puddled in her sandals. She tried wiping her legs with her napkin, but it was soaked through as well. "What happened there, Leo?"

Leo remained silent.

When Sid finally glanced across the table, looking for answers, she found Leo's eyes were as big as saucers and his face was contorted with fear. She lunged for him, clamping her hands on his shoulders and shaking him gently. "Leo! Leo, talk to me. What's happening?!"

Leo's lip began to tremble, and two tears spilled down his cheeks. "I think we spoke too soon."

Chapter Thirty-Seven

Sid grabbed cash from her purse and slammed it down on a dry part of the soda-soaked table. Then she bundled Leo into her arms and led him down the stairs to the ground floor and out of the restaurant.

Leo couldn't stop crying. He clung to Sid's arm, his fingernails digging into her skin. Sid was pretty sure he'd draw blood soon, but she didn't protest. They crossed over Cathedral Place and entered Plaza de la Constitución.

"Hattie!" screamed Sid. "Hattie!" She steered Leo in the direction of Hattie's usual hangout and found the old woman sitting under the big oak tree.

"Oh, my dear child," said Hattie as the pair approached. Sid tried to pry her arm loose from Leo's grip in order to offer Hattie a hand, but Leo wouldn't let go. Hattie got to her feet on her own and held out her arthritic hands to Leo, placing them on either side of his face. "My dear, dear boy. Let's make this right. Let ol' Mad Hattie help you make this right." She nodded and then stuck her arm out past Leo's head and shook her finger at the empty space behind him.

Leo knew who Hattie was scolding without him having to tell her. He also knew that, by the way Sid was holding on to him, he didn't need to explain anything to her either.

Hattie picked up her blanket and shoved it in her giant tote bag. "It's too crowded here. Too much noise. We got to go somewhere quiet." She patted Leo's shoulder. "We're gonna make this right, Leo. Mad Hattie's gonna help you make this right." To Sid, she said, "Take him to his granddaddy's house. We'll do it there. That's the best place. I'll be right behind you." She made a shooing motion with her hands. "Go on now. Don't wait for me."

Sid ushered Leo out of the park and wove through the streets of the Old City, trying her best to avoid those lanes and alleys that were overcrowded with tourists. Leo moved his feet in whatever direction Sid steered him and did his best not to trip and fall. Tears and snot were running down his face, and he wanted to lift his shirt and wipe it all away. But that would require him letting go of Sid, and he couldn't bring himself to do that just yet.

They reached the house on Saragossa Street in under fifteen minutes, but both Sid and Leo would have sworn it had taken hours. Burt was at the grocery store, stocking up for this afternoon's jam session with the Geezers, so Sid had to fish her own key out of her pocket. To do so, Sid let go of Leo with one arm. He whimpered slightly, and Sid worked as quickly as she could to jam the key in the lock and open the front door.

Hattie approached the house on the sidewalk, huffing and puffing from the effort of trying to keep up. "Take him upstairs," she called out. "To his bedroom. That's the best place."

Sid nodded, and she and Leo stumbled up the narrow staircase that was not meant to fit two adults abreast. Hattie came in behind them and closed the door. Once inside Leo's bedroom,

Sid and Leo sat on the bed, and Leo relaxed his grip on Sid ever so slightly. Sid winced when he pulled his nails from her skin. He hadn't drawn blood, thankfully, but there would be bruises forming soon.

Hattie came in the room, waving a smudge stick and blowing pungent smoke in all four corners. She placed the smoking bundle in an abalone shell that she pulled from her bag and set it on Leo's desk. Then she removed her sunglasses and rolled Leo's desk chair in front of the bed.

She placed her hands on Leo's knees and said, "Tell me what you saw, Leo." Hattie's voice was gentle, soft as velvet.

Leo's lip began to quiver again, and fresh tears spilled from his eyes. "I saw my dad," he cried. "At first, he was just the shadow. Same as before. Real, real dark. Standing right behind Sid." He let out a sob. "But then he changed."

Sid rubbed circles on his back, noting how frail and bony he felt beneath his thin Soundgarden T-shirt. "Breathe, Leo. Just breathe. It's okay."

A full minute passed before Leo could catch his breath and force the words from his throat. "I saw him. I saw my dad. He was . . . he was . . ." Leo hiccupped and fought with the last of his waning energy to say the words out loud, "He looked like Dru and Cameron." The tears flowed so fast that he could no longer see clearly. "He was in his uniform, but it was ripped and hanging off him. And he was gray and bloated, and . . . and there were parts of him missing. Just like Dru and Cameron. The fish or sharks or whatever had gotten him." Leo let out a wail and collapsed against Sid, forcing her to bear his weight in order to hold him upright.

Sid looked to Hattie for help, and Hattie nodded. "That's what I see, too." She patted Leo's knee. "I didn't tell you that part before 'cause I didn't want to upset you, but I think that's why he was wrapped in the shadow, 'cause he didn't want you to see him like that." Hattie nodded again. "It seems, now that I think 'bout it, that he was tryin' to protect you in his own way. Probably thought that seein' that dark shadow was less scary than seein' him like he is."

Leo lifted his head and blinked, trying to clear out the tears. "Is that how he's been this whole time?"

"I'm guessin' so," Hattie answered, "but let's see if we can help him. Whaddya say?" Leo sniffed and nodded. "Good, that's good." She reached out and tapped Leo on the arm. "I want you to sit up now, boy. Sit up and look at me." With a little help from Sid, Leo sat upright. Hattie smiled at him. "Now, let go of Miss Sidney and dry those tears."

Leo pulled the hem of his T-shirt up and wiped the tears and snot from his face. Sid rummaged through her bag and pulled out a pack of tissues, quickly plucking two and handing them to Leo. He blew his nose, tossed the wadded tissues in the trash can by his desk, and repeated those same moves as Sid handed him several more.

After a couple of minutes, Leo's breathing slowed, his tears stopped flowing, and he sat quietly on the bed, staring at the last few remaining tissues in the pack. "What happens now?"

"Now, we're gonna invite him in and ask him what he wants," Hattie replied. She patted Leo's knee again. "You're gonna see him lookin' terrible, but I want you to be strong. We can make this right. You just hold on and trust Mad Hattie, and I'm gonna help you make this right."

They sat quietly for several moments. Hattie closed her eyes, nodding her head every once in a while. Then her eyes popped open, and both she and Leo turned toward the foot of the bed.

Leo clenched Sid's hand in a death grip, and she almost yelped in pain. His breathing was ragged now, coming in shallow gasps.

Sid rubbed his back again. "Breathe, Leo. It's okay," she whispered. "We're right here. Just breathe." She felt his body struggle to take in more air, to wrestle his breathing back to normal.

Hattie turned to Leo, her brow furrowing. "Can you hear him, Leo?"

"No!" Leo shook his head. "I can't hear him! What's he saying?!"

"I'm gonna tell you. I'm gonna say exactly what he's sayin' to me. Tell you exactly what he's showin' me. All right?" Hattie's voice was once again soft as velvet. Leo nodded, and Hattie continued. "He's showin' me the deck of the ship. It's real noisy. There's a plane that's tied down on the deck." Hattie jerked to the side, and Leo knew that she was no longer looking at him. She was seeing whatever it was his dad was showing her.

"Boy, it's rainin' somethin' awful. I can barely see the others. Lots of people runnin' around, but I can barely see 'em. He says this storm came up fast. Faster than expected. And fiercer, too." She turned her head to the side. "Somethin's loose. Don't know what you call it. Some kind of rope or cable or somethin'." Hattie shook her head. "Your daddy's reaching for it. Fixin' it. Oh!" Hattie's hand flew up to her throat. "Oh my!"

"What?!" cried Leo. "What's happening?!"

"It was a big wave. A real big wave." Hattie turned her head again, eyes squinting. "It rocked the ship real bad." Her face fell. "Your daddy went over the side and into the water." Hattie blinked hard and turned back to Leo. "He hit his head, Leo. He was knocked out cold. He didn't know what happened to him. One moment he was workin', and the next he was gone from this world."

Leo and Sid sat in stunned silence, neither of them moving a muscle.

Hattie's brow furrowed. "He wants you to tell your granddaddy that it was an accident. Your daddy didn't jump." She blinked in surprise. "Leo, is that what ya'll been thinkin' happened to him?"

Leo bit his lip and nodded once. "Grandpa and Mom were worried that he might have . . . given up."

Hattie smiled and reached for Leo's hand, curling her crooked fingers around his own. "No, child, he didn't give up. He wants you to know it was nothin' more than a sad accident."

Leo nodded, tears spilling down his cheeks once again. "Okay. I'm glad he didn't give up."

Hattie squeezed his hand. "He also says he's sorry for not teachin' you more. He's sorry he didn't know what to do, how to help you." She blinked again. "Leo, he had the gift, didn't he?" Leo nodded, and Hattie clucked her tongue. "That poor, poor man." She was quiet for a few moments, gazing toward the end of the bed.

Leo blinked, clearing the tears from his eyes, and stared at his father. Gunner Roberts stood not more than six feet away, dripping water onto the bedroom floor. Leo focused on the nametag that was still attached to the shredded uniform. "Roberts, Roberts, Roberts," Leo recited over and over again in his head.

He forced himself to look only at the uniform because the rest of Gunner Roberts looked like something out of a horror movie. Grotesque was too kind a description. Leo couldn't hear his father's words, couldn't see the images. Gunner was reserving those solely for Hattie, probably trying to spare Leo the pain of knowing all the horrifying details. In a way, Leo was grateful to Hattie for bearing that burden and for serving as the go-between for him and his dad, but he was also a little resentful, a little hurt that she got to hear Gunner's voice in her head.

What Leo could feel was faint waves of emotions coming

off of Gunner's spirit. He knew that Hattie must be feeling them much more potently, but he caught bits and pieces. And they were strong enough for him to recognize Gunner's fear while on deck during the storm, his panic at not understanding his death, his despair at his family giving weight to the notion of him having died by suicide, and regret at leaving Leo to face the world of both the living and the dead all by himself.

Leo squeezed his eyes shut, trying to concentrate on his father's waves of emotion, which felt like barely more than a breath against his skin. It was all he had of his father, the only thing his father was willing to share with him besides the gruesome nature of his appearance. And then he heard Hattie chuckle.

"Well, there you are," she said. "Aren't you the handsome one."

Leo opened his eyes and saw his father standing at the foot of his bed. Gunner Roberts appeared healthy and whole—his skin tan, his eyes bright, his body strong, and his uniform clean and dry. He looked just like Leo remembered him. Gunner Roberts was larger than life, exactly as he always had been.

And no one seemed more surprised by this than Gunner himself. He stared at his hands, turning them over and back again, and then ran them down the front of his uniform.

"Dad!" Leo gasped and stood up from the bed on shaky legs. Sid held out her arms to catch him if he fell.

Both boy and spirit blinked at one another in amazement. Leo was as tall as Gunner now, if not as broad or muscled. Leo wanted more than anything to embrace Gunner and feel his father's strong arms wrap around him once more, but that wasn't how this worked.

"I miss you," Leo whispered, swiping at his cheeks. "Mom misses you, too."

"He knows," said Hattie in her velvet voice. "He's been

watchin' over your mamma. She's doin' fine. He says you need to forgive her. She's just doin' what she thinks is best, but she'll come 'round again." Hattie glanced sideways at Sid with her eyebrows raised, and Sid pursed her lips in a silent response.

"So you're not haunting me?" whispered Leo.

Hattie clucked her tongue. "No, he says he didn't mean to scare you. He was just tryin' to keep you from seein' what was out there at that golf course. Says you shouldn't be seein' horrors like that. That's why he wore the shadow. To keep you from seein'."

Leo nodded. "It's okay, Dad. I can handle it. I'm not a little kid anymore. I'm all grown up now." He could almost hear Gunner's laughter. The sound was faint, but Leo could just make out the warm, rhythmic chuckle that rang so familiar in his memory. If he hadn't been so grateful to hear it, he would have been offended that his dad was laughing at the idea of him being grown up. "I am, too," he muttered. There was the laugh again. And this time, it was accompanied by a strong wave of emotion that Leo knew was love.

"He says he's proud of you, Leo." Hattie smiled at Gunner. "Says you're growin' up just fine." And then she wagged a finger at the boy. "But don't be in such a rush. Enjoy bein' a kid for as long as you can."

Leo sniffed and nodded at his father.

"And you, Miss Sidney, this here gentleman says he's been watching you, too." She turned to Sid with a sly grin on her face. "Says he's grateful for you takin' care of his boy."

Sid looked over at the empty space beyond the foot of the bed. "You're welcome?"

Hattie suddenly frowned and turned back to Gunner. "Now, what's that nonsense?" She paused and then swatted the air in front of her. "I don't know what that means. Why am I supposed to say that?" Another pause, and then Hattie threw up her hands in surrender. "All right, all right. I give up." She heaved a sigh. "Sidney, I'm supposed to say somethin' else to you, too, but I ain't got no idea what it means. You ready?"

Sid looked up at Leo, who merely shrugged. "Yeah, okay," she said. "We've come this far. Why not? Let's hear it."

"Okay." Hattie shook her head. "Here it is." She held up her hands in front of her. "He's sayin' 'Brah voh zoo loo.'" Hattie shrugged and Sid frowned.

Leo burst out laughing. Both women smiled up at him in wonder. Sid noted that this was the first time Leo had smiled since he'd been presented with the massive platter of loaded nachos at Don Pedro's.

"What's so funny?" asked Sid.

Leo swiped at his eyes, happy to be wiping away tears of joy for a change. "It's Bravo Zulu." He grinned broadly. "It means good job. Dad used to say it to me all the time. He's saying that you're doing a good job, Sid." Leo clutched at a stitch in his side as he laughed and gasped for breath at the same time. "Clearly, he doesn't know you very well."

"Really?" Sid folded her arms and glared at Leo. "Any chance he's also telling you to quit it with the sarcasm?"

Hattie chuckled and shook her head. "Don't look for any help from this boy's daddy. Given how much that man's laughin' right now, I think he's Bravo Zulu-ing all that snark, too."

Chapter Thirty-Eight

After dinner, Leo sat on the wrought iron chair in Burt's backyard and typed out a text to his mom. She'd texted him toward the end of dinner, and Burt had been kind enough to let Leo out of dishwashing duty so that he could text her back now. So here he sat in the twilight of another hot and humid day in the Old City, listening to laughter spill from the house as the Geezers kept Sid and Kitty Lonigan entertained with their antics.

Earlier in the evening, the band had been working on a new song for their set, a cover of Free's "All Right Now," but no one seemed happy with how it was turning out. Leo thought it sounded fine, but what did he know. Not much, he admitted, at least not yet. Feeling frustrated, the band members had quit their jam session early in favor of drinking and eating. Eli took the opportunity to give Leo another lesson on the bass guitar, and Leo had the tender finger pads to prove it. To hear the laughter coming from the house, no one walking by would have had any idea that just a couple of hours earlier, Recent

Geezer's musical stylings had devolved to misplayed notes, rushed-down beats, and fits of swearing. Their antics had actually lifted Leo's mood, especially when Cesar Hernandez let rip exactly what he thought of the unnecessarily brief guitar solo in the middle of the song.

By the time everyone sat down to dinner, Leo's eyes weren't quite so red, and his face wasn't so splotchy. His mood was lifted even further when he got his mom's long series of texts, each one ringing out with a ping. Paizley wrote that she and Brooklyn were finally leaving Unicoi State Park after a much-needed break from their hectic travel schedule, and they were heading south first thing in the morning. They expected to arrive in Valdosta by late afternoon, where they would stay for a few days, and then they would head over to the Okefenokee National Wildlife Refuge.

Leo had actually looked that one up. According to Paizley, it was a natural wonder. Based on Leo's research, it was a swamp. And after spending the last few weeks surrounded by marsh and listening to the bloodcurdling song of alligators at night, the last place on earth Leo wanted to be was in a swamp. He didn't care if it was a natural wonder.

He'd typed back to her:

> ETA st aug?

Her response was:

> 1 wk

Leo had rewritten his next text over and over again, unsure of how to phrase what he wanted to say. His mom didn't like any discussion of spirits or ghosts or dead things that went bump in the night.

The few times he'd heard Paizley talk about it with his dad was when they argued about him, often with Paizley blaming Gunner for passing on his curse and then not teaching him what he needed to know to deal with it. Leo understood now that Gunner had no knowledge to pass along. Gunner had felt immense guilt about that while he was alive, and he continued to suffer such guilt in death, but Hattie had helped Gunner release that guilt.

Hattie also promised to help Leo, too, by teaching him how to handle his gift. For that was what it was to Leo now: a gift, not a curse.

Finally satisfied with his text, Leo pressed "Send":

> Saw dad. He looks good. At peace. Says he's proud of me. Proud of you too. Wants us to be happy.

Leo quickly typed another one and pressed "Send" before he changed his mind:

> It's ok that you left me with grandpa. I'm doing fine. I'm happy here. Hope you're happy too.

He put the phone face down on the wrought iron table and sat back, blowing out his cheeks. It was the right thing to do. Gunner had told him he needed to forgive his mother for abandoning him on Burt's doorstep, and Leo now realized his father was right.

Leo was beginning to heal. He was beginning to understand his gift and how to use it instead of being terrorized by it. He was also beginning to see a future for himself, one where he set up his own private investigation business and used his gift to communicate with the dead in order to solve mysteries, which his long list of clients would happily pay big bucks for.

Leo smiled as he pulled up the hem of his dad's old Sister Hazel T-shirt and wiped the sweat from his brow. He had had to change his shirt after Hattie left because the other one was soaking wet and covered with snot. This one would be soaked through as well very soon but thankfully only from perspiration. It was approaching mid-September, and the temperature in the Old City was still north of ninety degrees during the day and only slightly cooler in the dead of night. With the humidity, even at this hour, it felt like the upper nineties, and he wondered if it would ever cool off.

Leo inhaled the sweet smell of late summer—warm grass, burnt meat on the barbecue, and flowers beginning to wilt and rot from long days in the unrelenting sun. It was quiet in the backyard. The Geezers had ceased their jam session, and even the birds had gone quiet. That was fine with Leo. He was learning to appreciate silence.

A cold breeze ruffled his hair, and Leo spun around hoping to see his father, but it was only the spirit of Kitty Lonigan's husband. The old man was still wearing his seersucker suit and pink bowtie. Tonight, he carried a small bouquet of roses as he floated over the yard, looking like he was on his way to pick up his date for the evening. The spirit smiled and waved at Leo as he disappeared around the house on his journey to his widow's residence across the street.

Leo shook his head and smiled to himself. Two months ago, such an encounter would have sent him scrambling for his headphones and turning his music to full blast while he dove for cover wherever he could find it. Now, however, he simply interlocked his fingers behind his head and stretched his legs out in front of him, crossing them at the ankles. No need for loud music. No need for hiding places.

As content as Leo felt in that moment, he couldn't deny the sadness that came with saying goodbye to his father. It had been plaguing him all afternoon and evening. It would fade with time. Of course, it would. But right now, it was still prickly and raw. It was nothing compared to what he'd felt that moment his father revealed himself at Don Pedro's. The shock and horror of what Leo had seen had crushed him.

But it was Sid who had picked him up off the ground and held on tight. And it was Hattie who had worked to heal his broken heart and give his father some peace.

Leo chuckled to himself as he recalled Hattie trying to pronounce Bravo Zulu. Sid was flattered by the compliment; he knew that for certain. He could tell by the look on her face. Leo had laughed, not because Sid didn't deserve the praise, but because he was proud of his father for giving it. It had been a relief to hear his father's favorite commendation, and Leo was pleased that Sid was its recipient.

Hattie departed the house shortly after that exchange, once she felt certain that Gunner Roberts's spirit was at peace. She said that by communicating with Gunner and helping him to understand that he had not failed Leo as a father, Gunner's soul had begun to heal. And that was the moment that Gunner finally appeared to Leo as the strong, healthy man Leo remembered, no longer the dark shadow or the mangled corpse left to rot on the seabed.

And once Hattie left, Gunner Roberts slipped away as well.

Leo watched him float out of the house and across the front yard. When he reached the sidewalk, he looked back and gave his son one last parting smile. Then Gunner's spirit disappeared.

It took all of Leo's remaining strength not to run after his father, begging him to stay, but if Leo had learned anything in these last couple of months in the Old City, it was that only the living are meant to remain here. The dead should be allowed to leave once they are gone. Asking a spirit to remain is cruel, and helping them to move on is the best thing he can do with his gift.

That, and helping Sidney Stone solve mysteries, of course.

Author's Note

If you read the first book in the Old City Mystery series, *A Place for Good and Evil,* you will know that I endeavored to accurately portray St. Augustine's streets, landmarks, monuments, and historical sites. For this second book in the series, I have tried to do the same, including Anastasia Island and the surrounding waterways. That being said, I have taken liberties with respect to specific local businesses and establishments, and none of those appearing in this story are meant to portray real-life ones, whether in St. Augustine or elsewhere.

Regarding alligator poaching, such activity unfortunately does take place in Florida and is punishable by state law. I have no actual knowledge of any poaching activity having taken place on or near Anastasia Island, nor have I attempted to portray any such actual events that may have occurred elsewhere. If you are a resident of Florida or have spent any time in the state, you know that alligators exist everywhere here. They've been known to make appearances on golf courses and in people's backyards. You should assume that all bodies of water in this state have at least one alligator in them, whether

Author's Note

they are huge lakes, man-made canals, or small retention ponds. Better safe than sorry. Twelve-foot gators like Big Boy don't exist solely in fiction.

You may have noticed that I used the term "jon boat" to describe the flat-bottomed boat the alligator poachers use to approach the golf course via the marshland that buffers the Matanzas River and Anastasia Island. If you look up this term in a dictionary, you'll likely be redirected to "johnboat," which is the more universally understood term for this type of vessel and the standard form used in formal writing. However, here in Florida and in other regions, "jon boat" is the preferred term, colloquially speaking. To give this book a more authentic ring by staying true to the local vernacular (and to avoid being corrected by my friends and neighbors), I've opted to refer to Declan Chase's favorite watercraft as a jon boat rather than a johnboat. Full disclosure: I've done this against the excellent advice of my editor.

Even though I mentioned this in the Author's Note for *A Place for Good and Evil*, it bears repeating: my descriptions of the mediumistic abilities of Leo Roberts, Mad Hattie, and Valentina Ortiz are not meant to be a definitive statement. I researched paranormal experiences and spoke with people who have such gifts, but in the end, I created my own set of rules on how my characters would see, hear, feel, and experience spirits to best suit my stories. I believe that mediumistic gifts are as unique and varied as the people endowed with them, but for this series, I adhere to my own set of rules.

I should also mention that I am still waiting for someone in the Old City to create the perfect datil-pepper-glazed donut, exactly as I envision it in my stories.

Acknowledgments

One book turned into two, and now I have a series on my hands. It has been a pleasure to continue working with Sid and Leo and to watch them grow as characters. I am grateful that I get to spend so much time in St. Augustine, both literally and imaginatively.

There are so many people who have helped bring this story to life. In particular, I would like to extend my heartfelt thanks:

To my family for their continued love and support, despite my constant chatter about murder and ghosts.

To Christy Henry for her knowledge and expertise in those things that scare me more than the paranormal.

To my editor, Jessica Hatch, for her invaluable advice and guidance, as well as her enthusiasm for these characters and their stories.

To James at Bookfly for capturing the beautiful and haunting atmosphere of Florida that I've come to know and love.

To the members of the Reading Between the Wines Book Club for their continued friendship and support—especially Cathy Klein, Tracy Tripp, Meg Balke, Leah Maltz, Christine Schmitt, Renee Schreck, and Cecile Spiegel, all of whom were early beta readers and provided excellent feedback.

And last, but always first in my heart, to my husband, Matt for being my most important reader and best friend. I am grateful to be on this crazy adventure with you.

About the Author

Stacey Horan writes about things that scare her, and her goal is to keep writing until nothing scares her anymore. Stacey is the author of the *Old City Mysteries*, an adult paranormal mystery series set in St. Augustine, FL. Additionally, she has penned seven young adult novels, including two paranormal thrillers and an adventure/mystery series. Stacey also hosts *The Bookshop at the End of the Internet* podcast, which is dedicated to helping book lovers discover new authors.

You can learn more about Stacey at her website (www.staceyhoran.com) or on social media (@staceyleehoran).

Made in the USA
Columbia, SC
24 November 2024